Love promised for eternity as the day awakens . . .

MARRIE

P9-DLZ-222

featuring:

KATHLEEN E. WOODIWISS

the grande dame of romantic fiction, author
of nine *New York Times* bestsellers with over
32 million copies in print—from *The Flame
and the Flower* to *Forever in Your Embrace* and
Three Weddings and a Kiss.

JO BEVERLEY

four-time winner of the Romance Writers of
America RITA Award, winner of the Gold
Leaf Award, and the Career Achievement
Award from *Romantic Times*.

TANYA ANNE CROSBY

"A first class author"
Affaire de Coeur

"Truly touches the heart"
Pamela Morsi

"Weaves a hauntingly beautiful spell with
the stroke of a master's pen"
Romantic Times

SAMANTHA JAMES

nationally bestselling author, winner of the
Romantic Times Reviewers Choice Award, is

"A delight"
Affaire de Coeur

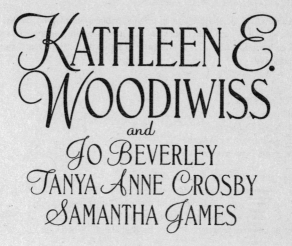

KATHLEEN E. WOODIWISS

and

JO BEVERLEY
TANYA ANNE CROSBY
SAMANTHA JAMES

Married at Midnight

AVON BOOKS ◆ NEW YORK

MARRIED AT MIDNIGHT is an original publication of Avon Books. This work, as well as each individual story, has never appeared in print. This work is a collection of fiction. Any similarity to actual persons or events is purely coincidental.

AVON BOOKS
A division of
The Hearst Corporation
1350 Avenue of the Americas
New York, New York 10019

Contents

The Determined Bride
Jo Beverley
1

A Kiss After Midnight
Tanya Anne Crosby
101

Scandal's Bride
Samantha James
199

Beyond the Kiss
Kathleen E. Woodiwiss
307

The Determined Bride

Jo Beverley

Belgium, 1745

"Madam, we must stop!"

Wet wind almost snatched away the shouted words of the clergyman clinging to one side of the rocking, racing cart.

"I *won't* give up now!" Kate Dunstable screamed back, though she was clinging just as desperately to the other side of the hay-lined cart, and was equally cold and exhausted.

Somewhere nearby in this bleak, cloud-squashed countryside was the father of her child. Nothing would stop her reaching him and compelling him to marry her properly before the child was born.

Before it was born a bastard.

She pushed her face closer to the jowly one of her companion. "They said the Buffs were up ahead. We must go on!" To the soldier driving the cart, she yelled, "Faster! Or we're likely to be benighted in the open!"

There had been some kind of fighting here today for they'd passed a cart loaded with wounded. So the driver eagerly whipped the two horses to greater effort, almost tossing Kate into the parson's lap. She braced herself, trying to cushion any impact with her legs, praying that her obsession wouldn't injure the child she so wanted to protect from shame.

The polite world was unkind to bastards unless they were the offspring of the nobility or royalty. Lieutenant Dennis Fallowfield—damn his black heart—was hardly royalty. He was gentry, though, unless that was just another of his lies. His child deserved a place in that world.

Connections. Perhaps a good school. An honest name. All the things that mattered.

"Madam, it is growing dark," the clergyman protested. "And clearly matters here are in some disorder. We should turn back."

"No, Mr. Rightwell. No, I say!"

Kate turned to look ahead through gathering dark made more impenetrable by the wind and drizzle, desperately seeking the ramshackle farmhouse apparently made temporary billet by Dennis's company. She shared all the clergyman's concerns, but her need was urgent.

She was already in labor.

"You are *mad*, madam," he muttered. "Mad, I say."

Kate suspected he was right, though if she'd known her time would come upon her so soon, she probably wouldn't have been crazy enough to set out on this wild journey.

The cart lurched violently, and fearing they would overturn, Kate flung herself in the other direction. She landed on top of Mr. Rightwell who whooshed as the breath was knocked out of him, then shoved her away, spluttering.

The middle-aged man had been rather chilly and urbane at the start of this enterprise, even though she'd virtually kidnapped him with her insistent demands that he officiate at her wedding. Now he was red-faced and furious.

"It will do precious little good, woman, to find

your prospective bridegroom and expire on the spot from exposure. I insist we turn back. Now!"

"Some shelter must appear soon." Kate struggled to sound rational or else he would take command and retreat. Surely they must come up with her quarry soon.

Was that . . . ?

"Yes! A light. Look. A light! That must be them."

It was only a flicker in the gloom, and too late she realized that it could be anyone, even the enemy French. But it was something and her strength was finally giving out.

They would have to stop here, whether Dennis was here or not.

Captain Charles Tennant was in his shirtsleeves, sitting on a beaten-earth floor staring into a leaping fire. The room had been the kitchen of a sturdy Flemish farmhouse, but the inhabitants had fired the place rather than leave it for the approaching armies.

Disobliging bastards, he thought.

One end had burned pretty well, but this end had largely been spared, meaning that the kitchen was weatherproof now they'd shuttered the windows and patched one hole in the ceiling. Though he'd twenty men crammed into the space, it was a better situation than many they'd been caught in.

For one thing, the men around him were alive, and their wounds were minor. They'd sent the more seriously wounded back down the line and buried the dead.

His mind sought back over the day's unexpected and disastrous skirmish. Could he have done something differently . . . ?

He shook his head. He'd learned ten years or more ago that such thinking did no good and sapped a man's ability to fight, to lead others into the thick of it. He was Charles the Bold, wasn't he? His company was the best, the bravest.

Those that were left.

Damn this mismanaged, meaningless campaign that had already cost too many lives and would soon cost more. Perhaps his own. He didn't fear death, but he hated graves. He wished he'd lived in ancient times when dead heroes were burned on funeral pyres. Better for the dead and for those left behind.

He shook himself and threw another piece of charred beam on the glowing fire. He loved fire. It was alive, hot, and dangerous—like the best moments in life.

Like the best women.

Hell, they had fire, fresh water from the well, and a few scraps of bedding to add to their own. This was surely soldier's heaven—

The door crashed open, bringing him to his feet in one bound. His sentry gasped, "Cart coming, Captain!"

"Cart?" Charles hastily dragged on his dirty white waistcoat and muddy, bloody, braided red coat. "Shut the damn door, Milwood. No point in freezing us all again."

The corporal hastily obeyed, leaning back against it, but then he hurtled forward when the door burst open and a wild creature surged in, swathed in a heavy cloak and blanket. "Is this the Buffs?"

Hands shoved the blanket back, and to his astonishment he saw the unforgettable—if ravaged—beauty of Kate Fallowfield. Tension gripped his gut in a way it hadn't in the worst of the fighting.

Damnation.

Deep, dingy shadows pressed under her eyes, made heavier by the dim light from the fire, but those eyes were still the most remarkable he'd ever seen. They were scanning the room, however, and now they fixed on him. "Where is he?"

Charles took refuge in anger. "What the devil are you doing out here? And in this weather. And in your condition. Are you mad? Shut the damned door, Milwood!"

As the corporal rushed to obey, another person spoke. "Indeed she is mad, Captain."

So at least Kate had not come alone. Then he saw who it was. A clergyman?

"I am *not* mad," snapped Kate. "Where is he?" She spotted the door leading into the other room— the room that was charred and roofless—and headed for it.

Charles caught her arm to halt her. "He's not there. Sit, Kate."

Though he made it a command, he was surprised when she obeyed, collapsing on the only seating in the room, a rough wooden bench. Since it was by the fire, he eased off her sodden cloak. It was good army issue and had kept her mostly dry, though hanks of her heavy blonde hair were dark with water.

"We have hot water and a bit of tea. Would you like some?" He signaled to his gaping men that someone get busy and make it.

"Thank you." She seemed a great deal calmer, though her hands were clasped tight together. "It will be very welcome. But I must know where Dennis is."

His men had been sitting like stuffed dummies anyway, but to Charles it felt as if the sudden intensity of silence must be answer enough. She was clearly so weary and focused on her need, however, that she was numb to it.

It was tempting to keep talking about tea and trivialities, but he went down on his haunches before her and took her chilled hands. "He's dead, Kate. We buried him a few hours ago."

He'd wondered sometimes how deep her feelings ran for Dennis Fallowfield. Now he knew. Her eyes went black with a kind of horror, and she swayed so that he swung up onto the bench to hold her. Then her mouth opened to let loose a banshee wail of loss the likes of which he'd never heard before.

"Kate, Kate, don't! You'll make yourself ill. The baby . . ."

She didn't even seem to hear him, but fell into a heartbroken weeping he could hardly bear. All he could do was to hold her swollen body tighter and tighter and beg her to stop.

Then, abruptly, she did stop, though her breathing turned strange.

"Kate? Kate!"

Slumped against him, she turned her ravaged face up to his. "I'm afraid I'm having the baby, Captain Tennant."

Charles found he was staring down at the immense bulge of her abdomen beneath a heavy brown wool gown as if it were a barrel of gunpowder licked by flames. "Good God."

"Having the *baby*?" cried the clergyman, straightening from where he had hunched over the fire. "You can't possibly . . ."

Kate didn't seem to hear the protests. She just stared up at Charles with the kind of hopelessness he'd seen sometimes in a dying man. "I did so want it not to be born a bastard."

She melted then into a weary weeping perhaps more heartbreaking than her previous agony.

Charles, however, was hard pressed not to point out that she could have thought of the problem a little sooner.

He gestured to Private Peabody to bring over the

mug of tea, praying for anything to help handle this. But even as he took the mug in his hand, Kate stopped crying and sat up, hands to abdomen, a frightened look on her face.

Charles ran a number of violently obscene comments through his mind. He was stuck in a storm in the middle of a running battle, with a birthing woman and no midwife closer than the baggage carts.

"Kate, you can't have the baby here."

Her face relaxed, and she was transformed by her smile—the quirky smile that crinkled her eyes and turned up the right side of her generous mouth. "And what, pray, do you suggest I do to prevent it?"

Charles looked around the crowded room as if one of his men might have an answer, and then started when she touched his hand, making him spill some of the tea.

"If that's for me, may I have it?"

He gave it to her. "How did you get here?"

"In a cart. It was going up ahead to collect more wounded."

So there was no immediate way of sending her back.

He realized Milwood was still in the room, gawking like the rest. "Get back on sentry duty!" he snapped. "And if that cart comes back, stop it."

"Yes, sir!" The corporal dashed out into the cold, wet night.

"You're a damn crazy woman," Charles told her, but he couldn't snarl when she was smiling so ruefully at him. "I thought you'd decided to go back to England."

Her smile faded. "I changed my mind."

"Dennis sent you away, didn't he?"

She didn't answer, but just stared into the fire.

"He wouldn't have changed his mind, Kate."

She looked at him then, and he'd never have thought that laughing, singing, sensible Kate could ever look so hard. "Oh yes he would."

He was about to vent all his feelings on her, when she caught her breath and he knew she was having another pain. She wasn't silent this time, though. "It's distracting," she gasped, "to have one's body take over . . . like this." Then she relaxed again.

"How much does it hurt?"

"Not much. Just a sort of pulling. It's more of a shock." She drained the tea and gave him back the mug.

"How long is it likely to be?" Perhaps they could carry her to a safer place, somewhere with women. But it was full dark by now and he couldn't know about enemy movements. Truth was she was safer here in shelter and guarded by a resolute bunch of redcoats.

"I have no idea," she replied with that wry smile. "I've never done this before."

"Come on, Kate. Women know these things. How long?"

"A day, perhaps, though it can go longer, or be very fast. But I don't know when it started, you see. It was only a little while ago that I was sure."

Charles had never felt so helpless in his life. He glared around at his men. "Can anyone think of a way to get a woman here to help?"

It was a damn stupid question and got the silence it deserved.

"I suppose we'd better make you a bed," he muttered.

The people who'd lived here had taken most of their belongings, but they'd left a rag-stuffed mattress and some moth-eaten blankets. As he was supervising the clearing of a corner and arranging the mattress there, he heard her say, "Here we go again."

He turned to see her arch slightly, which thrust her enormously distended belly further forward. She'd never been a lightly built woman, though every one of her generous curves had been perfect, but now highlighted against the fire, she was like some primitive earth goddess.

And just as terrifying.

One reason she terrified him was that he desired her, now, caught up in this primal force. She seemed almost one with the fire, burning with life, heat, and danger.

When she blew out a breath and relaxed, he took a deep breath himself. "Worse, eh?"

She turned, brushing a lock of hair off her face. It had presumably been pinned up when she'd started the journey, but now was a disordered tangle down her back. "Not worse so much as stronger. It's meant to be, so it can't be bad."

"Very philosophical, I'm sure. But pain is pain."

"So we cope as best we can. Is there more tea?"

He gestured for Peabody to get it. "Kate, you're in the middle of a military disaster here. With daylight and clearer weather, we'll be fighting again. Are you sure you can't hold out until we can get you out of here?"

"Captain, it's like being in the hands of the ocean and I am not about to play King Canute and try to cry halt. However, if your duty calls, you must leave me. I'm sure Mr. Rightwell will help as best he can."

Charles looked skeptically at the Reverend Rightwell, who was hunched in a corner clutching a mug of tea as if trying to dissociate himself from all proceedings.

Then he looked back at Kate. She'd spoken firmly, but he could see fear in her eyes. He didn't think he could be any help at all, but he squeezed her hand. "No one's going anywhere until morning."

Come morning, though, he would have to leave. His duty was to reunite with his regiment and be ready for action. He'd heard that births could go on for days. Could he bring himself to leave her here in labor?

He sent up an earnest prayer that this birth be fast. But how soon afterward could a woman travel on foot? And what about the baby? Peasant women seemed to travel with young babies. But, though Kate Fallowfield was clearly good country stock, he wouldn't describe her as a peasant.

She'd always been secretive about her origins, though Dennis claimed to have found her in a bookseller's shop in a small country town. She'd gone by the name Mrs. Fallowfield, but that was a common enough practice among the army camp followers. She spoke and behaved like a lady, but true ladies generally prided themselves on a kind of delicacy, whereas Kate Fallowfield had never seemed delicate at all.

She'd always impressed him with her decency, however, and he'd often puzzled about how she'd become Fallowfield's lightskirt. His lieutenant had been blessed with startling looks and an overabundance of easy charm, but he'd also had the morals of an alley cat. Charles would have thought Kate clever enough to realize that. Yet she'd stayed with him for well over a year now, and only left for England when he'd thrown her out.

Suddenly Charles realized her purpose. She'd battled fate and storm to get here with a clergyman in order to force Fallowfield to marry her. At pistol point, perhaps? Dammit, but he wished his lieutenant were alive. He'd hold a pistol to his head himself!

Fast on that thought, however, he knew he'd not wish such a husband on the most hard-mouthed jade in the army camp.

He watched another couple of pains come and go and then felt compelled to sit beside her. He'd held her when she was weeping, but it seemed awkward to touch her now. He'd never touched her before except in the most formal way.

"Would it help if I held you?" he asked.

She looked startled, and even might have blushed, but she nodded. He moved the bench a little so that they could both lean against the wall, then wrapped an arm around her. After a moment, she rested her head heavily on his shoulder.

"I was mad to come here, wasn't I? It just seemed so unfair . . ."

"It doubtless is unfair. If Fallowfield were still alive, I'd make him take his vows."

"I'm miserable because I can't seem to care that he's dead. He didn't deserve to die."

He rubbed her arm. "Perhaps no one does. Despite everything, he was a good soldier and died well." He wasn't sure if that was any consolation, but she was swallowed up in another ocean wave of labor and made no response.

Was there anything they could do for her? Back home as a lad he'd watched animals being born— horses, cats, dogs. He couldn't recall anything from that experience that might help here.

Trying to whisper, he asked, "Any of you men know anything about this?"

It was damned stupid to whisper when her ear was only inches from his lips.

The men shook their heads, and he saw genuine regret on many faces. They all knew Kate, and they knew her as cheerful and kind. It didn't hurt that she was so bloody beautiful, with clear skin, big blue eyes, and that mass of heavy golden hair, but the beauty went far deeper than that.

They'd missed her these past weeks since Fallow-field had sent her back to England. They'd missed her smiles, her joyousness, and her singing as she worked.

Even if the only flaw she possessed was to sing off-key.

"Then I suppose I must help."

Charles stared at Mr. Rightwell, still hunched in his corner. "You know about childbirth?"

The clergyman shrugged, and he did now look a little less morose and peevish. "I must make it clear that I have no professional qualification. I know nothing, really. But I have been at a few births in the course of my duties. Some devout women like to pray . . ."

Charles had hoped for more, but this was better than nothing. "What do we do, then?"

"As far as I can tell, very little. It is mainly a matter of waiting. The midwife generally comforts and encourages the woman, who is frightened and distressed . . ." He cast a dubious look at Kate, who was in the throes of labor again. She was a dead weight against Charles, looking more stunned than distressed.

Her hearing must have been working, however, for when it was over she said, "Some comfort and encouragement would be nice, you know."

Charles burst out laughing.

When he got a grip on himself, he took refuge in organization. He passed the duties of comfort and encouragement to Rightwell and went back to setting up a bed using the rag mattress. The best they could do for a pillow was to stuff a flour sack with odd bits of clothing, but soon they had a cozy corner shielded off from the rest of the room by blankets hung from a rope.

Charles then invited Kate to take up residence.

She moved to obey, but Rightwell held her back. "If you wish to take to your bed, madam, you must do so. But in my experience, the midwives encouraged the woman to stay sitting, or even walking, as long as possible."

"Walking!" Charles exclaimed. "Well then, why don't we march her back to the baggage carts! Damnation, Rightwell—"

"Language, sir!" snapped the clergyman. "You say you know nothing. I merely tell what I have observed. In fact, I questioned one midwife about these practices. She said that as babies have to come down, it generally helped for down to, so to speak, be down."

One of the men cleared his throat. "When me mam were birthin' young 'uns, Captain, she always seemed to be stamping around the place until near her time. Then she took to the bed."

The only pictures Charles had ever seen of women in childbirth had shown them in bed. But now he came to think of it, they seemed to also show the babe already born. Though his instinct was to make Kate lie down, perhaps with someone to gently wipe her brow, he said, "Right, then!" and seized her hands. "Up you come."

When she was on her feet, he put his arm around her and steered her up and down the small room.

She walked willingly enough, but said, "I never knew you were such a bully, Captain."

"When called for, Kate. I've no mind to be shot for desertion or dereliction of duty. I've even less mind to leave you here in distress. So let's get this child safely into the world."

The men were hastily scooting into corners, trying

to give as much walking space as possible, but it was still only about ten paces each way to the turn. They halted when labor hit her, then settled back to walking again. Though she clutched at him and her breathing spoke of pain, she denied any great distress.

She seemed to enjoy talking as they walked, and so he dredged his mind for light chatter. This was hard since he doubted she'd want to talk about Fallowfield and army life, or the time before she'd been seduced away from home and family.

At some point Private Chase pulled out his whistle and began to play a lively march. Charles wondered if a drummer might come in useful, too.

He looked over at Mr. Rightwell, who merely said, "As far as I can tell, Captain, it is going as it should."

He wanted to ask the man if any of these births he'd attended had resulted in death. Women did die in childbirth. He couldn't even say the words. Surely someone as strong and vital as Kate Fallowfield couldn't be dead before morning?

Soon they were stopping more than walking, and at last she groaned, "Ah, now it hurts."

He held her tighter, not minding the way she bruised him with her grip. He'd shed his jacket and waistcoat a while back, and now only his shirt protected his arms from her viselike fingers.

When she relaxed her grip and looked up at him, he saw fear, and this he understood. She was like a new recruit facing enemy fire. He said what he would say to such a terrified lad. "There's no turning back, Kate. The only way out is through it."

She blew out a breath, pushing hair away from her eyes. "That's easy enough for you to say!"

Charles laughed and found a string to tie back her straggling hair. "You've convinced me I never want to be a general. I'd rather be in the thick of it than out here watching."

"Whereas I've always been delighted not to be in the fighting."

"We soldiers value the women who are there to tend to us. Now, it seems, the situation is reversed. Is there anything practical we can do?"

She shook her head, swaying unselfconsciously against his shoulder. "I'm just glad I'm not alone—" But another pain took her, clearly sharper and stronger than before. When it finished, she was almost slumped against him. "I think I need to lie down . . ."

He swept her up and carried her to the bed. The next attack was on her before he put her down and she cried out with it.

By the time he had her settled, Rightwell had come to the other side of the bed. She was arching up, grimacing.

"Dammit, Rightwell. There must be something we can do!"

"I fear not, Captain. But I think that at last we are near."

"Pray God you're right. She can't go on like this. What time is it?" Even as he asked, Charles realized he had his own watch and pulled it out. Eleven. He'd thought it later. That left plenty of time before dawn and surely this writhing, sweating intensity couldn't last for long.

"I think . . ." said Rightwell.

"What?"

"In some cases, perhaps one of the women rubbed the mother's back."

"Then why the devil didn't you say so!" Charles immediately rolled Kate onto her side and started massaging her rigid shoulders.

"Er . . . lower, Captain."

"Lower? Where lower?" Charles moved his hands down to the center of her back.

"Er . . . just above . . ."

Charles looked for a moment at Kate's wonderfully rounded bottom, then put his hands just above it, pushing with his thumbs.

"Oh, God!" she gasped, so he snatched his hands away. But then she cried. "Yes! Harder! Harder!"

She sounded embarrassingly like a demanding woman in a spicy bed, but Charles pressed harder and harder and she rewarded him—like a woman in a spicy bed—with a groan that seemed almost of pleasure.

Since she wanted pressure, he started to use the heel of his hand, praying he wasn't doing any damage. At least she'd stopped that tormented arching.

As time went on, however, he began to dread that he was in fact ministering to a death. The baby was surely stuck inside.

Then, suddenly, it all changed.

Kate had almost seemed to be in a trance, but now her eyes opened and she grunted in surprise.

"Kate? What?" Charles looked at Rightwell, who actually smiled.

"This is just as it should be. I believe we are almost there, Captain. She is going to push the baby out."

Kate looked for all the world like a gunner pushing a cannon up hill, but then she relaxed and actually smiled at him, though she looked more drunk than maternal. "It doesn't . . . hurt much any more. Thank you for . . . for rubbing my back."

"I'm glad it helped." He had the strangest urge to stroke her face and kiss her simply because she was being so brave.

Rightwell cleared his throat. "Madam, are you wearing underwear?"

She turned dazed eyes to the man. "A shift, Mr. Rightwell. No corset. None fit." But then she was grunting and pushing again so that Charles looked down at her voluminous skirts expecting a baby to appear under them at any moment.

"Drawers," mouthed Rightwell. "Some ladies do wear them in the coldest weather. Er . . . at some point you are going to have to push back her skirts and . . . er . . . look."

"Me?"

"You, sir. You at least seem to know the lady. I am a complete stranger."

"Perhaps a stranger would be better!"

"You, sir."

"You, Charles," said Kate quite strongly, and he looked up to see that she was even smiling that tip-tilted smile.

"This is all damned irregular," Charles muttered, but he gingerly put his hands under her skirts—wool on top, then flannel, then cotton—and pushed them up to expose her open thighs. He was sure he was blushing and could only be grateful that the shielding blankets made this corner quite dim.

Then he realized they made it so dim he could hardly see anything. There certainly was no baby there.

He called for one of their precious candles to be lit and brought to him, then set it in the ground near her feet. When she grunted and arched with the next push, he saw the skin bulge between her legs. But there was no sign of the baby actually coming out.

It was surely stuck.

"Rightwell, come here and look."

"Certainly not, Captain. There would be no point anyway. You don't think I would actually have looked at a woman's private parts if there was no need to do so, do you?"

"It would have been useful if you had," Charles muttered. "How long should this take?"

"I think it can be quite a while."

Since there seemed nothing to be done, Charles lowered the skirts and moved to sit by her head and stroke her hair. "Poor Kate. It won't be long now."

She seemed half conscious, but she said, "Not poor . . . as long as the baby's safe . . ." But then tears swelled in her eyes and leaked onto her cheeks. "Poor innocent . . ."

He brushed them away. "Don't cry. I swear your baby will be safe." He wished he believed it.

"God, are you, Captain?"

He wiped more tears. "No, but a bloody good officer. I keep my men alive." Then he remembered the three burials that day. "I wish I'd kept Fallowfield alive for you."

"So do I. My child doesn't deserve to be a bastard." And more tears flowed even as she labored under the next push.

Charles knew that belief, faith, was key to many victories. Was Kate's misery over bringing a fatherless child into the world stopping the birth?

He stared at the clergyman, who shook his head. "A little while yet, I think."

"Not that. The question is, can I marry her?"

Rightwell's features set hard. "Are you saying *you* are the wretched father of this child?"

"No, dammit. But I could be, couldn't I? If we marry before it's born, it will legally be my child, and legitimate, won't it?"

"Legally, yes . . . Though there should be certain church formalities."

"But it would be legal, especially with a clergyman officiating."

"That is why I am here, Captain."

"Then let's do it."

"I don't know—"

"What possible reason can you have to refuse?"

"The lady's wishes, sir!"

Charles looked at Kate to see her watching him, dazed but comprehending. "Do you understand, Kate? Would you like my name for the child? I'm not saying I can be much of a husband. I'm not a family man. But if it would ease you . . ."

She disappeared into another of the appalling spasms but emerged to say, "Yes, please. If you don't terribly mind."

"Do it," Charles snapped to Rightwell.

It looked as if the clergyman might object again, but he swallowed it—perhaps because of the silent threat of violence Charles was sending him. He began to gabble from memory the rite of marriage, frequently interrupted by Kate's red-faced struggles and Charles' peeps under her skirts to check progress.

"Hair! I see hair!" he shouted. "Hurry up, dammit. Yes, I do. Of course I do. Yes, she does. Say it, Kate!"

She blinked up at him. "I do, I do, I do."

"Then I now pronounce you man and wife."

Impelled by the moment, Charles laughed and kissed Kate smackingly on her slack lips. She startled him by laughing herself, though it twisted into a groan and another writhing push.

Charles watched under her skirts and would have sworn the baby was going to push out, but then Kate relaxed and the hair disappeared again. It didn't seem right to him.

He pulled Rightwell to one side, hopefully out of Kate's hearing. "I thought you said babies should come down. She's pushing uphill!"

"Midwives often have birthing chairs, Captain, but we have no such thing here."

"So they do it sitting up?"

"Mostly . . . yes. In one case, the husband formed the chair."

"What do you mean, formed?"

"He sat on the chair, and she sat on his lap."

Kate had heard. "I should be sitting up?" She struggled up, and Charles went to help her. Though badly shaken by this whole event, he was a battle-hardened officer and it took only a moment to decide. He pulled her to her feet then turned to Rightwell. "Do you want to be husband or midwife?"

"You, sir, are undoubtedly the husband."

"Dammit, so I am." He swung her into his arms, thanking God he was a big, strong man. He took some pleasure from the thought that Fallowfield had been shorter and slighter and would doubtless have buckled. "Come on, Kate. Over to the bench."

"The bench?" It was just as if she were drunk.

"That's right. We'll have the baby out in no time." He sat with his back braced against the wall and arranged her in his lap, her legs spread wide over his. Then he realized they were facing most of his fascinated men.

"About face!" he commanded, and they hastily obeyed.

Soon only Rightwell was facing them. Clearly wishing he were somewhere else, the clergyman sat on the ground and tentatively peeped up Kate's skirts. She grunted again, but at least this time she didn't writhe or arch, but seemed to curl down upon herself. Caught in the moment, Charles began to urge her on as if she were a raw recruit in her first charge. "That's my girl! On and at 'em. Push, push, and never say die!"

She collapsed back on him, gasping, "Bully. I knew it."

"Officer. You can do it."

"Do I have a choice?" Then she was grunting and pushing again. Suddenly she gave a kind of squeal.

"What's happened?" Charles demanded.

"The head," Rightwell gasped. "It's out. Good God!"

"What's the matter with it?"

"Nothing. Nothing. But it's a *head*!"

"What the devil did you expect, man?" Then Charles realized that Kate, slumped against him like a sack of grain, was laughing. He turned her sweaty face to him. "I suppose you find us funny," he said.

"I find you wonderful. This is a most peculiar state to be in, though. I wish I could see . . ."

He pulled her skirts up and she looked down. "Oh God! It's my baby!"

"Now, what did *you* expect?"

But she wasn't listening. She was reaching down. He twisted to look too. It was astonishing. The baby was looking up, eyes open and seemingly as startled as everyone else.

"I wonder what *you* expected, infant," Charles whispered. "Not a bunch of rough, dirty soldiers . . ." But then had to gather his wits as another push hit Kate. Her skirts had settled over her thighs again, so he couldn't see, but he heard Rightwell gasp. "It's slippery! I almost dropped it. He. It's a boy!"

And the baby cried.

Kate grabbed her skirts up high to look. "Oh!" Then she reached out. "Here. Give him here! My baby!" All dreaminess seemed to have fled as she snatched the baby to bring it close, wrapping it in the layers of her skirt for warmth.

"Careful, madam," Rightwell said. "It's . . . er . . . still attached."

Kate was oblivious and the cord seemed long enough.

"Hello," she whispered quietly and Charles thought his heart would stop.

By some miracle all her ravaged weariness evaporated for the moment so that she was at her most beautiful, and she and the wizened baby were staring at one another like reunited lovers.

"Was that as hard for you as it was for me, beautiful one?" she murmured, stroking the baby's cheek. "Exciting, too, though, wasn't it? And tiring. Do you want to sleep now?"

A lilting lullaby drifted through the air. Chase and his whistle. Charles realized he was stroking Kate's tangled hair and had just planted a kiss on her cheek. It seemed wrong, but completely right.

After all, they were married. He was beginning to think that might have been a rash act bringing all manner of complications in the future, but remembering the peace it had brought her, he couldn't regret it. And she was right. This little innocent didn't deserve to have the stain of bastardy on him all his life.

With a swallowed laugh, he realized that it was as well that his uncle, Lord Jerrold, had a healthy son and heir. Society was inclined to look closely at the bloodlines and legitimacy of heirs to the peerage. Nor would it be right to bring a cuckoo into that nest.

Long life and health to Cousin Tom!

Charles pulled his wits together. No wonder they didn't let men into these matters. It was far too powerful a business. And, he now realized, the baby was still attached inside. His eyes met Rightwell's. "Does it just come out?" he mouthed.

"I believe so." But the man seemed as shaken and unsure of himself as Charles.

Charles looked up and caught some of his rough, tough killers trying to peep at the baby, faces as soft as the most doting grandmother. He glared and they hastily looked away again.

Then he looked dotingly at the perfect Madonna and child.

Reality intruded in time. Kate was no lightweight, and now the excitement was over, his legs began to complain. He wasn't sure he could move her, though, until the afterbirth separated.

Rightwell cleared his throat. "I do believe Mrs. Tennant should put the child to the breast about now. Since there is no question of a wet-nurse . . ."

"Mrs. Tennant," both Kate and Charles said together. Then they laughed self-consciously.

"Oh dear," said Kate.

"Oh, my dear," Charles replied with a grin. "Do as the doctor says."

"I think I'd like to, but how do I manage the gown?"

Charles muttered under his breath, thinking horses and dogs were a damn sight easier.

"Perhaps, Captain, you could carry the lady back to the bed."

"Do you think it's safe?"

"I believe so . . ."

"Hold on to the baby, then, Kate." He gathered her into his arms and praying his stiffened legs didn't give way, rose to stagger over to the shielded corner and the bed. He settled her on her back, but she immediately sat up, seemingly not at all tired. "Believe it or not, I feel splendid! Could you unbutton my gown, please."

Charles felt inclined to give her a lecture on proper womanly behavior, but when it came down to it, he had no idea what such behavior was in this situation. Certainly he could not imagine some of the fine, delicate mothers of his acquaintance—including his own—going through this enterprise, but he had to assume they had.

He saw now that she'd let out a gown with many panels of extra cloth so that it flowed loosely from the shoulders. But it was still fastened by buttons down the back. He undid them and eased the gown off, trying not to see more than he should. As she'd said, she wore no corset, so only her cotton shift covered her breasts. Blushing fiercely, she loosened the drawstring to expose a breast, and brought the baby close. "They said it would come naturally at the time."

The baby, young though it was, did seem to show the same instinct as any baby animal. It opened its mouth like a bird, trying desperately to find the source of food. Kate tried to guide her nipple into the mouth, but he judged it more luck than skill when proper attachment was made. Kate winced, but then seemed to settle to it, too, stroking the baby's damp hair and cooing to him.

Charles realized he'd been staring at her breast, and though there was nothing lascivious in his thoughts, he called for someone to bring one of his spare shirts. Unfortunately he had nothing clean, but some covering was better than none. He slashed it down the front and draped it around Kate's shoulders, covering baby and breast.

"Sir." Rightwell's rather tight voice intruded into Charles' contemplation. "Do you have any idea what I should do with this?"

Charles looked down and suppressed a laugh. The reverend gentleman was clutching what looked like a large lump of liver in his bloody hands.

Kate looked, too, and started blushing again. "Oh, Mr. Rightwell, I am so sorry. I never meant for you to be so *intimately* involved in this."

"I am pleased to have been of service, Mrs. Tennant." It was polite but unconvincing.

"Someone has to tie off and cut the cord," she said. "Then, I think, the afterbirth can just be thrown away. Also, I am not completely featherwitted. I came with a bag, and it does include some necessities for the baby and . . . and personal cloths for me."

Hoping it was not more complicated than it looked, Charles tied the rubbery cord with a strip of rag then sliced it with his knife. He half expected the baby to scream with pain, but it sucked on obliviously.

Rightwell went off to dispose of the afterbirth and Peabody hurried forward with Kate's bag. "Lovely baby, ma'am," he said with a bobbing bow, "and you're a gallant trooper!"

"Thank you, Private," said Kate, but Charles hurried the man back to the other side of the blanket even though there was nothing untoward to be seen.

He was beginning to feel quite shaken by all this. He'd wanted the baby born, but a mother and baby seemed a much more vulnerable package than a heavily pregnant woman.

This, legally, was his wife and child yet he had no idea how to take care of them.

"Could you take him, please."

Charles looked to see that Kate was holding out the baby, now bundled in cloth.

"Me?"

"I need to . . . to do something."

He saw the pad of cloth in her hand and understood. Reluctantly, very reluctantly, he took the tiny bundle in his hands. The baby was asleep now, peaceful but still looking more like an old man than a baby should. Ah well, not all babies could be beautiful, he supposed. It was still a precious mite.

And when he thought of it, a new colt could hardly be described as a thing of beauty, but they generally soon became so.

He looked up to find Kate relaxed back against the wall, watching him. The shadows under her eyes seemed darker, and her hair was a mess. She'd pulled a ratty blanket over her legs and clutched his dirty shirt around her shoulders.

She was still one of the most beautiful women he had ever seen.

"I suppose you want him back," he said, surprised at how reluctant he was to relinquish his burden.

"Eventually." Again, that bewitching smile twitched her lips. "Thank you, Captain."

"I don't feel I did anything much to the purpose."

"You were there. I needed someone I could trust."

He wouldn't be at all surprised if he were blushing. He thanked God for the shadows and his sun-darkened skin.

"Did I dream it?" she asked. "Or are we married?"

Tension coiled in him. It had seemed so right, yet she could hardly be said to have been in full possession of her faculties. "Yes, we are married, Kate. This little one is the legal son of Captain Charles Tennant unless his mother decides to contest the dubious honor."

"There is nothing dubious about it. I fear it is a terrible imposition on you, though. Such undisciplined weeping and wailing . . ."

"Hush." He leaned forward to place the baby in her arms. "I have no particular use for my unmarried status and am glad to surrender it in the cause. I fear it's more likely to inconvenience you than me. But war often takes care of such problems."

* * *

Kate held her precious child close, looking up at Captain Tennant—her husband, for heaven's sake—not at all sure what to say. She knew this campaign was not going well, and Dennis's death was proof of it. In a little while she was going to be very concerned over the safety of herself and her son, but for the moment she was more concerned about this man.

Charles the Bold, they called him because he seemed without fear. Even just walking through the camp he gave off a kind of energy, a readiness, an extra dose of pure life. He led the charge others quailed from. He captured positions others thought invincible.

In many ways Dennis had hated him—a kind of envy really—but he'd loved to serve under him because Dennis was above all a soldier. He wanted to be in the thick of things and victorious.

Part of the captain's boldness came from strength, she supposed. He was an impressively big man, lean and hard with muscle, dusted dark with virile hair. In the intimacy of army life she hadn't been able to avoid seeing men in various stages of undress and she'd sometimes feasted her eyes on the captain's fine form.

And felt guilty afterward.

His was a boldness of the spirit, though. She'd often seen his dark eyes light with the joy of a terrifying challenge. He didn't laugh much, but his smile, wide and carefree, had terrified her once or twice. It had generally been a prelude to him leading his men into appalling danger.

His smile now was just an ordinary one, yet he seemed to be expecting to die. She'd heard him say that since he didn't fear death, it could not dismay him. Now, he still didn't seem to fear death, but was he walking toward it?

She'd seen it happen a time or two. It wasn't suicide, and it certainly wasn't fear. Sometimes men just grew war-weary. They cheated death again and again until one day the game palled and death, like a teasing harlot, became not the enemy but the seducer.

Kate didn't have the energy to fight death at the moment, but she'd hate to think that their strange midnight wedding might have pushed him closer to the brink. "I would much rather you didn't die," she said simply.

"Then I assure you I will endeavor not to. I think this greedy lot may have left a little stew. Would you like some?"

"Yes please."

When he left her corner, she put the baby down on the bed and pulled back the blankets a little to peep into the room. Now the excitement was over, the men had rolled in their cloaks and blankets to sleep. Mr. Rightwell was sitting quietly by the fire. He looked up and smiled at her quite kindly, so she smiled back.

She'd almost kidnapped the poor man and dragged him along on this adventure.

The captain had squatted down by the hearth to scrape the last of the stew into the bowl, and the dying fire outlined him like a halo. She grinned at that. Saintly, he certainly was not.

Good, though. Yes, he was a good man. She'd lived with his company now for over a year and seen the way he cared for his men. A rough caring at times, and he could be harsh when called for, but caring all the same.

She dragged her eyes away from the sight of him and turned back to her baby. She'd wrapped him in cloths and a blanket for warmth, but she would have to put a baby clout on him before he soiled everything. She carefully unwrapped his tiny limbs and put the folded cloth between his legs, securing it with an outer cloth, tied at either side. She'd practiced this on other babies, but her own newborn was so tiny and delicate that she was afraid. She'd dearly like to have one of the women from the camp here to advise her.

Meg Fully, perhaps, who'd had a baby recently. Or Red Jess who'd had ten of her own and generally acted as midwife. These women had become her friends, though back home in Aylesbury she'd have crossed the street to avoid them.

Meg and Jess would scold her mightily for this mad venture, though it did seem that thus far she'd avoided disaster. Both she and her baby were alive.

The captain was coming over with the bowl and a spoon. Perhaps their marriage was the disaster she deserved. She couldn't think so. She did regret entangling him, but her child had a name now, and a respectable one.

She put the baby down again to take the bowl, murmuring her thanks.

He sat cross-legged on the ground by her bed, as graceful as a big cat. "There was only a crust of bread, so I broke it up into the broth. There's not much meat left, I'm afraid."

She took a spoonful. "It's good."

"It's not much nourishment after all that work. No wonder they call it labor."

"I admit I am hungry." She consumed the stew with indecent speed and could have eaten more if there'd been any. She knew enough to be grateful for what she'd had. One of the inefficiencies of this campaign was in the food supply. If there'd been meat in the stew it had probably been a rabbit one of the men had managed to snare or shoot.

She saw Mr. Rightwell find himself a corner and

lie down to sleep. "You must be tired," she said to the captain.

"So must you."

They both spoke softly to avoid disturbing the exhausted men.

"A little. But there's a kind of excitement. I don't think I can settle yet."

He nodded. "Like after a battle. But why not try? Lie down, and if you don't mind, I'll lie here by you in case you need anything in the night."

Because he clearly wouldn't rest until she did, Kate lay back on her lumpy bed and closed her eyes. She heard him moving and peeped to see he'd wrapped himself in his army cloak just a foot away and appeared to have gone to sleep.

She rolled, too, so that she could study her sleeping baby. Such a soft little face, yet so old-looking. Round cheeks, tiny nose, and closed eyes offered no hint of a resemblance. What would he look like as he grew?

By God, but I wish the captain was your father.

Taking the baby with her, she rolled so she could look at the captain again, placing the baby between them. The women at the camp had assured her that she wouldn't smother a baby in her sleep unless she was drunk. She prayed that was true for she had no cradle or other safe warm spot to put him in.

The captain looked less formidable lying down and with his eyes closed. She'd always been struck by his eyes, but now she realized they were framed by remarkably long dark lashes. His hair was dark, too, and fell in disorder around him, having escaped its ribbon. One lock straggled down over his eyes. She remembered him stroking her hair off her face many times during labor. She wished she were bold enough to do the same to him.

She was not Kate the Bold, though. She was Kate

Dunstable, very proper daughter of Augustus Dunstable Esquire of Aylesbury, Purveyor of Books, Pamphlets, and Writing Materials. Tears threatened. Childlike, she wanted her home and her mother at this moment . . .

She pushed such weak thoughts away, studying instead the man who'd saved her. She'd never have thought him the kind of man to involve himself in a birth. But then, what choice had he had other than to toss her into the dubious care of his men?

Suddenly, Kate lay back on the bed, painfully embarrassed. Giving birth had been the strangest, strongest, most exhilarating experience of her life. But now she thought of what she must have looked like—what she must have sounded like—and turned hot from head to toe.

No wonder they kept men out of these affairs!

The next thing she knew, a strange noise was dragging her out of sleep. An animal? A baby . . .

Her baby!

She jerked up and grabbed him. "Shhhhhh."

"What is it?" the captain asked sleepily.

"I think he's hungry."

" 'Struth."

Kate swallowed a chuckle as she exposed a breast and tried again the tricky business of attachment. The baby seemed willing to take a good firm grip of just about anything near its mouth but it took a few tries to get him on the nipple.

Then there were the strange sensations of suckling and a kind of tingling in response. Kate relaxed back against her lumpy pillow, relieved that the babe was silent and sucking away with remarkable strength and confidence.

Kate heard a faint snore and looked to see that the captain was fast asleep again on his back. The won-ders of birth and babies had palled a bit, she assumed.

The baby didn't feed long and soon they both drifted back to sleep.

The next time her son woke her, the captain sat up, rubbing his eyes. "Horses are definitely easier." He spoke softly, for the men were still sleeping, and the only light was the embers of the fire.

"I beg your pardon?" said Kate, the babe already suckling.

"Foals find their mother without having to demand attention." She could hear teasing humor in his voice as he added, "And they don't make such a stink."

Kate was only too aware that the baby had wet his cloth, but she retorted, "I have smelled a stable, Captain."

Clearly the infant had only wanted a light snack, for he soon slid off the nipple, fast asleep. Kate put him down and began to struggle to her feet.

Immediately, Captain Tennant pushed her down. "What the devil do you think you're doing?"

"I need water to wash him."

"Stay there. I'll get it. I put a jug by the fire last night so it will be a little warm."

He brought the bowl of water and a candle he'd lit in the embers. She thanked him, but added, "I don't think I need to lie abed, you know."

"Then why do they call it 'lying in'?"

"Are you always so logical?" She set about cleaning and changing the child, being especially careful in the dim light. "Perhaps women do usually keep to their bed for a few days. But that requires a bevy of female assistants to fetch and carry and a deal more security than we have here."

He rubbed his big hands over his face. "Gads, you're right. We have to get you out of here, though

I'm damned if I know how. If no transport comes by, you'll have to walk."

"I know."

"But can you?"

She looked up, hoping she looked and sounded calm and confident. "What choice do I have? Quite apart from warfare, I'm soon going to run out of clean cloths for him."

He touched her hair. "As soon as there's a trace of light, I'll send a couple of men to try to find some form of transport. I'd escort you, but . . ."

"But your duty lies elsewhere." She picked up her clean little tyrant and held him close. "I understand, Captain."

"You're a remarkable woman, Kate."

"Am I? I feel like a remarkably foolish one, all in all."

He stretched, hands brushing the rafters, then coiled down again to sit beside her, leaning on one raised knee. "What happened between you and Fallowfield, Kate? If you were willing to go to such lengths to force a marriage, why not sooner?"

Kate delayed by looking down and stroking her baby's tiny head. She could feel a light fuzz beneath her fingers, but now it had dried, the poor thing looked almost bald.

"You don't want to talk about it?"

She looked up then into those remarkable eyes, eyes that mocked cowards and fools. "It's just such a sorry tale. The truth is that until a short while ago, I thought we *were* properly married."

"What?"

She grimaced. "I'd heard tales of false clergymen and lying witnesses used by libertines to cozen virtuous young ladies, but of course such things could never happen to me. And certainly Lieutenant Den-

nis Fallowfield—handsome, charming, adoring—
would never resort to such deceit."

"He staged an elopement?"

"Certainly not!" Then the absurdity of her outrage
struck her and she smothered a laugh. She laid the
baby back down on the mattress and lay back on
her pillow. "I think you deserve to hear the whole
tale, Captain."

He lay back too, so that their heads were only a
foot or so apart. Pillow talk, didn't they call it? she
thought wryly.

"Could you bring yourself to call me Charles?" he
asked.

She would do almost anything for him, but that
was beyond her. "I really don't think so."

He just shrugged and lay there on his side, head
propped up on hand, attentive.

"Dennis was on furlough and visiting friends near
my home. Of course you know he had looks and
charm to turn any female head. It seems brash to
say so, but I too am similarly cursed."

"I don't think Dennis saw his attractions as a
curse."

"Perhaps not. I have always found beauty a cross
to bear."

"You certainly made a remarkable couple. Two
blond gods among mere mortals."

Kate couldn't be sure if his tone was ironic or not.
"Perhaps that was part of my appeal to him. Mainly,
however, I was a challenge. Many men of all stations
had wooed me and yet I remained unmarried. The
truth was that none of my suitors caught my fancy
and I was content enough with my life not to leap
into marriage. In time, however, the male species
began to see my unmarried state as a kind of insult.
I gather—though of course I only discovered this
recently—that the subject of my chastity came up

over a punch bowl and Dennis boasted that no woman had ever resisted him. Perhaps it was cheating of him to decide to win my chastity through marriage, but he courted me most assiduously and I proved as foolish as the rest of my sex. I accepted him even though he was charmingly frank about his lack of fortune."

"You mean he offered for you in form? Spoke to your father?"

"Yes, but we are quite simple folk." She couldn't bring herself to remind him that she was a shopkeeper's daughter. True, her father was an educated man and the shop was a bookseller's, but it was still a shop. Captain Tennant, she had heard, was connected to the nobility.

"I was of age, and my parents were not about to forbid me to follow my heart."

The captain's eyebrows rose. "So he managed a false ceremony in your own hometown. I didn't think Fallowfield a magician."

She grimaced at him. "No, of course not. But he was clever. He came up with a reason why we should marry elsewhere. A great-aunt with property to leave who would be pleased to see us marry in her private chapel. The journey took less than a day, and our middle-aged maid accompanied me to guard my virtue."

"Why didn't your parents travel with you?"

"My father is an invalid and my mother doesn't like to leave him. It didn't seem important since the next day we were to return home to celebrate the event with them."

"And?"

"And we spoke our vows in this musty old chapel which formed a kind of attachment to a decrepit house. Our witnesses were the ancient aunt and her equally ancient maid. The minister was the local parson who seemed a habitual drunkard. It wasn't the wedding I would have chosen but I thought it legal. I was even given a signed document to keep."

"So when you went home, everything seemed to be in order."

"I never went home. We stayed the night in a nearby inn and the next morning were awoken by a message demanding Dennis's instant return to his regiment. He was flatteringly upset and insisted I return to the comfort of my parents' home. I insisted on accompanying him. To this day I don't know which he truly wanted. He'd won his wager and taken my maidenhead."

"Wager?" His body seemed relaxed and yet she sensed the anger in him.

"Three hundred guineas. Dennis was often in debt, you know. His army pay was definitely inadequate for his tastes."

All he said was, "He's lucky he's dead. So, was there an aunt at all?"

"Apparently not. He hired three actors and used a deserted house."

"You know, in law there doesn't have to be a clergyman for marriage vows to be binding. The church courts don't like it, but the civil courts will uphold a union when there are witnesses to the vows being taken."

She smiled. "I've learned about such things. But what chance do I have, do you think, to find those actors and have them testify to my vows? The written record just disappeared."

"The cur. And you never forced him to acknowledge you as his wife. You called yourself Mrs. Fallowfield, but most of the army camp followers take their current protector's name. Why not, Kate? Why let him tell the world you were his doxy?"

She studied him. "I think you doubt my tale, Captain. I don't blame you. I did protest the situation, but he told me that he was not allowed to marry without his colonel's permission. I think that is true."

"Indeed it is. But the worst he'd have suffered would have been a blistering reprimand."

"He convinced me he'd lose his commission. And of course, it was only for a little while until the right moment to ask. He also reminded me that I had my marriage lines if I ever truly needed to prove my virtue. He was a most persuasive man."

The expression in the captain's shadowed eyes was disturbing, though Kate couldn't tell if it was anger, disbelief, or even disgust at her stupidity. She looked up at the dark beams in the ceiling. "They weren't bad times, you know. Dennis was always charming until pressed to be otherwise, and army life was an adventure for me."

"You were starved for adventure?"

She rolled her head to meet his eyes. "I wouldn't have thought so, but I think perhaps I was. Otherwise, I would have returned home after the wedding, wouldn't I, and not be in this ridiculous pickle."

"So, when did the bubble burst?"

She looked back at the ceiling. "When I realized I was with child. I was a few months into it before it really dawned on me. I wasn't sick as some women are. I just began to find my gowns too tight at the waist. Of course, I immediately told Dennis and pointed out that he must gain Colonel Purdue's approval of the marriage and make it public." She sighed. "The next few months were . . . difficult."

She started when he touched her cheek, then moved into his hand, looking at him. His expression was still enigmatic, but at least it was sympathetic.

He doubtless thought her a complete fool, but not a lying tart.

"I noticed Fallowfield grow more and more out of humor."

"Probably because I would not let the matter drop. He was alternately charming and terrifying so that I had no idea what to do, particularly when I was beginning to suspect that he was being unfaithful to me. When he was charming I truly believed that soon all would be put right. When he was angry, I was afraid of him. But then, since Dennis seemed so nervous of speaking to the colonel, and yet the man was quite kind to me, I said *I* would approach him."

He winced. "And that's when it all blew up."

"Exactly. He threw me out with just enough money to get me home. But first he explained that we weren't married at all, or certainly not in any way that I could prove. Of course I raced to find my precious piece of paper, but it was already gone. I doubt it would have served. It could have been written by anyone, anywhere. It's witnesses that matter."

He rolled onto his back. "He died instantly, you know. At the moment I could relish the memory of him perishing slowly and in pain."

She reached over and took his hand. "Don't. That serves no purpose. He was as he was. It was my fault for being so stupid."

He carried her hand to his lips, brushing a kiss softly over her knuckles. "None of it was your fault, Kate, none of it. I saw you leave, though. How did you come to be here?"

He still held her hand, and it was pleasant to leave it there. Dennis's hands had been strong but slender and he'd gone to some trouble to keep them soft.

Captain Tennant's hand engulfed hers in warm rough skin. It made her feel very safe.

"I headed back to England with a convoy of wounded soldiers. It was as if I were sleepwalking. I was numb. I didn't know what to do since I dreaded returning to my home in this state. But then one day I awoke. I realized he hadn't just branded me a whore, but he'd branded his child a bastard. It shouldn't matter. It doesn't matter in God's eyes. But it just wasn't right, and I was not about to let him get away with it."

The anger returned, the fierce flame that had carried her back across the continent, and had swept up poor Mr. Rightwell in the final stages. "I set off back to the army. I begged rides on carts when I could, and walked when I couldn't. I wouldn't stop or be stopped. Dennis was going to marry me properly before true witnesses, or I would tell Colonel Purdue everything and *ask* him to throw Dennis out of the regiment."

"And I always thought you such a sensible woman."

"Did you?" She realized she was gripping his hand tight enough to hurt, and let go. "I thought so, too. I suppose I did become a little wild, but what would you have done?"

He laughed softly. "For a host of reasons, it's hard for me to put myself in your position. But did it not occur to you to worry about a lifetime married to such a man, especially when you'd brought him to his knees?"

She sat up, hugging her knees. "No. It is rather daunting. But what else could I have done?"

"I don't know." He sat up. Slowly, he reached out to touch her cheek. She glanced at him, sensing something in the air, then feeling his hand coil around her neck. She stiffened under the tantalizing, intimate touch, but did not pull away. It did not feel wrong . . .

"And you've landed in the suds again, haven't you?" he said softly. "Married to me."

"I don't think so."

Those eyes studied her, studied her lips so she could almost feel them there as a touch. "I've been wanting to kiss you, Kate, from the first moment I saw you. This may not be the ideal moment, but it could be the only one we have. Will you permit it?"

From the first moment? What was he saying? "You've already kissed me a few times, Captain, and without asking permission at all."

"I wasn't sure you noticed. But I want to kiss you properly, Kate. Deeply, thoroughly."

Kate felt that perhaps she should object, though she couldn't think why. They were married, after all, absurd though it might be. And her lips were already hungering for a kiss. "I . . . I don't object, Captain."

"Charles," he said as he shifted closer so he could draw her against his shoulder. "Please try to think of me as Charles, at least for a moment or two."

His shoulder was very wide and hard. And yet comfortable. She was sure she'd rested against it many times during her labor, but this was the first time she'd been able to think about it. It fit her head better than Dennis's had. His arm around her seemed more cradling, more secure.

His lips were soft, though his bristles certainly weren't. It was the first time she'd ever been kissed by a man with stubble around his mouth, for Dennis's blond beard had been quite soft and he'd been fastidious about shaving.

She'd used to think Dennis's care over such things very attractive, but now she didn't mind the feel of bristles at all. Nor did she mind the insistent pressure of strange lips, or the first contact of a strange tongue with hers.

She let him take her weight and take her mouth and drifted on novel and highly pleasant sensations. His smell was different. His smell was actually quite pungent since it must be days since he'd had any chance to wash. That didn't seem to bother her, either. If anything it excited her, that mingled smell of sweat and blood. She didn't suppose she was any too delicate herself.

She even began to think that it would have been pleasant if there'd been a chance of taking it further. They were married, after all . . .

He drew back from the kiss, lids relaxed over smiling eyes turned almost dreamy. "I hate to stop, but if I don't I'll soon be in a state quite unsuited to our situation."

Kate pushed back flustered, not so much by his words but by the fact that they echoed her own. Intimacy with Dennis had been pleasant, but there'd been none of the fire she'd sensed in that mere kiss. Perhaps this, too, was an effect of birth.

If so, it was a very illogical one!

"I do like it when you smile like that," he said.

"Like what?"

His thumb brushed one corner of her mouth. "Your lips turn up just here."

"Do they? That sounds most peculiar."

"It's charming. I noticed it the first time we met."

When I was Dennis Fallowfield's doxy, she thought bitterly. She remembered Captain Tennant saying that he had wanted to kiss her then. She doubted his intentions had ever been honorable.

She began to regret their recent kiss and the message it might have sent him. Her body provided distraction. "I'm afraid I need to relieve myself, Captain."

It wiped away his lazy smile. "We've no chamber pot."

"I never supposed you had. I'm used to using the latrine."

"It's outside."

"So I would think."

He laughed. "Not even the most gallant knight errant could solve this problem for you, could he?" He stood and held out his hand. "Can you walk?"

"I think so." She put her hand in his strong one and was pulled to her feet. For a moment, she swayed, but then with the help of his arm she regained her balance. He wrapped her heavy cloak around her, then helped her over to the door that led into the ruined half of the building.

He turned away while she used the crude latrine, and only turned back when she touched him.

"All right?"

"Yes."

He wrapped an arm around her and she discovered that his shoulder was perfectly positioned for her head when standing up, too. His strong hand rubbed at her back, making her almost want to purr.

He spoke softly, almost to himself. "These things come upon us at the most damnable moments."

Before she could ask what he meant, he led her back into the warm room and settled her on the bed. Of course he'd meant that she'd summoned his desire at a time when he couldn't assuage it.

Without asking permission, he lay close beside her and gathered her into his arms. He was so big and warm that her instinct to resist melted in a moment and she drifted back into sleep.

She awoke alone on her bed to noises, misty morning light, and a deep weariness. Then she remembered her baby and turned to him.

He was gone.

So was the captain!

She ripped back the curtain and met the startled eyes of the soldiers all involved in packing their possessions. Clutching her blanket closer around herself, she desperately searched for her child.

She almost screamed. He was in the hands of a haggard dirty creature who was baring huge yellow teeth at him. But then she came to her senses. It was amiable Peabody, who couldn't help having teeth the size and color of a horse's.

The door swept open and Kate huddled further in her blanket as cool air blasted her. The door slammed shut. The captain had returned. In his red braided jacket and tall black boots he once more seemed the charismatic man she'd always found fascinating. And rather daunting.

Had they really kissed in the night? Had he confessed to having always wanted to kiss her?

She never would have guessed, particularly from the cool, assessing glance he flicked over her now. Whatever they had been to each other in the night, she was now a problem to be dealt with.

Belatedly, she realized that the weather outside, though chilly, had been clear and sunny. Traveling weather if she was up to it. She had to be up to it. Assessing herself, she felt stiffness and some tenderness between her legs, but no particular aches and pains. She'd probably tire easily, but she could try to walk back to camp.

Perhaps she looked afraid, for the captain's expression changed. He grinned for her in the devil-may-care way that the whole regiment recognized as a sign that Charles the Bold was about to take on death again. And win.

She hoped.

She'd married the man.

She must have been mad. She could never cope

with such energy, such risk-taking, and he could never have really intended to tie himself to a woman such as she.

In their last devastating encounter, Dennis had clearly told her that she should never have expected that even a son of the gentry would marry into trade, and he'd been right. Though she'd loved him for himself, she'd been extremely flattered by his attentions. Captain Charles Tennant was undoubtedly far, far above her touch.

He rescued the baby from the doting Peabody and came over, the child a tiny bundle in his big right arm. "We just wanted to let you rest as long as possible. But it's time to move."

No "Are you able?" she noticed.

Pushing weariness aside, she said, "It certainly is," and took the hand he extended. She was sure his pull contributed as much as her rather shaky legs, but she hoped he didn't notice. If he believed she could not cope, he'd be on the horns of a terrible dilemma.

How far could she walk today, though? Perhaps out of sight would be far enough.

"Are you in pain?" he asked curtly, shattering her hopes of looking indomitable.

"No. A little fragile, perhaps. Heavy inside. I'll be all right."

"Then what are you thinking?"

She smiled for him. "Nothing bad. Just that none of this seems real."

"Oh, it's real enough." He snapped a few commands to his men and they finished gathering their stuff in double time and rushed out the door followed by Peabody carrying a big pot of porridge. "They'll eat outside while we get you decent."

Kate bit her lips to control a smile. Charles the Bold was definitely back in form.

The baby, however, didn't recognize his authority and begin to wail. The captain scowled down at him then put the infant into her arms. "I suppose you'd better feed him. Don't take long."

Self-conscious in the daylight, Kate tried to slide the baby under his shirt, but the business was still sufficiently tricky that she gave up. A glance showed that he'd courteously turned away. "I suppose I had better name him," she said.

His back gave no indication of mood, but she thought there was a touch of humor when he said, "We certainly can't call him baby forever."

She liked that "we" but didn't place much dependence on it, and forever was not a concept that had any meaning for her at the moment. She looked down at the baby, who almost seemed to be frowning in concentration as he suckled. A fierce little thing. What name would suit him? Certainly not Dennis. And not Charles, either, tempting though it was. Her father was called Augustus, which she did not favor.

"Do you have any suggestions?" she asked.

"A good friend of mine died not long ago. His name was Stephen . . ."

Kate remembered Major Stephen Courtenay—a rather serious man, who liked to consider all the angles of anything. Dennis had found him infuriating, but no one had denied that he was honest, brave, and sensibly caring of all the men in his command. He'd been sincerely mourned.

She hadn't been aware of a close bond between the major and the captain, but the major would have been foil to Charles the Bold's occasional fiery impulses.

"Stephen, then," she said, but without a last name, for it seemed absurd to call the child Stephen Tennant. As absurd as to call herself Mrs. Tennant.

She left such conundrums for later.

The captain went to the door and called Mr. Rightwell. In moments the baby was christened, with Private Peabody and Corporal Milwood standing proxy for godparents back in England—Kate's sister Anne and the captain's cousin, Thomas.

When the others had retreated outside again, he went with them, saying, "I'll get you some porridge."

In moments he was back, and he started to spoon feed her as she fed the baby.

"In a hurry, are we?" she asked between glutinous mouthfuls. She was sure the stuff was nutritious, but she'd never before tried to eat it without sugar and cream.

"Yes." He pushed another spoonful into her. "I've to find my regiment and you must be out of here before the fighting starts."

As if summoned by his words, a distant boom stilled both of them. A cannon. Silence followed and so they both relaxed a little.

The baby—Stephen—had finished and so she quickly changed him, bundled him up, and placed him on the ground. Then she took off the captain's ruined shirt and began to struggle back into the bodice of her dress.

"Hold on." He came over, pulling out his sharp knife. "You've got to be able to feed him on the road." Pulling the bodice away from her, he slashed through over both breasts then helped her into it.

"I can hardly walk around like this!" she protested while trying to bundle her heavy hair up with the few pins still caught in it.

"With your cloak on top, you'll be all right." He brushed her hands away and began to drag a comb through her hair.

"Ouch!"

"Sorry. Hell, it's a mess." The next thing she knew, he'd just pulled it back and tied it with something, probably a piece of twine. "Once you get back to the baggage carts and the women you can get yourself in order again. There. You'll do."

"I see I will have to!" she retorted, but she was laughing. "You are a tyrant, sir."

A touch of humor lightened his grim face. "When I have to be. Can you use a pistol?"

"Yes."

He gave her one which she instantly recognized as Dennis's.

"I've had all his possessions put in the cart."

"Cart?"

"The one that brought you. It's on the way back and had room."

"You might have said! I've been steeling myself to walk."

He ignored that. "The pistol's loaded, so be careful." He suddenly stilled to look at her. "I've never been married before."

"Neither have I." She instantly regretting the sharp edge to it.

He brushed his knuckles down her cheek. "Don't be bitter, Kate. It never helps." His knuckles brushed over her lips. "Be bold instead."

"Very well." She stretched up to kiss him quickly but firmly on the lips. "Thank you, Charles the Bold. For everything."

He looked at her in some confusion for a moment before the officer snapped back into place. "Come. You must be off."

He gathered up her bundle and blankets while she picked up the sleeping baby. At the door she turned. Strange though it might seem, she was going to miss this place.

Then another distant boom shook the air, drag-

ging her back to the practical moment, and she hurried out to the familiar cart, now holding four
wounded soldiers, one of them in a very bad way.
Mr. Rightwell was standing beside the cart, clearly
intending to walk.

The men were already in line ready to march in
the opposite direction. Toward danger.

The captain picked her up and placed her in the
cart, her belongings beside her. "Doesn't sound as if
there's fighting between you and the main camp. If
you need anything, ever. Thomas Tennant. Marchmont Hall. Strode Kingsley. Got that?"

"Yes."

"God go with you!"

As if that were a command, the driver cracked his
whip, and the cart jerked off along the rough track.

"God go with you, too," Kate said softly to all the
soldiers marching briskly away from her.

On the slow journey back to the main camp, exhaustion felled Kate. The baby, too, seemed worn
out by his adventures and scarcely bothered her, but
the excited cries and welcoming arms of the women
stirred a smile.

Kate felt home and safe.

She slept. She woke when someone brought the
baby to feed, but never had to fetch him, or clean
him. He had learned the business as quickly as any
healthy animal and only needed her breast close to
suck lustily until he gave up, replete, milk trickling
from the corner of his soft sleepy mouth.

"Little glutton," she murmured to him as she
wiped away the dribble.

"That's men for you."

"All of them?" Kate smiled up at Red Jess who
was sitting ready to take Stephen away. Jess was a
strapping woman in her fifties who'd borne many a

child to many a man. Her red hair was fading into gray but nothing had faded her vitality.

"All of them," said Jess with a grin. "They're all greedy for something. Just find out what it is, and you've got them round your finger."

"Aren't we greedy for things, too?" Kate realized she was awake and alert again. A little part of her wished she weren't, for there were problems to be faced, but all in all it was good to be clear-headed and with energy.

"Of course we are. Affection and someone to care for, mostly. Why else do we put up with babies?" Jess grinned, showing strong teeth marred by only one gap. Kate had heard the tooth had been knocked out in a fight and she could believe it.

She liked Jess. She admired her. But she didn't want to be like her. She didn't want to spend the rest of her life with the army.

Clearly, during her semiconscious recovery, her brain had been working over the problems, and that was one of the answers. She was married to an army officer, though.

And that was another of the problems.

"What's the matter, luv?" Jess asked. "You're not in pain, are you?"

"No. Not at all. In fact, I think it's time to get up and get on with things."

"That's my girl." Jess scooped up the sleeping baby in one arm and extended the other to Kate. It was nearly as big and muscular as the captain's and brought back poignant memories of that strange night. Kate accepted the help to scramble up off the low cot bed, let the world steady, and then nodded. "Definitely better."

"You'll enjoy some fresh air, too. I'll just take the nipper off and freshen him up. You get yourself dressed. Shall I send someone to help you?"

"No, I'll be fine."

Kate hastily dressed, finding that she could squeeze into her less tight-fitting garments. Feeling almost normal, she stepped out of the tent into fresh air.

And into unnatural calm.

Mary Milwood sat by a fire stirring a pot.

"Where is everyone?" Kate asked her.

"Battle, ducks. Feeling perkier?"

Kate saw then the dark worry in the young woman's eyes. Mary called herself Gillet and appeared to be the true mate of Corporal Milwood. As with Kate, however, no one ever asked for proof.

So, there was a full battle going on, and the only troops here were the lightly wounded left to guard the baggage and the baggages, as it was put.

Oh God.

"Sorry about the lieutenant, ducks."

Mary's voice pulled Kate out of worry over Captain Tennant. She almost said, "Dennis?" but stopped herself in time. She couldn't pretend deep grief, however.

"It's all right," said Mary with a wry smile. "It's been clear awhile that it weren't all roses with you two. And he had sent you home. But still, he's dead. His son's fatherless."

It dawned on Kate then that no one seemed to know about the captain and their strange marriage. "What happened to Mr. Rightwell?"

"Who? Oh, that parson. Once he were sure you were in good hands, he went on his way. Important business in Brussels, he said."

Fortunately Jess reappeared at that moment with the well-bundled baby, and laid him on a blanket in a safe corner near a couple of older babies. Children ran around the camp like wild animals. They were happy and generally healthy, but it was not as Kate wanted her son to grow.

Dennis's son, legally the captain's.

What a tangle.

Other women appeared, all with some kind of work in hand, and sat to talk about men and babies. They didn't speak of the battle, even though cannon fire could be heard. None of these women were whores—available to any man. The whores kept to themselves in another part of the camp. All of these woman had a man involved in the fighting, and some of those men wouldn't come back.

Kate had been through this twice before in her time with the army. It didn't get any easier.

They wanted to hear the story of the birth, and it was as good a distraction as any. Her account of the men's panic, and Captain Tennant's command of the event had them all laughing. No one asked why she'd gone into a battle zone in such a condition, and she didn't mention her last-minute marriage.

Perhaps they guessed, but people never asked too many questions here.

Kate wished she could speak of it and ask advice, but it was impossible. Her desperation to have a legal father for her child might be seen as an insult by these women, who stuck by one man at a time but rarely bothered with legal ceremonies. She also didn't want to claim to be married to the captain until he was here to support the story. True, this time she had her marriage lines, but with Mr. Rightwell gone, her witnesses were the captain's own men. If they denied the whole thing, then where would she be?

And did she even want to be the acknowledged wife of Captain Tennant? Did he want to be husband to her?

What moon-madness had seized them?

The battle proved to be as bad as everyone had feared, but the captain wasn't among the dead. He wasn't among those returning to the camp, either, and by the time the army moved to safer ground, Kate still didn't know exactly where he was.

She could have asked, of course, but she hesitated to draw any particular attention to their situation. Everyone was accepting her as Dennis Fallowfield's unofficial widow, her child as his son.

For three weeks she waited for word from the captain. Silence in itself was telling. Their marriage had been mere impulse, and he must be regretting it.

Then one day the company paymaster gave her the sum of fifty guineas. "Widow's allowance," he said, but accompanied it with a wink.

"Lieutenant Fallowfield arranged for this?"

"Let's just say it's fair and aboveboard." And though she pressed him, he would say no more.

Dennis had always been short of funds, and when he'd given her ten guineas for her journey home, he'd acted as if he was squeezing out blood. Any official money would only go to a legal wife.

Walking back to her tent—Dennis's tent—Kate was sure the money had been arranged by the captain. He'd managed to arrange money for her, but sent no message? It was as good as a message. It said, "Go away."

She remembered then that his last words to her had been about a cousin in Strode something. At the very least that translated into, "Go back to England."

He must be waiting for her to leave before returning to his regiment! Though she couldn't blame him, tears ached around her eyes.

She hid the hurt and arranged to return to England with a slow train of wounded heading for the coast and a naval ship. She'd work her passage by nursing the men.

She'd be glad to be home again, she assured herself, home with her friends, her family, and the peace of her father's shop. If Captain Charles Tennant wanted to speak to her about their situation, he could always find her there.

Six weeks later, Kate stepped onto English soil, tears of joy in her eyes. It had grown on her over the weeks, this need to be home. The feeling had only confirmed, however, that she was done with army life. That certainly complicated her marriage.

She put that aside for the moment and concentrated on getting back to Aylesbury. She had a baby to cope with, but she also had help. Red Jess was with her.

Jess had spent nearly all her life with the army, and if she'd ever kept track of her men, she'd stopped years ago. She'd married quite a few of them, too, and laid their bodies out. Kate had been surprised when the woman appointed herself her companion.

"I'm getting old, Kate," Jess had said. "I have a fancy to go home again. If I tire of it, I can doubtless come back."

Kate hadn't really believed the speech. Jess radiated vitality, and her ability to draw men hadn't waned at all. She hadn't argued, though. She'd discovered that a baby was a lot of work. An extra pair of hands would be very welcome.

Perhaps she would have been better without extra hands, though, and her mind occupied by work. Instead, the journey had given too much time to think.

Everyone in the army had thought her Dennis's doxy, but been happy to treat her as a widow, and Stephen as a normal child. But the army was used to irregular unions and illegitimate children. In Aylesbury, they cared about marriage lines and such. She believed that she would be treated as Dennis's legal widow, since she had left home to marry him. Could this belief hold, however, for the rest of her life? For the rest of her son's life?

She'd like to think so, but she doubted it. Partway through the journey, she'd thought of Dennis's family. Apart from his bogus great-aunt, she'd never met his relatives, but he must have some. At some point she would be expected to contact them and inform them about Dennis's son.

Even if she didn't they might hear about her. They'd doubtless drag her into court as an impostor!

Kate was by nature impeccably honest, and though in her heart she had truly been married to the man, she would feel as if she were living a lie.

The honest act would be to tell the truth. But that involved telling her parents and all who knew her that she'd been a fool and had no proof that she'd ever been legally married to the father of her child. Even if they believed her, her reputation would be tarnished, and her son would be viewed as a bastard.

Unless, of course, she made her marriage to Captain Tennant public.

How could she do that to him, though? He must be feeling like a man waking up after a wild drunk wondering what follies he'd committed under the influence.

All in all, she thought wearily, as she hauled the baby and a couple of bundles from the wharf to a nearby inn, it might have been simpler to stay with the army, where no one looked at these matters too closely.

At the inn, Kate took care of the baby while Jess booked places for them on the coach to London, from whence they would go to Aylesbury. Her mind continued to run round and round the problems like a chicken with its head cut off. And just as uselessly.

Straightening from bending over Stephen on the bed, she sighed. Perhaps her problem was just lack of sleep. The baby was waking her three or four times a night these days, and though Jess sometimes tended him, Kate always had to feed him. A good stretch of sleep was a long-forgotten fantasy.

When she was home it would be better.

As soon as they were settled into the crowded coach she dozed off, only to be awakened by a demanding cry. At least she'd grown adept at putting Stephen to the breast discreetly, and Jess had shown her how to alter her dresses to make it easier.

She still had the big shapeless one in her baggage, though, the one with the roughly cut slashes over each breast.

It was alarming the way the captain still dominated her thoughts.

She worried about his safety. He'd not been seriously wounded in the battle. That was all she knew. Irregular fighting had continued however, with some deaths.

Surely Charles the Bold wouldn't surrender to the dark. He was so vital, so strong, in mind as well as body. This was illogical, she knew. Dennis had loved life, but death had seized him.

She stroked Stephen's head beneath the big shawl that covered both baby and breast. He had hair now, but so fine and blond as to still be scarcely visible. She'd begun to detect a resemblance to Dennis in his soft features, too. How could she put Captain Tennant in the position of having to claim as his oldest son a child so clearly not his own?

But how could she live a lie?

Her head was aching with all this by the time they

reached London and settled into a room at the Black
Anchor Inn.

"I think I'll nip out and see if there's any news of
the Buffs," said Jess, and was gone before Kate could
object.

She shrugged. Probably Jess had ex–army friends
in London that she wanted to meet. Men. Though
Kate was fond of the woman, she had no illusions
about Jess, who enjoyed the company of men a lot.

Kate wasn't sure she did. Once the bloom had
worn off, Dennis had just been a problem to be han-
dled—a problem rather like an unreliable pistol,
likely to fire at unpredictable moments. Looked back
on, the last months of their relationship had been
exhausting.

As for other men, in the army she'd stayed with
the women and not spent much time with the other
soldiers. She'd only noticed the captain because he
was so unignorable—big, graceful, powerful. A
force, really, creating waves wherever he went.

Waves could leave people battered, as she was.

Not all men were so disruptive, though.

She sent her mind back before Dennis, to her years
working in her father's bookshop, chatting to the
customers, mostly male. She'd enjoyed that, especially talking to the older gentlemen. The young
ones tended to embarrass her with attentions, not
always honorable. She'd particularly disliked flattery from married men. It had made her feel soiled.

And now here she was, to all intents and purposes
a soiled dove.

Tears of weakness threatened and she blew her
nose.

Damn all men!

But perhaps not Captain Tennant.

Jess came back late and a little drunk, but Kate
pretended to be fast asleep. Stephen, for a blessing,

only woke her once in the middle of the night so that she felt a little more like herself the next morning. A maid brought breakfast to their room and as they sat to it, Jess pulled a much-folded news-sheet from her pocket.

"One of my friends had finished with this, luv, so I thought you'd like it. Thought you might read it aloud like, since I don't read much."

A touch of color in the woman's weather-worn cheeks confirmed that she didn't read at all. Kate hadn't seen a recent newspaper in over a year and so she picked it up willingly enough. Holding it one-handed she read out bits of political and court news. Seeing Jess enjoyed the sensational news of trials and hangings, she read those in detail.

Then she stopped.

"What's the matter, luv?"

Kate scanned the brief item again. "There's an account here of the trial of Jem Suffolk for highway robbery and murder. The victim was apparently a certain Thomas Tennant of Essex, heir to Viscount Jerrold."

"Did you know this Jem Suffolk?" Jess asked, her mouth full of excellent ham.

"No, of course not. It just struck me that Tennant is the same name as Captain Tennant." And Thomas was the name of his cousin.

"Oh, aye. And the captain's connected to some lord or other. He's what they call a black sheep, though I've never seen the point in calling 'em that. Black wool's valuable for weaving."

"Do you know what his relationship is to Lord Jerrold?" Kate asked, a nasty sinking feeling threatening to disgorge the ham and eggs she had just eaten.

Jess shook her head. "But in line to become a lord 'cept for a few others. Or that's what they say."

Kate clung to that "few others," but when she climbed into the Aylesbury coach she knew she certainly wouldn't tell anyone about her strange marriage just yet. If Captain Tennant were now closer to inheriting a title, the question of his legal heir would become a touchy one indeed.

Aylesbury hadn't changed.

After a moment, Kate wasn't sure why she'd thought it would have, but she'd changed so much, gone through so much, that it caught her by surprise. The White Hart's sign was still so faded as to be hardly readable, and she immediately saw a number of people she knew.

And who knew her.

In moments a crowd had gathered.

"Why, it's Miss Dunstable!"

"Kate!"

Then they saw the baby and remembered. "You married, didn't you? Home to see the family? What a nice surprise!"

Kate took a breath and said the words. "My husband died."

Silence fell, then she was enveloped in a new babble, a caring, loving fuss that carried her along the High Street toward her home.

"Oh, you poor dear."

"A soldier, wasn't he . . . ?"

"Still, you have a child."

The crowd turned into a lane to stop before the double bow-front of her father's shop.

Augustus Dunstable Esquire, Purveyor of Books, Pamphlets, and Writing Materials.

It, too, hadn't changed.

Tears started to escape and Kate bit her bottom lip.

The commotion had been heard and the door

swung open, bell jingling, to reveal Kate's mother, short, plump, abundant gray hair tucked into a cap.

"What's amiss . . . ? *Kate!* Husband, it's Kate. And with a baby!"

Kate hardly knew what happened next until she was ensconced in the small parlor with a teacup in her hand. Her mother was crying by now, with happiness to see her and ecstasy at the tiny grandchild in her arms. Her father in his wheelchair was smiling and nodding, though as usual saying little. This certainly was not the time to embark upon her sorry tale even if she'd intended to.

"Oh dear," said her mother for perhaps the tenth time, "it is so sad about poor Lieutenant Fallowfield. Such a charming young man. I did have doubts, dear, about you marrying a soldier. But so brave, I'm sure. And this little one his image. His very image! I'm sure it will be a consolation to his family."

Kate's mother didn't put stress on the words and Kate let them flow by. It was as she'd thought, however. Life was not to be simple.

She'd thought of Dennis's family as a problem to be avoided. Her mother was right, however. They were doubtless grieving and could be comforted by knowledge of his child.

He'd casually mentioned that his family lived in the Midlands, but nothing more than that. As far as she knew he'd never received letters from them, or sent any. He'd certainly received no funding, for he'd often lamented having to live on his army pay.

Perhaps he didn't have close family. She clung to that. In fact, she was driven to say, "Dennis had no family."

"No family?" asked her mother, looking up from the baby. "Oh, the poor man! But what about that great-aunt?"

"Oh, yes. Well, he had *her*." Kate was about to say

that the old lady was dead when she realized that would raise questions about the supposed inheritance. "But she's a recluse and very unpleasant. I'd not want to take a baby there."

To her, the words sounded wooden and she was sure she was coloring with guilt. She hated to lie.

"Perhaps when he's older, dear," said her mother. "There was an inheritance wasn't there? It would be foolish to deny little Stephen the chance of it."

"I suppose so."

Perhaps everything could be put off until Stephen was older. In time, surely some solution to this tangle would occur to her.

Jess, it appeared, had a mind to stay with Kate for a while, and since her parents had few servants, it was convenient to have her play nursemaid and general help. "But good behavior, Jess," Kate warned. "My parents are well-respected here and I'd not want any scandal."

"I can be proper as a church cat when I've need to, Mrs. Fallowfield," said Jess, addressing her as a proper servant should and even bobbing a curtsy.

It occurred to Kate for the first time that Jess must believe that she'd never been married to Dennis. That she was lying to everyone. It was tempting to raise the thorny issue, but even more tempting to ignore it.

Kate did such a good job of ignoring everything that it was three days before she made herself go into the shop and pick from the shelves a guide to the nobility of Great Britain.

As well as running the bookshop, her father was a collector of books and the store operated as a sort of library open to the public. He kept reference books of all kinds, and genially assisted people to find the information they needed.

Kate was equally adept at searching the books for facts.

She flicked through the guide to the page devoted to Viscount Jerrold. Montague Arthur Tennant, born 1683. Married 1709 Mary FitzMarshal. Issue: Mary 1710, Catherine 1713, Thomas 1715, Eliza 1720, Elizabeth 1727.

Only the one son? But Thomas had been thirty at his death. Surely he would have married and produced sons of his own?

Her eyes scanned down over details of the estates owned by Lord Jerrold to find the section on the heir.

Thomas Arthur Tennant. Married 1742 Sophie Earlingham. Issue: Mary, 1743.

Kate flipped back to the title page. This was last year's issue! He could well have a son by now. Please let there be a son.

Then she calmed herself. Even if there was not, Captain Tennant might not be next in line. Nothing in this book could tell her, though. What she needed was a directory of notable families.

She soon found one, but it was ten years out of date. It might suffice. This book was arranged by district, and she turned to the page on Strode Kingsley, Essex.

The principal house of the area was Marchmont Hall, home of Montague Arthur Tennant, Viscount Jerrold, and his family as given above. At Oak House lived the Dowager Lady Tennant and Miss Eliza Tennant, doubtless one of the dowager's daughters acting as companion. The dowager would be Lord Jerrold's mother.

At Grailings lived Mr. Charles Tennant, his wife, two sons and two daughters. The sons, in order of age, were Charles and Arthur. She noted that the captain was just thirty-one years of age.

Kate slowly closed the book.

Unless Thomas had sired a son shortly before his tragic death, Captain Charles Tennant was now heir, after his father, to a title.

"What are you digging around in there for?" asked her father amiably. "There's no need to work, my dear, now you have a babe to tend to."

Kate emerged, hoping her smile looked convincing. "But I like to, Papa. And with Jess and Mama both doting on Stephen, I'm hardly needed except at feeding time."

He chuckled. "Yes, your mother is in heaven, isn't she? Thank you for coming home, Kate."

"Thank you for letting me."

He raised his gray eyebrows. "Would we turn you away? But you have a duty to your husband's family, too. Is that who you were searching for?"

Of course, he would know exactly what books she'd been consulting. "Yes," she lied, feeling like the worst sinner. "I didn't find anything, though."

"Ah well, some people are sadly without near kin. There is that great-aunt, however. In due course you must contact her and ask about family."

It was a command, and the matter would not be forgotten. How had she ever thought to manage this deception?

A customer came in and she went to serve him, happy of the distraction. Of course she was offered sympathy and lured into conversation about her time with the army. At least she could talk of such matters without outright lies.

The days soon fell into a pattern that would have been pleasant except for nagging guilt and the fear that at any moment her illusion would crack open to reveal her a liar. And to plunge her and the captain into disaster.

She'd checked other books and found that, as she

feared, inheriting a title was not simple. When a new peer applied to take his seat in the House of Lords, a committee investigated his claim. Normally this was just *pro forma*, but sometimes they dug deep. In one case, a man had been cut out of the title because his parents hadn't been married at his birth, even though they'd tried to forge documents later. In Stephen's case, they might insist that he was the rightful lord even if neither she nor the captain wished it.

She clung to the hope that Thomas Tennant had had a son, but still hadn't found a way to find out more about the Tennant family without raising suspicion.

Nor did she know whether the captain was still alive.

She was avoiding the papers that lay out on a table in the shop for all to read. Thank heavens Jess couldn't read, or she'd be poring over the army news. She often begged Kate to read such items to her but Kate always found an excuse.

Horribly, she couldn't help thinking that it would be so convenient if the captain was dead. At that thought, however, she experienced a real physical pain in her chest. She hardly knew the man, so why did he seem such an important part of her world?

He is your *husband* after all, a little voice reminded her.

A fact I'm sure he'd much rather forget.

Perhaps not. No one forced him. Perhaps he'll want to be married in truth.

And acknowledge a son not of his blood? And a wife from a shop?

Then perhaps he'll contact you and tell you what he wants you to do.

Perhaps he will, thought Kate, pushing the matter yet again to the back of her mind.

When Charles Edward Stuart landed in Scotland, however, attempting to raise that nation in support of a Stuart claim to the throne, she found she couldn't resist the papers any longer. The rebellion was all anyone wanted to talk about, and she was as interested as they.

The recall of troops from the continent to face this new threat was an essential part of the story, but she didn't see anything about the Buffs. When she came across important news, however, it was quite incidental.

The name Tennant leaped out at her. It was among a list of officers giving up their commissions, and the editor of the paper had added a special note.

Major Charles Tennant—so he'd been promoted— had resigned his commission in order to support and assist his elderly uncle, Lord Jerrold, grieving over the cruel murder of his son and heir Thomas Tennant by the highwayman Jem Suffolk, hanged for the crime at the Colchester Assizes. Major Tennant was now heir to the viscountcy.

Well, there it was, and it must even mean his father was dead. He was next in line.

And he was now in England.

That fact created an absurd little fizz inside her until she realized that he hadn't contacted her.

His silence, added to the fact that he was now heir to a title, should have simplified matters. She must keep silent for his sake.

It plagued her conscience, however, so that strife in Scotland faded to insignificance alongside the warring loyalties in her mind. Kate's mother must have noticed, for one day she pushed her down into a chair in the parlor and said, "Kate, tell me what is the matter."

Kate tried to find the strength to lie yet again, and

failed. She told her mother the whole sorry story, most it through tears.

"Well!" said her mother, fairly quivering with outrage. "If Dennis Fallowfield were still alive, he'd wish he wasn't!"

Kate laughed and blew her nose. "That's what Captain Tennant said."

"He sounds like a man with some sense of right and wrong. So, Kate, what are you going to do?"

Her mother was an amiable, soft-seeming woman, but Kate knew her sense of right and wrong was firm. Sitting on the moral fence would be unacceptable. "What do you think I should do?"

"It's for you to decide, dear, but you cannot hide from it. Your captain—or major as he is now—is caught in this dilemma, too. He is married and thus cannot marry again. Yet he may wish to. He may feel it his duty to provide an heir for this title."

"He has a brother . . ."

Her mother fixed her with a look. "You would condemn him to chastity or a life of sin?"

Kate hadn't quite looked at it that way, since she knew perfectly well that the captain had not led a life of chastity. It was true, however, that he might want a family of his own.

She gnawed on a fingernail, a habit she thought she'd broken in childhood. "But if we make our marriage known, Stephen will be his legal heir."

"There must be a way of getting around that."

"Perhaps, but only by making a horribly public scandal of the whole thing. It would brand me a whore and Stephen a bastard to the world. Must I really do that?"

Her mother turned pale. "The poor innocent. If only we could find those actors who played aunt, companion, and clergyman. They'd still serve as witnesses."

"And what, do you think, is the chance of that?"

"As likely as a rain of fish. Oh Kate, poor Kate."

"But what am I to do, Mama?"

"I think you must go to see Major Tennant and discuss the matter. Perhaps he can see a way out of the situation. Even if not, you owe him the chance to have a say."

"He could have found me if he'd wished to speak of it!"

"Perhaps *he* feels *you* don't want the matter raised. Come, come," she said briskly, "no good will ever be done by shilly-shallying and talk might clear the air."

"Talk might dig me deeper in the hole," Kate muttered, burningly aware of one possibility. That she might be Major Tennant's true and only wife and therefore have to save him from a life of chastity or sin. The thought was terrifying, but it carried a certain wanton appeal.

In the weeks after the birth she'd thought herself drained of all desire. Time had healed, however, and now at moments her body longed for a man. She would have expected her desire to be for Dennis, who had been a satisfying lover on his good days. Instead, memories of lying in Captain Tennant's arms, of that long and stirring kiss, spun off into more erotic fantasies.

It was really all most embarrassing.

"Perhaps I should wait," she said, rising to fuss with the copper molds on the shelf. "Stephen's too young to be an easy traveler . . ."

"Stephen's six months old and able to do without you, now that you're no longer breast-feeding him. He's taking pap and goat's milk well."

"I can hardly travel cross-country alone."

"Take Jess."

"I hate to leave you . . ."

"We coped before, and can again."

Kate pushed back a lock of escaping hair. "You're determined on this, aren't you, Mama?"

"It's right, my dear."

Kate sighed. "Yes, it's right. And as with a trip to the toothpuller, it will be horrid, but I'll feel better when it's done."

Her mother stood. "Good. I pray it will put an end to this moping around. But don't tell your father why you're traveling. It will only fret him. We'll just say you're going to visit an army friend."

"Lies, Mama?" Kate teased.

"Not exactly." But her mother's color was high. "You know how he frets."

"Just as much as you do." Kate hugged her mother, who was a head shorter than she. "Is that what love is, all this protection?"

Shrewd blue eyes looked up. "Love? Is that why you're trying to protect this Charles Tennant?"

Kate could feel her color flare. "Love? I hardly know the man!"

"I met your father at the Michaelmas fair." Kate's mother's eyes became unfocused as she looked into the past. "Of course, we had seen one another about. But that was the first time we really noticed, if you know what I mean. We spent most of the day together, and we both knew. Sometimes it's like that, Kate."

Kate shivered with a kind of recognition.

"But what if it's impossible?"

Her mother patted her cheek. "Few things really are, dear. You go to this Strode Kingsley and talk to your young man."

Aylesbury to Strode Kingsley was not a great distance as the crows fly, but by stagecoach it would require another journey into and out of London. So

Kate used some of the remaining fifty guineas to hire a post chaise for herself and Jess to travel cross country.

Jess was mightily impressed. "Very nice," she said, settling into one of the two red-upholstered seats. "I've never traveled post before."

"Nor have I." As the coach pulled out of the inn yard into the road, Kate added, "You've always known about Major Tennant and me, haven't you?"

Jess shrugged. "Rumors reached the camp before we left. Didn't surprise me. I'd seen the way he looked at you now and then." She clutched onto the strap. "Lordy, we're going fast."

"The advantage of traveling in style. How do you mean, looked at me?"

Jess turned to her. "All the men looked at you, and that's no lie, but the captain, he had that look in his eye. Not just admiration. Not just lust. More than that. Can't describe it if you don't know it. It's when you know a man's yours for the wink."

"You must be mistaken! We scarcely ever spoke."

"What's that got to do with it? He was hardly going to make a play for a fellow officer's woman now, was he? Especially when relations weren't too cordial between them at the best of times."

Kate tried to make Jess's comments fit her memories. "They didn't like each other, did they?"

"Never did, and less so when the lieutenant came back with you. But he was a good soldier, the lieutenant, and in a strange way the two of them worked well together in the fighting. The captain would never risk messing that up over a woman."

Kate smiled ruefully. "That puts me in my place."

Jess shook her head. "You gentry folk. Everything has its place. Do we worry about the men's feelings when there's a baby to be born?"

"I certainly didn't."

"So I should hope. And look at marriage. I gather you were upset because the lieutenant didn't marry you, but what good is marriage and those so-called sacred vows? Does the parson come around and tell a man he's to worship his wife and hand over all his worldly goods? Not bloody likely. But he'll preach about how a woman should obey her husband. Can't see the sense in marriage, myself."

"It gives a woman legal protection, and it makes her children legitimate."

"And who makes life difficult for poor little bastards?" Jess was warming to her subject, and Kate couldn't help feeling that she'd be a fine orator. "The church and the men who make the laws, that's who! And as for protection, a few words don't make a man respectful or faithful. It's how they treat you that counts. And if they treat you bad, you land 'em one, or just go find a man who appreciates what he's got. If you're not married, there's nothing to stop you."

Kate burst out laughing. "Oh, Jess! How true. It doesn't work that way in Aylesbury, though."

Jess grinned. "So I gather. When I've got you settled, I think I'll get back to the Buffs. Things are a deal simpler in the army."

Kate had already ascertained that Strode Kingsley had a small inn, the Jerrold Arms, and had written to request accommodation for a few days for herself and her maid. The innkeeper greeted her courteously and his curiosity about her purpose was subtle enough to be ignored.

She was astonished that he didn't seem to see that she was pulled tight as a harp string.

From first rolling into the tiny village she had expected to see Major Tennant at any moment. She'd studied the few people on the evening street in search of him. What foolishness. There was no reason he should be there when light was fading.

She was worried that she wouldn't recognize him, yet certain that was impossible. True, she'd be hard pressed to draw an accurate picture of his face even though she had some talent, and her memories of that wild night in the farmhouse were almost dreamlike. But for all her time with the Buffs she'd been aware of his presence—his height, his broad shoulders, his walk. Yes, his walk. For a big man, he moved gracefully, seeming more comfortable in open spaces than when confined. And he walked confidently, as if sure of his place on the earth.

She would recognize that walk.

Surely she would recognize his features, too, unless he had relatives who very closely resembled him. She could never forget that combination of dark hair and dark eyes along with a very determined chin.

Jittery, Kate decided that evening, was the only way to describe her state. If it wouldn't be outrageous, she'd storm up to the Grailings immediately and demand to see him. It was bad enough, however, to turn up unexpectedly in the middle of the day. She couldn't possibly do it in the evening.

She picked at an excellent dinner glad that at least Jess was doing justice to it. After prowling their room for a while she announced she was going out.

Jess heaved to her feet somewhat reluctantly, so Kate waved her back. "I'm just going to walk up and down the street a little before the sun goes down. In such a small place I won't even be out of sight of the inn."

She swung on her cloak and went down the stairs, which emerged into the one open tap room. She was aware again of the curious looks from the innkeeper and his patrons. Any new face would be remarkable in a small village like this, and she knew her face was remarkable in any location.

Trying to look uncaring, she strolled to the door and almost collided with someone coming in.

She looked up into dark, well-remembered eyes. Startled eyes.

"Kate?"

"*Oh.* Oh no!" She turned away, hand to face, and heard herself babble another embarrassing, "Oh no!"

He seized her arm and turned her back. "If you try to persuade me that this encounter is entirely by accident, you will stretch my credulity, you know."

At least a smile lurked in those eyes, allowing her to rally. "I'm sure, sir, that any number of people stop in this charming inn for no particular reason at all."

"They must all be ghosts, then, for we never see them. How are you, Kate?" His hand remained on her arm, and those eyes were fixed on hers.

Despite hot cheeks, Kate tried to be cool. "Very well, Captain. My maid is upstairs." It seemed important that he knew she had one. Then she realized who the maid was, and turned even hotter. Then she realized she'd called him "Captain."

This was not how she'd planned this important encounter.

His lips twitched slightly. "I have the feeling that I should go out and come in again when you've had time to compose yourself."

Kate took a deep, steadying breath. "I did come to speak with you. I intended to call upon you tomorrow."

"That would, of course, be delightful. But for the moment, why don't we stroll outside, since I assume that to be your purpose." He held out his arm, and she placed hers upon it. A flickering glance at the

locals showed them to be deep in their ale pots but
looking smugly satisfied that they'd solved the problem of the mysterious visitor.

"How are you, Kate?" he asked again as they began their walk down the simple lane that was the
nearest thing Strode Kingsley owned to a road. The
repeat of the question comforted her. Perhaps he
was as flustered as she.

"Very well. And you?"

"In prime twig. The baby?"

She smiled up at him. "Is beautiful and healthy.
He's sitting now."

"I presume that's on schedule or ahead of it, since
you look pleased."

"He is a little ahead."

"You make an excellent proud mama, Kate. And
you're looking well. I assume you have a suitable
place to live."

"I'm living at home, of course." She felt her color
rising. "Everyone thinks . . . I let everyone think that
my marriage—to Dennis, I mean—was acknowledged. That I'm just a war widow."

"I'm sure that was simplest."

Was that reserve in his voice? "Yes. But it was
mainly you I was thinking of." They'd come to the
end of the village, and a curve in the road brought
them out between fields gilded by the setting sun.

He paused. "Me? Why?"

She studied him as she explained. "As soon as we
arrived in England I heard about your cousin. I wondered about the implications. I wasn't sure it would
be wise . . ."

"To advertise the fact that we were married? Why
ever not?"

Yes, it was reserve. Or even leashed anger. Why?
"You can't want Dennis's son to be heir to your uncle's title."

He separated from her and leaned back against a rough fence. The flaming sun glowed along the edge of his strong cheek, and down the length of his body, reminding her disturbingly of him by firelight. "Perhaps you regretted your involvement with me."

"No, of course not! I was, am, very grateful."

"Grateful. You are very welcome, I'm sure."

"Well, really! If you *wanted* to see me again, Captain—Major—you had only to visit."

"I would have been pleased to do so if I'd had any idea of your hometown or your maiden name. Have you any idea how many booksellers there are in England?"

Kate put a hand to her unsteady chest. "You've been looking for me?"

"A good officer does not mislay his wife."

"I'm not really your wife . . ."

"A fact I am very aware of."

His meaning caught her breath. "You can't want to—"

He pushed sharply off the fence. "I see the notion is distasteful. We'll say no more—"

"Stop!" She physically blocked his way, terrified he would storm away. "I didn't mean that."

He didn't push past her, but he was rigid. Guarded.

Gathering her courage, she placed a hand on his chest. "I'm not accustomed to even thinking of . . . of fully being your wife, Captain. Major, drat it!"

Perhaps he relaxed a little. "If you called me Charles, it would solve one of your problems."

She licked her dry lips. "Charles, then."

"Thank you. Now, about fully being my wife?" Perhaps it was just the setting sun that made his eyes look hot. Kate didn't think so. She felt rather hot herself, and the evening sun gave little heat. But what did she want in this regard?

"It is not . . . not entirely out of the question," she whispered.

He covered her hand, and through two gloves she clearly remembered his touch—big, strong, callused from his trade of war. "I, at least, have thought about it. God, have I thought about it. I want you, Kate."

"As your wife?"

One eyebrow quirked. "You *are* my wife."

"But it's so complicated!"

"Is it? It seems quite simple to me." He tilted her chin and kissed her. It was a slow advance, allowing room for retreat, but when she put up no resistance, he pushed forward and captured her entirely.

They'd kissed in the night, two strangers brought too close, too soon, but needing contact in the dark hours.

This time, it was as if it were a first kiss, and she tasted him with interest and with wonder. How different he was to Dennis, who had kissed greedily, or else with planned seductiveness.

Charles kissed as if exploring, and relishing what he found. Or perhaps it was just that she felt that way about him. His arms came around her tight and strong and it was as well she had no mind to escape, for it would have been impossible, especially with her hands clutching his shoulders.

He turned her, pressing her back against the fence. His raised leg captured her on one side as he molded her body to his in a sensuous possession the like of which she had never encountered. Clothes hardly muted the intensity of such an embrace.

When he released her swollen, tingling lips, she felt dazed, and he looked it.

He trailed kisses from temple to jaw. "I don't want to trap you, Kate. But we are married." He was breathing as if he'd just run a race.

"You really want me as your wife."

He laughed and pushed against her, so that even through her petticoats she could feel his erection.

"As your *wife*," she repeated, studying his face. "In sickness and in health. Till death us do part. I'm a shopkeeper's daughter, Charles."

"And I'm the black sheep. I'm sure my family expect me to marry badly, and you aren't bad at all."

"Except that I bring the complication of a son who isn't yours and yet is, legally, your heir."

"What's your solution then?" Perhaps unconsciously he pushed against her, almost hurting her against the rough fence. "Do we hide our marriage and both set off blithely into bigamy?"

She pressed away from him, but there was nowhere to go. "I don't know. That's why I came."

The pressure increased suddenly. Then he stepped back. "I see. You are seeking a way out."

It was as if a chill wind blew.

"For *you*."

"But I don't want a way out. I want you. In sickness and in health, Kate. Till death us do part. I wanted you nearly the whole time you were with Dennis. I watched you move. I listened to you singing. I was aware of you every bloody minute. I saw how you treated all the men with kindness. I thought of getting wounded just to have you nurse me. I saw you cry when one of them died. I love you, Kate."

She turned away. "Oh, don't!"

"Are you saying you cannot feel that way for me?"

At the hurt in his voice, she had to turn back. "No! I'm saying I don't want you to hurt as much as I do. It can't work, Charles. Stephen's looking more like Dennis every day. He's going to be the exact image of him when he's a man. We can *never* pretend he's yours."

He put his hands on her shoulders. "Kate, I've faced the enemy from thirty feet and not flinched. I won't let this ruin our lives. Be with me. Be my wife. And we will win."

"Some battles cannot be won..." But this was Charles the Bold before her, the man who could inspire raw recruits to valor, and turn a forlorn hope into a brilliant success. Could she resist?

He kissed her again, quickly, passionately. "That's for tomorrow, Kate. Tonight we seal our marriage with our bodies. Tonight I know you in the depth and heat I need, I've longed for, and you learn me so that nothing can ever part us short of death. Say it will be so. Say it."

"It's madness..." But the power of his will battered hers. She didn't know if she were ally or enemy here, but he *would* prevail.

And she didn't want to resist. She'd been sleepwalking through the past six months, only half alive because this man was not by her side. She didn't see how she could live the rest of her life without him.

"How?" she said, and it was surrender. "Where?"

She looked around but he shook his head. "In a field? In a barn? Kate, we are *married*! I've already told my family, and had the devil of a job coming up with reasons for your long absence. You have a very frail and sick father, by the way."

He was tugging her back toward the street but she resisted. "You *told* them?"

"Of course. They were suitably dismayed." Victorious, he was grinning.

Kate broke free to put hands on hips. "*What* did you tell them?"

He sobered a little. "Just that you were the widow of a fellow officer. That wasn't what dismayed them.

And that you are the daughter of a bookseller. That didn't upset them, either."

"Then what did? Our scrambling marriage?"

"I didn't tell them about that. They are just sure you'll be impossible because I married you. My mother and sisters do not think much of me. Because of some youthful indiscretions, they always think the worst."

Kate melted, wanting only to hold and comfort him. "Why do I think that I am not going to enjoy meeting them?"

"It need only be briefly, thank God, and another day. I'm living with my uncle at Marchmont Hall. We rub along well enough." He put an arm around her and began to propel her toward the inn. "Let's collect your bags and your maid and move you there."

"The maid is Jess," she said. "Red Jess."

"I know."

"How?"

"When I got back to camp I was told. It's been my one ray of hope. I always knew that Jess couldn't stay away from the army, and when she returned she'd be able to tell me where you were."

"If you'd come back quicker, I'd have still been there."

"I had duties." But he wasn't looking at her.

"I can read and you can write."

He looked at her then. "Believe me, I've regretted the delay. I was thinking about it all, Kate. I wasn't sure you'd want to be tied down by that scrambling ceremony. I wanted to find out how binding it was."

"And?"

"Very, unless we swear all my men and Mr. Rightwell to secrecy."

"Oh dear."

"Not at all." He swept her into the inn, smiling.

"Gentlemen," he said to the locals, "I'm pleased to present to you my wife."

Eyes widened, and startled glances bounced around the smoky room. This, clearly, they had not expected. But then they all grinned. "Congratulations to you both, Major!" declared the innkeeper. And chancing a wink, he added, "Congratulations well deserved indeed."

"Thank you. Mrs. Tennant wasn't sure I was at home. Now she wishes to remove to the Hall. Please have her bags and maid brought down and lend me your gig to transport them."

"Right you are, Major!"

"And a round of ale for all here."

As the small room echoed with cheers, Kate trembled. Thus are the bridges burned, she thought. How like Charles the Bold to make retreat impossible for the nervous raw recruit.

In moments Jess came clattering down the stairs. "Captain! Major, I should say. I'm right glad to see you." She did mute this familiar greeting with a demure curtsy that made him laugh.

He pulled her to him and kissed her heartily. "It's good to see you, too, Jess. And thank you for taking such good care of my wife."

At the word wife, she winked. "It's been an experience. A bit tame, though, if you see what I mean."

"I'm sure I do. Come on. There's the gig."

They squashed together on the seat, Kate in the middle, and headed off briskly down the lane. The sun was a deep fiery red now and the shadows of houses and trees lay long and dark across the road.

He pointed to a solid square house near the road. "The Grailings. My family home."

Soon they turned in between gates to wind up a driveway toward a larger, less organized house.

Marchmont Hall. The center was probably Jacobean, but two wings had been added more recently. Not a particularly elegant house, but with charm.

Kate couldn't imagine it as her home, however.

"I know nothing of managing such a large establishment," she told him.

"That's the least of our worries, love."

And there, she supposed, he was right.

Back by the fence he'd swept her into his madness, but now all the problems were crowding back to harry her. There was no retreat, though. Like a ruthless officer, he'd made sure of that.

Did raw recruits facing the flash and fire of enemy muskets feel this spurt of anger at their charismatic leader?

He drew the gig up before the gleaming mahogany doors and a groom ran from the side of the house to assist him. Jess climbed out by herself, but Charles insisted on helping Kate down. He kept hold of her unsteady hands. "The only way out of this is through, Kate. Up and at 'em."

"Have you ever lost a battle?"

"Yes."

"You could lose this one."

"We can't lose, Kate, as long as we have each other."

"That's simply not true. And what about Stephen?"

"He'll win, too. I promise."

"How?"

"Trust me, Kate?"

Damn him, he'd found a new weapon—a genuine appeal in his eyes. What could she say but, "Yes, I trust you."

She allowed him to lead her into the house.

It was not, she knew, a spectacularly grand house, but it was finer than any she'd been in. The door opened into a spacious tiled hall whose walls were darkly paneled and hung with assorted weaponry arranged in decorative wheels and lines.

When Jess had been introduced to the housekeeper and sent off to the servants' quarters, Kate looked around at the swords and pistols. "Expecting an armed assault, are you?"

He smiled at her. "At least we're ready for the Jacobites."

That gave them something rational to talk about as he led her up wide stairs to the second floor. "I must introduce you to my uncle."

"And what does *he* think of me?"

He stopped by one of a line of panelled doors. "He's still grieving for Tom. I don't think he cares much about anything."

Kate's resistance melted. What an appalling homecoming this must have been for him. His mother and sisters expected the worst, and his uncle must see him as a poor substitute for a beloved son.

Then she wondered if summoning her sympathy was an officer's trick, too.

He pushed open the door and gestured her into a small sitting room furnished in heavy, dark brown brocade. An old man sat hunched near the fire looking older than sixty. He turned, showing a lined, weary face and straggly sliver hair. "What is it?" At the sight of a stranger he made the effort to stand.

Charles immediately hurried forward to settle him again. "Don't disturb yourself, uncle. I just wanted to introduce you to my wife. I didn't expect her so soon, but she surprised me."

Lord Jerrold's eyes were dark, too, she noticed, and when they fixed on her she thought they might once have had his nephew's intensity. She went forward and curtsied. "Good evening, my lord."

"Got a beauty at least, didn't you, lad? And she *looks* a lady."

"She *is* a lady."

Kate stiffened her spine. "In the sense of good manners, I am, yes. But I am also the daughter of a bookseller in Aylesbury, Lord Jerrold. And not the least ashamed of it."

A crack of laughter escaped the viscount. "I suppose a man like you needs a filly with spirit. Is she fertile?"

Kate gaped, but Charles merely said, "Kate has a son. We'll have to see if we can repeat the miracle." Charles gave Kate a sideways glance that made her toes curl.

"That's the main thing. Sons. And don't forget to name your first son Tom. You promised."

"I won't forget," Charles said, gently. "I want to show Kate to her room now, uncle."

"Aye, you do that. And see she has everything she needs." He then sank back on himself, once more staring into the flames.

Charles led her out of the room and further along the corridor. "If you wish, you can choose from five spare rooms, but I suggest this one." He led her into a pleasant chamber with cream damask curtains and hangings. "It conveniently adjoins mine. However, the sheets are doubtless not aired, so . . ."

Kate found herself in his bedroom with the door firmly shut behind them.

The hangings here were blue, and only a riding crop on a table and a book by the bed showed any sign of occupancy. "I don't have a fire lit in this mild weather. I will if you wish, but I can think of better ways to keep warm."

Kate clutched her cloak around her as if she were, in truth, cold. "You are brash, sir."

"I am bold. I want you, and I intend to have you, Kate."

"Whether I am willing or no?"

He flinched as if she'd hit him. "Of course not! Are you unwilling?"

She turned away, for he could so easily weaken her. "I don't know. I came here to *talk* to you."

"What good will talk do? Is there some aspect of our problems that I haven't considered? I doubt it. The only thing of importance is whether you love me and want me."

"That's childish talk."

He turned her to face him, to face those intense, compelling eyes and the leashed vitality that could overwhelm armies. "Kate, this isn't just any love. As soon as I saw you, I knew. You walked into the camp on Dennis's arm, smiling up at him. It was a cool, sunny day and you were wearing something pale. Bone-colored with braid. Everyone stopped to look because new people always stirred interest. Everyone kept looking because you were so damn beautiful. I looked and I felt sick. I knew at that moment, and I knew I couldn't have you. I knew I was going to have to watch you with another man. See you kiss him. See you going into his tent together at night." His hands tightened on her shoulders. "Tents don't cut off sound, you know."

She did know. She'd always tried to be quiet, but Dennis liked noise. She'd come to realize that he liked to show off and it had always embarrassed her. She remembered a number of occasions when she'd caught Captain Tennant looking at them as they headed for the tent, or in better days, toward a room in a billet. She'd felt even more uncomfortable then.

She covered her hot cheeks, but he pulled her hands down.

"We have our chance, Kate. The only thing that

will make me lay down my arms and retreat is if you tell me you want to be free."

Reason told Kate to keep resisting, but everything else surrendered to the power of his hunger for her, and her need of him.

"I watched you, too. I can't say I noticed you that first day, but once I did, I was always aware of you. It bothered me. I thought it was just that you're the sort of man people notice. After all, I was married. I *couldn't* be so aware of another man."

He pulled her against him. "Ah, Kate. But now *we're* married. You're supposed to be aware of me." He looked down into her eyes, cradling her face. "We have the moon and the stars, beloved one, but I need to make it full and complete. Somewhat desperately," he added, making her burst out laughing.

Doubts lingered, but Kate pushed them back. She wanted him as desperately as he wanted her, and they *were* married.

Taking a deep breath, she stepped back out of his arms, unhooked her cloak, and let it slide to the floor. When he reached for her, she held up a hand to stop him. Then she unfastened the two buttons at the waist of her overgown and slipped it off her arms. That joined the cloak, leaving her just in two petticoats and her corset over her simple cotton shift.

Watching her fixedly, he leaned back against the bulbous post of his bed. "I've been running mad this past half year, Kate, thinking you'd managed to disappear off the earth."

"I'm sorry. It never occurred to me that you didn't know my name and my hometown." She untied her petticoat laces and the top quilted one slid away. "I didn't talk of them because I knew my parents would be devastated to hear of my living as a soldier's kept woman. But I think I expected you to know all about me by miracle." The second petticoat of red flannel fell, leaving her just in corset, knee-length shift, and stockings.

He stayed still, though she could see his chest rise and fall and his cheeks were flushed.

He swallowed before he spoke, but his voice was still husky. "I've hired people to search for you. I've been waiting for Jess to return to the Buffs. I didn't expect her to stick it out so damn long . . ."

Since Kate and her mother didn't employ a personal maid, she wore corsets she could get into and out of herself. Her hands trembled, though, as she unfastened the hooks, for the power of his need was beating against her like the fierce heat of an oven and this did seem the last bastion of decency.

The fact that he'd seen her without a corset before didn't help at all.

When she opened the corset and shrugged out of it, he groaned. A giggle escaped her and she clapped a hand over her mouth. "I'm sorry."

He was grinning, even if his eyes seemed to burn. "Don't be. I'm in a state of the most delicious agony."

She expected him to seize her then, but instead he wrenched brass buttons out of holes and dragged off his jacket. As he tore off his waistcoat, one button actually popped and rolled away. By instinct Kate scrambled to trap it before it was lost. When she stood he was laughing.

"Oh, Kate! I adore you."

Then she was in his arms, and his shirt-covered torso was wonderfully familiar. "I like you in your shirt, Captain . . ."

"Back in memories, are we, love?" He tugged on her hair so she had to look up at him. "Am I not allowed to take it off then?"

"Are you saying you are mine to command?"

"Always."

"I'll remind you of that at inconvenient moments, sir."

"Ah, Kate." Rough-light, he traced the right corner of her mouth. "That smile. I've longed for that smile. Command me. Command me to kiss you and love you and make heaven with you . . ."

Despite tears in her eyes, Kate said, "You are so commanded, Major Charles Tennant."

Kate had never been kissed like this before—to the edge of pain, to the edge of breaking, to the edge of ecstasy just from a kiss. As they landed on the bed she heard cloth rip and had no idea if it was hers or his.

His mouth and hands roamed her, not gently but with tight-held control so she feared he'd break. So she met him in fierceness, using nails and teeth until he did break and was in her, deep in her, shuddering, hot, heavy, hard.

Wonderful.

She choked on a cry and moved before he did. He laughed, though it turned into a groan as he met her hips. Then they pounded together as if eternally practiced in the rhythm, losing it together as orgasm gripped them. Collapsing together in a shuddering, sweaty tangle of perfectly matched limbs.

Kate sprawled on her back, one arm over her eyes, mind scoured clear of all but one thought. "It's never been like that before. Never. That fierce . . ."

His hand moved to rest with simple possession over her left breast. "It's never been like that for me, either, Kate. I'm a big man. I'm usually very careful. I assure you, I can be gentle in season."

She moved her arm to smile at him. "I'm sure you can. So can I. But I'm a strong woman. I can take it. You . . ."

"We're made for each other."

"Yes, I really think we are." But thought was re-

turning. "That doesn't mean we don't have problems."

He moved his hand to cover her lips. "For tonight,
it does. Let's try gentle . . ."

And he proved to her that he could be gentle in
season, stroking and teasing until she was a puddle
of sweet need, which he amply fulfilled. In turn,
much later, she loved him in turn, delighting in re-
ducing the mighty officer to a man conquered by
desire.

It was mid-morning when they acknowledged the
new day.

Kate sat up in bed and knew her hair was a tangled mess, and that her pins could be anywhere. She
gazed around at a scene from a wild debauch.
Clothes draped the room as if a whirlwind had
passed through, and her shift was completely ripped
down the front. One of her stockings draped from
the top bar of the four-poster bed!

The bed-coverings must have worked loose in
their activities and been pulled around them again,
for they were all hanging at odds, and mostly trail-
ing on the floor.

She leapt out of bed and began to straighten
things.

"What are you doing?"

She turned, his waistcoat in her hand, to see him
sitting up in bed, smiling at her.

Naked, his shoulders seemed to span half the bed,
rounded and contoured with muscle. Dark hair
feathered his strong chest, disappearing into the disordered bedclothes that covered his hips and most
of his legs. His long hair straggled onto his shoulders, as unkempt as hers, and a dark shadow
marked his cheeks.

Never had a man looked so beautiful to a woman.

"You can eat me if you want," he said with a very

tempting smile. "It would be more to the purpose than what you're doing."

"You must be worn out! Or should be."

"Should I take that as a challenge?"

"No!" She realized she was stark naked and his waistcoat didn't conceal much. She was tempted to grab her cloak, but knew he'd be hurt. She'd undressed for him last night, hadn't she?

His smile turned tender. "All right, I'll admit it. I need to recoup my strength. I suppose you're in the same state. That was a truly remarkable night." He slid out of bed and began to straighten it. She went to the other side to help. Their eyes met across the sheet they were pulling tight.

"This feels very comfortable," he said softly. "Very right."

"Yes, it does, though you don't make good corners, you know."

They both laughed, and the smiles lingered as they completed the bed. But then he folded it back and came around to her.

"What—"

Kate was picked up and tucked into the bed. "Stay there."

"Bully." But Kate stayed and watched as he found his robe and slipped it on. It was a rather dull gray. She pondered what color would suit him better, planning to make another for him.

He disappeared into the next room, returning with her valise. He dug out her nightgown and tossed it to her. "Put that on, and I'll command some breakfast for us."

Kate clutched the night dress but looked around at the wild room. "Here?"

"I'll soon have it tidied."

"I should—"

"It can be your turn tomorrow."

Kate slumped back, silenced by his confidence. Tomorrow. Another night like last night, and then tomorrow.

They still had to face today.

While he was out giving orders, she pulled on the night dress, then climbed out of the bed. He returned as she was finding her comb and hairbrush in the valise. Sitting at the dressing table working on tangles, she fired the first shot of reality. "If I came to live here, Stephen would have to come too."

In the mirror, she saw him turn to her. "Of course he would."

She swiveled to face him. "You wouldn't mind?"

"I'd mind any other arrangement. I mind the fact that you haven't brought him with you. He must be a different child to the one I saw born."

"Yes, he is. But you can't acknowledge him as your son."

"Later, Kate." He turned away to gather up his coat and her flannel petticoat. "We'll talk about it later."

Kate sighed and turned back. Time wouldn't change anything, but perhaps that was reason enough to put off the reckoning.

He had the room in pretty good order by the time two maids arrived with trays of food. Though well-trained, they couldn't hide their interest and excitement at Kate's arrival. They arranged covered platters, coffee and chocolate pots, and pots of jams, then curtsied and left.

"I suppose I'll be a nine-days wonder."

"Begging for compliments?" He led her to the table. "I'm sure your wonder will last more than nine days."

"You know that's not what I mean!" She raised a cover and found eggs and bacon. "I'm astonishingly hungry."

"Nothing astonishing about it." He helped himself to a huge amount of food and ate with relish.

Kate ate a bigger breakfast than she ever had in her life.

And all the while they talked—about army friends, his decision to come home, and her family in Aylesbury. They avoided talk of their marriage.

When they'd finished, he said, "I've ordered you a bath next door, and Jess should have your clothes unpacked. When you're ready, come to the drawing room. It's to the left at the end of the corridor. We'll talk there."

Kate went without complaint. The idyll was over.

A long bath was welcome, and delayed the fateful hour. Kate had to climb out eventually, though, for even with a fire in her room, the water grew cold. She dressed carefully in the light brown merino she had intended for her formal meeting with Charles Tennant. Jess helped her tidy her hair into a simple knot, and then settled a demure lace cap on top of it. The cap was trimmed with lace and ruffles, but couldn't be called frivolous, she assured herself.

Taking a deep breath, she went into the corridor and followed it to the left to a half-open door. When she pushed through it, she found herself in the drawing room with Charles awaiting her, standing by a lit fire.

Midday sun shafted through four long windows hung with cream brocade, and glowed on light-oak paneling and a white-painted ceiling. It was a charming, comfortable room, part of a house that until recently had presumably been a happy one.

"What happened to your cousin's wife and daughters?" she asked.

"They are living with Sophie's family at the moment. I'm sure they will at least visit here."

He was dressed much as he had been yesterday,

in green coat, long white waistcoat and breeches, and brown tan-top boots. He'd shaved, and his hair was tamed back into a neat ribbon. All the energy was there, though, threatening to shatter her good sense.

She sat in a chair quite close to him. "So, what are we to do?"

"I think our best course is to tell the world that our marriage occurred after your baby's birth."

Kate gripped her hands together and made herself consider it. "It makes him a bastard."

"Everyone seems willing to accept that you were married to Fallowfield."

"That's only because no one has questioned it."

"Who's likely to?"

"His family? For all I know, there's an inheritance at stake."

Now she'd surprised him. "You don't know?" he asked.

She shook her head. "He never spoke much of his family and since coming home, I've . . . I've been too frightened to look."

"Kate, there's no inheritance. His father was a corn factor, I believe, who married a lady. Doubtless the father had the same charm as the son. They were both carried off by a fever when he was quite young and he was sent to a school paid for by his maternal uncle. All the uncle did for him in the end was to buy him a commission. So I doubt anyone is going to take an interest in his son."

For a moment, Kate surrendered to the pleasant prospect, but then she sat up straight. "But the only birth documents I have are those provided by Mr. Rightwell, and *they* state that he is your son!"

"We'll find Rightwell and have the matter corrected. If you were married to Dennis when the child was conceived, that overrides who you were married to later."

"But *he'll* want proof that I was married to Dennis!"

"Plague take it, are you always this difficult!"

Kate snapped to her feet. "And are you always so self-deceiving? There *is* no easy way around this. Either my son is a bastard, or he is your son and heir." She took a deep breath and made her decision, bitter though it was. "He can be a bastard. He certainly is a child of his mother's folly. I expect the support and patronage of a peer of the realm will mitigate any stain upon him."

"Which only leaves your reputation sullied . . ."

"Perhaps I deserve that."

"Never." His hand formed a fist against the mantelpiece. "Kate, what if we can find proof of your marriage to Dennis?"

"Proof?"

"Those actors."

"There are probably more actors in the nation than booksellers! How do you intend to find those three?"

"We could advertise. Post bills."

"Charles! It's a forlorn hope."

He smiled in a way she remembered from the army. "I'm the master of the forlorn hope," said Charles the Bold. "First, we'll go to the place you were married . . . Where was it?"

"Worleigh, but—"

"That's not far from here. We'll ask questions. Perhaps the actors were local."

"But—"

"If we find witnesses to vows, no matter who they are, the marriage would be legal."

"And Stephen would be Dennis's son." Kate was almost caught up in his spell, but only almost. "I go odds we find a decrepit house, and no one who even remembers a mock wedding over two years ago."

"So you'd rather give up without trying?"

At that, Kate raised her chin. "Never. By all means let us try."

"That's my girl." He pulled her in for a kiss. "Don't forget, I'm a genius at the forlorn hope."

Kate's memories of Worleigh were faint, but she remembered the name of the place in which she'd said her vows—Thornford House. She and Charles had come alone in his curricle, traveling almost entirely in silence. Kate could not bear to talk of hope or the future, but was not interested in anything else.

She suspected he felt the same.

She tried to hold onto hope until they turned in between crumbling stone pillars and gates rusted open. It was a wild-goose chase. The house was still deserted. The drive was rutted, and overgrown by unkempt trees and straggly shrubbery.

"Other vehicles have passed this way," Charles pointed out as he steered around a particularly large hole. Kate looked and saw that he was right. Since the last rain, wheels had rolled down this drive. It gave her a tiny bit of hope.

At first glance, the rambling old house killed it, but then she realized that behind dense ivy, no windows were broken. A wisp of smoke curled up from one of the half-dozen chimneys.

"Someone's here!" she announced.

"Probably just a servant," he cautioned as he halted the vehicle and jumped down. "We won't find our actors here, but there may be a clue."

Kate scrambled down by herself. "It's more than I ever hoped for. It's something." As he tied the reins to a tree, she marched up to the door and rapped the iron knocker, causing a shower of rust.

Paint was peeling from the door, but even though most of the leaves had fallen and were piled in drifts around the house, the steps were clear of them.

She plied the knocker again, loudly.

"Perhaps we'd better go around the back," said Charles, coming up behind her. "If it's a servant, they doubtless just live in the kitchen."

Kate scowled at the knocker, but took his hand to pick her way along a rough path round the house to the back. There they saw the promising sight of a well-tended kitchen garden, and when they knocked on a back door, it was opened by a surly old man.

"What d'yer want?"

He held the door half-closed so they couldn't see into the kitchen, but warm air and a smell of soup or stew wafted out.

"We'd like to speak to the mistress of the house," said Charles.

"Why?"

Kate's heart gave a little skip. He hadn't denied such a mistress.

"Private business." Charles became the officer. "Open up, man! You can't keep a lady standing here."

The man instinctively stepped back, and they were in before he could collect himself.

It was a large old kitchen, with smoke-blackened walls and simple wood furniture, but it was fairly clean and well-tended. In front of an open hearth, two old women sat on a settle hunched in shawls.

One of them straightened. "What business have you here?" It was not a servant's voice. Then she peered at Kate. "Don't I know you?"

Heart beating fast, Kate went closer. "I'm Kate Dunstable, Miss Heston. I was here two years ago to marry your great-nephew, Dennis Fallowfield."

"Hah! Now I remember. Yours is not a face anyone would forget, gel. What do you want?"

"I'm afraid Dennis is dead, ma'am."

"So I hear. Do you want money? You'll not have
it from me."

"No, I don't want money." Kate was gripping her
hands tight together. The aunt was real. Was it possible the marriage was too? Had Dennis *lied* to her?

God, why had that never occurred to her?

"What do you want, then? Speak up."

"I . . . I have lost the documents of my marriage,
Miss Heston. I am looking for the witnesses."

"Well, here we are. Myself and Aggie here." She
gestured to the other woman, who nodded vaguely.
"Her wits are going. Fine companion she's turned
out to be. Does nothing but eat."

Rather dizzy with relief, Kate asked, "And the
clergyman?"

"Reverend Trowlip. You'll find him down at his
parsonage, I suppose, nursing a brandy bottle. Such
a fuss as he made about coming here to wed you
two in my own chapel. Seems to think I should go
to his church. What's wrong with a lady praying to
God for herself in her own chapel? All he wants anyway is money for 'glass.' Money for windows and
things, you might suppose, but it all goes for bottles." She stared up at Kate. "I did tell you I have
no money, didn't I?"

"Yes, and I'm sorry for it. Can we help you in any
way?"

The old woman jerked back in surprise. "We?"
She peered behind Kate. "Who are you, sir?"

"Major Charles Tennant, ma'am. A fellow officer
of your great-nephew, and husband to his widow."

"Indeed! I like your jaw, young man, but you'll
still get no money of me!"

"I assure you, we wouldn't take it if you offered.

You so clearly need every penny. But Dennis and Kate did have a son."

"Ah-ha!" Miss Heston emphasized the explosion with a thump on the arm of the settle. "Now I see it. You want my money for the boy. How old is he?"

"Just six months."

"Bring him here when he's ten. No younger. I can't abide young children. And don't bother bringing him if he don't have manners. Can't abide brats. If he can make a bow and say please and thank you, I'll consider leaving him my pittance."

The old lady's sour words didn't bother Kate at all, for hope and relief were spreading through her like the warmth of the fire. In fact, she went forward and took a clawlike hand. "That's very kind of you, Miss Heston. I'll be sure to bring him here to see you. He should know his father's family."

The old woman scowled up at her, but didn't remove her hand.

"And," added Kate, "I now regard you as my family. If you have need of anything, you must send word." As if by magic, Charles passed Kate his card with Marchmont Hall, Strode Kingsley on it, and she placed it in Miss Heston's unresisting hand.

They found their own way out into the sunshine.

"I was really and completely married to him," Kate said in wonder. Then she added sharply, "The loathsome toad!"

"Indeed. A nasty trick to steal the documents and deny it. I suppose he just found marriage too restricting. I apologize on his behalf."

"But *why*? Why court me and marry me, then . . . ? Oh God, it was all just the wager."

He took her hand. "He never could resist a challenge, and your unassailable virtue must have seemed an exciting one. I'm sorry, Kate."

"I'm just sorry that I proved such a disappointment to him."

He drew her into his arms. "Don't. It wasn't your fault. None of it was. He wasn't a man for domesticity. I was considerably surprised when he turned up with a regular woman. I'd probably have keeled over with shock if he'd announced that he'd married. But I'm sure he intended to play honestly with you at first. He was a gentleman." He rubbed her back comfortingly. "Perhaps it was us all along."

She looked up then. "What do you mean?"

"A few times he accused me of wanting to steal you. Even of having an affair with you—"

"The wretch!"

"He read my wishes correctly. Especially when he started going to other women."

"I suspected it. Especially as I grew big with child." Kate wondered why—with all the other betrayals—this one hurt so much.

"Perhaps he sensed that what you had together wasn't perfect. Put it behind you, Kate. I want domesticity, I want marriage, and I adore you. And I will be completely faithful to you, till death us do part."

"You'd better be," Kate said, pulling out of his arms and deliberately using her smile. "Let's go and talk to Reverend Trowlip."

The plump, red-faced, elderly clergyman confirmed the marriage without hesitation, though he railed at Miss Heston's practice of only using her decrepit private chapel. In return for a couple of guineas, he copied out his record of the marriage and signed it for them.

"For glass," he muttered as he pocketed the coins. Kate suspected that Miss Heston was right, and the glass was in bottles rather than windows.

She didn't care. She didn't have a care in the world!

As they walked back toward the curricle Charles said, "All we have to do now is to amend the birth record."

"Will that present any difficulty?"

"None at all. A man can't be declared father to a child if he couldn't have been legally married to the mother at conception."

Kate leaned against the side of the curricle, almost weak with relief. "It's over? It's settled?"

"It's over. It's settled." He took her hand. "But do you know what? I want to marry you again, with all pomp and ceremony, and with the whole of Aylesbury as witness. So you can never get away."

Kate looked up at him, tears in her eyes. "Jess warned me about that. She thinks marriage just ties a woman down."

"I want you tied down. I want to be tied down with you. Gads, this is beginning to sound decidedly odd!" He raised her hand to his lips, watching her with those remarkable eyes. "Marry me, Kate. Marry me with pomp and ceremony and forever."

Kate went into his arms. "Oh yes. Yes, please. Till death us do part."

Jo Beverley

In writing *The Determined Bride*, JO BEVERLEY finally managed to use the knowledge and experience gained teaching woman-centered childbirth classes, and in giving birth to her own two children. These days, however, she's a full-time writer with sixteen romance novels to her credit—four of them RITA Award winners—and a member of the Romance Hall of Fame. Her most recent novel is *The Shattered Rose*, a medieval romance.

A Kiss
After Midnight

~

Tanya Anne Crosby

Prologue

❧

England
Summer, 1850

They called her the *little princess of Blackstone.*

He just called her brat.

She was no princess, o' course, just a duke's daughter, but even his own da called her that out of pity, because they kept her locked away in a schoolroom all day, where she learned to tally and read at the age of seven as though she were some bloody bookkeeper.

That's what his da said.

Thomas just kept his mouth shut, because no one knew she stole away from her studies to meet him each day. No one ever looked for her, and Thom supposed they kept her locked away in that rotten schoolroom because her da just didn't wanna see her. That's what he thought, all right. Her da was a rotten old bugger, who yelled more'n he breathed.

Nah, she was no princess . . . she was just his best friend in the whole bloody world.

Laying belly down upon his pasteboard sled at the crest of their favorite hill, Thomas peeked through the tall grasses at the little girl sitting down below. His heart raced as he shimmied nearer, parting weeds and silly flowers to get a better look.

Every day he'd come to meet with her here, same time, same place—ever since the day they'd met in the garden his da tended for her father. He'd been eight then, she'd been seven, and they'd become fast friends, racing through the mazes together and rolling beneath hedges, giggling as they escaped hideous creatures in pursuit—mostly her bellowin' da.

But now that he was thirteen . . . his heart was beginning to do strange things whenever he saw her. It beat so fiercely at times he thought it might grow legs, burst from his chest, and race away. And his breath . . . hells bells . . . he could never seem to catch it anymore. It was happening again just now, his body reacting strangely. He knit his brows as he watched her, and he drew in a breath, sucking a weed up his nose. He sneezed it out in disgust, and glowered down at her.

Damned if she didn't look sad, he thought, though he really couldn't be certain at this distance—until she slumped forward, and her sobs reached his ears. He frowned and lifted himself up from the ground, slapped at his clothes to relieve them of the dirt. Abandoning his pasteboard, he started at once down the hill. She'd prolly tripped over that silly dress she wore and couldn't get back up, he thought with a smirk. He missed the clothes she used to wear. . . . the way they used to play together, scuffling in the dirt.

She didn't seem to notice him even once he was standing over her, so preoccupied was she with her caterwauling. Thomas simply stood, waiting for her to look up. Used to be that he woulda simply popped her on the head and took off, and she would have run screaming after him. Now, he couldn't bring himself to touch her. Her hair was so pretty, curls, perfectly arranged in such a manner that even her earnest wailing couldn't properly muss it. He stood there, mesmerized by the way the sunlight glistened over the lustrous coppery strands.

Dammitall.

He had the sudden most disconcerting urge to sit down beside her and embrace her . . . stroke her beautiful hair and comfort her. It wasn't like her to cry. He remembered the time she'd scolded him for sobbing after he'd run into the naked statue in her father's garden—the one with the silly leaf over his man things. He'd grown a knot on his forehead the size of an apple, but she'd told him to grow up and had boxed his ears soundly. Devil take her, if she'd been a boy, he woulda just boxed her right back.

But she wasn't a boy.

And it was becoming more and more apparent. His heart lurched and beat a little faster at the thought. She was his best friend, and she was a bloody rotten girl—and if the fellows ever discovered he still met with her here every day, he'd never hear the end of it. His face warming, he stood there, wondering if he should speak up . . . or maybe tap her on the head to gain her notice.

For the first time in all the years he'd known her, he felt like scurrying away before she could chance to spy him. Longingly, he gauged the distance to the crest of the hill and considered dashing back and diving behind it for cover. He didn't move however, simply stood before her, his feet pasted to the ground. And then she suddenly glanced up, and Thomas felt a sudden leap within his breast.

Watery green eyes stared at him.

She gave a little shriek at the sight of him, and he leapt backward in alarm, responding with a yelp of his own. But she didn't move, and he thought for certain she prolly couldn't in that silly dress she wore.

"You scared me!" she accused him, and didn't look a bit grateful for his presence.

"I . . . er . . ." He glanced away at the hill where his pasteboard sat waiting, feeling suddenly timid, as though she'd caught him at something he wasn't supposed to be doing—and that didn't make any sense, 'cause he wasn't doing anything a'tall. He merely wanted to show her his new pasteboard . . . wanted to take her sliding, hear her gleeful giggles and shrieks. But the thought of being so close to her, putting his arms about her middle, made his chest hurt somehow. "I saw you weepin'," he finished lamely.

"Well!" She glared at him, her brows drawn together in that familiar scowl. Her hands went to her hips.

It almost eased him to see the spark of anger in her eyes. Almost, but not quite, because there was something different about the way she looked today.

"Well what?" he snapped, annoyed that she was staring at him as though he were some wart-covered frog.

"You could have said something!" she announced somewhat less petulantly, and then added sullenly, "I've been waiting for you."

As she had done without fail for the past four years, so why did the thought suddenly make him feel so light-headed?

"Well," Thomas countered, trying to sound cool and collected. "I'm here, aren't I?" He swiped his damp palms upon his trousers, and frowned at the strange catch in his voice.

"Did you . . . um . . . fall?" he asked her. "Is that why you were crying?"

"No." Her voice was oddly subdued, and her eyes misted once more.

He scratched at his head, and asked, "Aren't you hot?"

"Hot?"

"Well, you look hot to me."

"No."

"Then why are you crying?" he asked her, and knelt before her upon the grass.

She shrugged.

"What's the matter, brat?" he taunted her. She shook her head, fat tears sliding from her lucid green eyes, and Thomas sobered. "Toria? What's wrong?"

She began to weep in earnest, casting her head into her lap, and Thomas, without another thought, scooted closer and placed an arm around her shoulders. He lowered his head to her wet cheek, and whispered against her face. "Toria . . . what is it? It can't be so bad as all that."

"Oh, but it is!" she wailed, and buried her head more deeply into her crossed arms. Thomas moved closer, heat rising into his face as he did so. She shrugged away a little in her hysteria, elbowing his cheek in the process, and his face burned hotter as he realized how close he'd been. He winced but didn't move away. He couldn't. She smelled nice, like a field of flowers after a gentle rain. He tried to concentrate upon her words, but couldn't quite manage the feat.

"Don't you understand?" she sobbed.

God only knew, he didn't. He hadn't heard a bloody word she'd said. He didn't know his body anymore—it was a strange beast these days—or his voice—or even the little girl he'd known for an eternity. He rubbed at his cheek to soothe the soreness.

"I might never see you again!" she exclaimed, her head still buried within her arms, and her sobs muffled there.

Good grief, she was even beginning to act like a girl. "Hells bells, Toria!" Thomas declared, reasoning with her. "You see me every day!"

"Not anymore!" she whispered brokenly, shaking her head sadly, sobbing as she lifted her face to look at him.

He frowned. He somehow understood she was telling him something important, but couldn't concentrate with those green eyes focused upon him so intently.

"My father says no more! Oh, Thomas!" she whispered woefully. "He says I may never see you again, and he's going to make your papa send you away!"

Her words registered at last.

Thomas blinked as comprehension dawned. "Send me away?" She nodded, her cheeks streaked with tears, and Thomas felt the blow of her words like a fist to his gut. "Why?"

"Because he says 'tis unseemly that I should play with you—a boy, at that!—and if your papa wishes to remain employed at Blackstone, he must send you far away!"

"Send me away?" Thomas felt numb. "Where?"

"Away to school, I think," she revealed, her brows slanting sadly. "He says your papa will do it because he knows what is best."

Thomas sank from his knees to his bottom and declared, "My da will never send me away!" Even as he spoke, he knew it was a lie. His da had seven mouths to feed, including his own, and his da would do whatever it took to be certain the entire family was safe and sure. If the duke of Blackstone meant to send him away . . .

He stared for the longest time at the windflowers dancing with the gentle breeze. "When?" he asked quietly.

"I don't know," she cried, and threw her arms

about him, embracing him. "Oh, Thomas!"

"Hells bells," Thomas exclaimed, and sat, benumbed with emotions he couldn't begin to untangle. He really thought he hated her da, but he wasn't about to tell her so. He put his arms about her, returning the embrace, uncertain whether the tears that stung at his eyes suddenly were for the family he knew he would leave . . . or for the best friend he didn't think he could live without.

They sat there, embracing, the two of them, and Thomas didn't feel the least bit ashamed for the kiss he bestowed upon her temple.

She peered up at him, her green eyes glistening with her tears.

Thomas looked down into her face and simply stared, memorizing every line of her face, the curve of her lips, every last freckle upon her nose.

She'd been his best friend for five years, his confidant, his playmate. And now he realized with the knowledge that he was losing her . . . in his heart he'd begun to think of her as something more . . .

"Promise you'll never forget me!" she implored softly, her tears spilling onto his shirtsleeve.

"I promise I never will," he swore. And meant it with every piece of his soul. He plucked a windflower and pressed it into her hand. "Promise you'll never forget me, Toria."

She hugged him tighter.

"Promise!" he demanded.

"I never will!" she vowed, shaking her head adamantly. "Oh, Thomas, you know that I never will!"

"I think . . . I think I love you," he whispered, blinking with a bewildered sense of self-discovery.

"I think I love you, too," she whispered in return.

And together they sat, embracing, words much too difficult to speak between them.

Someday, he would come back for her.

Someday, he would be good enough—not a mere gardener's son.

Someday . . .

Chapter 1

June 1, 1863

> *Dearest Mr. Smith,*
>
> *I realize it has been some time since our previous correspondence....*

Lady Victoria Haversham tapped her quill upon the cherrywood desk, and sighed a little despondently. Frowning pensively as she stared at the black ink stain that remained, she tried to determine the best course of action to be taken.

Confound it all, she was running out of time!

She simply must be wed come two weeks hence! And here she was practically on the shelf—practically, ha! At twenty-four, she *was* on the shelf! She hadn't gone through the *rite de passage* as her friends had, because her father had suffered his unfortunate attack at the very age she would have begun her ceremonies—not that she held that against him, mind you. It certainly hadn't been his fault that his heart had failed him. And neither had she cared for the silly girlhood ritual, at any rate. It was just that ... now ... at this very instant ... she found herself regretting ... Her face screwed. Well ... perhaps not regretting precisely, as she truly didn't wish to be wed even now.

Certainly, it wasn't her choice of preference.

She continued to tap the tip of her pen upon the desk, staring at the letter, not entirely certain why she was writing the old gardener. He rarely responded to her letters anyway, as he didn't know how to read. She knew dear George often held her letters until his parson came to visit, because the few times he'd replied, the letters had been composed by the parson himself. It was simply that . . . even after all these years, she felt a stronger connection with the old man than she did to anyone else.

Strange that . . . And then perhaps not so strange, after all. She'd never been close to her mother, nor to her father. Not really.

Victoria swallowed her grief as she looked about the room—her office now, though it had once been her father's. The somber colors, deep blues and darkest golds, and the heavy draperies had always given her a strange sense of ambivalence. On the one hand they were familiar and comforting, and on the other . . . made her feel quite like marching across the room and ripping them all down like some mad woman, only to let in the sunlight. She had them drawn just now as far as they would go—not far at all—revealing the vivid green lawns and the sunlit beds of wildflowers brilliant in bloom. All of it hers now.

At least for the time being.

Devil take her father! Whyever should she have to wed simply to keep what was already hers? It was absolutely unbearable! How could he have placed her in such an untenable position? How could he have cared so very little?

Lord only knew, all she'd ever wished to do was please the scoundrel—her mother, too—though neither of them did she ever manage to make proud. Her mother had been a delicate woman, striving so hard to win her father's favor, yet never succeeding in the endeavor. And it seemed her greatest sin of all had been to bear him a daughter, and then to cock up her toes before she could bear him his precious son. Her father had never forgiven her for it—not her mother, nor Victoria either. Until the very day he'd breathed his last he'd lamented his lack of a male heir to carry on the family legacy. With his dying breath he'd wept for his nonexistent son, while Victoria had remained at his side, gently brushing the hair from his forehead.

And yet . . . not for an instant had Victoria suspected he would turn from her so completely.

In truth, her father had never spoken an ill word to her; he'd simply never been a doting father. He'd been a man who'd abhorred weakness of spirit, had determined that if he couldn't have his male heir, then he would, at least, force his only daughter to rise above such abhorrent female failings.

Victoria had tried so hard to rise to his expectations.

She'd studied her letters diligently, had exercised her numbers until her eyes had crossed and her head had ached. She'd worked them well—had an aptitude for numbers, so her professors had said. Under her father's tutelage, she'd even managed the household accounts—had managed them well, she'd thought. Gad, but her reward had been a handful of pats upon the head, and an occasional, "Good show, Victoria." Inconceivable how very much of herself she'd placed within her father's hands. Every precious ounce of her self-worth had depended upon those rare pats of approval.

No more.

The day his will had been read she'd realized the

utter folly of her pride. All of his *good shows* had amounted to nought more than flapdoodle. In the end, he'd preferred to entrust his estates to a brother he abhorred, or a perfect stranger, rather than to a daughter who had labored all of her life to be all that he'd wished of her. Very simply, if she failed to wed before midnight of her twenty-fifth birthday, every last farthing she owned would be surrendered to her bloody uncle. Everything. Not simply the inheritable estates—which had already been forfeit—but everything. But that alone wasn't so unbearable, it was the fact that with it, she would lose her freedom as well. So her choice, it seemed, was to lose some of it now to a husband she no more wanted than she wanted chin hairs . . . or to an uncle who would take as much joy in caging her as had her father.

Given such a straight corner, there was no choice to be made . . . none at all . . .

At the stroke of midnight precisely two weeks hence, for better or worse, she would, indeed, be wed.

And yet . . . She worried her lip as she considered, for she was far from finding a suitable candidate. She shouldn't have put this off so long.

Lord, but it didn't seem fair that a man could, if he so chose, live his life as he saw fit, answering to no one but himself. Her brow furrowed as she lifted up the quill once more, setting it to paper. She finished the letter to the old gardener, hoping that in detailing her abominable situation to her dear old friend, some answer would bring itself to light.

. . . forgive me, please, if I've overburdened you, dear sir, she finished.

. . . as it certainly was not my intention to do so. It is simply that at times, like a mathematical equation,

*it helps me to see the problem drawn out upon pa-
per. The solution will present itself soon, no doubt.
And I've my agent working diligently upon the matter as well. Never fear.*

Delicately tapping out a period at the end of her
sentence, Victoria reached up to dip the drying quill,
and her gaze was caught at once by an instant of
movement out upon the lawn. Behind a distant oak
she spied two figures embracing. Lovers. She
blinked, watching them, fascinated, though modesty
should have compelled her to turn away. It was difficult to tell at such a distance just who the lovers
were, but she thought it might be Robbie, the new
stable hand—comely lad—and perhaps Bethany, the
cook's daughter. As she watched, Bethany ducked
under and out from Robbie's embrace, and hid herself playfully behind the tree. Robbie wasn't quick
enough, for he suddenly found himself staring at her
from behind the fat oak. The two of them circled the
tree as Victoria watched; two lovers at play.

Her heart squeezed a little painfully, and she
sighed softly. Blinking, she continued to watch.
She'd never been one to woolgather much, and
prided herself upon her pragmatism, but this moment, she couldn't help but feel a mite wistful over
all that might have been and never would be—a direct result of her circumstances, no doubt, for it had
been a long, long time since she'd daydreamed of
lovers . . . or stolen kisses beneath perfect moons . . .
or of children laughing about her skirts.

She glanced down at the pen in her hand. Those
things were better not considered at this late hour,
she reprimanded herself. It was much too late for
girlish fancies! She wouldn't be marrying for love—
not that she might have at any rate. Good Lord! did
she know anyone who had married for love? Not

her own mother and father, for certain! No, such musings were best left for giggling schoolgirls— something she had never, ever been . . .

Save once . . .

She recalled a time when she would leap from her bed each morn, eager to discover all the mysteries the day should hold . . . eager to share each and every jewel of discovery with a mischievous little boy with whom she'd fancied herself in love. He was Thomas, the gardener's son, a fair-haired boy with an adorably wicked face, and eyes that fairly twinkled with life and mirth.

What a silly little girl she'd been.

Sighing at her childhood foolishness, Victoria stared down at her own meticulous script. Dare she ask after him now? Something like butterfly wings fluttered within her belly. It seemed rather silly to do so, as George's response was always a simple, "Thomas is very well, thank you." Thomas himself never sent his regards in return.

Her gaze was drawn back to the window, to the sprawling lawns beyond the leaded glass panes, but remained unfocused upon the present. The faint, distant ring of laughter reached her ears . . . laughter that brought a wistful sting to her eyes.

"Promise you'll never forget me!" she recalled beseeching him.

"I promise I never will," he'd sworn.

So much for childhood promises.

Blinking away the sting in her eyes, she forced her gaze away from the window, and shuddering free of pointless reveries, penned a brief closing to her letter, signed her name, and folded the paper. She set it aside at once.

There was no time to waste, as she still needed to pen a letter to her agent. She trusted Philip Goodman well enough to manage the inquiries and initial interviews. He was already aware of what she expected of him; she needed now only draw out a list of her requirements for a suitable spouse—first and foremost, he need be a commoner. If her father had imagined for one instant she would marry some distinguished bore only to keep what was already hers, he'd been sorely mistaken! After all her years of dealing with pompous men—men who wanted nothing more from her than quick, sweet smiles and dutiful silence, Victoria intended to marry just whomever she pleased! Her father's will *hadn't* specified *who* she might wed, and she fully intended to have the final say in this matter. Never again would a man manipulate her life! Not if she could help it!

Victoria only hoped her father would wail in his grave over what she was about to do. Resolved, she opened a drawer and drew out another sheet of paper. Arranging it before her upon the desk, she dipped her quill within the inkwell, and began a very precise letter of instruction to her agent.

Chapter 2

London, June 5

It was certainly true that one could take the man from the country, but one could hardly take the country from the man.

The London apartment was furnished modestly, with rugged pieces that served only to emphasize the meagerest of beginnings. Thom made no apologies for his provinciality. It was part of who he was. No matter the formality of his education, he was still a boy in ragged breeches, and would surely go to his grave with figmental holes upon the soles of his shoes.

He struck a match, sinking back into his favorite chair as it flared. He lit the cheroot, and sucked sweet smoke into the back of his throat as he surveyed the familiar room.

His da had taken up woodworking after retiring, as London hardly offered occasion to "get the dirt under one's nails." A simple wooden rocker sat beside the hearth, evidence of his father's labors; draped over it was the plush quilt his mother had lovingly stitched for him all those years ago, "for those cold nights away at school."

It was just the two of them now, he and his da, as his mother had passed on some years before.

He'd thought a move from the country where his da had been alone would prove beneficial, but damned if his old man hadn't been behaving strangely of late. All day, he'd been coming into the room at intervals as though he had something to say, and then departing, shaking his head like an absent-minded old fool—something his wily old da certainly was not. At sixty-eight years of age his old man was as shrewd as they came. Thom supposed he *did* have something to say, but it certainly wasn't like him to keep it to himself. His father had certainly never had much difficulty in speaking his mind.

It wasn't long before his da peered into the room once more; this time he entered carrying a small carton before him. "Are you busy, son?" he asked.

Thom eyed his father somewhat discerningly. It didn't take a mastermind to deduce he was not. "No," he answered anyway.

"Good. Good." His father approached with his box, and for the first time in his life Thom thought his da appeared old. His mother's death had aged him, surely, but somehow, in the space of these few days, he seemed . . . wizened. He didn't speak, nor did Thom. He simply watched as his father placed the small open carton upon the table beside him. Concern for his father kept his attention from the box for the moment.

Thom sat up within the chair, and withdrew the cheroot from between his teeth. It was only then he noticed the folded parchment clutched within his da's fist, and his gaze converged upon it. Somehow, he understood that its contents were the source of his father's agitation. He handed the letter to Thom and then sat within the facing chair. Waiting, it seemed.

"What is it?"

"Open it," his da bade him.

Thom set his cheroot down within the ashtray, and then did as his father requested, unfolding the parchment. The date upon it was five days past, the scribble unfamiliar. He started to turn the paper over to find the signature, but his father prevented him with a hand.

"Read it first, Thom," his father directed him rather sternly.

His brow's drew together as he turned the paper over to begin.

"*Dearest Mr. Smith,*" he began aloud. "*I realize it has been some time since our previous correspondence . . .*" And then he lapsed into silence as he continued, the tone of the letter becoming entirely familiar.

> *I'm quite certain I don't know why I'm writing to you with this dilemma, dear sir, but you have always seemed so inclined to listen to my ravings—do you remember all those hours I rambled away so, while you tended the roses? I must have worn your patience thin, and yet you listened to me ever mindfully, imparting now and again such wonderful jewels of wisdom for me to ponder. Did I ever thank you properly?*

Thom peered up from the letter, eyeing his fidgeting father with some bewilderment. He wasn't entirely certain he wished to continue, but curiosity, and something more, got the better of him and he continued, his heartbeat quickening.

> *It seems that once again I find myself rambling to you, albeit upon paper—though I do hope you'll bear with me. Good Lord, how to begin . . . From the first, I suppose. By the time you read this I shall be most likely wed—not that I wish to, you see, but it seems I've hardly any choice in the matter. I have*

already written my agent with the necessary terms,
and he is even now conducting a rather unconven-
tional search on my behalf. For a husband ...

The letter continued, explaining rather directly the
terms of her father's ludicrous will. It expressed with
some vehemence, her distaste for the proviso, and
her reluctance to comply. And yet, her tone was
wholly resigned.

He peered up once more, not quite certain how it
was he was supposed to react to the letter's disclosure. Or to his father's apparently well-kept secret.

"You've corresponded with her before?"

His da nodded, indicating the carton at his side.
Thom peered into it, finding the answer to his question. It was filled to brimming with old letters.
Though his brain went suddenly numb, his hand
reached into the carton, withdrawing a letter ... addressed to his father ... from Victoria. And then another. And yet another. He cast an unsettled glance
at his da as he removed the fistful of papers from
their storage box.

In all these years, he'd never dared seek her out—
not even for a fleeting glimpse—not since the day
he'd left Blackstone at her father's dictum.

He'd been handsomely compensated for his departure, of course—his father, as well. Thom had
been afforded an education the likes of which no lad
of his station might ever have dared even to covet.
And his father had been given a substantial enough
pension so that he might be able to enjoy the last of
his years without working his fingers to bloody
nubs. Thom might have been grateful for that much,
but instead he'd chosen anger as his balm. He'd wal-
lowed in it, sworn by it.

His father had continued on as gardener at Blackstone for less than a year after his own departure to

Eton. No time at all for Thom to get over his resentment enough to ask after Victoria. In his anger and youthful pride, he'd vowed to eradicate her from his memory, and to vindicate himself to the bloody world. And so he'd committed his years to furthering his assets and his influence, resolving to show Blackstone that he could make money enough to provide for any man's daughter. Somewhere along the way, he'd forgotten his raison d'être. Growing his business and his money had become objectives in themselves, and he'd stepped upon heads aplenty to gain whatever he'd desired. And yet he'd never truly forgotten her.

That much was painfully clear to him as he stared at the elegant scribble of her pen.

"She spent much time after you left reading within the rose arbor," his father explained. "I got to know her very well."

Thom couldn't be certain what he was feeling. It was unreasonable to love a mere memory so fiercely. And yet there was no denying the churning feeling in his gut, or the anger he suddenly felt at his da for keeping the letters from him. "You never said." His tone was clipped and cool, restrained.

It was a long moment before his father seemed able to respond. "I thought it best, son," he answered in a gruff voice. "Her da gave us so damned much money to leave her be. He didna even want me near her, and so he asked me to go, too. Your ma and I decided it was best to hide the first letters."

"The first letters," Thom said, eyeing his father coldly. "What about the rest?"

His father shrugged, seeming suddenly fragile and melancholy. "It seemed the right thing to do."

What good would it do him to be angry now? What was done, was done, and the time to make things right with Victoria long since past. Thom felt a sense of emptiness as he reached into the box, his eyes scanning the addresses. "None to me?"

"None to you," his father answered.

Why did that suddenly dishearten him all the more? Provoke him, even? "Then you did nothing wrong, did you? These letters are addressed to you, not to me. It was your right to show them to me, or not to, wasn't it?"

Again, his father shrugged. "I think you should read them, Thom," he said only, "before you decide what to feel."

Christ, but he suddenly needed to read them. Damn, but he'd regretted all this time never knowing how she'd fared, never having asked, never having dared to insinuate himself upon her life. He'd gone through his years shoving her image from his memory, trying not to think of her a'tall, because every time he did, he saw her face as he'd left her that day at the foot of their favorite hill— and he'd felt the anger anew that he'd been judged and found unfit for the company of the *little princess of Blackstone.*

They'd been little more than children then . . . but Thom believed he'd loved her in the purest sense of the word. She'd been his very best friend, his confidante, and none of the proper lovers he'd known since—even in their maturity—had ever come close to filling the void that Toria had left behind.

So much time had passed . . .

He began to read, commenced with the letters that he already held, and found that they'd been written within the past two years; no mention of him, a'tall. He pulled out more, and found one that had been written soon after his departure. The entire letter was an inquiry of him: *How did he fare at school? Did he ever ask of her? Did he like his new friends? and had anyone thought to send him a blanket? because in the winter one could never have quite enough.* He glanced up, his gaze drawn at once toward the rocker, to the blanket his mother had sent him that first winter. His eyes stung suspiciously. Victoria's concern for him, even after all these years, warmed him, pricked at his heart.

His da seemed to know what he was thinking. "Your ma wept for weeks after you left, feeling help-less. It wasn't until Victoria suggested sending the blanket that she found an outlet. She commenced to stitching it for you at once, and she and your sisters worked night and day to complete it."

Thom turned to look into his father's eyes; they were weary and red-rimmed over the memory he'd shared, but full with affection. "I've never said this to you, Thom. And perhaps I'll never get the chance to say it again . . . but I love you, son. Anything your mother and I did, we did because we thought it was the right thing to do."

"I know da," Thom said, and numbly reached into the box again. He searched and found a few more written around the same time: more of the same page-long inquiries.

There was a long instant of silence between them. "I realize that it's been a long time, son, but read them all, and I think you'll know what to do," he said. "A man must do what he must, you realize?"

Thom nodded, and was vaguely aware that his father left him at some point to peruse them in pri-vacy.

The majority of the letters had been written in the first three years of his departure to Eton. And then they had slowly dwindled. The last few years her letters had been sparse, nor had she asked after him any longer.

A tinge of melancholy filtered through him.

If he closed his eyes . . . he could almost remember

the way she'd looked the day she'd told him she could no longer see him ... the anguished expression upon her face ... her beautiful hair aglow beneath the noonday sun, her green eyes sparkling with those precious diamond-like tears.

He could hardly forget the way it had made him feel.

For the first time in his life he'd been made painfully aware of the differences between them. Somehow, in all their childhood together, he'd managed to overlook the disparaging differences in the sizes of their homes. He'd managed to forget ... when she'd smiled at him ... that he'd had holes in his breeches, and sleeves that were entirely too short ... while she, on the other hand, had worn silks with fragile white lace. He'd failed to comprehend what it had meant that whilst she'd had servants to tend her, his family served.

That day, in his childhood innocence, he'd promised never to forget her. God only knew he'd tried, despite his vow.

She'd promised never to forget him, too.

He stared at the letters scattered now about him; so many letters. She'd kept her promise for so long, and he'd failed her.

He could still make amends.

It wasn't too late.

His father was right, he did know what to do. She needed a husband, did she?

The hell she did; Victoria Haversham needed someone who would set her free once they were wed. And he was that man.

He'd talk to Philip Goodman first thing in the morn. She didn't seem to understand that whatever contract her agent might draw up for her, no matter how solidly worded, it would be much too easily breached. Any man with suitable connections might render the prenuptial bootless with so little trouble it would make her head whirl. As an attorney Thom understood how effortless that undertaking might be. By law, once a husband and wife exchanged vows, the wife lost, to all intents and purposes, all rights over any property she possessed. Everything she owned came into the control and disposal of her husband—everything, even so far as herself—prenuptials be damned!

Thom was determined to ensure she was protected against such thievery. He refused to allow her to lose everything when she'd labored so long and so hard to earn what little her father had bequeathed her.

Neither did Thom need her money. Thanks to her father's *generosity* and the success of his firm, he was comfortable enough.

But knowing Victoria . . . she was proud and wise and barefaced . . . he determined it would take nothing short of cunning to coax her into accepting his aid.

Well, Philip Goodman owed him. With Philip's help, Thom intended to present Victoria Haversham with a bargain she could hardly refuse. He wasn't the man she bloody well would have chosen to wed were her circumstances different. He knew that. But circumstances weren't different, and he wasn't the least bit repentant for employing whatever Machiavellian tactics were needed to bring about the one thing he hoped would redeem him.

Whatever it took, before these nine days were through, he planned to be wed to Victoria Haversham.

In fact, he decided it couldn't wait until morning. He left the scattered letters where they lay, and found his coat at once, with the express intent of paying Philip Goodman a midnight visit.

He didn't bother to tell anyone where he was off to, but George Smith knew his son very well. The old man smiled as the front door slammed shut, and took himself off to bed, anticipating his first good night's rest in some time.

Thom would take care of everything, he knew, and Victoria Haversham would find herself in good hands.

"All's well that ends well," he chirped, and climbed the stairs to bed.

Chapter 3

Lord, she couldn't imagine what could be keeping them!

Victoria tried not to pace, but she couldn't very well keep herself from it. The clock had last struck after five, and still they'd yet to arrive—Philip Goodman and her spouse to be—whoever the devil he might be!

Her stomach fluttered at the very notion of what she was about to do: wed a perfect stranger.

Well, it couldn't be helped, she assured herself. No use fretting over it now.

She tried to recall everything Mr. Goodman had related of him—not very much. Perhaps if she knew more of him, she wouldn't be so ill at ease just now. As it was, she knew only the basics; that his name was Thom S. Parker, that the two were close personal friends, acquaintances since their days at Eton. She knew that he was an attorney. And not very bloody much else. It seemed Mr. Goodman had gone to Mr. Parker for counsel and had left his office with the perfect spousal candidate—Mr. Parker himself. Mr. Parker had, in fact, helped to draw up the necessary papers to ensure Victoria's position in this conjugal union. She might have doubted that particular arrangement, save that she trusted Philip Goodman's judgement to the utmost degree.

Besides, she'd never be so witless as to simply take a man's word in this matter of her life; she'd had the papers looked over by objective parties, and despite that they'd been found to be in order, she'd attached her own addendums, as well.

At any rate, there hadn't been any need to continue the search, Mr. Goodman had assured her. Thom S. Parker came highly recommended. And yet, Victoria would have felt ever so much better had she at least been able to interview the man herself. Somehow, it hadn't worked out that way—and here they were in the eleventh hour, and still she'd yet to set eyes upon him!

Perhaps he was a horrid little troll? short and squat, with a florid face and a bulbous nose, and he was afeared she'd be repelled by the prospect of wedding with him? Well, she might have set his mind at ease at once, as she didn't have any intentions of carrying on with him as though they were man and wife! She was wedding for one reason, and one reason alone; to save her inheritance.

She glanced up at the clock—one quarter after the hour—and fretted. Famous! As it was, they wouldn't be arriving in Gretna Green until almost midnight! And no, that wouldn't do a'tall!

They simply *must* be wed *before* midnight!

It was with no small measure of relief that she heard the door knocker, at last. Praying that it would be Mr. Goodman with her little troll, she rushed toward the foyer, swinging the doors open to find that Godfrey had already answered the door, and was even now allowing her long overdue guests entrance.

Philip Goodman entered first, brushing the night's fine mist from his coat. Her fiancé entered next, and Victoria, much to her dismay, found she could merely gape from the doorway of her office.

Lord, but he was no troll.

In fact, whatever Thom S. Parker lacked in breeding, he certainly bore in good looks. He was a splendid specimen of a man, to be sure, with gilded locks that were brushed at the ends with a paler shade of sunlit gold. He wore his hair unfashionably long, wavy locks that fell like lustrous silk below wide-set shoulders in total defiance of convention—something that quite appealed to her, if the truth be known. She drew in a breathy sigh as she stared, unaware that she did so.

Oblivious to her presence, the two men bade Godfrey announce them. Victoria tried to find her voice, to assure them that it wasn't necessary, that she was perfectly *aware* of their presence already, but words wouldn't seem to come.

Bronzed and well hewn, like that of a common laborer's, Thom Parker's face was in stunning contrast to the pristine white stock he wore. Dressed in a somber black evening coat and trousers, he cut a dashing figure. And then, good Lord, those eyes—he glanced her way suddenly—uncanny blue, they hinted at the most devilish thoughts. Their scrutiny fair left her breathless.

He smiled, making her feel just the slightest bit disoriented. Good Lord, with no more than his glance and the slightest curve of his lips, he'd managed to make her head reel and her heart leap against her ribs. In fact, she had the sudden disconcerting sensation of having walked into a bloody wall! She, who had sworn men were every one the same, one little different from the next, had somehow, in the space of mere instants, found herself abashed at how very *different* this one seemed to make her feel.

Much too warm.

And heady.

And dizzy.

Positively dizzy.

She was going to have to work at remedying such things. Resisting the urge to fan herself, Victoria pushed away from the door frame. She focused her gaze upon Philip Goodman. "At last!" she admonished them. She turned to address the butler, keeping her gaze carefully averted from Mr. Parker. "Have the carriage brought about at once," she directed him.

"Yes, mum," Godfrey said, and bowed as he took his leave.

She turned again to address Mr. Goodman, studiously avoiding Mr. Parker's gaze, as she determined it most detrimental to her composure. Lord-a-mercy, but it would have been so much easier to face him had he been a bloody toad! As it was, her limbs were trembling. "We've no time to waste!" she apprised them both, trying to retain control, despite the fact that she suddenly felt scattered.

"Do forgive our tardiness, Lady Victoria," Mr. Goodman appealed, removing his hat, shaking it off, and clutching it before him rather anxiously. "I'm afraid we managed to run into a bit of . . . bedlam," he explained, and peered up at his companion rather uneasily. Victoria didn't dare follow his gaze, though she had the provocation to, as she thought Mr. Goodman seemed a trifle suspicious.

"Bedlam?" she asked him.

His brows lifted. "Well, yes, but . . . nought for you to be concerned over, Lady Victoria. 'Tis bedlam of a personal nature, I assure you. Quite personal—and tedious—and—"

"Never mind, then," Victoria said. "I see."

"At any rate," Mr. Goodman continued. "I should like you to make the belated acquaintance of Mr. Thom Ssss . . . Parker."

Victoria wrinkled her nose at his emphatic pronunciation of the man's middle initial, thinking it rather peculiar. Perhaps he was trying not to sneeze? By the screwed expression upon his face it was entirely probable.

"I'm so very sorry it took me so long to get him here. You see, I just couldn't seem to get myself together."

"Never mind," she said, sucking in a breath. She braced herself as she turned to her husband to be. "He's here now, isn't he?"

"That I am, Lady Victoria. Please accept my apologies, as well. I'm afraid I cannot allow Philip to take all of the responsibility here, as it has been quite a chaotic week for me, as well." She dutifully proffered her hand, and he clasped it within his own. His gentle touch sent instant quivers down her spine.

She cleared her throat discreetly and said a little breathlessly, "Mr. Parker . . ." And then suddenly forgot what it was she was going to say.

His full lips curved into a delighted smile, and Victoria was wholly flustered to find that her gaze focused upon his wickedly sensuous mouth. She forced her gaze to lift to his eyes as he brought her fingers to his lips, brushing the back of her hand . . . with the softest lips . . .

Good Lord, whatever was the matter with her?

"You're as lovely as they say," he murmured.

She was? "I am?" she asked, though she hadn't meant to speak the question aloud. And then she realized what she'd said, and amended hastily, "Why, thank you!" Good Lord, that's what they all said! It was simply a pleasantry, she reminded herself. Surely her brains were addled!

His eyes twinkled with mirth, and he chuckled

softly. Victoria didn't allow herself the discomfiture of embarrassment.

His eyes—up close, so vivid a blue that it was unsettling—remained focused upon her own, and Victoria had the strangest sensation of having looked into them before. Some time long ago . . .

A trick of the imagination, no doubt, as she certainly would have remembered Thom S. Parker.

"You're quite welcome," he replied softly.

Another shiver raced down her spine at the sound of his voice. Rich and low, it seemed to whisper directly unto her heart, for the beat of it quickened unmercifully. "I—yes, well—'tis so wonderful to finally make your acquaintance!" Victoria stammered, and then recalled herself to the task at hand. "Now, then! Now that proper introductions have been made, perhaps we should be on our way?"

"As to that, Lady Victoria . . . I'm afraid I won't be going along," Mr. Goodman announced.

Victoria tore her gaze away from Mr. Parker. "You'll not?"

Philip Goodman fidgeted nervously. " 'Fraid not, Lady Victoria. Something's . . . er . . ." He peered up at Mr. Parker, again somewhat uneasily. "It seems something's come up."

Something like panic gripped Victoria at the prospect of sharing a carriage with Mr. Parker. Alone. All the way to Gretna Green. "You'll not be coming with us?"

"I promise to remain a perfect gentleman," Mr. Parker interjected, reassuring her.

"Yes, of course," Victoria agreed, swallowing with some difficulty, though she was entirely certain it was true. He wouldn't dare be otherwise. And certainly if she would trust him enough to wed him, she would have to trust him enough to simply ride in a carriage together with him. That wasn't at all what concerned her. No, it was rather the prospect of being alone with those bewildering blue eyes.

It wasn't until he winked at her that she realized she was staring once more. "Unless you feel we require a chaperon?" he suggested with a devastating smile.

Victoria's cheeks warmed. "Oh! but, of course not! We should manage quite fine without you, of course," she assured Mr. Goodman.

"Jolly good, then!" Mr. Goodman exclaimed. "And I believe I hear the carriage drawing up as we speak." He extended his hand to Mr. Parker. "Thom," he said. "Be well, my friend!" And then he turned to Victoria. "Next time we meet, Lady Victoria, I expect you shall be Mrs. Thom Sssss . . ." His face screwed and he shook his head, looking most annoyed with himself, as he finished, "Parker. Demme!" he exclaimed, and popped his hat back upon his head. "Felicitations to the both of you!" he said. "And if you'll please excuse me, I shall be well out of your way." He hastened to take his leave.

Victoria blinked as she watched him go, certain he was developing a terrible stammer. Poor man. Perhaps he was working too hard. "Well, then," she said, turning to her intended. "Shall we go, as well?"

"Certainly," her heretofore unseen fiancé said, and moved to open the door for her. "After you," he insisted, and Victoria had the sudden, most goatish thought that if she were to be forced to stare at another face across the breakfast table, it might as well be one so pleasing to the eye. And, Good Lord! Thom Parker certainly was that. And furthermore, she refused to feel guilty for such shallow thoughts. Men were so salacious and superficial all the time, were they not? Why not women, too?

Resisting the urge to run screaming up the stairwell, to lock herself away for the rest of her natural life, she smiled as she retrieved her shawl from where she'd placed it upon the banister, took a deep breath, and preceded him out the door.

She only wondered why such a man as he would agree to a proposal such as the one she'd offered. It was a mystery, indeed. Perhaps he was a spend-thrift, anticipating an endless source of funds. If so, he was sorely mistaken, as she was quite frugal with her finances, and she wasn't about to hand him an open bank draft.

Or perhaps he was simply a womanizer, who found a commitment free marriage wholly desirable. In such case, she could only hope he would be dis-creet. She certainly couldn't expect him to remain faithful when she never intended to share his bed. Her face burned at the very notion.

At any rate, it was far too late to turn back now.

Marrying Thom Parker was the only thing left to do.

Chapter 4

She didn't recognize him.

Thom hadn't truly expected her to after all these years, though he'd hoped there might be some small glimmer of recognition in her eyes when first they met again. He admonished himself that it was ludicrous to be disappointed over something so absurd. Thom was a common enough name, and he'd used his mother's maiden name as a surname, besides—damn, Philip, for nearly giving him away. Nor did the man he'd become bear any resemblance to the youth he'd been. She had no bloody cause to be reminded of him a'tall, he assured himself.

It was apparent, by the crease in her brow just now, that she wasn't particularly thrilled at the notion of spending five minutes alone with him, less the entire carriage ride to Gretna Green, and even less exchanging vows with him.

And devil take the woman! she couldn't have chosen a more effective way to get her point across than to wear black to her own wedding. Gad, but it had been all he could do not to howl in laughter at her cheek when first he'd spied her standing there in the doorway. Not that it wasn't a perfectly lovely gown—in fact, though its color was the expression of mourning, the cut of it sent his pulses skittering and his heart to racing like a green boy with his first lover.

If the truth be known, he was pleased enough to see shades of the mischievous giggling girl she'd been—if nothing else, in the simple fact that she'd chosen such a flippant manner in which to choose her husband. The little minx. Though Blackstone's title and patrimony were not hers to give, nor even to keep, the unentailed estates alone amounted to a bloody fortune. She knew good and well that with her father's name and money backing her, she could choose her husband at will, and was certainly doing so with all abandon. Flouting in the face of society, she'd chosen but a lowly commoner to wed.

She'd chosen him.

He'd made certain of it.

Silvery moonlight sluiced within as the carriage turned along a bend in the road, illuminating her face along with the blush upon her cheeks. Even by the pallid starlight, it was more than apparent that her color was high, and he smiled wistfully, wishing he were privy to her thoughts. She turned to look at him, and he didn't glance away—even knowing that perhaps he should . . . lest she spy the truth manifest in his eyes. He fully intended that she should learn his identity, but not until *after* they were wed.

Damn her father for a despotic old fool, for Thom could see in the stern lines of her face that she'd forgotten how to laugh. He'd like to kiss those pursed lips and make them tremble sweetly. He'd like to ease the stress from her brow with the caress of his fingertips.

He'd like to be wedding her in truth, and not for convenience's sake alone.

While he'd been prepared to follow her dictates to the letter—to make this marriage one wholly of convenience—he was no longer convinced it was propitious for her. And perhaps he should, but he damned well didn't feel the least compunction for what he resolved to do. A passionless marriage would merely serve to drive Victoria deeper behind that haughty facade she wore so easily. Watching her now, he was blindsided with the undeniable truth. He wanted her. Loved her still. And he was going to employ every and any advantage to win her.

Only he wanted her to win too.

Though her demeanor was haughty and her hair pulled much too tightly back, every curl pasted into place, deep in her heart Victoria Haversham was still that carefree child, struggling to be free of her father's restraints. Thom needed only look into her eyes to see the little girl he'd once known staring back at him. Lord, but what he wouldn't give just now to hear the elfin lilt of her laughter . . . to run his hands through that luscious hair.

A familiar longing embraced him as he sat there watching her, and he marveled that this connection between them could remain so strong.

On his part, at least.

He shifted within the carriage seat, stretching his legs, and her eyes met his through the shadows. He forced a smile, though the effect of her beautiful gaze, even in the heavy shadows, sucked the breath from his lungs.

Christ only knew he hadn't expected to feel so acutely.

"Do you believe in frankness, Mr. Parker?" she asked abruptly.

"Over duplicity, and ambiguity? Of course," Thom replied, wondering at such a pointed question.

"Then please forgive my plainspokenness," she implored him, "but I was wondering . . . well, you see . . . I know what it is that I hope to gain from this union. And I know what it is Mr. Goodman claims you hope to achieve, but I believe I'd like to hear it from your own lips."

For a moment, Thom was taken aback by the abruptness of her question.

"I fully intended to conduct my own interview with you, you see, but Mr. Goodman seemed rather reluctant for me to meet you."

Thom knew, of course, precisely why Philip had put off their meeting—at his request—lest she somehow recognize him—but he wasn't about to say so.

"I thought, perhaps, it was because you were a toad," she announced rather flippantly.

Thom practically choked at her disclosure. "Did you now?" The little vixen. "You thought me a toad?"

"Of course, I did." She tilted her head. "Mightn't you have thought the same had I been so disinclined to show my face?"

He grinned. "Perhaps, I would, at that," he was forced to concede. "And did you find me a toad, after all?" he asked her rather baldly, thinking to disarm her with playful banter.

He certainly didn't anticipate her response. She lifted her brows pertly. "I won't be ill over my breakfast, if that's what you're asking. No."

Thom couldn't help himself; he threw his head back and roared with laughter.

"You didn't answer my question," she pointed out quite cheekily, her tone perfectly serious, despite his obvious mirth.

" 'Tis simple enough, really," Thom answered between chuckles. "You need my name, and I need yours."

"Nothing more?"

His laughter faded to an engaging grin. "Nothing more."

The little minx. She'd grown into a stunning beauty, with those exotic high cheeks and those entirely too kissable lips. And that wit—sharp as it ever was. And Christ, that hair . . . deceptively dark within the dimly lit coach, but Thom knew only too well the way it looked when the sun played upon its unbound length, bringing it to shimmering life. Vixen.

He could spy her face at intervals by the flashes of moonlight that illuminated the coach. She was staring at his mouth, he thought, and God help him, it was all he could do not to draw her into his arms and kiss those sweet, pouting lips as he craved to do. The only thing that kept him from reaching out, cupping her face into his hands, and tasting the sweet warmth of her delectable mouth, was the simple fact that it wasn't merely her body he wished to win, but her heart, as well.

"Though I believe I've changed my mind," he remarked softly.

Her brow furrowed, and she bit into her lip at his pronouncement. God, but he had the almost irrepressible urge to reach out and lift her chin, to lean forward and offer his own love bites. He wanted to slide his tongue across the seam of her lips, slip within to trace those satiny white teeth. He wanted to drink deeply of the sweet elixir of her mouth, and never to stop.

Damn, but he wanted to taste her.

She was frowning rather fiercely at him now. "Changed . . . your mind? Whatever do you mean, changed your mind, sirrah?"

Victoria's heart beat madly as she awaited his response.

His lips twitched slightly, though he didn't bother

to move from his reclined position, she noticed. He sat there before her with an indolence that both calmed and provoked her at once.

"I believe I've a condition to add to our bargain," he said.

The cad. A condition? "How very amusing!" Victoria exclaimed and laughed softly.

He said nothing, merely stared, his gaze wholly unreadable through the shadows.

It took her an instant longer to realize that he was perfectly serious, and then she gasped in outrage.

"A rather innocuous condition," he added reassuringly.

Capital! Victoria thought, her hackles rising. The cad *would* wait until they were so near their destination, with scarce few hours left before midnight. *Money in all probability!* Rotten knave. "And what, prithee, might that *innocuous condition* be?" Victoria asked him, her anger mounting over the lackadaisical way in which he continued to recline and watch her.

He grinned, his teeth flashing white through the shadows. "It occurred to me," he remarked, seeming unmoved by her sarcasm, "just now . . . as you were staring at my mouth—"

Victoria gasped. "I certainly was *not* staring at your mouth, sirrah!"

His eyes slitted. "—that I should very much like to kiss you . . . and yes . . . I believe you were."

Victoria sucked in her breath with indignation. *The rogue!* She had, in truth, though she could scarce admit as much. She drew trembling fingers away from her mouth, and forced her gaze to meet his eyes, only to find them twinkling with an unsettlingly familiar light.

"How dare you?" she asked him. "How dare you make such a roguish demand!"

"Roguish?" His brows lifted. "Merely because I should wish to kiss my bride? I think not."

Victoria's heart began to pound traitorously. Good lord, he *wished* to kiss her? *And he'd called her his bride; she hadn't thought of herself as precisely such until this instant.* The very thought left her reeling. "I believe you take this much too far, sirrah! And no!" she declared. "The answer is no! I'd say you are in no position to make demands!"

"Of course I am," he answered easily. "You need me," he reminded her.

Victoria glared at him. It was certainly true; she did need him. But she was too angry, and much too offended by his impertinence to concede the fact.

"Wherever would you find yourself another groom at this late hour?" he pointed out unnecessarily.

Victoria continued to glower at him, wholly unsettled by their most unseemly exchange. "You might have spoken up before now to voice this unreasonable demand—as any gentleman would have!"

"Unreasonable?" he asked her.

"You know very well that it is!"

"For a groom to wish to kiss his bride?"

Victoria straightened within the carriage seat. She didn't know any other way to address the issue than to speak plainly. "We are both quite aware that this is merely a marriage of convenience, sirrah. A kiss is only reasonable between lovers—and that we are not—nor shall we ever be!"

"I see." He managed to appear a little injured by her vehemence—and how dare he make her feel like a shrew for having to point out simple facts! "I somehow managed to forget," he replied rather dryly, and straightened within the seat. He stretched out his long legs before him. "Thank you for reminding me. In any case, I can see now that the prospect disturbs you so. Forgive me for asking."

"It hardly distresses me," Victoria countered, her cheeks burning in chagrin and anger. "I simply find your approach distasteful, Mr. Parker!"

"Do you?" he asked her, blinking.

"Yes, I do!" Victoria replied quite fiercely. She was suddenly quite certain she was *not* going to cow to his ungentlemanly behest.

"Why should a simple kiss frighten you so?"

"It most assuredly does not frighten me," she answered as calmly as she was able.

His gaze never wavered from hers, and his lips curved into a knowing smile. "You're certain you aren't?"

A shiver coursed down her spine at the husky softness of his voice—not familiar, though strangely intimate, even so—not particularly soothing either—not when he was asking for kisses whilst they sat alone in a dark, unchaperoned coach, en route to their wedding! It made gooseflesh tingle upon her arms. Rich and low, his voice seemed to whisper somehow into her heart and the beat of it quickened unmercifully.

"Of course, I'm not afraid!" she answered, drawing in an unsteady breath. "Not a'tall!" She averted her gaze and willed to slow the traitorous beating of her heart.

"Then why should a simple kiss distress you, Victoria?" he persisted, his voice low and entreating. " 'Tis a small enough favor to ask—not as though I am asking you to share the marriage bed with me."

The mere mention of a bed made Victoria's heart leap into her throat. The thought of the two of them together upon it made her swallow convulsively. Her gaze reverted to his face. She studied it through the shadows. "Surely you don't intend to ask for such a thing?"

He didn't answer.

Panic filled her. "Because the answer would most assuredly be no!"

"Of course not," he replied easily. "And I certainly would understand how *that* might, indeed, frighten you. But a simple kiss . . ."

"It most assuredly does not frighten me!" Victoria persisted. "It merely does not appeal to me, is all!"

His brow arched a little higher. "No?"

"No!" Victoria assured.

"Still and all . . . I do hope you'll reconsider the request," he suggested. "That is . . . if, in fact, you aren't afraid," he added softly.

It was a challenge. A gauntlet cast at her feet. One Victoria could scarce ignore.

If the truth be known, she'd never considered herself so fetching that a man should crave so much to kiss her. The fact that he wished to, somehow, did, in truth, appeal to her. She smiled softly, though her composure was hardly returned, and said with more aplomb than she felt, "Mister Parker . . . I repeat, I most assuredly am not afraid of any mere kiss."

"Of course not," he yielded. "But do call me Thom, if you would," he suggested. "After all, we are soon to be wed. Whatever will the parson think when he hears you speak to me so formally?"

Victoria's lips twitched at the thought. "I don't suppose it would seem so very appropriate to call you Mr. Parker, now would it?"

"Not very," he agreed. "So, then, Victoria . . . may I call you Victoria?"

Why did she feel he was baiting her? And yet it was a simple enough request from a husband to a wife. Victoria frowned. "Certainly, you may."

"Thank you," he said, and continued to stare, unsettling her. "So, then, Victoria," he persisted, "won't you reconsider the request?"

Victoria swallowed convulsively, and somehow managed to find her voice. "Request?"

"The kiss," he reminded her.

Warmth crept into her breast. Shadows permeated the small carriage, but there was no mistaking the glitter of amusement in his eyes. Her flush crept higher with the realization. And yet she couldn't seem to tear her gaze away. "That's it? Just a kiss?"

"No more," he swore.

She was suddenly grateful for the obscurity of darkness to hide her blush. Those full lips of his curved a fraction more, and Victoria was doubly unsettled to find her gaze drawn to his wickedly sensuous mouth once more.

She couldn't seem to help herself.

How could she possibly say no? He was to be her husband, after all, and it was no longer a demand, but a request . . . Certainly that deserved a reward of sorts? It'd be best if he learned straightaway that demands would get him nothing, that requests would garner him so much more.

Whatever harm could a simple kiss come to?

It wasn't as though she needed to be in love with the man to kiss him, she reasoned.

And she certainly wasn't. She wasn't even entirely certain she believed in love. If one couldn't touch it, or smell it, or see it, one couldn't be entirely certain it even existed. Could one?

"Very well," Victoria relented. "A kiss . . . and no more . . . once we're wed."

He grinned, looking entirely too much like the little boy who'd coaxed the mouse from the cat's jaws, and she wanted suddenly to take it all back.

She wouldn't, however.

For better, or worse, she owed the cad a kiss after

midnight—but just a kiss, no more—and it certainly didn't mean a bloody damned thing! That concluded, she lapsed into a brooding silence for the entire remainder of the journey.

However had he managed to make her agree to such a thing?

Chapter 5

Gretna Green had been highly overpraised, Victoria determined upon their arrival. Her mood was pettish, her bottom numb from travel, and her companion entirely too high-spirited for her liking.

Lord, but tales would have had the village be some grand sanctuary for lovers, with parades to greet runaway sweethearts, and grand huzzahs for their mad, courageous dashes over the border. As it was, the sleepy village was little more than a handful of clay houses with their carefully thatched roofs.

The streets were abandoned, save for a single barking dog, a stray mule, and a drunkard swilling his whiskey outside the town's only two-story structure.

Victoria wasn't particularly impressed.

Then again, neither was she some starry-eyed bride.

They arrived with little enough time to spare. Mr. Parker—Thom—she wrinkled her nose at the awkwardness of using his given name, even in her thoughts—alighted before her. Her legs numb from the jouncing ride, she stumbled out of the carriage, and into his arms.

"Oh!" she exclaimed in surprise, and was helpless to do anything but allow him to steady her upon her feet. His hands grasped her at her waist, his fingers

147

strong and lean and firm. Victoria tried not to construe anything into the way that his fingers slid upward along the sides of her ribs ... and lingered there just an instant too long.

She refused to be caught up in the delusion of this elopement—refused to consider it a lover's clasp. Certainly, it was nothing more than a friendly assist—and the look in his eyes as she peered up to acknowledge his aid was nothing more than a trick of her overweary mind. He wasn't staring at her as though he were waiting for her to confess her undying gratitude and love, she assured herself, nor was he considering that shocking kiss he'd finagled from her. It was her own monstrously wicked mind that imagined he restrained himself from lowering his head to hers just now ... and brushing his lips ever so softly against her own.

A frisson raced down her spine at the merest thought.

Gracious! Whatever was wrong with her? Victoria admonished herself. It certainly wasn't like her to be so fanciful.

It was that bloody kiss she'd been contemplating for most of the journey! she decided. Moreover this *was* her wedding night, business arrangement though it was. Perhaps it was only natural she have such soppy notions?

"We'll have done with this soon enough," he promised. "And then we shall acquire ourselves a room at the inn."

Why did even that sound so scandalous?

The images that came immediately to mind made Victoria chasten herself for a silly romantic fool. And yet her heartbeat quickened at the vision of the two of them embracing so. Lord only knew, he *was* an exquisite-looking man.

He'd yet to release her, and Victoria could scarce find her voice to ask him to do so.

"There will be plenty of time to rest then," he assured her.

"Yes, of course." She nodded. "But we'll have to have separate rooms," she felt inclined to point out.

He made some sound that sounded suspiciously like laughter. "Of course," he agreed amiably. "Separate rooms."

He released her then, and proceeded to give the driver instruction. When he was done, with a gentle hand upon her elbow, he guided her toward the single street occupant who, she assumed, might better lead them to the marrying house.

"What if they will not perform the ceremony so late?" she fretted, her legs feeling suddenly as unsubstantial as water. "Goodness only knows, we should have departed Blackstone long before we did!" She wavered a little on her feet, feeling suddenly as though she would swoon.

She couldn't believe she was actually going through with this!

He placed an arm about her shoulders, steadying her, and though it gave her a little start, she allowed it. She didn't have much choice, lest she fall flat upon her face, for she felt suddenly more anxious than she'd ever been in all of her life.

"Don't worry, Victoria . . . I'll take care of everything," he assured her.

"But what if they should refuse us?"

"They won't," he asserted.

"How can you be so certain?"

He peered down at her, his blue eyes shuttered by the darkness, and yet the intensity there was more than apparent somehow. "No one could refuse you anything," he told her with certainty.

Victoria tried to gauge his expression. Perchance did he think her too bold?

Well, she didn't care! It was the only way she knew to accomplish anything at all in this man's world.

And yet his gaze didn't seem particularly reproachful. He was, in truth, peering down at her rather strangely. She would think . . . rather fondly, even . . . if she didn't know better.

"Money speaks, remember?" he pointed out quite reasonably. "And we both have an ample supply of it. They'll not refuse you," he maintained.

Why did she suddenly feel so disheartened? He certainly couldn't have intended the remark to be a doting one! "Perhaps so," Victoria agreed. "Though it must be done before midnight," she reminded him a little snappishly. "What if we cannot get these laggards to stir from their beds?"

"Never fear . . . they'll smell the gold in their dreams, I'll warrant."

Victoria clasped her hands together fretfully. "And what if they do not?"

He gave her a sidelong glance and a disarming grin. "Then I shall, personally, go and drag them from their beds, Victoria. Have no fear."

Though she understood he was jesting with her, Victoria grimaced. Why was it that something so simple as the way he said her name sent quivers down her spine? She reached up to tug her bonnet more firmly down upon her head, telling herself that it was the chill Scots wind that made her shiver so ridiculously.

They approached the drunkard, though he never stirred from his seat beside the door, rather he simply watched them, looking rather mystified by their presence. Victoria felt a surge of irritation, eager as she was to be finished with the task at hand. Lord, but it simply wasn't fair that she should be forced to give over her life into the hands of a man simply because she was a woman!

Well, she reminded herself, she certainly didn't intend to!

"I shall speak to him," Thom suggested.

"I shall do it!" Victoria informed him at once, her expression quite mutinous. "I believe, sirrah, that I am perfectly capable of addressing the man!"

Thom knew better than to chuckle at her ready defiance, endearing though it might be, and so he ceded graciously, "As you wish." But he couldn't quite wipe the smile from his face as she turned to address the drunkard.

"How do you do, sir?" she asked the man.

"Fine as a fiddle, can ye no' see?" he replied. The drunkard lifted his flask of whiskey for her perusal. "Hoozyersel' hinnie?"

"Well enough," Victoria answered quickly, and without pause. "Good sir, I thought perhaps you might direct us to the marrying house?" she told the man, dispensing at once with idle talk.

"The marryin' h-house!" the drunk sputtered, staring up at her rather stupidly.

She nodded. "Yes, sir, the marrying house."

The drunkard took another swig of his sour-smelling whiskey before bothering to reply. "Och! But I dinna ken why everyone is lookin' for the marrying house!"

"I'm certain I don't know, sir. But we are, alas, and are in quite a terrible rush, besides. Do you happen to know where it is?"

"Och, lass, everyone iss in a rush!" he admonished her, slurring his words. "Do y' see what hurryin' did tae me? I'm a drinkin' me whiskey oot in the blessed cauld while me wife is snug in her bed all cozy and warm!"

"I really am terribly sorry, sir," she relented. " 'Tis only that we really must be wed by midnight, you see! Perhaps you might wish to join her . . . *after* you direct us to the parsonage?" she persisted.

"Och, nay!" the drunk declared, "but even if her tongue wouldna lash me back oot the door, I canna walk through walls! She's locked the door." He took another hearty swig from his flask, mumbling something to the effect that women were born with unprecedented tempers.

Thom could almost see Victoria's hackles rising over the disparaging remark. He wanted to remind her that she was conversing with a drunk, but refrained.

"I see. So she's locked you out?" Victoria asked.

"Thass what I said!" The drunk took another swig of his whiskey, and exclaimed, "Stubborn fashious wench that she is!"

"I, of course, would never presume to know why she would do such a thing, dear sir, but—"

"Victoria," Thom interjected, placing a hand gently upon her shoulder, "perhaps I should handle this?"

She shrugged free of him, as though he were a pesky bug. "*I believe I am quite capable, sirrah!*" she assured him at once, her voice beginning to rise. She turned again toward the drunk. "The marrying house, sir . . . you see, we are sorely in need of directions, if you please . . . and then we shall leave you to your . . . er . . ."

"Och, noo, laddie!" the drunkard exclaimed, having watched the exchange between them with keen interest. He stumbled forward within his chair, waving a finger at Thom, dismissing Victoria's presence suddenly as he presumed to lecture him. "Are ye certain ye wish to wed this lass? Seems tae me ye go' yersel' a pawky one here, son. 'Tis no' too late to run, you know?"

Not that Thom particularly wished to, but it was time to step in, he realized. Victoria wasn't going to get anywhere with the man. He placed a hand quite firmly upon Victoria's shoulder, drawing her back. "Quite certain, old man," he said, "I can handle this particular lass just fine." He winked at the drunk. "If you know what I mean."

"I beg pardon!" Victoria exclaimed, her hands going to her hips in indignation.

The drunkard crooked a finger at him, ignoring Victoria completely. "Aye, weel . . . thass what I thought too." He sighed loudly. "Sae ye're lookin' for the parson, are ye noo?"

"Yes!" Victoria replied at once. She glared up at Thom. "And we are in a terrible . . ."

"Rush," the drunk finished for her. "O' course!" he exclaimed. He cocked his head up at Thom. "And ye're certain ye dinna wish tae be waitin' 'til the morrow, son?"

"No!" Victoria answered, sounding perfectly furious now.

Thom squeezed her shoulder gently. She shrugged away once more. "No," Thom replied. Victoria peered up him, frowning, her eyes casting daggers at him. He grinned down at her, his brows lifting. "I said no," he pointed out.

"Verra weel," the drunk relented, lifting himself from his seat. He began at once to pound upon the door beside him.

"Oopen up, Constance!" he demanded. "We've customers! Ooopen up this instant!" He banged upon the wooden door, shaking it, but never budging it. After the longest interval, a thin, pink-faced woman answered. She threw open the door, and glared at the drunk as though she would murder him where he stood. In her hand, she held, of all things, a horsewhip. "We've customers," he told her matter of factly, unshaken by the strap she wielded in her hand.

Tom, for his part, couldn't help but wince. The woman said nothing, merely cast the door open wide, glaring at the three of them each in turn. 'They're wantin' tae be wed t'night," the drunk told his wife.

"Now?" the wife asked.

"O' course now!" her husband declared. "Why d' ye think they're standing here?"

"Verra weel," she relented. "Come in."

Victoria merely stared. "*You* are the parson?" she asked, sounding utterly shocked.

"Aye!" the wife exclaimed in disgust. "He's the bluidy parson while he's no' otherwise occupied with his whiskey!" She turned to her husband. "I thought I told ye tae sleep wi' yer bluidy bedfellows at the bluidy rotten tavern!" she railed at him, lifting the horsewhip and snapping it in the air after her obliviously drunk husband. She left the door wide for Victoria and Thom to follow.

If they dared.

Victoria peered up at Thom in stunned surprise, lifting her brows. Thom offered a shrug. "Marital bliss," he replied, and chuckled.

She made no move to enter the house, and he had the sudden urge to shove her in the door. Surely she knew it was too late to change her mind; he already had his heart set on this. He lifted his brows. "Does it not warm the cockles of one's heart?" he said, and grinned down at her.

She blinked up at him, bemused, those green eyes enchanting and her expression much too familiar, and he felt suddenly like that thirteen-year-old with sweaty palms.

"He's the pastor!" Victoria exclaimed suddenly, evidently in shock and wholly unaware of his thoughts, his deception, his identity.

No matter his motives, he was doing the right thing, Thom reminded himself.

He nodded, leaning slightly closer to capture the elusive scent of her, a subtle mingling of jasmine and woman. The brisk air had pinkened her cheeks and the tip of her nose. He wanted to kiss the bridge of it . . . work his way down to her lips. God, but he craved that kiss with a desperation he could taste. "I believe I determined that already," he said, and resisted the urge to cleave her to him suddenly, kiss her fiercely.

"Capital!" she exclaimed. "Whatever is this world coming to!" She narrowed her eyes at him. "You don't happen to share the pastor's inclination to imbibe, do you, Mr. Parker?"

He forced a light-hearted smile and winked down at her. "Will you toss me out of bed if I do?"

She averted her gaze at once. "You know very well we'll not be sharing a bed together, sirrah!"

Thom's brows collided. Had he known that? He was no longer quite certain he had. Perhaps his brain had, but his heart had believed elsewise, he realized suddenly. Perhaps not tonight, nor tomorrow . . . but someday . . .

"A simple kiss hardly a lover makes!" she declared.

Thom heartily begged to differ . . . perchance it was only the beginning, but it was a beginning, nonetheless. He'd never kissed a woman he hadn't meant to bed. A slow smile turned his lips as he heard his father's voice speak to him: *A man must do what he must, you realize?* Perhaps he'd not entered this bargain with the intent to win her heart, or perchance he had, but he suddenly resolved to do just that.

So, she fully intended to kiss him, did she?

He couldn't have justified it had he tried, but he suddenly felt unreasonably giddy and more than a little bit reckless as he smiled down at her. "True enough, Victoria," he ceded with a wink. "A kiss hardly a lover makes," he agreed. He swept his hand in a gesture urging her to enter. He arched a brow, when she still didn't stir. "Unless you're afraid and have changed your mind?"

"Afraid, bosh! Whatever would I have to fear?" she exclaimed, and brushed past him, marching after the pastor and his wife.

Thom smiled, and followed, heartily pleased she still reacted so defiantly to a challenge. It would make his seduction go all the easier, for certain.

And God save his rotten soul, he fully intended to seduce his bride.

And more, he was going to relish every bloody last minute.

Chapter 6

"Verra well, then, *Lady* Victoria Haversham." He stressed the title before her name as though it were a blasphemy. "Did you come here of your own free will and accord?"

"I did, of course!" Victoria replied. Goodness only knew, she understood this was the right thing to do, that it was the only course of action that would ensure her future to any degree, but it certainly didn't alter the fact that within mere moments she would be entered into holy wedlock with the stranger towering at her side. She couldn't help but be terrified out of her wits, but she refused to show it.

"And you, Thom . . . I'm afraid I can't read your scribble," he complained.

"Parker," Victoria offered.

The pastor eyed her sternly. "Whatever! Did you come here of your own free will and accord?" he asked Thom.

"Well, of course he did!" Victoria exclaimed, anxious for the ceremony to be ended, and wholly terrified that Thom would change his mind at the very last instant. "Do you see shackles upon his wrists?" she asked. As though she could possibly force the man standing at her side to do anything at all against his will!

Once more the pastor refused to acknowledge her,

and Victoria chafed. "Really, sirrah! You don't believe I could drag him all this way by brute force?"

"A woman's tongue makes a frightful lash," the pastor replied somberly. He turned to look at his wife, and muttered, "They dinna need horsewhips."

Victoria peered up at her husband to be, trying to gauge his expression once more. There was nothing, not the tiniest suggestion of his thoughts. She wondered if he were suffering regrets—wondered, too, if he thought her tongue wicked as the pastor plainly did. More than anything, she found herself, much to her dismay, wondering in particular if he were thinking about that kiss.

Her face heated at the possibility.

"Och, Duncan!" the wife chimed in. "Ye dinna see that the laddie is sae unhappy, noo d'ye? Gae on with the ceremony sae we can all gae tae bed!"

Victoria stared at the whip in the woman's hand, wondering if she truly would use it upon her poor husband. No wonder he was so discontented.

"I did come of my own accord," Thom answered, and Victoria breathed a sigh of relief. She rather thought he seemed to be enjoying this repartee entirely too much, and felt like elbowing him in the ribs for playing along with the obnoxious man.

The pastor merely shook his head, as though to lament Thom's decision. "Verra weel, then, my son . . . de ye take this woman tae be your lawful wedded wife, forsaking all others, keeping tae her as long as ye baith shall live?"

"I will," Thom replied, his voice firm, but wholly lacking in emotion. Victoria contemplated why that should disturb her so. For goodness sake, it wasn't as though they were madly in love with one another . . . it was a marriage of convenience, she reminded herself, no more.

"And Lady Victoria . . ."

"I will," Victoria replied quickly, and handed him the ring at once.

The pastor looked up from his volume and raised his brows. In disapproval, Victoria thought. Too bad. She was in a hurry, and this was entirely too disconcerting.

" 'Tis late," she reminded him, "and we really must make haste!"

The pastor shook his head, casting a dubious glance at Thom as though to be certain he should, in fact, continue. Victoria resisted the urge to stomp upon the pastor's blessed foot, knowing it would merely waste more precious time. Time they didn't have to spare. He reached out, received the ring from Victoria's trembling fingers, and handed it to Thom. " 'Tis still no' too late, son," he whispered ominously.

"It most certainly is!" Victoria screeched in response, sounding more like a fishwife than she might have cared to. She cast an uncertain glance at Thom, hoping his opinion hadn't somehow been swayed.

The pastor sighed once more, shaking his head. "Gae ahead and place it upon her finger son," he directed Thom.

"Please," Victoria urged him, thrusting out her hand impatiently. Before she could possibly change her mind—before the pastor could manage to scare Thom away. But she worried for naught, it seemed, for Thom peered down at her, his demeanor wholly composed—easy enough for him, she thought, as it wasn't precisely his future at stake. She frowned at that. He winked at her as he slid the ring over her fourth finger. It slid the length so very slowly, sending quivers down Victoria's spine, and for an instant, she forgot where they stood. He nestled the ring around her finger, his touch lingering, and then he withdrew his hand. Victoria swallowed convulsively at the caress. She shuddered with total awareness of the man who stood at her side.

In mere moments he would be her husband . . . and there *would* be a part of her life she would indeed share with him.

A sense of panic enveloped her. Lord, but she knew this man scarce at all!

And yet somehow . . . somehow . . . she felt an uncanny connection to him.

How much dare she give? How much would he take?

Her fingers trembled as he held them.

"Noo, Lady Victoria," the pastor was saying, "repeat these words after me . . . with this ring I thee wed, with my body I thee worship, with all my worldly possessions I thee endow in the name of the Father, the Son, and Holy Ghost. Amen."

Victoria suddenly couldn't speak. Lord-a-mighty! She couldn't very well promise him her body! And yet the very thought suddenly filled her with warmth unlike anything she'd ever experienced. It sent her pulse skittering and set her heart to hammering. For that matter, neither could she promise him her money, as she planned to keep it all for herself. Elsewise, why, indeed, would she be wedding him at all?

She blinked up at him once and saw a stranger— a stranger she knew no better than she did this confounded scotch-drinking Scots preacher. She blinked once more and saw the warmth nestled in the oddly familiar depths of his gaze. Blinked yet a third time, and his face blurred out of focus.

Good God, she couldn't do this!

But she must, she reminded herself. There were

no choices to be made here! She was no child to go running in fright! She had always taken the brass ring in hand, and tonight was no different. She had, in fact, contemplated this option thoroughly, and it had been her most sensible choice.

So then . . . what was she waiting for?

"I thought ye were in a hurry, Lady Victoria?" the pastor said, sounding quite inconvenienced now.

She was, of course. They were. She simply couldn't seem to get the words past her constricted throat. She was vaguely aware that Thom had withdrawn a timepiece from his vest pocket. He flipped it open, glanced at it, and then closed it quickly and replaced it. She didn't particularly relish the frown upon his face. It filled her with a sense of impending doom.

He gave her a nod, urging her to continue, and Victoria inhaled a breath, and blurted, "With this ring I thee wed! In the name of the Father, Son, and Holy Ghost! Amen!"

The pastor slapped his book angrily shut. "Ye canna change the words, Lady Victoria!"

"I mostly certainly can and have!" Victoria informed him at once, with greater conviction than she felt. "Please, go on, sirrah!"

"Please do go on," Thom insisted quietly, coming to her defense.

Victoria smiled up at him a little tremulously, uncertain as to whether she should be grateful for his compliance, or panicked. He was staring once again at her mouth, reminding her of their private agreement as surely as though he'd spoken it aloud. She lapped at her lips gone dry, and averted her gaze.

The pastor glowered at Thom as though he were a goose gone mad. "Are ye bluidy daff, mon?" he exclaimed. "What are ye wantin' with a wife if ye canna have the best o' what comes wi' her, lad?"

"Oh, leave them be, Duncan!" the pastor's wife demanded.

"Och, never mind!" the pastor muttered crossly. He thrust his book into his wife's hands. "Forasmuch as this man and this woman have consented to be together by giving and receiving a ring, I therefore declare them to be man and wife before God and these witnesses"—he waved a hand indicating his children—"in the name of the Father, Son, and Holy Ghost! Amen! Gae tae bed!" he commanded his wife and children quite irascibly. "And dinna bar the door, Constance!" he said sternly to his wife, With no small measure of disgust, he added, "You may noo kiss the bride!"

Victoria blinked up at her husband, disconcerted by the knowledge that they were now wed . . . she and this intimate stranger. There was something about him so very familiar, and yet he was truly no more than a stranger. He was staring down at her now, his expression as untelling as ever, but she distinctly sensed he might be waiting for his kiss.

Good Lord, she felt suddenly much too hot. Couldn't catch her breath.

A promise was a promise, she reminded herself. Certainly, she could do this. It was a simple enough thing, after all. Drawing in a fortifying breath, she puckered her lips, and lifted her face, squeezed her eyes shut, and waited . . . anticipating the touch of his lips.

"I believe I've changed my mind," her husband said.

Victoria's eyes flew open. Her brows collided. "Whatever do you mean you've changed your mind? You cannot change your mind; it's much too late to change your mind!"

"You don't wish to marry her?" the pastor asked,

sounding more than a little bemused, and perhaps a bit hopeful. Victoria cast him a withering glance.

"I have married her," Thom replied evenly. "I just don't wish to kiss her, is all."

Victoria's face began to burn.

He didn't wish to kiss her, after all?

The pastor mumbled something quite uncharitable beneath his breath. "God's bloody teeth! That'll be half a guinea!" he demanded of Thom. "In all me bluidy days, I ha'e never seen the like! Guid luck son! Ye're gaein' tae need it!" he declared, and with that Thom withdrew the appropriate payment, offered an extra coin for the pastor's troubles, thanked the man, gathered the necessary papers, looked them over, and then led Victoria out of the marrying house, leaving the pastor to complain bitterly, and his wife, having forgotten the whip for the time being, to soothe his temper.

Chapter 7

She was brooding, and it was all Thom could do not to chuckle with pleasure.

Unconscionable though it might be, he was quite satisfied with the reaction he'd wrought from her. She sat there before him just now, looking wholly bemused, her thoughts clearly whirling behind those delightfully bewitching eyes.

Damn, but he felt as giddy as he had before she'd said her goodbyes that day so long ago; he was again that little boy, dashing toward the hill, pasteboard in hand to show her.

As on that fateful day, not all had gone as he'd anticipated this night either: They'd gone to the inn directly. Hoping to procure a single room for the both of them, Thom had bribed the clerk to deny them two. Unscrupulous though it might be, he couldn't seem to muster the least remorse for his underhandedness. His only regret was that Victoria had refused the arrangement out of hand, opting to make the return journey to Blackstone, instead.

No matter. He could wait.

The rewards to be reaped, he knew, were entirely worth his patience. He would simply bide his time, and Victoria would come about eventually.

He knew she would, because he could spy it within her eyes, see it in the way she watched him.

"The man was dyspeptic," Victoria declared suddenly, breaching the silence between them at last.

She didn't bother to turn and look at him.

Thom suppressed a chuckle. "You think so?" he asked rather coolly.

"Quite!" she avowed. "He was ill-tempered, bigoted, and rude, to say the least!"

"He was smashed."

She turned to look at him, then, and Thom sucked in a breath at the incredible loveliness of her face. "Smashed?" Illumined by the bloodless moon, her face was pale, her eyes incandescent green.

"Soused," he explained. "Drunk."

"Yes, well, I don't believe there was any need to reward him so well. Do you?" she asked.

He wisely refrained from pointing out her own peevish mood, and disclosed, "My timepiece revealed one quarter past the midnight hour as we exchanged our vows. I thought it prudent to leave him appeased, as he's the only one now who might gainsay us."

"Oh!" Victoria exclaimed, and her face seemed to pale all the more by the moonlight. "You don't think he will, do you?" Her sea-green eyes were suddenly full of concern. Wistful, perhaps, but he wished to believe it was for more than her desire to keep her bloody estates. "He did place the correct hour upon our certificate, did he not?"

Thom nodded. "He did." Still, he withdrew the papers from his vest and offered them to her, hoping she wouldn't note his signature—not that she could possibly make it out in the darkness of the coach. "Examine them for yourself."

"Thank you," she said, and took the folded papers from his hand, never averting her eyes. "I never even thought to ask," she confessed. "It never . . . occurred . . . to me."

She seemed to lose her train of thought. As he lost his own every time she merely glanced his way.

It was good to know he wasn't alone in his temptation.

After all these years, she was like a feast to his starving senses. The whispering black silk of her wedding gown made him yearn to reach out, to draw the sleek garment into his ready fingers. The soft scent of jasmine filling the air made him long to bury his face into her hair, against the curve of her neck . . . taste her flesh . . . place his tongue upon the pulse at her throat, feel it beating beneath his lips. The even fainter scent of peppermint . . . exhaled in his direction by soft, tantalizing sighs, made him thirst to kiss her.

All in all, he was in a dangerous state of mind . . . for a man who'd only just vowed to give his wife time . . .

"Well . . . they do seem to be in order," she yielded softly, though without ever having glanced down at the papers in question. Thom could scarce help but notice, and he smiled, his lips curving with a fierce sense of satisfaction.

He followed her gaze down to the papers she held . . . at her breast . . . and couldn't help himself. He focused upon the neckline of her gown, low and inviting, and groaned inwardly. He closed his eyes, his senses reeling at the bloody temptation.

The hazy moonlight was playing with his vision . . . his mood . . . conspiring . . .

God help him, he was only a man, no saint, and he was suddenly dizzy and his mouth had gone bloody dry, besides.

She didn't know him anymore, he reminded himself. She needed time. He needed to give her that time. It was the right thing to do.

He repeated the litany until he was certain he

must believe it, but his body remained tense as a caged wildcat in heat.

Her gaze was still focused upon him when he re-opened his eyes, and he swallowed and held himself still ... because if he moved ... if he so much as stirred ... he was going to reach out and draw her into his arms, seduce her right here within this bloody rotten coach they shared.

Blinking, Victoria handed the papers back to him, her hands trembling, her thoughts in chaos.

She hadn't bothered to look at them, she realized—but then again she couldn't see the accursed print in the darkness of the carriage, at any rate, so why bother?

And Lord, it shouldn't matter, but somehow it did ... why had he so suddenly refused to kiss her?

Had he found her wanting? Did he regret binding himself to her? And why should it even bloody matter what he felt for her? or what he thought of her?

She'd chosen him solely because he'd offered her this union without the usual bindings—without duty, without attachment.

And yet, never in her life had a man looked at her with such intensity of expression. Never in her life had she experienced such a fluttering within her belly, such a tightness within her breast ...

As she did this very instant.

Her heart beat a staccato as she stared at his lips ... at his face ... at his deep-set eyes and brows that tilted so devilishly with his sinfully beautiful smile.

Her brow furrowed. Why hadn't he kissed her?

The question plagued her, though she told herself it was absurd. Perhaps he had found her wanting, after all. Somehow, the possibility weighed like stones within her belly.

Maddened her as well, if the truth be known!

He sat there now, looking much too unrepentant, and she suddenly felt like boxing his ears. Good Lord! she couldn't recall the last time she'd had such a furious temptation—yes, she certainly could! and couldn't suppress a sudden giggle over the memory of a little boy who had once vexed her so relentlessly that she had cursed the encumbrances of her femininity that she could never seem to catch him to properly do so.

"Laughter suits you," her husband said.

Victoria blinked, and was momentarily taken aback by the compliment.

"Whatever are you thinking of?"

Victoria narrowed her eyes at him, refusing to be subdued by simple flattery. How dare he rebuff her before that ill-tempered man! "A childhood memory—nought you should be concerned with!" She lifted her chin, and sat forward within the carriage seat. "Not that I'm particularly upset over your change of heart, mind you!" she said, before she could stop herself. "Or your motives, for that matter—but I hardly appreciated the humiliation of your declination, sirrah!"

He lifted his head and leveled his gaze upon her. "Pardon?"

Victoria inhaled a breath. "It was certainly your prerogative to change your mind—again, might I point out!—however, you might have advised me in advance—before I managed to make myself appear quite the perfect ninny!"

"It was my prerogative to change my mind?"

"Of course! Though you might have advised me you cared to do so!"

He knit his brows. "Advised you . . . that I cared to do what, precisely?"

"Kiss me!"

He lifted his brows.

Victoria was at once chagrined over the path in which their conversation had veered, and by the way her declaration must surely have sounded. "I mean to say! You might have said ... then ... before ..."

He lifted his head to peer at her through the shadows, looking entirely too composed, while she, on the other hand, in an instant, had managed to feel even more the fool for her outburst.

She groaned. Good Lord, how must she sound to him? As though she desired his kiss, after all?

"I rather thought you would be relieved?"

The mere slant of his brows sent her heartbeat to bedlam. Victoria shrugged, and mentally attempted to compose herself. "Well, of course I was relieved," she assured him much too quickly.

His lips curved a fraction more, and she cursed him to perdition for it. "Really?"

"Of course!" Victoria asserted. "I simply might have wished—"

"Because I could remedy it easily enough, you realize."

Victoria froze. "Remedy?" Her voice sounded strangled, even to her own ears. She stared at his face through the shadows, trying desperately to discern his expression.

He sat up a little straighter. "If you should like that kiss, after all," he submitted, his expression perfectly sober, and more than a trifle compelling. "I am quite willing," he revealed.

"How absurd!" Victoria exclaimed, but scarce could she tear her gaze away from his face ... his mouth. Her heart beat like thunder in her ears. If he couldn't hear it, as well, then he was surely deaf. "However could you think so, sirrah?"

He leaned forward, and Victoria sucked in a startled breath at his sudden advance. And yet ... she didn't withdraw backward into the seat, wasn't able to move suddenly. She swallowed convulsively. So close, he somehow made her head swirl and her breath short.

"Perhaps," he revealed softly, "by the way you are once again staring at my mouth."

"I most certainly am not!" Victoria argued, though she knew it was a lie. She irrefutably was, for she was decidedly aware of those sensual lips moving as he spoke, and nothing else. Scarce could she seem to remember, even, to breathe. She had to remind herself to do so.

Her imagination? Or did it seem as though he leaned forward?

Closer.

She swallowed any words of protest, as his hand reached out suddenly to touch her face . . . so softly, she might have thought his caress formed of simmering mist, a heated, tentative brush of whispering flesh that made her breast swell with pent up breath. She gasped at the touch, and blinked as the tips of his fingers slid down to her chin, slid beneath, and ever so gently leveled her face to his. Victoria lowered her lashes, afeared suddenly to look into his eyes.

"No?" he asked her softly, his voice little more than a whisper.

"N-No," she croaked, and closed her eyes. She couldn't seem to help herself—nor could she move away. Whatever was it about this man that drew her so? That made her yearn to be so bold? To be held by him? What is it that made her long to be kissed . . . by his wickedly beautiful lips.

"Perhaps 'tis only me, then," he confessed.

"O-Only you?" she stammered, her heart pounding now.

"Because you see . . . I cannot seem to stop myself

from staring at those luscious lips of yours."

Victoria dared not breathe at his confession. "No?"

"No," he murmured, and asked softly, "Would you deny me if I asked you please, Victoria?"

"Please?" Thoughts didn't seem quite able to form; her brain seemed suddenly as muddy as the puddles she used to trample through as a child ... with ... some glimmer of memory surfaced, but fled as quickly as it appeared, leaving Victoria to feel an overwhelming desperation to chase it.

He moved closer, until their mingled breaths were a teasing veil between them, and she knew he was going to kiss her. And more, she wasn't going to refuse him. Her breasts tingled in anticipation of his kiss, tiny prickles of fire that inflamed her and stirred liquid heat within her belly.

"Would you like me to kiss you, Victoria?"

Her body slumped forward, and she sighed, no longer able to think clearly at all. His soft voice mesmerized her, delighted her, sent delicious shivers racing up and down her spine.

"Yes," she whispered softly, lapping at her lips gone dry. "I ... I believe I surely must ..."

He chuckled at her artless response.

Her eyes were closed, her mouth slightly parted, giving him a tantalizing glimpse of the glistening nectar within ... the sweet dew of her lips, and his own mouth went suddenly dry as dust.

So bloody much for good intentions.

Damn, but how could any man refuse a mouth so full and luscious as hers? How could he expect to turn away from temptation when she sat so bloody close, smelled so sweet? When the gentle rise and fall of her breast, and her quickened breath, were but tantalizing glimpses of the passion he knew full well lay tempered within? What chance had he of convincing himself that this could possibly be wrong when it felt so right?

And she was his wife.

No matter that it was for convenience sake alone, his body wasn't aware of the distinction. And his brain had quit working some time ago, besides. Christ, but he'd wanted this too long . . . needed too much . . . had waited a bloody lifetime . . .

She couldn't possibly know how much he yearned to take . . . how much he needed to give . . . how very much he craved to kiss her . . .

Reaching out slowly for fear that he would startle her, he slid his fingers across the velvety softness of her neck. He felt her shudder and sucked in a breath. His heart hammered against his ribs. Cupping her nape and drawing her close, he anticipated the taste of her lips with a hunger that belied the gentleness of his touch.

She made some sound deep in the back of her throat, a soft, whimpering sigh that heated the blood in his veins to a feverish pitch and hardened him fully. His nostrils flared. More than anything, he longed to taste her soft, beautiful body . . . every inch of it . . . inhale the scent of her into his long-deprived lungs. He growled, a fierce sound of unrepentant triumph, as he allowed his lips to descend at last to the lips he'd only dreamed about for so long. And Christ, he was lost the very instant he tasted her upon his tongue.

He couldn't possibly have known how very sweet she'd be . . . how very supple her lips would feel beneath the play of his own. Nothing could have prepared him for the silky warmth of her mouth, and the glorious mysteries held within.

He didn't think he could stop with a single kiss.

No more could he do so . . . than he'd been able to forget those bewitching eyes . . . or her brilliant smile . . . or her laughter . . . or even the impertinent tilt of her head . . . and the stubborn lift of her chin.

God, but he wanted to make her laugh again, wanted to cherish and protect her always . . . wanted to draw her within his very soul.

So easily was she undone.

Victoria moaned softly as his lips pressed upon hers—velvet steel against her lips, insistent and sleek, coaxing her to open for him.

She slid her hands about his neck, entwined her arms there, and he groaned savagely, sending shivers down her spine. He swept her up into his arms, lifting her as though she weighed no more than a child of three—no time for protests, no time even to think. She found herself seated scandalously within his lap, his arms bracing her for the onslaught of his mouth.

"You cannot know," he whispered fiercely against her mouth, "how very much I have wanted this. From the instant I first laid eyes upon you, Victoria . . . open for me," he demanded, and slid his tongue across her lips, persuading with masterful strokes.

Victoria swallowed and did as he bade her, her body thrilling to his declaration. Her heart leapt within her breast. Hardly did she dare imagine he should want her at all. His tongue slid within to drink of her mouth, liquid heat between her lips, exploring . . .

Whimpering softly, she allowed her head to loll backward while his hands held her face in an intimate lover's embrace that made her heart cry out and her soul weep. Never had she been held so tenderly. Never had she known a mere touch could be so exhilarating.

Nor had she imagined she would yearn to give her soul to the first man who should hold her so ardently—but heaven help her, she did.

"Give me your tongue, Victoria," he whispered into her mouth, and she could do nothing but obey, offering it tentatively at first, and then more boldly. He could have asked her for anything in that instant, and she would have given it gladly. He made some sound, part groan, part chuckle, when she thrust it at him awkwardly, and then ever so gently suckled it . . . until Victoria thought she would die with the soul-stirring sensations that spiraled through her body. "That's it," he coaxed her, leaving her tongue only to suckle next at her lips. Shiver upon shiver rushed down her spine. He nibbled at them gently, nipping and tugging with his teeth, and then suckling once more to soothe the erotic sting.

Victoria clung to him, afraid she might tumble backward into the undiscovered abyss of her own desire.

Wrapping his arms about her waist and folding his hands at the small of her back, Thom attempted to reign in his lust . . . for Victoria's sake. His heart pounded like cannon fire against his ribs. God, but she was making this entirely too easy for him.

Not that he wouldn't normally appreciate such enthusiasm, he acknowledged to himself, but he wanted no regrets. He should stop now, he knew. He should drag her away and set her neatly upon her own seat, safely out of his reach, away from harm, but he couldn't seem to make himself obey. The delicate fingers that were curled about his nape clutched at him a little too desperately . . . and the fingers combing through his hair . . . teased a bit too unmercifully, if unknowingly.

Bloody hell, he didn't want to stop.

Remaining reason began to fade.

His vision hazed. His mouth grew parched and he sipped urgently of her mouth to quench his ungodly thirst. His hands took on a will of their own,

unlocking at her back, and sliding to her waist . . .
such a deliciously tiny waist. He tested the width
with his hands, and slid his hands up along her ribs,
discovering them each by turn, as well. He stopped
only when his thumbs touched the curve of her
breasts.

He envisioned himself bending low, ripping her
bodice with his teeth, and tasting her flesh . . . lower
to her belly . . . until she lay unclothed . . . and was
wholly undone.

Burying his face against her throat, he groaned
and commanded himself to stop.

She sighed and curled up like a kitten within his
lap, entirely unaware of his lascivious intent. Damn,
but she trusted him to keep his word, to kiss her
and do no more. The thought made him smile. He
held her, stroked her cheek with his thumb.

He cleared his throat. "Sleepy?" he asked her, after a moment.

"A little," she murmured, sounding quite con-
tented.

Christ, he was anything but. And he sorely
needed something to take his mind off of his baser
thoughts. He couldn't help but wonder what she
was thinking.

He gave himself a mental shake. "How about we
play a little game?" he asked her, recalling a particular contest they used to play together. Perhaps it
would jog her memory.

She didn't stir. "Game?" she asked with another
breathy sigh. "What sort of game?" She yawned
daintily and started to rise, but he held her firmly in
place.

"No need," he told her. "Rest. It's been a long
night, and we've yet a ways to travel before we return. Now . . . how about . . . I shall say a word, and

you tell me the first thing that comes to mind," he directed her.

She settled back and peered up at him from between thick, dark lashes, scrutinizing him. "I remember that game!" she said after a moment. "I used to play it as a girl!"

Thom had to resist the temptation to answer, *I know.* "Really?" he said. "Then you know exactly what to do."

"I always did like to play that," she confessed.

Again he had to resist the urge to answer, *I know.* "Good," he said. "Laughter," he began.

"Children," she answered at once. "That one was easy." He smiled when she nuzzled him, making herself more comfortable.

"My turn!" He smiled at her enthusiasm. "Blue," she said.

"Sky," he answered. "Play," he countered.

"Work."

Thom frowned at her reply.

"Books," she said.

"Boring," he answered, and chuckled.

She chuckled as well. "They're not so very boring," she demurred.

"I rather suppose it depends upon what you're reading. The books I read are quite tedious," he maintained. "Kisses," he offered.

"Nice," she whispered, without pause.

"Regrets?"

"None." She sighed softly, and cuddled deeper within his embrace.

"You?" she asked.

"What do you think?" he asked her, and tickled her ribs playfully with a finger.

She giggled softly. "Stop! Stop! You're not playing right! You cannot answer a question with a question!

Nor was that one word, it was four. Answer properly!"

"No."

"Was that no, you will not answer properly? Or no, you have no regrets?"

"No, I have no regrets."

"Did you see the look upon the parson's face when you refused to kiss me?" She laughed softly. "I rather think he was addled. He didn't know what to make of us."

"I'm sure," Thom said, and smiled.

She giggled, and then quieted. For an instant, the two of them simply sat together in silence, lulled into a languor by the rocking coach and the soothing darkness. They sat together with the comfort of two lovers used to sharing the same breath. But he wanted more than to simply be her lover. He wanted to recapture what they'd shared so long ago.

"Friend," Thom said, after a long moment.

She remained silent.

"Friend?" he said again.

She didn't respond.

"Victoria?"

Still she didn't respond, and Thom glanced down to see that her eyes were closed. She didn't move, nor did she even seem to be breathing. She'd fallen asleep. Damn. He was rather enjoying her answers.

"Brat," he whispered, and settled back within the carriage with his sleeping wife cuddled within his lap.

Gad, but she was his wife . . . after all these years . . . he smiled at that, leaned his head back, and closed his eyes to savor the feel of her within his arms.

Chapter 8

Victoria awoke within her own bed the next morn, with only vague memories of how she'd arrived there.

She'd fallen asleep within her husband's arms, it seemed, while playing that silly game. Well, she hadn't precisely fallen asleep *during*, she'd only pretended to, unable to respond to the word *friend*. In truth, she'd only had one true friend in all of her life, and he happened to share the same name with her husband. Her response, at once, had been *Thomas*, but she'd caught herself before speaking it. And then he'd called her brat, and she'd suddenly found herself lost in memories, and had drifted to sleep.

Her dreams had been a mélange of old memories and new; of sweet child's play, and lusty, heart-stirring kisses.

Good Lord, but she'd been a wanton last night, practically throwing herself into her husband's arms after begging him to kiss her! Whatever had she been thinking?

And yet, she had shamelessly revelled in every instant of his embrace, every sweet caress of his lips.

She sighed as she glanced at the closed door between her suite and that of her husband's. She couldn't help but wonder if he'd found his way there last night. Was he there even now? or per-

chance down in the dining room taking his breakfast? And did he think her a bloody goose?

Something about Thom Parker made her good
sense scatter to the winds. With little more than a
glance from those compelling blue eyes, he made her
head swirl with perfectly wicked thoughts and her
body behave altogether strangely. It was a good
thing he'd had the sense about him to stop before
she'd had the opportunity to do something entirely
foolish.

Having determined so much, she descended to
breakfast, ready to face him. And if her cheeks were
pink with chagrin, she admonished herself, well and
good! It would serve as a reminder next time not to
abandon herself so shamelessly to temptation. But
she prepared herself all for nought.

She entered the dining room only to find herself
quite alone, and exhaled the breath she'd not realized she'd held. Her arms dropped at her sides, and
a strange heaviness entered her breast.

Certainly it was not disappointment that made her
feel so?

Was it?

The table was set, a steaming breakfast arranged
upon the buffet, the servants only waiting to serve.
And yet she lingered in the doorway, frowning at
the emptiness of the room.

It was certainly the same as it had always been.

So why had she expected it should be different
this morn?

A certificate of marriage did not a family make.

Nor were kisses promises.

So what had she expected to find this morn?

A husband who greeted her with a hearty *good
morn* and a kiss, or two?

A somewhat repentant rogue with deep-set blue
eyes and a smile that made her knees weak?

She lingered a moment longer, contemplating the answer to that question, and then suddenly didn't feel like breakfast at all.

Oblivious to the confounded looks the servants gave one another, she turned and made her way to the rose arbor.

It had taken him the better part of the morn to find himself a pasteboard, but with the child's toy in hand, Thom was ready at last to face Victoria. In his other hand he carried a horsewhip, both of them gifts for his lovely new bride.

It took some searching, but he discovered her within the garden, kneeling over a particularly unsightly bush, her back to him. The sight of her there upon her knees, pruning shears within her hand, took him slightly aback. So, too, did the appearance of the rose garden. Gad, but it wasn't at all the way he recalled it. His brow furrowed as he surveyed the garden in which he and Victoria had spent so many hours as children.

It was the most pitiful excuse for a rose garden that Thom had ever had the misfortune of setting eyes upon in his life. In his father's day, the bushes had been lush and vivid, every color of rose peeping out from leaves so plush they deceived the eye. How many times had he forgotten the thorns behind their shining facades and leapt into the midst of them to hide from Victoria, only to leap back out howling in surprise?

The memory made him smile, for then as now, he suspected Victoria had more to do with his embarrassing lack of judgement than did the deceptive rose bushes. She'd always had a way of turning his thoughts inside out.

Armed with props, and with a singleness of purpose, he made his way toward her, sidestepping overgrown, leafless, thorn-filled vines that sprawled across his path like wicked writhing garden snakes.

The rose arbor had always been Victoria's pride and joy.

Ever since she'd been a mere child, anytime she'd felt herself a little unhinged, this was the place she'd come. With over fifty species of roses in bloom, it was loveliest in the waning summer. The most delightful fragrances filled the air, soothed her troubled soul.

She surveyed the garden with a critical eye.

Of course, it wasn't precisely what it had once been, and her brow furrowed, for she had certainly done the best she knew how to do. She could get the roses to bloom, but she just couldn't seem to get the leaves to stay on the infernal stems. She glowered down at the bush she was currently pruning. Drat thing! No matter that she gave it her time and her attention, it didn't seem to wish to thrive.

She sighed wistfully. No one had been able to get the roses to flourish like Thomas's father had. Her shoulders slumped as she stared at the naked, thorny limbs, trying to remember them when they'd worn more verdant attire. They'd never been the same since Thomas's father had abandoned them. It was, she thought wistfully, as though they were grieving. They'd gone through a procession of gardeners since, and not a one had been able to resurrect them. Victoria had finally taken them into hand four years ago, after dismissing the last gardener her father had hired.

She wondered if Thomas's father had gotten her letter—wondered, too, if he'd consider returning were she to beg.

She didn't dare wonder about Thomas.

Never dared wonder about Thomas any longer.

Lord-a-mighty, he likely had long since forgotten

her—likely had a brood of children, too—and a hearth that was surrounded by love. He surely had a wife to whom he chirped *good morn* to, and a daughter who clung to his neck, exclaiming, *I love you daddy* at his back.

And she . . . well, she had her own Thom to contend with now . . . a man who eschewed breakfast with his wife.

A man whose mere voice could melt the stars from the sky. A man with lips that drove her to madness, and eyes that . . .

Thomas had had blue eyes, she suddenly recalled.

And he'd called her brat.

"Victoria?"

Startled from her musings, Victoria turned to spy her husband standing behind her, and gasped in surprise at the bedraggled sight of him. She grimaced. At least she thought it was her husband. Her brows drew together in dismay. The man standing before her certainly didn't appear at all the man she recalled from last night. Were it not for those singular blue eyes gleaming out at her, she would never have believed it to be him, a'tall.

He had mud streaked upon his face—an overabundance of it, in fact—as though he'd either fallen flat upon his face, or washed his cheeks in a mud puddle. And his trousers—Good Lord, his trousers—they were shredded at the knees and too short besides! She looked closely and saw that the hems had been rent, until they were much too short to wear. She wrinkled her nose, and lifted her gaze to his shirt to find the sleeves, too, had been shorn—grass and dirt stains adorned the front of it. And those wickedly gentle hands that had roamed her body so knowingly last eve were caked with dirt, as well.

"Good gracious!" she exclaimed in horror at his

appearance. "What in heaven's name has happened to you?" She thought he must surely have been assaulted by bandits. Though even then she wasn't entirely certain why he should look so . . . draggle-tailed.

"Thom?"

He chuckled softly. " 'Tis only me," he assured her.

"You look ghastly!"

He shrugged his shoulders. "Then I should make a perfect addition to this garden," he told her. "It is a rather nasty piece of work, I should say." He drew his muddy brows together into a frown, and it was all Victoria could do not to giggle as dry mud sprinkled from them. "What in damnation has happened here?"

Victoria tipped up her chin in indignation. " 'Tis quite an enchanting garden, I'll have you know," she proclaimed, affronted that he could not see it, as well. She waved a hand, indicating the roses, and then noticed for the first time that he'd come bearing gadgets within his hands. Her gaze, curious and perhaps a little wary, settled upon the whip in his left hand, and remained focused there. "They are . . . rather glorious in bloom," she disclosed somewhat distractedly.

"And when are they in bloom?" Thom asked, nonplussed.

Good God, he thought she must be utterly blind!

Most of the garden was nought more than distorted, rambling vines, overgrown and fragile in appearance . . . as though no hand had bothered in years to turn their soil. His father would weep to see them looking so abused.

Victoria seemed not to notice. "Why now, of course. Do you not see?"

Not at all, though he humored her and looked about once more. Naked limbs waved back at him with the soft afternoon breeze. He grimaced in disgust.

"Over there," she said pointing to the most hardy of them all, and then shading her eyes. "Is quite an interesting specimen. It is the *Rosa Gallica Officinalis.* Do you see it?"

The Apothecary Rose. Thom knew it well. The damned bush had but a single puny flower and sparse foliage. It was one of the hardiest roses to be found, ancient as the devil. And Victoria had somehow managed to strangle the bugger.

"Interesting story it bears," Victoria elucidated. "Reputedly brought to France from Damascus by a weary crusader for his lover. 'Tis believed to cure many diverse ailments," she told him.

"Really?" Thom remarked, trying to appear engaged by something other than her beautiful mouth. He could scarce seem to forget the way it'd felt against his lips.

"And that one," she said, pointing to a singularly unattractive bush, "is the *Rosa Mundi.* Legend has it that it was named for Henry the Second's mistress, the Fair Rosamund." Her gaze returned to him, and her cheeks began to bloom. "I'm afraid I cannot seem to make it produce much."

He smiled wanly. *Much* was an incredible understatement. More like not at all. Gad, he could scarce believe his eyes.

"And then, of course, there is this one," she said, indicating an ambling vine that seemed to have the meandering will of a garden snake, and the viciousness of an adder. Somehow, in the short time he had been standing there listening to her speak it had managed to wrap about his pant leg, and when he tried to shake it off, it sank its thorny teeth into his flesh. "Bloody damn!" he exclaimed.

"Oh! Let me get that for you!" Before he could stop her, she was at his feet. Thom stood there, trying like the devil not to allow his mind to wander. Against his will, visions of her loving him from her knees assaulted him, heating his blood, making him shudder with desire anew. He stared down at the pate of her head, and lapped at lips gone dry.

"This one is my particular favorite," she confessed somewhat sheepishly, leaving off with his pantleg and attending the wayward rose. She lifted the frail limb and clipped it in twain. "It is *La Seduisante*. Also known as *Incarnata*, *La Virginale*, *Cuisse de Nymphe*, or—"

"The Great Maiden's Blush," Thom supplied.

Her head popped up. "You know roses?" she asked, peering up at him, sounding surprised.

"Not much," Thom admitted, "but a little. I know this one."

"Really?" She turned her attention to the rose once more. "I'm not at all certain what's wrong with it," she admitted. "It simply does not wish to bloom. I thought perhaps a little pruning would do it good." She snipped a sickly looking blossom and studied it.

Thom thought perhaps it needed to be put out of its misery, once and for all, jerked up by its roots and tossed into the dung heap.

"Perhaps," he agreed, smiling down at her. His gaze focused upon the pruning shears. "So you've been tending this garden yourself?" he asked her, with no small measure of surprise.

"I'm afraid I have," she admitted. "I cannot seem to find anyone able to tend it well enough."

His brows collided. God only knew, she hardly

could find anyone who could tend it worse. He refrained from saying so, however, and came to his haunches beside her.

"This garden is quite special, you see," she revealed, and began to pluck the rose petals one by one.

A feeling like fluttering birds launched within his gut. "Is it?" he asked her, trying to remain calm, as a memory suddenly surfaced . . . of the two of them seated before this very rose, plucking petals from the blossoms. His heart hammered. "Why so?"

She seemed to lose herself in thought for an instant, and he wondered . . . hoped . . . she was remembering, too . . .

"She hates me so, she hates me not, she hates me so, she hates me not . . ."

"I do not hate you, Thomas!" she had exclaimed, *frowning, as he'd tossed the discarded petals into her lap. "I just do not particularly relish slimy, croaking frogs upon my head!"*

"Very well," he'd yielded easily enough. *"I shall never do it again, Toria."*

"Good!" she'd shouted, *"because if you do . . ."* She'd *held her skirt between her two hands, lifting her skirt slightly so that all the petals gathered into a small pile in the center. "I shall have to put snakes down your pants!" And she'd thrust up her skirts as she'd surged to her feet, tossing rose petals into his face. He spat them out of his mouth as she ran away, giving Thomas his first tantalizing peek of lean stockinged legs . . . perfect ankles that had vanished within the blink of an eye, leaving him to stare in open-mouthed wonder over his first glimpse at the glorious difference between boys and girls.*

It had set his heart to pounding and turned his brain to something close to mush.

Even now, all these years later, his reaction was the same. Her hair was swept up today into an artful arrangement that displayed the back of her neck to particular advantage. It was all he could do not to bend and nibble at her nape. He sucked in a breath, and recalled to mind his purpose in seeking her out today.

She continued to pluck petals, blissfully unaware that his eyes were crossing with lust at her back, and he murmured softly, "She hates me so, she hates me not . . ."

Her head snapped up, and she peered over her shoulder at him in surprise. "What . . . what did you say?"

He smiled softly at her. "You're plucking petals . . . just something I used to say as a child."

She blinked, and stared at him for the longest instant, looking bemused, and then returned her attention to the blossom in her hand. "I used to know," she began, and his heart raced. "Well, I spent some of my happiest days within this garden," she revealed, sounding wistful suddenly. His gaze moved to the pruning shears she held within her hand. She set them down at her feet and took a frail vine between her fingers, examining it.

God, so had he . . . spent some of his finest hours here . . . with her . . .

"Alone?" he dared to ask, trying to sound casual.

"No . . . with my dearest friend." She turned to look at him then, her green eyes flashing, and he knew. The friend she referred to was none other than a certain randy little boy who had cast frogs into her hair and called her brat.

She was tending this garden in memory of him.

He was moved beyond words, his brain gone black with her unconscious confession.

"Victoria," he said, standing.

"Yes?" She peered up at him.

He set the whip under his arm, freeing his hand.

He proffered it to her. "Will you come with me?"

"Come with you?" She lifted up her hand to his. "Wherever to?"

"I've something I wish to show you," he said, and dragged her after him, giving her no time to object.

Chapter 9

It was all Victoria could do not to trip over her skirts to keep up with Thom. She must have been out of her wits to go traipsing behind him without even eliciting the first explanation.

"Just a little further," he urged her.

"*Where* are we going?"

"You shall see," he replied, tormenting her with his elusiveness.

"I must be mad!" Victoria exclaimed. It had been years since she'd ventured this far into the park-lands. So many years. Not since she'd been a child.

He brought her to the crest of a hill, and then set down the pasteboard he carried in his hand.

"Now sit down upon it," he demanded of her.

Victoria stared up at him in disbelief. "I mean to say, I think *you* must be mad!" she amended. "Whyever should I sit down upon *that*?"

He winked at her, grinning. "To humor me," he suggested. And then persisted, "Sit down, please?"

Victoria frowned. She could scarce refuse him when he looked at her so . . . so . . . engagingly . . . with his head tilted so like that of a pleading little boy. "Very well," she relented somewhat grudgingly, and sat down upon the pasteboard, feeling like a complete goose. "Now what?"

He began to laugh suddenly.

Victoria peered up at him in sheer exasperation, her hands going to her hips in outrage. "Did you, perchance, bring me all this way to make me sit upon paper, only to snicker at me like some ungracious oaf, sirrah?"

To her dismay, he continued to chuckle and Victoria decided she'd had just about enough. She made to rise. "I thought you wished to show me something," she said. "Apparently, I was mistaken!"

"No!" he said, choking upon his laughter. He thrust out his hand, urging her to remain where she sat. "Ah, but, Victoria! 'tis merely that you look . . ." He shook his head. "Absolutely enchanting!" he declared, and began to laugh anew. "Sitting there upon that pasteboard . . . you have no idea what good it does my heart."

"You mean to say I look a merry-Andrew!" Victoria countered, wholly vexed with his amusement at her expense. "Well, look at you!" she demanded, waving her hand at him. "You did not see that I laughed so rudely at you, sirrah, when you came to me looking like . . . like *that!*" She waved a hand once more in disgust, and made again to rise. For the first time, she noticed his feet. "And you have no bloody shoes!" she exclaimed.

He knelt down beside her, laughing uproariously now, placing a hand to her shoulder to soothe her. "I lost them," he told her between chuckles. "Hold," he said, while he groped behind her, feeling for the pasteboard at her back. He moved his hand to her sides. Victoria only belatedly realized that that hand was beneath her dress.

"I beg your pardon!" she exclaimed, smacking at his probing hand in scandalized horror. She pinned it beneath her skirt under her own, and glared at him fiercely. "What is it you think you are doing?"

He grinned at her, a rather infectious grin that Victoria had no intention of allowing to disarm her. "I simply need to know how much room is left upon the pasteboard."

"Whatever for?"

His eyes twinkled with a devilish light. "You shall see."

"No I shan't!"

He tilted his head at her once more, giving her that little boy look and smile that melted her will. "Trust me," he said.

Victoria frowned at him. "Whyever should I?"

He sobered at that. "Because I am your husband," he suggested, "and I would never do anything to harm you?"

Victoria shook her head vehemently. "Try again, sirrah!"

"Because I *need* your trust," he told her. "Please Victoria?"

He didn't play fair a'tall, Victoria decided and glowered at him. How could she refuse him when he begged her please, and frowned so pitifully? She lifted her hand, but gave him a warning glare. "Very well," she relented. "Do what you will."

His grin returned, brighter than before, and the sight of it made her heart leap painfully. Good Lord, Victoria admonished herself. However was she supposed to keep her wits about her when he smiled at her so?

He groped about beneath the pasteboard, beneath her dress, and Victoria sat there feeling quite flustered, resisting the urge to slap him again. His hands skimmed her thighs, and she flinched, her bottom, and she winced, and then between her thighs. She gasped at his forwardness, and slapped at his hand beneath her skirt, realizing belatedly that it was the wrong thing to do. Dear God . . . she swallowed convulsively, and peered at his face from the corner of her eyes. He was grinning wickedly, flashing perfect white teeth. The cad! She squeezed her eyes shut. And yet . . . heaven help her, this touch was nothing at all the same as the night before . . . and still . . . her breath quickened, and her heart began to pound unmercifully.

"If you'll simply lift your hand up . . . I shall move mine, Victoria," he whispered at her ear.

For an instant, Victoria couldn't respond. In fact, she thought she might die precisely any moment, so painfully was her heart leaping now.

"Of course," he yielded softly, his breath sweet and warm against her face, "I don't particularly *wish* to move it, you see . . ."

Victoria blinked, and released his hand at once. He laughed softly.

"Now scoot forward," he demanded of her.

"Scoot?"

"Yes, Victoria, *scoot*." He placed a hand behind her, and quite boldly shoved her bottom forward, when she didn't respond quickly enough.

"Oh!" Victoria exclaimed.

He sat behind her then, and before she could even think to protest, wrapped his legs about her, entrapping her between them.

"Now," he commanded, "close your eyes!"

"This is entirely preposterous!" Victoria protested fervently. "Whatever in heaven's name are we doing?"

"You shall see," he only said. And then, "Trust me, Victoria."

Her eyes were wide with anticipation. "You keep saying that!" she contended, but somehow she did trust him.

"We're not quite done yet. Are your eyes closed?" he asked her.

"Not yet . . . now they are. And now what?"

"Now," he murmured against her face, sending shivers down her spine. He took her hands into his own. "Hold on to me tight."

Victoria didn't even have time to ask why. Within the instant he had shoved them forward. She screeched hysterically as they went flying out over the hill. For an instant, she was wholly terrified, but he wrapped his arms about her and held her close. And then they were racing down the hill upon the pasteboard, the wind in her face, and Victoria couldn't contain a sudden peal of laughter. It was glorious. Freedom. She opened her eyes and watched the horizon fly by, and giggled madly.

They ended at the bottom of the hill in a scattered heap, both of them laughing uncontrollably. Neither of them could seem to stop for the longest interval. Victoria lay back upon him, wholly unconscious of where she was, laughing like a schoolgirl in his arms.

"Oh, my! That was unspeakably delightful!" she confessed.

He held her against him, a smile in his voice, his chuckles subsiding. "You've no idea how long I've wanted to do that with you, Victoria."

"With me?" She peered back at him, surprised, confused.

"With you," he affirmed, nodding, smiling.

"I don't understand," she said. "We've only just met. How can you possibly—"

"Shhhh," he urged her, placing a palm gently over her lips to shush her. He sat up with her, and turned her about to face him. "I've come bearing gifts, as well," he told her, and handed her the whip he'd somehow managed to hold onto in their flight downward.

Victoria scrunched her nose at the wicked-looking device. "Whatever is that for?"

"For you to keep me in line," he said, grinning broadly, looking at her quite like a wicked little boy who deserved his strapping, but knew his mother would never give it.

Victoria couldn't help but chuckle at his expression, at his outrageous gift. "Like Constance?"

"Gad, but I hope you never have to use it," he admitted. "Though I give you leave to if you must."

Victoria tossed it away, her heart suddenly a little heavy. It wasn't the same, she knew. Their marriage wasn't the same. "I'm certain I shan't have to," she declared. "It's not as though—"

"We love each other?" he finished for her, idly plucking a flattened windflower from the grass beside them. A cacophonous silence fell between them. Her brows drew together as memories accosted her. She peered about at the place, the familiar landscape . . . the skyline above . . . the circle of trees . . . the hill they'd only just come racing down . . . the windflowers all swaying with the breeze. Her heart began to hammer. She stared at the windflower he twirled between his fingers, and swallowed convulsively, afraid to look at him suddenly, afraid to hope.

"Toria," he said, "I think I do."

Victoria's heart thumped furiously. She blinked, peering up into his eyes, recognizing him. How could she not have known him before? Blue eyes that seemed so familiar . . . familiar because they were. She understood everything suddenly; the filthy shirt, the torn breeches, her unholy attraction to him. "Thomas?"

" 'Tis me," he whispered.

Time slipped away suddenly, and it was as though they were there together all those years before.

It *was* him.

"Oh, my dear God!" She choked on a sob, and

cast herself into his arms, unable to keep herself from it. "I cannot believe it's really you!" she cried. "I cannot believe you've come!"

"It's truly me," he assured her, holding her tight, and then disclosed, "And I still love you, brat."

She clutched at his dirty shirt. "How can you possibly?" she asked him.

"I never stopped," he said easily. "I told you I'd never forget, and I never have." He pressed the windflower into her hand, and then reached out to do what he hadn't the nerve to do all those years before. He took a wayward lock of her hair between his fingers, and brushed it from her face.

Victoria wrapped her arms about his neck and held to him fiercely. "I love you, too," she whispered, crying softly now, clutching the windflower within her clenched fist. "And I never forgot," she swore. "I never forgot!"

"I know, my sweet, Victoria," he whispered. "I know . . ."

And he bent to seal their whispered vows with a simple, sweet, if slightly muddy, kiss.

"Victoria," he murmured, reaching out and gently tracing the curve of her breasts with his palm. He revelled in the feel of supple flesh beneath his fingers. "I'd like to make you my wife, in truth," he whispered, and bent to kiss her throat. "Stop me now," he commanded her. "Or not at all."

"Not at all," Victoria murmured, almost too softly to be heard. But he heard, and his heart nigh thudded to a halt. Thunder bolted through him.

It was all the reassurance Thom needed. He caught her wrists and drew her hands down . . . asking her without words to free him, wanting her to know without any doubt just what it was he was asking of her.

For an instant, he thought she might refuse him.

She froze and lifted her gaze to his face. He heard her swallow, and then, with trembling hands, she moved to obey. Gulping his relief, he slid his hand down, skimming her tiny waist, her hip, her thigh. He gave her leg a reassuring little squeeze when she peered up at him, her eyes wide and full of uncertainty, and then he continued his path down her leg, her calf, clutching the hem of her dress within his hand, lifting it slightly, watching her expression for some sign that she would protest. She didn't stop him, merely stared back, her eyes shining with love and glazed with passion.

"I-I cannot seem to," she stammered, her face flushing prettily when her hands began to quake and fumble with his breeches. Thom grinned down at her and reached to undo them himself, while his other hand continued to lift her skirt slowly. He heard her intake of breath, saw her lashes flutter closed, and he urged her back upon the grass, following her down. She moaned softly, lifting her face into the brilliant sunlight, surrendering to him, and his body quickened at the sight of her.

Christ, but she was beautiful. After all these years, it was difficult to believe she was truly his. At last. And yet, there was no denying the vision of loveliness lying there before him, with her glorious hair mussed from their play, woven like softest silk through the scattered windflowers. He reached out to thread his fingers through the shining strands, and sucked in an awe-filled breath.

Her eyes remained closed, but her desire was more than apparent upon her face, and Thom rejoiced in it. God, but he wanted to please her—for the rest of his bloody days he wanted to please her . . . with every last beat of his heart, he wanted to please her . . .

More than anything he wanted to make her smile and laugh.

Always.

Everything he had, he wanted to give her.

His fingers moved upward to find her ready for him, and his heart jolted with a pleasure so fierce it bordered upon pain. Still he had to ask. "Victoria . . . do you understand what it is we are about to do?"

It took Victoria a befuddled instant to realize he was speaking actual words, and yet another to determine just what it was he was asking of her, so lost was she to her body's pleasure . . . to the way his hands made her feel.

Good Lord. Did he think her a ninny? "I rather think I do," she answered, frowning at him, though her thoughts were any moment in danger of scattering—like pigeons taking flight.

"Do you?" he asked.

Her face heated. "Of course," she answered, trying desperately to cling to a single coherent thought, for his hands were working their magic, making her dizzy, stirring her body to incredible life. "We're consummating our marriage," she said with a shuddering whisper.

"We are, at that," he answered with a chuckle.

And there at the foot of their favorite hill, they did exactly that.

Tanya Anne Crosby

TANYA ANNE CROSBY is the author of six best-selling historicals for Avon Books: *Angel of Fire, Sagebrush Bride, Viking's Prize, Once Upon a Kiss, Kissed,* and her most recent title, *The MacKinnon's Bride.* All have garnered excellent reviews, and have graced such bestseller lists as Walden Romance and *USA Today.* She makes her home in Charleston, South Carolina, with her husband, two children, and their two feuding dogs.

Scandal's Bride

Samantha James

Chapter 1

London, 1820

Had she known what fate awaited her, she'd never have kissed him.

But Lady Victoria Carlton, only daughter of the marquess of Norcastle, did not act out of a mere frivolity of nature. Oh, no. In all truth, she was desperate to seek an end to her predicament.

She was convinced her only hope lay in scandal.

Unfortunately, there was precious little time. Papa had informed her this very morn that she must choose a husband by midnight tonight.

Or else *he* would.

It was not an idle threat—of this, Victoria was very certain. Much to Papa's vexation, she had passed through several Seasons, turning down each and every one of the marriage proposals that had come her way. But now Papa's patience had come to an end. He'd received three proposals during the last fortnight. He was usually not a tyrant, but when in one of his testiest moods, he was an imposing figure—there was simply no crossing him. And since she had no engagements other than the Remingtons' ball that evening, it must be soon. *Very* soon . . .

The ball was a typical gala affair. A din of voices rose in the air. Dozens of couples swirled across the floor in time to a lively waltz. The ballroom and adjoining salon had been decorated with huge clusters of pink and red roses.

With a deep curtsy, Victoria laughingly retreated from the arms of her latest dance partner. Her steps carried her to the edge of the salon, near the terrace doors. It wasn't so crowded there, and she needed time to think. Good heavens, time to *act*, for only a few hours remained before midnight.

There was a touch on her arm. Victoria turned to her good friend Sophie Mayfield. Two years her junior, Sophie had just come out this Season. Sophie gazed at her, her brown eyes softly beseeching. "Victoria, I beg of you, please do not do this. Perhaps your father is right. Perhaps you should have chosen a husband long ago. Certainly it's not from a lack of suitors—"

"Pompous and selfish young bucks dazzled by the size of my dowry, and none of whom I cared to spend the rest of my life with." A finely arched blond brow rose high as she spoke. Though her tone was light, the strength of her resolve was not.

She had entered her first Season with stars in her eyes and romance in her heart—with the dream of catching a dashingly handsome young man, of having him fall madly in love with her. Vivid in her mind was the certainty that marriage would follow, and they would live out the rest of their lives in blissful enchantment.

Another dear friend, Phoebe Tattinger, had shared that very same dream.

It was Phoebe who found her prince first. She'd tumbled head over heels in love with Viscount Colin Paxton the instant they met. Victoria did not envy Phoebe her good fortune—no, not in the least! How could she, for never had she seen Phoebe so happy! She discounted the rumors that Colin's proposal

stemmed from his desire to marry an heiress, though
Phoebe was indeed an heiress. Colin loved Phoebe—
she was as certain of it as her friend.

Phoebe's joy had not lasted even three months after the wedding.

A pang swept through Victoria. She tried not to
remember, yet she couldn't help it.

She and Phoebe had been out walking in Hyde
Park one day; Phoebe had only recently learned she
was with child. For that very reason they'd stopped
to rest, sitting on a secluded bench with a view of
the pathway, where they could watch the members
of the *ton* strut and parade their fine feathers on this
sunny spring morn.

A man and woman passed by. 'Twas very clear
both gentleman and lady were of an amorous inclination. One lace-gloved hand lay tucked into the gentleman's elbow. The other was snugly enfolded
within his. Even as they watched, the couple stopped,
touching their lips together in a sweet, binding kiss.

Phoebe had laughingly commented. "It must be
the air in London, Victoria. *Everyone* is in love these
days—"

But all at once her voice choked off. Victoria's regard snapped back to the pair in question.

The man was Colin, Phoebe's husband.

Never in her life would Victoria forget her friend's
expression. She had watched as Phoebe's heart shattered into a million pieces. She'd held her while
Phoebe cried throughout the day. And she had
waved good-bye when Phoebe departed for the
country two days later.

Colin remained in town, where he continued his
association with his ladybird, the Lady Marian Winter, a widow.

Since that day, Victoria had lost count of the
women who had been associated with him. For the

most part, Phoebe remained in the country. Victoria had seen her only a few times since that horrible day, but the change in Phoebe was sobering indeed. She was no longer lively and vivacious. There was no light in her eyes, no dazzle in her smile, where before there had been sunlight bursting in her heart and soul.

Slowly, her attention was drawn back to Sophie. "Oh, come now," Sophie was saying. "Victoria, when I think of your suitors—why, none have been so terrible! And this very moment, your father has offers from three prospects. What about Viscount Newton—"

Victoria's generous mouth had turned down. "A man whose arrogance I cannot abide," she finished succinctly.

"Well, then, what about Robert Sherwood?"

"A cad, Sophie, and you know it as well as I."

"But there's still Lord Dunmire's youngest son Phillip—"

"Boorish and dull, Sophie. I should grow weary of my own voice were I to marry him. And I'm told he gambles to excess."

"Victoria, I beg you reconsider."

"There's nothing you can say to change my mind, Sophie."

"But your reputation will be ruined—"

"Quite," Victoria pronounced grimly.

Sophie sighed. " 'Tis because of your friend Phoebe, isn't it, that you refuse to marry? But I would remind you, Victoria, not all men are scoundrels such as her husband."

"I'm quite aware of that, Sophie. Indeed, there are times I enjoy their company very much." It was true. Oh, she laughed. She danced, but she was no longer the innocent she'd been when she entered her first Season.

Her chin came up. "But I would remind *you* that you are only in your first Season, and I am not so naïve as I once was. I have borne witness to countless infidelities—husbands with mistresses, wives with lovers. I've seen fortunes lost and amassed with the turn of a card. The *ton* is filled with despicable men whose vices are exceeded only by their monstrous ego."

"And so you will *never* marry?" Sophie remained unconvinced.

Victoria's gaze turned cloudy. "I would never bury myself in the country as Phoebe does," she said slowly. "But long ago I abandoned my foolish notions about love and marriage. I've learned that marriages are made to gain money, power, position, or land—perhaps to breed an heir—perhaps any and all of these."

Sophie fluttered her fan in utter distress. "But you will spend your life alone, Victoria, with no husband, no children. Why, I find the thought simply unbearable!"

Victoria said nothing. She couldn't deny that Phoebe's painful experience had left its mark, for she had no wish to suffer a betrayal such as Phoebe had done. She would not allow any man to use her as a pawn, for his own gain . . .

Her heart twisted, for there was a part of her that was torn in two—a part of her that could not disdain love entirely. Her parents had loved each other, something she never doubted for an instant. Though it had been nearly ten years since Mama died, Victoria still remembered shared, subtle glances between them, a lingering touch on the shoulder that spoke with such eloquence . . .

If she were ever to wed, it must be to a man she could love enough to trust . . . ah, but could she trust enough to love?

She had no answer.

She knew only that she could not spend her life as Phoebe did, in melancholy despair, hopelessly in love with a man who shared nothing of her feelings . . . never being loved in return . . .

She *would* not.

She would far rather spend her life alone.

But now Papa was insisting she marry . . . oh, she truly did not wish to defy him!

And so she turned her attention back to her mission, which was simple. Were she embroiled in scandal, her suitors would want no part of her—neither those present nor prospective. As for Papa, surely he would consider her totally beyond redemption and would at last cease his efforts to see her wed.

Twisting her white lace handkerchief between slender gloved fingers, Victoria directed a fervent prayer heavenward. *Forgive me, Mama.* Her poor dead mama would be horrified at what she proposed to do, yet Victoria could see no other way. All she needed was a gentleman to help her carry out her plan, such as it was.

The only problem was *who.* In all truth, she couldn't quite summon the nerve to approach a gentleman with whom she was already acquainted. It must be a stranger then, for she knew she'd never have the courage to face him again. With that singular thought high aloft, she scanned the sea of bodies. Faith, but there must be *someone* . . .

A figure brushed by, elegantly clad in black. The man was tall, long of limb and broad of shoulder, a study of lean, masculine grace. Victoria caught her breath, for it was as if he'd been lifted from the very essence of her mind—from those dreams she'd cast aside long ago. Her gaze followed him as he passed through the terrace doors and out into the shadows of the gardens.

Something leaped in her breast. There would be no better time. There would be no better *man*. Anticipation sparked within her. If all went as planned, by midnight her fate would at last be her own.

She turned to Sophie and saw that Sophie had again gleaned her intent. Her friend looked ready to cry.

Victoria lightly squeezed her shoulder. "Don't look like that," she scolded gently. "I shall be fine, you'll see. You have only to come to the terrace in a few minutes' time, but make sure someone is with you as well. And don't forget, you must pretend to be horrified at finding us—"

"I *will* be horrified!" Sophie's eyes were huge. "Victoria, when I think of what you are about to do . . . throwing yourself at a gentleman . . ."

"Shhh," Victoria cautioned, then summoned a smile and pinched poor Sophie's cheek. "Wish me luck, love." With that Victoria turned and fairly flew through the terrace doors.

It was a moment before her eyes adjusted to the dimness. The man stood perhaps ten paces distant. His hands were locked behind his back, his dark head slightly inclined as he stared out into the night. Victoria had to force her feet to do her bidding. But a rustle of skirts warned of her presence. Before she could say a word, the stranger spun around just as she came to a halt.

Wide sapphire eyes met those of steely gray. Victoria's eyes flew wide, and she clutched at her skirts. It was all she could do to stand her ground. Her heart knocked wildly, both in fear and anticipation. All sense of reason fled her mind. The moment was upon her, yet she knew not what to say. She knew not what to *do*.

It was he who spoke first. "If you're looking for

someone, I fear you're destined for disappointment. I'm the only one here."

"Oh, but I'm hardly disappointed. You're the very one I sought." The words tumbled forth before she could stop them. Victoria colored as she realized how rash—and how audacious—she must surely sound. But she couldn't tear her gaze from his face. She was tall for a woman, yet he was half a head taller than she. And he really was stunningly handsome, with winged brows as black as his hair, and a square, masculine jaw. His eyes were most unusual, like clear crystal with a glimmer of silver. She found herself thinking that he would be quite irresistible if only he smiled . . .

But now it seemed she was the one who merited a closer look. The stranger proceeded to inspect her from the shining blond coronet atop her head to her narrow, slippered feet. Though Victoria had always prided herself on her ability to remain unruffled no matter the circumstances, there was a sharpness to this man's gaze that rendered her distinctly ill at ease.

A dark brow hiked upward. "Indeed," he responded coolly. "To my knowledge, we've never met."

"No," she agreed. "We have not." Her mind was turning frantically. However was she to accomplish her mission without sounding like a brazen hussy?

"You sought me out, yet you don't know who I am?"

"Yes. You see, I have a favor to ask of you."

"A favor. Of a man you do not know."

"Precisely. You see, I find myself in a situation only you can help me with."

His eyes narrowed. "How so?"

Victoria forced a light, buoyant laugh, even as she battled the urge to turn and flee. "Men are very fond of gambling, are they not? Well, you see, my friend Sophie proposed a rather outrageous dare, a dare I simply could not refuse. She dared me to kiss the first stranger I met tonight. And so, kind sir, I wonder if you are willing to oblige me."

The moment was tortuous. Victoria held her breath and waited.

Nor did she have long to wait.

"Oblige you? Ah, but we have not *met*, have we? You have no idea who I am. I haven't the faintest idea who you are, and I do believe it's best we keep it that way." His smile was cutting. "In short, my lady, I think it best if I remove myself from your silly, schoolgirl schemes."

Victoria understood; truly she did, for already she had recognized that this man was not a carefree, frivolous young buck like so many others in the *ton*. He was older, for one, and his bearing was that of a man who knew what he wanted and knew it well.

Panic flared high and bright as he stepped past her. It appeared he had every intention of returning inside.

"Wait!" she cried. "I beseech you, please do not leave!"

He swung back to face her. Victoria cringed inside, for his expression was no less than forbidding.

"Young woman," he said sternly, "please do not make this more difficult than . . ."

Victoria never heard the rest. A medley of voices came from behind him, near the terrace door.

She had been polite. She had *asked*. And now it seemed she must take the matter into her own hands. Quickly, before she lost her courage, she flung her arms around him and pressed herself against him.

Strong hands clamped down on her waist. Victoria felt him stiffen, but she didn't give him the chance to do more. She tangled her fingers in the hair that grew low on his nape, pulled his head down and levered herself upward in one fluid move.

Her lips met his. Her eyes squeezed shut.

The world seemed to tilt and spin. A hundred different sensations bombarded her. His mouth was soft, while his body was hard. She battled the strangest urge to clutch at him wildly, to press herself against him and feel even more of him against her . . . In her heart she was appalled at such a wickedly unladylike thought, yet she could not deny the hungry surge within her.

In some distant corner of her mind, she heard his swiftly indrawn breath; she sensed that he was as startled as she. Though his fingers bit into the soft skin of her hips, he didn't thrust her away. An odd little quiver shot through her, for she'd never thought to find pleasure in this moment—yet pleasure there was, a world of it, intoxicating and sweet. Her lips parted, a silent invitation . . .

Behind her there was a gasp . . . That would be Sophie, she thought hazily.

Aware they were no longer alone, Victoria reluctantly broke off the kiss. She levered her heels to the floor and prepared herself for the sight of Sophie standing there, pretending to be horrified. With a breathy little sigh, she opened her eyes . . .

Only to confront her father's blistering regard.

"Oh, dear," she whispered. Sophie was behind Papa, her eyes huge. Their host, Lord Remington, was there as well.

The stranger, too, had turned toward the door. Oddly enough, one lean hand remained anchored on her waist, the gesture almost protective. "Good heavens," he said irritably. "Who the devil are you?"

Papa straightened himself to his full height. "I am the marquess of Norcastle," her father said grimly. "And I'll thank you to unhand my daughter."

Chapter 2

✦

An hour later the three of them filed into her father's study. Though his features were stoic and tight-lipped, Victoria knew he'd never been angrier. It wasn't his way to rage and shout. Indeed, she thought half-hysterically, she almost wished he would!

The dark stranger sat stiffly beside her—only now she knew his identity. He was Miles Grayson, earl of Stonehurst. Clasping her fingers in her lap, Victoria dared to steal a glance at him . . . oh, and how she wished she had not! His shoulders were as rigid as a soldier's, his profile as cold as the sea.

Yet she couldn't deny that Miles Grayson had been remarkably civil, and very decent, thus far. Nor was it Papa's way to make a scene. Papa had quietly requested that the earl accompany him to his town house that they might discuss the matter further.

But a man could only be pushed so far . . .

The proof was in her father.

Victoria's stomach was churning. She felt very much like a child about to be punished for some misdeed. But this was no childish prank. She'd been caught kissing a gentleman—scandalous behavior in polite society! She reminded herself that sullying her reputation was what she had intended . . . yet somehow it had gone terribly awry . . . she'd never dreamed that Papa would actually *see* it . . .

And she had the awful sensation it wasn't over yet.

"Now." Papa's voice rang out. "I will not ask either of you to explain yourselves, since 'tis very obvious what the two of you were about." He turned his formidable gaze to the earl. "The *ton* is filled with foolish young wastrels who dally whenever and wherever they please and care not a whit about the consequences. 'Twas my belief that you, sir, were above such outlandish behavior—an honorable, respectable man whom I have held in the highest regard. Frankly, my lord, I am appalled at your behavior."

Beside her, the earl said nothing. But Victoria did not miss the way one hand clenched into a fist.

Then it was her turn to bear her father's displeasure as he turned baleful eyes toward her. His tone was stern. "As for you, Victoria, there are no words to express my disappointment."

Victoria could not bear to look at him. In all her life, she had never been so ashamed. "I-I'm sorry, Papa." Swallowing, she slowly raised her chin. "But indeed, you are right. The *ton* is filled with wastrels who dally where they may. Well, I have no wish to marry such a man—"

Her father cut her off with a sound of disgust. "And I would never allow you to marry a scoundrel, Victoria. But you should not spend your life alone and—"

"I would rather spend my life alone than marry a man who would further his own interests by marrying the daughter of a marquess, for that is what happened to my dear friend Phoebe—her husband chose her for her fortune." She spoke with heartfelt candor. "I simply have no desire to marry—not Viscount Newton, not Robert Sherwood, not Philip

Dunmire. And that is why I-I did what I did. I thought they would each withdraw their suit when they heard what had happened. And I thought you would consider me beyond redemption and cease your efforts to see me wed."

"Hmmmph!" Her father's mouth compressed. He directed his attention to the earl. "Have you anything to say, my lord?"

Victoria interrupted before Miles could say a word. "I assure you, Papa, the earl had no idea what I was about!"

From the corner of her eye, she saw the earl stiffen. "I am quite capable of speaking for myself," he said curtly. One elegantly shod foot tapped on the carpet. "You have my sincerest apologies, my lord. My behavior with your daughter was most reprehensible. Beyond that, I fear I can offer no more."

"Now that's where you're wrong, my lord." The marquess drummed his fingers on the desktop. "Because I am not prepared to let the matter end here."

An ominous foreboding descended over the room. Victoria's eyes darted between the two men, who beheld each other in rigid silence. Why didn't Miles Grayson speak up and agree with her? Why didn't he tell Papa that he hadn't kissed her—'twas *she* who kissed him! For in truth, the blame was not his at all.

"Papa," she said in desperation, "did you not hear? It was I who kissed him!"

"Either way, Victoria"—her father's tone was biting—"the earl appeared ever so willing. Or am I wrong, my lord?"

Miles Grayson's jaw might have been hewn of iron. He spoke not a word, neither agreement nor denial.

"Very well then," Papa went on. "My daughter's

reputation has been compromised, and I will not permit this scandal to go further. The only question that remains is how to rectify the damage."

He fixed his gaze on his daughter. "Since your mother died, I have provided for you the best I knew how, Victoria. I am proud to say, you have disappointed me in only one thing—your reluctance to take a husband. I have been patient. Through three Seasons I have waited for you to do what is expected of you, I have bided my time whilst you turned up your nose at first one suitor, then another, for I could not bear to see you unhappy. But you are a woman now, Victoria. And you must live with the consequences of your actions."

He transferred his attention to the earl. "Now then. I believe it's best if we speak privately, my lord. Victoria, a moment alone with the earl, if you please . . ."

Victoria needed no further urging. She leaped to her feet and fled.

Miles was furious—with himself, the marquess, and his troublesome daughter. He'd only accepted Lord and Lady Remington's invitation because Lord Remington had stood as godfather to him. But going to the ball had been a monumental mistake.

His trips to London were rare, usually confined to business only, for he'd grown tired of society long ago—the parties, the false gaiety, the endless gossip, the never-ending pretense of manners and goodwill. He much preferred the solitude of Lyndermere Park, his estate in Lancashire; he enjoyed far more the company of farmers and shepherds . . . and of course, Heather.

He'd very nearly departed London for Lyndermere Park that very morning. He hated the noise and grime of London—and he missed Heather. His mouth twisted. God, but he should have listened to his instinct. Then this would never have happened . . .

The marquess's voice cut into his thoughts like the prick of a needle. "I have a proposition for you, my lord. Would you care to hear it?"

Miles's smile was a travesty. "Not really," he drawled.

"Nonetheless," the marquess stated with icy precision, "you will."

Miles shrugged.

"Now. What I propose is very simple. I want you to marry my daughter."

Miles's smile was wiped clean, his reply heated and instantaneous. "You're mad."

"I assure you, my lord, I am not."

Miles forced a calm he was far from feeling. "What!" he said scathingly. "I heard you say quite distinctly, my lord, that your daughter is in her third Season. I cannot help but wonder what's wrong with the chit that she's been unable to find a man willing to marry her."

The marquess only barely managed to restrain his temper. "I would be careful were I you, my lord. When you insult my daughter, you insult me as well, and that is not wise. And surely you have eyes. Victoria is a beauty, as comely as any. She has had numerous suitors, more than I can recall. And I've had in my hand this past fortnight three offers for her hand."

"Then let one of them marry her!"

Leather creaked as the marquess leaned back in his chair. "Ah, but they did not dishonor her, sir. *You* did."

Miles very nearly retorted that the chit had no one to blame but herself. But just as he opened his mouth, a voice tolled through his mind. *Papa, did you not hear? It was I who kissed him!*

The girl had been remarkably forward—and incredibly fetching. And that kiss . . . An unguarded taste of innocence, sweeter than ripe summer berries, a hint of heaven . . .

At first he'd been too startled to move. And then—God above but he couldn't lie—he hadn't wanted to. Desire struck the very instant their lips met—strange, for he was not a man to yearn for a woman so quickly—and so intensely. He'd wanted to snatch her against him. Plumb the depths of her mouth with his tongue while his hands explored the lithe ripeness of her body . . . But something had stopped him. Perhaps the innocence he'd sensed in her . . .

No, he thought soberly. He hadn't expected to like it so much. He hadn't expected to want her sweet, stolen kiss to go on. And on . . .

He could have stopped it. He could have ended it at any given moment . . .

His lips tightened. "I accept my part in this. But do you really expect me to *marry* her?"

"I will make myself very clear, Lord Stonehurst. If you don't, you will live to regret it."

Miles clenched his jaw so hard his teeth hurt. "A threat, my lord?"

The marquess shrugged. "Call it whatever you like." Shaggy brows drew together over his nose. "I understand you have a daughter."

Miles had been about to tell him to go straight to hell. But at the mention of Heather, he froze. "My ward," he said curtly. "Heather Duval. She's been with me since she was a very young child. Her parents were killed in a carriage accident." His tone was level, as level as his gaze. But his heart had leaped high in his chest. The marquess couldn't possibly know . . .

The marquess frowned. "Ah, now it comes to me!" he explained. "You were once betrothed to the former Lady Margaret Sutherland, were you not?"

"What of it?" His voice was clipped and abrupt. Miles couldn't help it.

"But you broke off the engagement only days before the wedding, as I recall."

"Marriage between Margaret and I would have been a mistake." Miles felt compelled to defend himself.

"Ah, but Margaret's mother was most distressed. I remember her telling me that Margaret had gone to Lancashire to visit you. Did she and your ward not get on well, my lord?"

Miles's tone was tight. "That, my lord, is none of your affair."

The marquess paid no heed. He tipped his head to the side. "Who did you say the little girl's parents were, my lord?"

"I didn't," Miles said from between his teeth.

"Hmmm. Odd, but I suddenly find myself most curious, my lord. Most curious, indeed."

Miles's eyes glinted. "You bastard," he accused baldly. "I'll tolerate no one prying into her past."

"And there'll be no need if you marry my daughter." The elder man's tone was as smooth as oil. He didn't take his eyes from Grayson's face. "Well, my lord? Do we have a bargain?"

Miles was up and on his feet in a surge of restless anger. Damn him. He couldn't possibly know . . . Yet he couldn't take the chance the marquess might find out the truth. Oh, it wouldn't hurt him. But Heather's life would never be the same—and he wanted only the best for her. She would *have* only the best.

"Let it be done," he muttered.

"Excellent!" proclaimed the marquess. "Now, I think the wedding should take place posthaste...." He rose and opened a massive oak door and called for his daughter.

Victoria walked slowly into the study, feeling for all the world as if she were entering a dungeon of darkest doom. The earl stood near the window, arms crossed over his chest; he made no acknowledgement of her presence. As for her father, Papa's expression told the tale only too well—he was pleased with the outcome of his discussion with the earl. His words bore out her suspicion.

"The earl has some news for you, my dear."

Miles Grayson turned and gave her a stiff bow. "It seems we are to marry, my lady. I trust you'll understand that I am less than overjoyed."

Victoria's face drained of all color. "Marry," she echoed, her tone half-strangled. "No, it cannot be. You—you cannot want this."

"No." His mouth twisted. "But your father is a persuasive man."

Stricken, Victoria looked at her father. "Papa. Papa, *please* do not make me do this."

She didn't acknowledge the spasm of pain that passed over his face. The marquess shook his head. "I warned you, Victoria. I warned you but you would not heed me. And so I have no choice."

A horrible knot of dread coiled in her belly. He was right. She'd been caught. Caught in a trap of her own design.

Nor had Papa lied. He'd said if she did not choose a husband this very night, then he would. And as she soon discovered, Papa was determined to see the deed well and truly done...

This very night.

A vicar was summoned to the town house. He took his place in front of the massive marble fireplace, his Bible in hand. Smiling and sleepy-eyed, he glanced between the two men. "Shall we proceed, my lords?"

Papa gave a curt nod. Stoic and silent, the earl stepped before the vicar. His posture was wooden.

He spared no glance for his bride-to-be, standing in the shadows at the back of the room.

Victoria stifled the urge shrink away into the darkness of the night. But then Papa was there, offering his arm. Her steps heavy, Victoria crossed the carpet, feeling as if she were being led to an early grave. As she took her place beside the earl, a feeling of sick dread tightened her middle. Her mind screamed silently. How could this have happened? She was about to marry this man—Miles Grayson, earl of Stonehurst. Sweet heaven, she was to *marry* him, a man she'd not set eyes on before this very night . . .

She stole a glance at him, only to regret it. His profile was as rigid as his spine, his expression grim and angry. There was scant comfort in knowing he wanted this marriage no more than she . . .

She hadn't wanted to marry, most certainly not this night. And she would never have wanted it like this, in this sterile, lonely room at midnight . . . Despair pierced her breast. If it had to be, she'd have wanted it differently . . . Four prancing steeds would have delivered her to the steps of the church. She'd have walked down the aisle in a long, flowing gown of satin and lace. Friends and acquaintances would have filled every pew. Sophie would have been there, beaming at her shyly, and Phoebe, too . . .

The ceremony passed in a haze. She roused only when her hand was laid within the earl of Stonehurst's. She nearly snatched it back—his skin was like fire.

Then all at once it was time for the vows. The earl spoke his in clipped, staccato tones.

She whispered hers.

In the corner, the clock began to toll the hour of midnight.

Victoria watched numbly as the earl pulled a gold, crested ring from his smallest finger and slid it onto hers. The ring was heavy . . . as heavy as her heart.

At the very last stroke, the vicar raised his head and cleared his throat. "I now pronounce you man and wife," he intoned. "My lord, you may kiss the bride."

Chapter 3

❦

Victoria's numbness receded. Aware of Miles Grayson's burning gaze on her profile, a flurry of panic took hold, swift and merciless. She sought to withdraw her hand but he wouldn't allow it. His grip tightened. An unpleasantly strong arm slid about her waist and caught her up against him.

His head swooped down.

His mouth crushed hers, fierce and devouring; it was a kiss far beyond Victoria's limited experience. Oh, she'd allowed a few of her gentleman callers a chaste peck on the lips·now and again—and thought herself quite daring!

But this was different. Her husband's possession of her mouth was far from worshipful. She could feel the rampant, seething fire of his emotions in the hot brand of his mouth on hers, filled with stark, relentless purpose. He meant to defile her—to dishonor her.

Gasping, she tore her mouth free. She knew it for certain then. He raised her head, and both triumph and challenge glittered in his eyes. Victoria's spine went rigid. She would have slapped him were it not for the sharp rap of Papa's voice.

"A word of warning, my lord. Although Victoria is now your wife, do not forget she is my daughter.

Misuse her and you'll feel my wrath—and I promise, you'll wish you had not!"

The earl was undaunted. Instead his mouth curled in what could only be called dry mockery. "My lord, I could hardly forget," he drawled. "I trust you'll forgive our hasty departure." He turned to his bride. "Countess, I suggest you hurry and have a maid pack a bag for you. Our wedding night awaits."

Victoria's eyes flew wide, then slid back to her father. This couldn't be happening! she thought wildly. Miles Grayson had no right to take over her life like this! *Ah, but he does*, whispered a niggling little voice.

And they all knew it.

Her bag was packed and ready all too soon. The earl's carriage clattered around to the front of the house. With a steely-fingered hold about her elbow, the earl proceeded to lead her outside. But as he would have handed her up and into the carriage, she broke away.

She rushed back to where Papa stood on the steps. Throwing her arms around him, she clung to him unashamedly. "Papa," she choked out. "I cannot do this. I cannot bear it!"

The hand that smoothed her hair was not entirely steady. "Shhh," he whispered. "It will be all right, Victoria. I know it."

"He is so hard. So cold!"

"I know what he seems at this moment, child. But he is not. Dear God, do you think I'd give my only daughter to such a man?"

An ache rent her breast. In her heart, Victoria knew her father wanted only what was best for her. Yet she couldn't see what good could possibly come of this marriage.

"Victoria!" From the shadows behind her, the sound of her name sliced through the night.

Victoria paid no heed.

Papa kissed her cheek, then squeezed her shoulder. "Go now, Victoria, and remember. You now have a husband, but I will always be your father— and I will always love you."

Though her throat was hot with the burning threat of tears, somehow those words gave her the strength she needed to turn and retrace her steps. This time when the earl handed her into the coach, her head was high, the set of her shoulders proudly erect.

The interior of the coach was thick with an oppressive silence. Victoria felt the earl's gaze on her— dark and angry—like the man himself, she thought with a shiver. Despite her resolve, she was sorely tempted to fling open the door and flee.

Soon the carriage rolled to a halt before a fashionable red-brick mansion in Grosvenor Square.

"Our humble abode, countess."

Victoria gritted her teeth. The wretch was baiting her—and enjoying it immensely. She disdained his hand and alighted without his assistance. The door was opened by a stoop-shouldered butler and they were ushered inside a wide, flagstoned entrance hall.

Miles wasted no time imparting the news. "Nelson, meet my wife, the former Lady Victoria Carlton. Would you please show her to the gold bedchamber?"

Nelson was all agog but recovered quickly. "Certainly, sir." He picked up her bag and inclined his head toward his new mistress. "Please come with me, my lady."

Victoria brushed past the earl without a word. The bedchamber she was shown into was lovely. The carpet was of pale cream. Deep yellow brocade draperies framed the windows. A matching counterpane covered the bed. Under other circumstances

Victoria might have exclaimed her delight aloud, but not now.

What was it the earl had said? Her mind flew like wind across the fields. *Our wedding night awaits.* She shivered. He hadn't meant anything by that, had he? No. Of course not. After all, their marriage had hardly been planned. Surely he would not expect her to—to behave like a bride. Or—God forbid—to share his bed . . .

"I trust this room suits you?"

The voice startled her. Victoria whirled around to see her husband standing in the doorway. He leaned with careless ease against the doorjamb, one lean hand curled around a glass of wine. Despite the lateness of the hour, he looked as elegantly handsome as he had hours earlier.

The room does, she longed to shout. *It's you who does not.*

She nodded.

"Good." There was a small pause. "Will you join me for a drink in the drawing room?"

She politely declined. "I think not. It's been a tiring night."

"A tiring night! But you saw the fruition of your plans, didn't you? I should imagine you'd want to celebrate." His tone was falsely hearty.

Victoria stiffened. "Celebrate? I fail to see what there is to celebrate," she informed him archly.

"Oh, come now, countess. This was your plan all along, wasn't it? To trap me into marriage."

Her jaw closed with a snap. It was all she could do to maintain a civil air. "It's just as I told my father, my lord. I wished to marry no one—least of all you," she said cuttingly. "Indeed, it was the very thing I sought to avoid."

"Ah, and you went about it quite admirably,

didn't you?" Mockery lay heavy and biting in his voice.

Victoria's face burned painfully. "A mistake, my lord. A costly one for both of us, I admit, for I misjudged my father grievously. But perhaps you may draw comfort from the fact that you stand to gain far more than I. My father is a wealthy man. My dowry is a fortune unto its own. I should imagine *you* would be celebrating." Her gaze lowered to the glass of wine in his hand. She smiled with acid sweetness. "But you are already, I see."

Her barb struck home. His mouth hardened. His grip on the fragile stem of the glass tightened so that the skin of his knuckles shown taut and white; Victoria was certain the stem would snap at any moment.

He straightened. "This seems as good a time as any to tell you of my plan. I suggest we dwell under the same roof for as long as it takes to appease your father. In time, I have no doubt you'll be able to charm him into seeing this marriage was a mistake. When that happens, the marriage can be annulled and we'll go our separate ways. Is that agreeable?"

"Quite," she snapped.

"So be it," he said. He started to turn away, only to pause.

"A word of advice for you, countess. I shouldn't force my attentions on a gentleman—let alone kiss him—the way you did me in the Rutherford's garden. A man"—his smile was but a travesty—"I fear there is no polite way to put this . . . a man finds such boldness distasteful." With that he left her.

Victoria was speechless with rage. She glared at the door through which he'd just passed. Miles Grayson, earl of Stonehurst, was the most odious, hateful man alive!

*   *   *

This was war.

Her pride had been stung, the gauntlet cast. Her husband had insulted her, cutting her down with naught but the lash of his tongue.

Oh, she would do as he said. They would reside beneath the same roof, for the sake of her father. But they would share nothing else—not a single meal. Not a room.

But if he thought to make her cower, he would be sorely disappointed, for Victoria was determined not to wilt away, to hide in the corner.

So it was that the next morning, she summoned the earl's staff and introduced herself . . . and promptly rang for the carriage. While she waited in the entrance hall, she stopped before a gilt-framed mirror and retied the satin strings of her bonnet, humming a merry little tune.

"Going out so soon, my dear?"

Victoria very nearly choked herself.

Thank heaven her recovery was mercifully quick, even though her heart pounded and her mind turned wildly. He thought her bold and audacious, so that was what she would give him. Giving a final tug on her bonnet strings, she turned and bestowed on him a smile that would surely melt the hardest of hearts.

But not her husband's.

"Well, Victoria?" He stood before her, an imposing figure garbed wholly in black. Her stomach fluttered strangely. He seemed taller than ever, lean and muscular. Seen in the full light of the day, she could detect no flaws in his countenance, save the almost wicked slant of his brows. Indeed, he was so very handsome he nearly took her breath away. But there was no mistaking the disapproval inherent in his regard, and that fired more than a twinge of resentment.

She gave a trilling little laugh. "What!" she said breezily. "Did you think I'd be given to vapors? If so, I'm sorry to disappoint you."

His eyes seemed to sizzle. "On the contrary, Victoria"—he spoke with precise deliberation—"you are exactly what I expected."

She paid him no further heed as she swept out the front door. Minutes later the carriage drew up before Sophie's house. When the butler announced her, Sophie thrust aside her embroidery and leaped up.

"Victoria! Oh, I'm so sorry . . . I-I don't know how it happened . . . your father followed me onto the terrace and asked your whereabouts. And suddenly there you were . . . ! Oh, I've been so worried. Mama rushed home from shopping this morning with the news you'd wed the earl of Stonehurst! Is that who you were with in the garden? The earl of Stonehurst? I told Mama she must surely be mistaken . . . she is, isn't she?"

There was no need to answer. Victoria practically fell into Sophie's arms and collapsed into tears.

Within the day, their marriage was the talk of the *ton*.

Within the week, the talk of London.

Victoria had feared she would be ostracized, for the *ton* was notorious for turning a condescending eye to those who committed the slightest *faux pas*. Yet the ladies sighed with envy, for they thought marriage between Victoria and Miles Grayson grandly romantic—and quite a catch! As for the gentlemen, they merely smiled quietly to themselves, for they were well aware the earl of Stonehurst had captured a covetous prize—a wife who possessed both beauty *and* money.

All in all, her social calender changed little, for invitations continued to arrive daily. But Victoria felt very much the intruder in her husband's house; oh,

not because of the servants, for they were only too
anxious to please. No, it was Miles. She couldn't forget he disdained her very presence in his home, her
so-called role as wife. And so she stayed away as
often as she could. On those rare occasions she encountered her husband, he was unfailingly polite,
yet chillingly so.

One morning, she accompanied Sophie to a seamstress on Bond Street. While Sophie and the seamstress went back to the dressing room, Victoria idly
sifted through a handful of hair ribbons in the far
corner of the shop. The doorchime sounded, and she
glanced up. Two matrons stepped within; one was
Lady Carmichael, the other Lady Brentwood.

Her greeting died on her lips.

"Why, I've never met such a gentleman as Lord
Stonehurst in all my days," Lady Carmichael was
saying.

Curious, Victoria ducked her head low and listened intently.

"I find him utterly fascinating," Lady Carmichael
went on, "and *most* charming."

"Yes, indeed." This came from Lady Brentwood.
"Charles has had numerous business dealings with
him. Why, only last evening I distinctly recall he told
an acquaintance there's no man he respects or ad-
mires more than Lord Stonehurst—and Charles is
not a man to give his praise lightly."

But Lady Brentwood had not finished. "As for his
marriage to Lady Victoria Carlton, why, many a
man would have left her to her own devices, no matter the harm to her reputation. The haste with which
they married simply proves that he is a noble fellow
indeed." She gave a trilling laugh. "To say nothing
of handsome!"

Victoria's lips tightened. Handsome, oh, exceed-
ingly. That she couldn't deny. But charming? Noble?

They did not have to live with the subject in question. Little did they know—why, the man was a veritable fencepost!

"I do hope Victoria appreciates how lucky she is to have landed such a catch!" said Lady Carmichael. "I find it rather odd that she continues to go about as if she'd never married! Why, my Theodora sobbed the night through when she heard Stonehurst had wed."

Victoria's head snapped up. She was sorely tempted to tell Lady Carmichael that her Theodora was welcome to Miles Grayson, earl of Stonehurst!

But she was unwilling to fuel gossip any further, and so she maintained her silence, keeping her presence hidden until the two ladies had left the shop.

But the conversation nagged at her throughout the next few days. Was Miles truly so respected among the *ton*?

For the first time she began to see her husband in a different light . . . and reluctantly admitted that to her knowledge, Miles was neither a cad nor a bounder. He didn't overly frequent the gaming tables. She heard no tales of wild or reckless behavior, nor did he drink to excess. If he had a mistress, he was so discreet she never even suspected. Indeed, it seemed her husband possessed none of the vices she might have despised in a husband . . .

Soon she began to feel guilty, for neither malice nor spite was in her nature. What need was there to live together as enemies? One morning as she prepared to go downstairs, she decided perhaps it was time to make the best of their situation. On impulse, she tapped on the door of his room. When he bid her enter, she stepped inside . . .

Only to stop short at the threshold.

Apparently he'd just come in from riding. His riding jacket lay in a heap upon the bed; a rumpled white shirt lay next to it.

All at once her mouth was dry as dust, her gaze riveted to his form. Victoria had never seen a man in a state of dishabille, not her father or any other.

His hips were incredibly narrow, his boots spattered with mud. His fawn-colored breeches were like a second skin; they clung to his thighs, cleanly outlining every muscle. But it was what lay nestled between those iron-hewn thighs that drew her gaze in a manner most unseemly . . . the swelling there hinted at a masculinity that—were it unfettered and released from constraint—promised a sight to behold indeed . . .

Egad, whatever was wrong with her! Stunned by such audacious thoughts, she tore her gaze upward, only to realize that his naked torso was no less disconcerting.

His shoulders were strong and wide, the muscles of his arms smooth and tight and sleek. A mat of dark curly hair covered his chest and belly, disappearing beneath the waistband of his breeches. Her mind ran wild. Oh, but there was beauty in the male form, of a kind she'd not thought to find . . . most certainly not in her husband!

"Was there something you wanted, Victoria?"

His regard was cool and unsmiling. Victoria swallowed, praying he hadn't noticed her staring. Quickly she gathered her courage—and her senses. Yet still her voice was a trifle breathless.

"There is a garden fete at the Covingtons this afternoon. I-I wondered if you would care to attend with me?"

His reply was most emphatic. "I am not one of your London peacocks to strut at your side for all to admire you, countess. If you wish to attend, then go.

But do not trouble me about such trivial matters again."

Victoria felt as if she'd been slapped. Stupid, foolish tears stung her eyes. She blinked them back, and somehow managed to salvage her pride. Raising her chin, she matched his disdain with dignified aplomb.

"As you wish, my lord," she stated levelly. With a swish of her skirts she turned and was gone.

By the time she reached the dining room, a seething resentment had replaced the hurt. So much for her peace efforts, she reflected bitterly. She had tried, and she could do no more.

The next step—unlikely though it was—was up to Miles.

So it was that in the days that followed, Victoria went riding in Hyde Park. She attended birthday parties and routs. She waltzed until the wee hours of the morning at Almack's. The Lady Carmichaels and Lady Brentwoods of the *ton* could gossip all they pleased about the state of her marriage. When queried about the whereabouts of her husband, she would simply shrug and say lightly, "It's hardly the thing to be in each other's pockets. Besides, what marriage these days is a love match?"

Never had she been so miserable.

One man in particular, Count Antony DeFazio from Italy, was frequently at her side. No matter where she was, more often than not he was there as well. Eventually—unfailingly—he would make his way over to her. Sophie thought he was to-swoon-for handsome. In all honesty, Victoria supposed he was. Yet somehow when she looked into eyes as dark as midnight, she was reminded of eyes the color of storm clouds . . .

It was most distracting—and highly vexing.

In any case, Antony was charming and warmly attentive. He complimented the rich gold of her hair, the creaminess of her skin, the remarkable blue of her eyes. He was an outrageous flirt, but when it seemed her husband wanted nothing to do with her, his praise was balm to her wounded pride.

But her husband was not as heedless of her activities as she thought.

Miles remained in the background, watching all unfold with mounting displeasure. Even before that disastrous night at the Rutherfords, he'd heard rumors of his new wife; in his estimation, she was a lady of fashion who thrived on attention. He couldn't help but think of Margaret Sutherland, the woman he had very nearly married. Once the toast of London, he'd fallen victim to Margaret's sultry beauty, her vivacious charm.

He'd not be so foolish again.

His mouth turned down. No, Victoria was no different than Margaret. Indeed, how could she be anything but shallow and vain? In the end, Victoria would prove herself selfish and hurtful, and Miles would not expose Heather to such a woman.

You judge without evidence, whispered an irascible little voice.

Hah! What more did he need? Why, they'd been wed nearly a fortnight and the chit had not spent one evening home!

Still, he was reminded how Victoria had stood up to her father and announced that *she* had kissed him. Odd, how she'd tried to protect him. Rather honorable, really, to say nothing of noble and courageous . . .

But Miles was a man who didn't need the glitter of London to be happy. He'd chosen a more simple life in the country, an infinitely more satisfying life. Margaret would never have been happy anywhere but London. Neither would Victoria, which was yet another reason he was convinced they had no future together.

That very thought was high in his mind as he strolled inside his home that evening. Nelson hurried to greet him.

"Good evening, my lord."

"Good evening, Nelson." He handed the butler his gloves and cane.

Now came the inevitable question... "Is the countess home?"

... and the inevitable answer. "No, my lord." The butler's eyes flitted away.

"I see. And where is she this fine night?"

"My lord, she mentioned something about a ball at Lord and Lady Raleigh's. I believe the invitation arrived last week."

It was then Miles saw it—a calling card on a silver tray. He picked it up and read the name—COUNT ANTONY DEFAZIO. Sheer red misted his vision, for Miles had also heard the count's name bandied about—in conjunction with his wife's!

"The count was here?"

"This afternoon, my lord. He and the countess took tea together. Then he returned to escort my lady to the ball."

So now the chit was entertaining her admirers in his very house! A stark, blinding fury came over him. He damned himself for giving in to it, even as he damned his errant wife for her part in it.

He jutted out his jaw. "Nelson, have the carriage brought round."

In all her days, Victoria didn't know when she'd been so bored. The lilting music all sounded the same. The crush of faces around her had blurred to indistinction, and she found the scent of fresh flowers almost cloying. If she had to attend one more wretched affair like this, she would surely scream.

Whirling around the dance floor with Antony, she prayed he would unhand her. Her head ached and her feet hurt. All she wanted at this moment was to go home . . .

Home, she thought with a pang. There was a painful catch in her breast. She no longer knew where she belonged. Papa had foisted her off upon the earl, and the earl would just as soon be rid of her . . .

The dance ended. One hand possessively at her waist, Antony would have led her from the floor. But Victoria gently broke away. "Oh, there's Sophie!" she exclaimed. "Please excuse me, count, but I must have a word with her." She gave him no chance to protest, but breezed away in a swirl of skirts.

Across the room, she kissed Sophie's cheek. "Thank heaven you appeared when you did, Sophie. Antony is sweet, but he can be a bit much at times."

"Oh, Victoria, but he is so dashing and handsome! And just think, he is quite entranced with you."

Victoria smiled slightly. She found two seats at the edge of the dance floor and sank into one of them, wriggling her toes gratefully. "Granted, he is quite pleasant to look at, but there are times when he's really quite full of himself, Sophie."

Sophie gave a wistful sigh. "Still, that I could be in your slippers tonight . . ." She had yet to sit, and her gaze drifted out to the dance floor once more. All at once she gasped.

"Victoria, look! He—he's here!"

Victoria accepted a glass of champagne from a tray. "Who, love?"

"Your husband!"

Your husband. Victoria's heart lurched. She very nearly dropped her glass of champagne.

"Victoria, what if he saw you dancing with Antony? Do you think he'll be angry? Do you think he'll be jealous?" Sophie gasped. "He's coming this way and . . . oh, dear . . . I don't think I wish to be in your slippers after all! Victoria, I could almost swear . . . he *does* look rather jealous."

Her gaze tracked Sophie's. Sure enough, Sophie was right. Miles was there, already bearing down on them. But judging from the expression on his face, she guessed he wasn't jealous at all . . .

He was positively livid.

Chapter 4

Yet no trace of it showed in his demeanor as he stepped up before them. He bowed low, a gesture of graceful elegance. "Victoria, I had no idea you were here." He turned to Sophie, chiseled lips drawn into a devastating smile. "Who is your companion, my dear?" Victoria saw a dreamy appreciation enter Sophie's eyes and nearly groaned.

She hastened to her feet, and lay her hand on Sophie's arm. Her stomach twisted in dread but she was determined not to show it. Lifting her chin, she matched his smile. "My lord, this is my dearest friend in all the world, Miss Sophie Mayfair. Sophie, my husband, Miles Grayson, earl of Stonehurst."

"Miss Mayfair, I do hope you don't mind if I steal my wife away. Can you imagine, married nearly a fortnight and we've yet to dance together."

He allowed no protest, but set aside her champagne, captured her hand, and pulled her onto the dance floor. Victoria glared her outrage. " 'Married nearly a fortnight and we've yet to dance together,' " she quoted. "I wonder, my lord, whose fault that is."

"The opportunity could hardly present itself when you were not present, countess."

"My lord," she said sweetly, "I could say the very same of you."

He chose to be silent for several moments. His arm was hard about her back. He held her close—far closer than was proper!—so close she fancied she could feel the muscled breadth of his chest. She felt suddenly giddy . . . from the way he whirled her around, she told herself.

It was then she noticed they had attracted more than an idle number of glances. "We're being watched," she murmured. Her gaze caught his. "Should we give them something to talk about?"

"My dear, I do believe you already have." He sounded almost angry.

Shuttered behind his oh-so-pleasant facade was an anger even deeper than she'd realized. Her heart bounded clear to her throat.

"In fact," he went on, "I do believe we should continue this discussion at home." He whisked her off the dance floor.

Victoria was suddenly not at all eager to leave. She tried to twist away without making it appear she did so. "But I came with—"

The arm about her waist tightened like a band of steel. "I know who escorted you. Nonetheless, you're leaving with me."

There was a tap on Miles's shoulder. "Excuse me," said a thickly accented voice, "but Victoria promised this next dance to me."

Victoria held her breath while Miles squared off to face the count. But he only shook his head and said easily, "Then I'm afraid you're out of luck, old man. Because my lovely wife has promised the night to me—along with every other night."

A very red-faced count fell back, murmuring his apologies.

Victoria clamped her mouth shut. When they were alone in the carriage, she vented the full force of her wrath. "I do not recall promising the night to you, my lord. Not this night or any other."

"Ah, but I beg to differ with you, countess. Or do you forget our wedding vows so soon?"

Victoria lapsed into silence. Drat the man and his facile tongue, she decided furiously. Why must he always have his words so ready at hand?

Once they were inside his home, he ushered her into the salon and closed the doors. Ignoring her, he removed his coat and unwound his cravat, dropping them onto the back of a chair. Her stomach dropped clear to the floor when he proceeded to undo the top buttons of his shirt. She balked. Surely he would not . . . But no. Why, the thought was ridiculous. He'd made no secret of his distaste for her. Of course he had no intention of asserting his husbandly rights . . .

Stifling a pinprick of hurt, she seated herself in a velvet wing chair while he poured two glasses of wine. He turned to face her.

Silence mounted, thick and heavy. Victoria's heart lurched, for he stared at her most oddly. Why, she could almost believe that he *was* jealous . . . But no. She was mistaken. That familiar glacial coolness was very much in evidence as he presented himself before her. He wordlessly extended a glass of wine.

Victoria opened her mouth to decline but he cut her off abruptly.

"I suggest you take it, countess. You didn't get to finish your champagne, remember?"

She would rather not, she decided uneasily. Indeed, she would far rather put this entire night behind her and pretend it hadn't happened, for there was an air of danger about her husband that sent warning bells ringing all through her.

He wasted no time. "You had a caller this afternoon, did you not?"

Her chin lifted a notch. "What, my lord? Am I not allowed to have callers?"

"Of course you may. It's this particular caller I have a problem with, countess. So tell me, who was he?"

Lying was not an option. He already knew. "Count Antony DeFazio," she ventured calmly.

"It's my understanding you've been seen with the count on numerous other occasions. Are you aware of his reputation?"

Her smile was as false as his had been earlier. "Why, yes, indeed I am. Antony is a wonderful dancer. An engaging conversationalist, to say nothing of being an immensely charming escort—"

"That's not what I mean and you know it."

Victoria shrugged. "Men have mistresses and ladies have lovers," she stated daringly. " 'Tis the way of the world."

"Well, it's not my way." Suddenly he was there before her. For the second time in just a few short minutes, her glass was set aside. Without further ado, she was hauled up and out of her chair. Strong hands imprisoned the fragile span of her shoulders.

"You've had free rein these past few weeks, Victoria, but no more. I will not have you behaving in a way that will cause embarrassment or dishonor to my name—to *your* name," he emphasized.

Temper flared but she held it in check. "And what behavior might that be?"

"Dancing with Count Antony DeFazio. Receiving him in our home when I am not present."

"Our home?" she retorted archly. "This is *your* home, my lord."

"It is also yours," he countered, "at least until such time as your father ceases to peer over our shoulder."

The soft line of Victoria's mouth thinned with suppressed fury. "Is there more, my lord?"

"Indeed there is. You will not cavort with the count—nor any man—for all to see."

"Why, my lord," she stated with acid sweetness. "I could almost believe you're jealous." She mocked him. She knew it, and was secretly appalled at her daring. But another part of her, deep in the recesses of her being, yearned to hear him say it was true— that he *was* jealous of DeFazio. And—God help her—that very same part of her desperately wanted the strength of his arms hard around her back—the brand of his mouth upon hers, hot and searing, banishing these angry words so that nothing else mattered.

Oh, it made no sense! She wanted to be rid of him—and he of her . . .

"Well, my lord. *Are* you jealous?" She was aching inside. Quivering. Praying as never before . . .

"Of course not. Why, the very idea is nonsense."

He denounced her baldly—heaven help her, a knife in the heart. But she wouldn't let him know it, not in a thousand years.

"Nonetheless," he went on, "I mean what I say, Victoria. I won't allow you to meet DeFazio again."

Her eyes narrowed. "You forbid me?" she said pleasantly.

"Call it anything you like. Either way, you won't be seeing him again. Nor will you stay out till dawn."

Anger flared at his imperious tone. "Till dawn," she sputtered. "Why, I did no such thing!"

"Nor will you."

"You can't stop me!"

"Oh, but I think I can."

"What will you do? Lock me in my room like a child?"

"If that's what it takes, yes." He was deadly serious. "You need a firm hand, Victoria. You are wild and reckless and I'll have no more of it."

Victoria gasped. "You presume to know me quite well when you know me not at all." She wrenched herself free. Her eyes smoldered, twin flames of pure fire. "Why do you even care what I do—and with whom I do it?"

He stood before her, a pillar of stone. "A ridiculous question, countess. I care because you are my wife."

"The wife you didn't want." Victoria spoke bitterly. Odd, but it burned inside to hear the words aloud.

"Regardless of the circumstances, we *are* wed. And you will mind your manners and your tongue—"

"I need no lessons in manners, my lord earl. Certainly not from you—a man who's been too long in the country!"

"I mean what I say, Victoria. I'll not have you making a spectacle of yourself, running wildly about town with a man like DeFazio—"

Victoria cried out indignantly. "Why, I do believe if it were up to you, I'd stay here in this house and—and mold!"

His smile was utterly maddening. "A vast improvement, I daresay."

Tears stung her eyes, tears she blinked back furiously. "I'm going home to Papa," she announced. She sought to step past him, only to find herself snared by the elbow and whirled around to face him.

She flung up her hands between them. "Let me go!"

He caught her up against him. His smile had vanished; his expression would surely have curdled cream. "You are not leaving this house, Victoria."

"Oh, yes, I am. I'm going home! Papa did not dictate to me like this."

"Well, perhaps he should have. Perhaps then we would not be in this wholly untenable predicament."

It was the wrong thing to say. Miles knew it the instant the words left his mouth, for Victoria's face whitened. For an instant, she looked as if she'd been struck. And then she did the one thing he never expected.

She burst into tears.

For the space of a heartbeat, Miles could only stare. He'd been prepared for a fiery rage. A spiteful defiance—anything but this.

She sobbed as if her heart were broken.

He wrapped one arm around her slowly. Her body was pliant and limp as he directed her to the small divan just to his left. He sat, cradling her against his side, her head nestled against his shoulder. He spoke not a word, but stroked the shining cap of her hair, holding her as he might have held Heather.

In time, the sobs eased to deep, jagged breaths. He stilled the movement of his hand, resting it between the narrow plane of her shoulder blades. "Now," he said quietly. "Would you like to tell me what distresses you so?"

Oddly, she made no move to distance her person from him. "It's . . . everything."

He studied her as she glanced up at him. It struck him how exquisite she was, even with her features ravaged by tears. "Everything?"

She expelled a sigh, her breath misting warmly across the line of his jaw. "I hate knowing how I displeased Papa. And I—I regret that I chose to involve you in my foolish scheme. But I did and—and now you're utterly miserable."

Miles wiped the pad of his thumb across her cheek, then held it up for her inspection. "I beg to differ with you, Victoria. I do believe you're far more miserable than I."

She smiled. Oh, a shaky smile, at best, but a smile nonetheless.

But all at once her breath caught audibly. She withdrew from his arms and sat up. She didn't meet his regard; it was as if she couldn't bear to look at him. "It's just that I . . . I feel like I don't belong here." A tear traced a lonely pathway down her cheek as at last she lifted her head. She spoke, her tone very low. "I-I know you hate me for ruining your life—"

"Stop right there. I don't hate you, Victoria."

Her eyes clung to his. "Truly?" she whispered.

"Truly."

And indeed, Miles had never been more certain of anything in his life. His eyes darkened, roving over her face. Her skin was flushed, her eyes still damp and bluer than ever, her lashes deeply spiked and glistening. God, she was sweet. Yet this was not a disobedient child he'd held in his arms. He could still feel the soft, womanly imprint of her curves against his. He wanted to kiss her again, he realized suddenly. But a kiss was what had got them into this mess . . .

And indeed, he wanted far more than just a kiss.

These last weeks had been hell; knowing she slept beneath his very roof sheer torment. He had only to walk into a room and the lingering scent of her perfume sent him into a tailspin. He lay awake long into the night, his manhood rock-hard and nearly bursting. His dreams were as wantonly erotic as a youth's; he indulged his every fantasy.

Ah, yes. In his dreams he knew her body as well as he knew his own. He felt her come alive beneath his hands; with lips and tongue he teased the tips of her breasts to quivering erectness. The soft down between her legs hid flesh that was damp and sweetly wet. And when at last he came inside her, she moaned into his mouth. God! but she was like warm silk around his turgid shaft.

But it wasn't only the pleasure of the flesh that Miles envisioned. He imagined what it would be like to hold her through the night while she slept, their passion in check. He longed to wake with her sleep-flushed and warm, her sweet curves tucked against his own.

But he'd not force himself on any woman, let alone his *wife*.

And so he held himself very still, uncertain of himself in a way he liked not at all. He watched as her fingers plucked at her skirts. "We haven't tried to make this situation more palatable, either of us," she said.

She was right, he realized. He was not an ogre, though he'd behaved like one thus far. A sliver of guilt stabbed at him, for he disliked knowing he was responsible for her unhappiness.

"It's true we don't know each other very well," he said slowly. "I admit, I've behaved rather abominably these past weeks."

"And I rather shrewishly."

"No." They looked at one another, for they spoke at the very same time.

Victoria had caught her lip between her teeth. All at once the tension was no longer quite so evident.

"Nor have we chosen to rectify the situation, either of us," Miles went on. "But . . . perhaps we should."

This was crazy. Dangerous. She was no different than Margaret, a voice in his head warned. They simply did not suit. And God knew, he wasn't the only one who would end up hurt. There was Heather to think of . . .

"I-I would like that, my lord."

"So would I," he heard himself say . . . and knew it for the truth. "Your social calendar, countess. I suspect it's quite full?" His tone was deliberately offhand, yet his heart was suddenly thudding.

"Indeed it is. For the next week, in fact." Her reply was rather breathless.

"Then I fear we have a slight problem, for I am at a distinct loss as to how I might persuade you into crying off for just one evening—to have supper with your husband." As he spoke, he reached for her hand where it lay atop her silk-covered thigh. He felt her start of surprise. Slowly, giving her time to withdraw if she wanted, he laced his fingers through hers.

But she didn't pull away, as he thought she might. Instead, she stared at their hands, at his fingers entwined with her own. Then she raised her head and smiled, a smile that held him spellbound.

"My lord," she said softly, "you have only to ask."

Chapter 5

Odd, that such a simple thing as supper with her husband could bring about such excitement.

By seven o'clock the next evening, Victoria was happier than she'd been in days—why, weeks! She labored over her toilette in a way that she hadn't even done for her come-out ball. Indeed, she could scarcely sit still as her maid dressed her hair, twisting it into a smooth gold coil atop her crown. Her gown was of pale blue silk, long and flowing; beneath the high-waisted, low-cut bodice it fell in dozens of tiny pleats.

At last she was ready. As she descended the stairs, Miles was just exiting the library. When he saw her, he stopped short at the foot of the stairs. Victoria held her breath, for his gaze was riveted upward. She was half-afraid to glance at his face yet neither could she stop herself.

But then she could have pinched herself in sheer delight, for though he spoke not a word, it appeared he very much approved of what he saw.

She was suddenly very glad she had taken such pains with her appearance.

When she reached the last step, silently he extended his arm. Lightly she placed her fingers on his sleeve.

In the dining room, Nelson had seated them opposite the other, at each end of the long table. Miles frowned and said something to the footman. Plate, silver, and glass were hurriedly swept up and placed directly to the left of his.

Victoria could never quite remember exactly what she ate. Dishes were set before her, then removed. It might have been straw, for all that she knew.

It was over dessert when she finally tipped her head to the side and regarded him.

"Why have you never wed?"

"My dear, correct me if I'm wrong, but I do believe I *am* wed."

She wrinkled her nose. "You know what I mean. Why did you never wed before now?"

A dark brow arose. "Why do you ask?"

"Well"—her tone was earnest—"you're a bit old to have never married."

She had shocked him. It was only then she realized she must have reached for her wine glass just a bit too often. Her fingers stole to her lips. "Oh, dear me, I can't believe I dared to say such a thing. I-I did not mean to be so rude, truly."

Miles shook his head. "It's quite all right." There was a brief pause. "It was several years ago, but I was, in fact, engaged to be married."

"Then why didn't you?" This, too, emerged before she thought better of it.

"It simply wasn't to be." Though his tone was light, his features had turned rather solemn. "And since that time, well, I never found a woman I wished to wed."

And he still hadn't, she acknowledged with a pang. He would never have married her if his hand had not been forced. The realization caused a sharp, knifelike twinge in her chest.

Why it should hurt so—why it even mattered— she didn't know.

But she didn't allow it to show when supper ended and they arose. She was surprised but pleased when he invited her to play chess, and then all was forgotten. Victoria had always prided herself on her skill at the game—Papa had taught her when she was barely out of short-coats. But like Papa, Miles was a clever opponent, and it took all her concentration to pose a substantial challenge.

Miles won, but Victoria didn't mind. This was the most enjoyable evening she'd passed in weeks.

A short time later, he escorted her upstairs to her room. At her door, they stopped. He stood close, so close were she to draw a deep breath her breasts would have brushed the lapels of his coat. There was an odd tightening in her chest. The evening had passed in such accord, she wondered almost frantically if tonight would be the night he would make her truly his wife. And if it were, how would she feel . . . ? She was afraid—oh, not of him, but of what he would do—to be sure. And yet, a shiver of excitement coursed along her veins.

"Victoria."

The sound of her name startled her. Eyes like silver dwelled on her upturned face. She glanced up, swallowing a gasp.

"Yes?" The word was but a breath. All the world seemed to totter on this one moment.

A half-smile curled his lips. "I merely wished you goodnight, countess. And—sleep well."

With that he was gone. Her hopes plunged. She gazed into the shadows after him, her spirits forlorn.

It seemed she had her answer after all.

A week passed in much the same fashion. Supper, then chess. Sometimes a glass of wine in the salon. Victoria gladly put aside other engagements to sup with her husband.

Just being near him made her stomach clench—

not that he was unsightly. Lord, no! The sweep of his neck was long and corded, his jaw taut and strong. His brow was broad and regal, his lips beautifully chiseled. No longer was his mouth so sternly set as it was during those first days of their marriage. He didn't smile often, but when he did . . .

But it wasn't enough to be with him. She wanted him to touch her. She ached for him to hold her as he had the night she'd cried, to feel his arms snug and tight about her once more.

She couldn't deny what her heart was telling her.

Something was happening. Something strange. Something wonderful.

Something . . . impossible.

Oh, there was no doubt that Miles's reserve had thawed. He was unfailingly polite, occasionally teasing, no longer coolly remote. With every day that passed, he treated her with an ever-increasing familiarity. But Victoria wanted more. She longed to be treated like a woman.

She longed to be treated like a wife . . . *his* wife.

It was a point that caused her no end of frustration. Other gentleman had been drawn to her. Other gentlemen had found her face and form attractive. Why not Miles? And perhaps most difficult of all, what was she to do?

Painful though it was, she couldn't forget what he'd said the night they wed.

A word of advice for you, countess. I shouldn't force my attentions on a gentleman—let alone kiss him . . . a man finds such boldness distasteful.

Perhaps it was time she did something she'd never dreamed she would do. Something she'd never thought she would *have* to do.

Seduce her husband.

She'd indulged in mild flirtations now and again.

But to go about seducing a gentleman was something she'd not dared to consider.

So how did one go about seducing one's husband?

Miles was different than the men she knew. It was apparent almost from the start that he was not a man to spend his evenings dining and gambling at the various gentleman's clubs. No, he was not a bold and strutting London peacock.

So, Victoria determined, she must be industrious in her efforts, without being obvious. Persistent, without throwing herself at his feet. Sophisticated, like a *femme du monde*, for perhaps that was the sort of woman he wanted.

With that in mind, she knocked lightly on the door to his study one afternoon. Without waiting for him to bid her enter, she strolled within, as if she'd done so a hundred times before. Miles sat behind a huge mahogany desk, his quill poised over the open pages of a thick ledger. His head came up at her entrance.

His eyes flickered. Clearly he was startled to see her.

"Victoria. What brings you here?"

She positioned herself directly before him. "I'm here to take you away from such drudgery as this." She nodded at his ledger. Her tone was airy and gay, or so she hoped. Inside she was a quivering mass of nerves.

Leather creaked as he leaned back in his chair. "Oh?"

"I thought we might take the curricle, you and I. I know a lovely spot just outside the city, and I thought we might have luncheon there."

"This afternoon?"

"Yes."

"Why?" There was no bite in his tone, just blunt curiosity.

Her face felt stiff from smiling. "Because it's a lovely day outside."

He hardly looked convinced.

"And because I-I'd like to share it with you." So much for sophistication, she thought dryly. But at least it was out, though all in a rush.

But she had captured his undivided attention. He looked at her then, and in a way that had never happened before. Something kindled in his eyes, something she dared not name for fear it was otherwise. She thought surely her heart would burst the bounds of her body when he put aside his quill, arose, and came to stand before her.

Time hung suspended, a never-ending moment. A lean, dark hand lifted toward her face. His lips parted, as if to speak.

But whatever he was about to say was not to be. The doors were swept wide and Nelson stepped in.

"Your lordship, we've just received a note from your tailor asking if he may stop by this afternoon, if at all possible."

"It will have to wait." Victoria's heart skipped a beat, for his gaze never wavered from hers. "I'm spending the afternoon with my wife."

Several hours later they lounged beneath the shade of a stout oak tree, replete from the meal Cook had packed. Victoria sat upon a soft down blanket, her skirts spread out around her.

There was a farmhouse nearby. A low stone fence traversed the fields. Errant shafts of sunlight winked through the branches, bathing them in warmth and sunshine. As she had just told Miles, this place was one she knew well. When Mama was still alive, she and Papa had brought her here often. Even when Mama was gone, she and Papa had continued to visit.

Miles lay stretched out beside her, leaning back

on an elbow. He'd removed his neckcloth and discarded his jacket. In polished boots, skin-tight
breeches and shirt, an aura of undeniable masculinity clung to him. Conversation was like the stream
that flowed nearby, lazy and idle and meandering.

"There's a place much like this near Lyndermere
Park," he murmured.

"Lyndermere Park?"

"My estate in Lancashire."

"Lancashire! What a long way from London. I
didn't know you had an estate there."

There was a brief pause. "Actually, I live there
most of the year. I usually stay in London only a
month or so while attending business matters."

"Well, I can certainly see why. London becomes
quite tiresome at times." She pulled a face. "Hot and
smelly in summer. So dreary and cold in winter."

Miles made no comment.

"So," she went on lightly, "if you were in Lyndermere Park this very moment, what might you be
doing?"

The makings of a smile tugged at his lips. "I might
well be mucking through a field in search of a lost
sheep."

Victoria chuckled. "You? I can't imagine you chasing after lost sheep."

"And I can't imagine you in anything but silk and
ribbons, the toast of the Season."

His voice was so quiet, almost somber, that she
glanced at him sharply.

"Miles?" She probed very gently. "What is it?"

His lips continued to carry the slightest trace of a
smile. "Nothing, Victoria. You needn't concern
yourself."

Something was wrong. She couldn't see it in his
features. But she could *feel* it.

Unthinkingly she placed her fingertips on his

sleeve. "Miles," she pleaded softly, "if something is troubling you, I wish you would tell me."

His gaze dropped to her hand, then returned to her face. "Do you, Victoria?" Slowly he sat up. His tone was almost whimsical. "And what would you say if I told you I lusted after my wife—now. This very moment."

A smile grazed her lips. "I would say . . . you need lust no more."

In one swift move she was caught up hard against him. For the space of a heartbeat, his eyes blazed down on her. "Do you have any idea what you're saying? Do you?"

Her fingertips splayed wide across his chest. Beneath she could feel the strength of muscle and bone. "Yes," she whispered recklessly. Dangerously. Uncaring that all she felt lay vivid in her eyes. "*Yes.*"

That one word was like a trigger being pulled. His arms locked tight around her back. Then his mouth came down on hers, and it was just as she'd imagined it. His kiss was fierce, yet wondrously so. She could taste passion, heady and sweet, and a driving need that matched her own.

Her heart rejoiced, for nothing had ever felt so right—nothing.

Blindly she clung to him, caught in the tempest of emotions gone wild and rampant. She felt herself seized by a strange, inner trembling. Her breasts seemed to ache, for what she didn't know. Lean male fingers traced the deep rounded neckline of her bodice. Victoria's heart slammed to a halt, but she didn't pull away.

The pad of his thumb just barely grazed the peak of her breast.

Fire seemed to blaze from the place he touched so fleetingly, but now she knew what she so longed for. Time stood still while those devil fingers circled and teased first one nipple, then the other, until those soft pink crests stood thrusting and erect. Her breath was but a ragged tremor. *Miles*, she thought yearningly. *Oh, Miles . . .*

But there was more. No protest found voice as he tugged loose the drawstring of her bodice. The neckline of her gown was swept from her shoulders, exposing the rounded softness of her breasts. He stared down at her, at pink swelling flesh that no man had ever seen before.

Victoria's eyes locked helplessly on his face. She prayed that she would find favor in the eyes of her husband. But all at once his features might have been carved in stone.

"No," he muttered, as if to himself. And then again, with a fierce bite in his tone: "This isn't right. Dammit, this isn't right." He nearly flung himself from her.

She felt his withdrawal like a blow. Stunned and confused, Victoria sat up slowly. "Of course it is," she said faintly. "We—we're married!"

His jaw clenched hard. His gaze veered away from her. "It's time we left," he said curtly. His profile was stark and unyielding.

Her fingers were shaking as she tried to retie the strings of her bodice. He didn't want her, she thought numbly. She'd made a fool of herself for nothing. She had *thrown* herself at him for nothing.

At last she was ready. Through eyes that were painfully dry, she stared at him. At a loss for words, for understanding, she struggled for both. "Miles," she said, very low. "Miles, please tell me—"

"We're leaving, Victoria. *We're leaving.*"

His voice sliced through her as cleanly as a knife. Despair clamped tight around her breast, raw and bleeding. Choking back tears, Victoria picked up her skirts and ran toward the curricle, her heart in shreds.

Not one word passed between them the entire way home.

Once there, Victoria fled to her room. Only then did the tears come, slow and scalding.

Chapter 6

At first Victoria was devastated . . . little wonder that she avoided Miles over the next few days—or did he avoid her? It was only later, when she could react to the incident with her mind and not her heart, that she realized . . .

His kiss had not lied. He had felt something for her. She hadn't imagined the fire in his kiss, the longing in his arms.

Something was holding him back. That was the only answer. Yet what could it be? *What*? Another woman? She didn't believe it. She *couldn't*.

Her husband was a quiet, private man, a man who would not reveal his every side for all to see; she had concluded that Miles was not one to trust lightly. Yet neither would she have deemed him a man of secrets. So why was it only now that he had spoken of his home in Lancashire?

It was odd . . . or was it? Perhaps it was only that the days had swept aside the boundaries between them.

Only now the barriers were back, as staunchly formidable as ever.

Still, she was determined not to sit home and wilt away. When an invitation to a ball given by Lord and Lady Devon arrived one morning, she decided she would attend the event, to be held the next week.

Supper that night was a dismal affair. Yet Victoria took quiet note of Miles's attention upon her, his regard unsmiling—and enigmatic. Yet once—once—she caught the flare of some unknown emotion on his face . . . He stared at her with eyes that seemed to burn her very soul.

Hope burgeoned within her. As a footman removed the roast hare she'd hardly touched, she managed a bright smile.

"We received an invitation today from Lord and Lady Devon. They are giving a ball the Thursday after next. I should very much like to attend."

His reply was brief and to the point. "Then do so."

A pang swept through her. Gone was the man who had held her fast against him, whose mouth had covered hers with a passion unbridled and uncontrolled, a hunger fierce and unchecked. Everything within her cried out the injustice—she hated the cold, indifferent stranger he had become.

Her smile slipped. Icy-cold fingers linked together in her lap, for she was not prepared to let the matter rest so easily. "Miles," she said softly. "Will you attend with me?"

"I think not, Victoria. You are fond of such affairs. I am not."

They spent the rest of the meal in strained silence. Victoria pleaded tiredness soon thereafter. She excused herself and fled to the sanctuary of her bedchamber, blinking back tears.

She did not sleep. In anguished turmoil, she paced the length of her room, back and forth. But one thing was clear . . . This could not go on. *They* could not go on like this.

It seemed she had but one choice.

Miles had come upstairs some time ago; she could still hear him stirring in the room next to hers. Quickly, before she lost her nerve, she tapped on his door.

He opened it. A winged black brow arched. "What is it, Victoria?" His tone was gruff, his manner impatient.

Her eyes were riveted to his face. His expression was remote and scarcely encouraging.

"May I come in?" she ventured.

He wanted to refuse. She could see it in the flicker of his eyes, yet he opened the door so she could step within. She advanced several paces, then turned to face him, thankful he couldn't see her knees trembling.

"I don't mean to intrude," she said quickly, "but I thought we might . . . talk."

"Oh? And what is on your mind, Victoria?"

Her eye ran over him nervously. She was still fully dressed, while Miles wore only a maroon velvet dressing gown. Loosely belted at the waist, there was a generous slice of bare chest exposed. Her stomach fluttered, for she had the oddest sensation he wore not a single stitch beneath. Her mind balked. Did he *sleep* naked? Victoria couldn't help it; her imagination ran away with her. His body would be like his chest, all long, hair-roughened limbs. And all she could think was that he would be as breathtaking *without* benefit of clothes as he was in his most elegant attire . . .

She gestured vaguely. "I know our marriage did not start off well," she said, her voice very low. "But I'd begun to think it was not such a mistake after all—and not so very long ago." She paused, but Miles said nothing. He merely remained where he was, his hands at his side, his expression impassive.

Victoria swallowed, forcing herself to go on. Faith,

but this was the hardest thing she'd ever done! "Indeed, Miles, I-I thought things were progressing quite well. I-I thought everything had changed between us. That day in the country, when you—you kissed me. Or"—her voice fell, no more than a wisp breath of sound—"have you forgotten?"

His tone was harsh. "It *should* be forgotten."

In but an instant her wistful longing was shattered. Her control grew perilous. It was all she could do not to run crying from the room. "Why should it be forgotten? You—you act as if you are ashamed of what happened."

The cast of his jaw was rigid. "It shouldn't have happened, Victoria. Need I say more?"

Pain was like molten fire in her lungs. "Yes," she said raggedly. Recklessly. "Yes! Why is it wrong to—to desire me? To kiss me? To hold me? Miles, I-I don't understand."

Her voice caught as she struggled for words, for composure. Then suddenly it was all coming out in a rush. "I-I wanted you to kiss me, Miles. I wanted you to touch me and—and never stop. I wanted to be your wife in . . . in every way. Oh, Miles, I-I thought you wanted me, too!"

His features were cast in stone. "I think you forget, Victoria. If I had not stopped, there could be no annulment. Did you consider that?"

Victoria stared at him unblinkingly. Her lips were trembling so that she could hardly speak. "Is that it?" she whispered. "You still wish an annulment?"

Miles said nothing. He merely stood there, his posture wooden, his eyes downcast.

She persisted. "Do you want an annulment, Miles? Do you?"

Time slipped by. And in that deepening silence, she could almost hear her heart breaking . . .

Her throat clogged painfully. "You do. You do,

but you don't have the courage to tell me to my face. Look at me, damn you." Her chin climbed high. Tears shimmered in her eyes, tears that betrayed the cost of her jagged cry. "Look at me and *tell* me!"

He looked at her. For one heart-stopping, frozen moment, their eyes collided . . . and what she saw there—what she *didn't* see there—shredded the last of her control.

He didn't need to tell her. It was over, she thought brokenly. She meant nothing to him. She never had . . .

She never would.

She rushed forward with a low, choked sob. Escape was her only thought. But in her headlong flight, her fingers were clumsy. She twisted the doorknob frantically, but it refused to open . . .

Then suddenly *he* was there, a looming presence at her side, a hand on her arm.

"Victoria—"

"Don't!" she cried. She tore herself away and whirled on him. Suddenly her eyes were blazing. "Just leave me be," she whispered fiercely. "Do you hear, Miles Grayson? Just leave me be!"

The latch finally lifted. The door opened. Victoria fled blindly down the hall to her chamber. She flung herself on the bed, her heart bleeding.

In the morning her pillow was still wet with tears.

But she was dry-eyed and determined. She was a woman scorned, a woman who would not offer herself again. No, she would not beg or plead . . .

She, too, had her pride.

Nor would she wile away in misery.

She saw little of her husband, and soon the day of Lord and Lady Devon's ball arrived. In an attempt to boost her spirits, she had indulged herself with a new ball gown. Though she was not given to pettiness, it had proved immensely satisfying when she'd informed the seamstress the bill was to be sent to her husband.

She was waiting in the entrance hall for the carriage to be brought around when Miles suddenly appeared.

Eyes the color of storm clouds flickered over her. Only moments earlier her maid had commented that she'd never seen her mistress appear more entrancing. The gown was of white satin shot through with shimmering silver threads that brought out the highlights in her hair. The style was off-the-shoulder and daringly low cut; it emphasized the pale fragility of her neck and shoulders.

Her heart quavered, for despite the odds, she had prayed nightly that he would tear down the barriers he'd erected between them; that he would choose to alter their stalemate.

But all he said was, "Going out for the evening, countess?"

Summoning an icy strength, Victoria met his regard head-on. "Yes. If you recall, we were invited to Lord and Lady Devon's ball. You told me you didn't wish to attend."

Miles made no reply, but he did not appear pleased.

She took a deep breath and prayed she wasn't about to make a horrendous mistake. "Do you disapprove of me going alone, Miles?"

"It's hardly the first time you've done so. Why should I disapprove?"

But his expression revealed otherwise.

Some devil seized hold of her. "Oh, and by the way"—she smiled sweetly—"please inform the staff there's no need to wait up for me. I shall undoubtedly be quite late."

She experienced a certain grim pleasure at seeing

the lightning change in his expression. She could almost hear the crack of thunder in the air. Relishing her brief moment of triumph, she picked up her skirts and swept outside to where the carriage now awaited her.

"Damn!" With an exclamation of disgust, Miles pushed himself away from his desk. He'd just spent the last few hours tending to his correspondence—or trying to. His efforts had proved quite futile.

He strode to the side table where he poured himself a generous glass of port. He grimaced as the brew slid down his throat.

No doubt Victoria was having the time of her life. He had no trouble picturing the scene that was surely even now taking place at Lord and Lady Devon's ball. No doubt she was surrounded by half a dozen young pups, eagerly fawning over her. Or perhaps she was with that cad, Count DeFazio!

The thought that DeFazio might be helping himself to his wife made him clench his teeth. Not that Miles could blame the oily-tongued Italian rake. When Victoria had come down the stairs tonight, he'd felt as if he'd been punched in the gut. Her gown set off to perfect advantage the gleaming slope of bare, slender shoulders. She'd looked particularly delectable, and he'd felt a stab of pure possessiveness—along with no little amount of male pride—that this woman was his.

That's right, you pompous ass, sneered a voice in his head. *She's yours. So why aren't you with her?*

His lips twisted. "Why indeed?" he said aloud.

He had no one else to blame but himself. He could be with her now, this very moment. He *should* be with her. Moreover, he *wanted* to be with her.

But it wasn't so easy, he argued silently, for he was still struggling with his dilemma.

Do you want an annulment, Miles? Do you?

His insides twisted in dread remembrance. Dear God, he couldn't say yes. He couldn't say the words. Yet how could he say no . . .

I-I wanted you to kiss me, Miles. I wanted you to touch me and—and never stop. I wanted to be your wife in . . . in every way. Oh, Miles, I-I thought you wanted me, too!

The memory of that night still haunted him. He could still hear her, her voice raw. And he could still see Victoria, her face so pale, fighting back the tears she thought he didn't see.

His heart squeezed. He'd never meant to hurt her. God, if only he could, he'd make it up to her . . .

You were so convinced she was shallow and vain, jabbed a voice in his brain. *But you were wrong. You know it and still you refuse to see it!*

Long fingers tensed around the glass. He *was* a fool, he admitted at long last, for these last few weeks had been a revelation. Victoria was strong-willed and spirited, even a bit headstrong, but not wild. A bit reckless perhaps, but most assuredly not rebellious. The admission provoked a slight upward curl of his lips. She had a bit of a temper, but no less than his own.

His smile withered. She wasn't like Margaret. She wasn't!

But experience had left him wary, and it was that which held him back. There was so much at stake— too much to allow for another mistake.

A pang of guilt shot through him as he thought of Heather. He'd been gone from Lyndermere Park too long already. It was time he returned home to Lancashire. To Heather. Oh, he'd sent letters and gifts he knew would entertain and cheer her, but he knew how terribly she missed him when he was away . . .

Which only brought him full circle. What was he to do with Victoria?

Take her with him to Lyndermere? Or leave her here in London? Everything within him rebelled at leaving her behind. But it wasn't just her reaction to country life that he feared. What about Heather? What would Victoria think of Heather? That was his foremost concern—he could not allow Heather to be hurt as Margaret had hurt her.

He should have told her, he thought heavily. Perhaps he should have told her long ago and let fate take its course.

His gaze sought the clock on the wall. Just after eleven. The ball was in full swing. Victoria wouldn't be home for hours . . . What was it she'd said?

Please inform the staff there's no need to wait up for me. I shall undoubtedly be quite late.

Lord, but she'd been so cold . . . but no colder than he had been to her.

It was then that an awful thought crowded his mind—and his heart.

Had he lost her? Had he? *You fool,* the voice inside him chided. *You've no doubt driven her straight into the arms of that scoundrel DeFazio. And you have no one to blame but yourself*

No. *No.* He couldn't lose her. He *wouldn't.*

His glass slammed down on his desk. He strode to the corridor and threw open the door. "Nelson!"

The servant hurried out from the kitchen. "Yes, my lord?"

"Please see that my evening jacket is laid out. I shall be joining the countess at Lord and Lady Devon's ball."

"Very good, my lord." Nelson smothered a smile and trotted away. There was a considerable amount of wagering going on belowstairs regarding the outcome of lord and lady's current state of affairs. He had the sudden feeling a rather tidy sum would soon line his pockets . . .

Victoria didn't care if she had provoked Miles—all the better if she had! Yet several hours later, her defiance had given way to something else entirely. Oh, she danced and laughed, chatted and smiled. But all in all, it was the most tiresome affair of her life. As she confided to Sophie, were it not for her friend's company, she'd have quit the affair long since and gone home. Indeed, as she stood on the edge of the ballroom with Sophie, she was just about to voice that very intention.

There was a tap on her shoulder. It was Count Antony DeFazio.

"Dance with me," was all he said. His arm snug about her waist, he whisked her onto the dance floor.

Dark eyes roamed her face. "I've missed you, *cara*."

"Have you?" Her tone was polite but detached. Manners alone dictated a reply.

"Oh, yes, *cara*. Never have I been so lonely!" he proclaimed grandly. "Did you not hear my heart call out to you?"

Lonely? How Victoria stopped herself from rolling her eyes, she never knew. Why, he must believe her a dimwit to fall for such drivel!

"But enough of me. Where have you been these past days?"

"Actually"—she spoke very demurely—"I've spent many a delightful evening at home with my husband."

He laughed. "Oh, but I can make you happy as he cannot." The arm about her waist tightened. His voice deepened to intimacy. "I can make you forget any man but me. Shall I show you, *cara*?"

Victoria was speechless. How had she ever thought this man charming? Apparently he was convinced she was joking, the cad! Such ego deserved a dressing-down.

"Rubbish," she said forcefully.

He blinked. "I beg your pardon?"

"Rubbish," she stated baldly. "You see, Count, there is only one man who can make me happy. Of a certainty that man is not you."

Her partner was left standing in the middle of the ballroom. He gaped at her, stunned and open-mouthed.

Amidst gasps and whispers, Victoria strolled across the floor. Oh, she was fully aware her conduct was scarcely commendable. No doubt her name would be on every tongue the rest of the night and well into the next day. Still, it was worth it, she decided rebelliously, and she didn't regret that she'd given Antony the dressing-down he deserved. Perhaps he wouldn't be so arrogant in future.

The thought kindled a smile, a smile she maintained as she breezed her way across the ballroom, intent on fetching a breath of air in the garden.

There was a touch on her elbow. Thinking it was Antony, she spun around, prepared to loose on him the full force of her disdain.

"I thought I made myself quite cl—" she began.

The rest died unuttered in her throat. Because it wasn't Antony at all . . .

It was Miles.

In an instant she was whirled back onto the dance floor. "You mustn't look so shocked, countess." Miles's eyes were somber, but his voice held a trace of mirth. "Lord knows you've just given the gossip-mongers a juicy little tidbit. I should hate to give them another."

"My very thought, my lord," Victoria echoed

faintly. Her heart pounded a bone-jarring rhythm. Her mind was all agog. What on earth was he doing here?

Miles glanced toward Count DeFazio, who glared at the pair, then pointedly turned his back. "Your tongue is rapier-sharp tonight, I take it. I pray you'll not turn it against me tonight."

He bent his head low. Warm breath rushed across her skin . . .

He kissed the side of her neck.

Victoria's pulse was clamoring, her emotions a mad jumble. "To-tonight?" she stammered.

"Yes, sweet," he said softly. "Tonight."

And then he said the words she'd never thought to hear. "You were right, Victoria. I *was* jealous, jealous of every moment you spent with DeFazio. But I have the feeling you made another assumption— only a quite erroneous assumption, I fear." His gaze pierced hers. "I don't want an annulment, Victoria. Not now. Not ever."

Her heart stopped—along with her feet. Was she in heaven? Surely it was so, for this couldn't be happening . . .

He kissed the tiny hollow before her ear. "Did you hear me, sweet?"

Her eyes clung to his. His regard was so tender, his words so sweet. She nodded, for she could do no more.

"Good," he said gently. "Now dance again, love."

Hope flowered in her breast, hope that warmed her like the heat of summer sunshine.

"Are you . . . certain?" She ventured the question cautiously, then held her breath.

"Very." Quiet as his tone was, beneath was a gravity that left no doubt he meant what he said.

Yet even while hope burgeoned still further, a pang rent her breast. Never had she been so afraid!

Her eyes slid away. "Why," she said, her voice very low. "Why not?"

"The reason is simple, Victoria. I am your husband."

"A reluctant husband," she said unsteadily. "And as I recall, you made your feelings for me quite clear. You—you found me distasteful." She fought to keep the hurt from her voice and wasn't entirely successful.

The arm about her back tightened. His gaze was unerringly direct. "No, Victoria. Never distasteful. Never that."

But Victoria could not forget so easily. A rending ache seared her breast. "What then if not distasteful? You wanted nothing to do with me," she said haltingly. "You said it . . . it wasn't right."

"And what if I was wrong? What if I was a fool? What if I told you that I wanted you then? That I want you now. That I will *always* want you."

The music and voices around them faded into oblivion. There was a note in his voice she'd never before heard; it might have been just the two of them. She was half-afraid to speak, lest it be a dream.

"Then you must show me," she whispered.

And God above, he did.

She scarcely noticed they had glided to a halt. She had one paralyzing glimpse of glowing silver eyes before his dark head descended.

He kissed her then, there before all the *ton* to see. Slowly. Leisurely tasting, as if they had all the time in the world. Victoria couldn't have moved if she'd wanted to. It was as if he had some strange power over her. The pressure of his mouth on hers was magic. Bliss beyond reason.

By the time it was over her head was spinning. Her hands had come up to clutch at the powerful lines of his shoulders. As he raised his head—reluctantly, it seemed to her—she realized the room had gone utterly quiet.

And every eye in the ballroom was turned to the two of them.

She didn't know whether to laugh or cry. "Oh, dear," she murmured, catching her lip between her teeth. "I do believe we've caused yet another scandal."

Miles hiked a brow in sardonic amusement. "Scandal be damned," he said baldly, "for I should very much like to escape this crowd and take my wife home—if that meets with her approval, of course."

Victoria wanted to weep with relief and happiness. She raised shining eyes to his. "It does indeed, my lord. It does indeed."

He pressed her hand into the crook of his elbow. "Then let us be off, countess."

Together they strolled from the dance floor. But it seemed Miles was not yet ready to leave, for he snared two glasses of champagne from a passing footman.

Heedless of the gazes which had yet to leave their figures, he touched the edge of his glass to hers.

"To my beautiful wife," he stated for all to hear, "and to a long and happy marriage."

His head came down. He rested his forehead against hers. As his gaze captured hers, heat shimmered between them, as hot and blazing as a fire. Only now his words were a velvet whisper, for her ears alone . . .

"And to the night ahead . . ."

Chapter 7

Miles's bedroom door clicked quietly shut. Victoria had stopped in the middle of the room. She was quick to flash a beaming smile at him, but he knew she was nervous. Nor had he missed the way her eyes flitted to and from the four-poster on the opposite wall. His own dropped to where the creamy skin of her breasts swelled above the lace of her bodice. Blood rushed to his head and loins, firing his desire into a raging need, swelling his manhood to an almost painful fullness.

He tightened his shoulders, fighting to hold himself in check. Slowly he expelled a long, pent-up breath. He could wait, he cautioned himself. He *must* wait, for he knew full well Victoria was a virgin, well born and gently bred. He didn't want to shock her, nor did he want to frighten her.

He extended his hand. "Come here," he said softly.

There was a rustle of skirts as she breached the distance between them. Shyly she placed her hand within his. Her fingers were ice-cold.

Raising his free hand, he curled his knuckles beneath her chin and tipped her face to his. His tone was very quiet. "You know where this will end, don't you? There will be no annulment after this night."

Her eyes clung to his. "I-I know."

"And this is what you want?" He searched her face intently.

She didn't retreat from either his gaze or his question. "Yes," she said breathlessly. "Yet still I wonder, my lord, if you are certain that is what *you* want."

In bringing her here, Miles realized he had made not one, but two choices. The first was to make her truly his wife. He wanted that, he realized. He wanted it so much he could taste it. As for the other . . .

He could no longer hide the truth from her. But there was time enough to tell her about Heather. For now, Miles wanted the moment to stay just the way it was—the two of them alone, secluded from the world, with no one to think of but each other.

"Do not doubt me, Victoria. My choice was made when I came after you tonight." He spoke very quietly. "I have no regrets and it's my hope you will have none either."

The wispiest of smiles touched her lips. "I've known for quite some time what I want, my lord. I am here . . . and I am yours."

Miles needed no further encouragement. He caught her up in his arms and carried her to the side of the bed. Lowering her to the floor, he let her body slide against the hardness of his, then turned her mouth up to his. He fed on it endlessly, like a feast before a starving man. His fingers slid into her hair. It tumbled about his hands, thick and heavy and silken.

It was he who dragged his mouth away. Holding her gaze, he shrugged off his jacket, waistcoat, and shirt.

He saw the way her eyes widened at the sight of his naked chest. Two spots of color bloomed on her cheeks. He sensed her uncertainty, but her fingers fluttered to the neckline of her bodice.

His hand engulfed hers. At her questioning glance, he shook his head. "No," he said. "Let me."

He undressed her down to her shift, so sheer the outline of her body was clearly visible beneath. He pulled her close, suppressing a groan, letting her grow used to the feel of him. His mouth sought hers, at first slow and exploring, then with mounting urgency.

But suddenly she drew back, burying her face against his shoulder.

He smoothed the tumbled gold of her hair. "What, Victoria? What is it?"

The breath she drew was deep and uneven. "Oh, I know 'tis silly, but . . . we have been a long time coming to this moment. What if I should do something foolish? What if I should do something wrong?"

He caught her hand and brought it to his lips. "You need not worry, Victoria. You are perfect. In every way. In all ways." There was a small pause. "And now, countess"—it was his turn to tease as he tugged slender arms up and around his neck—"I would very much like for you to kiss me."

Her head came up, only now there was a faintly teasing light in her beautiful blue eyes. "What is this, my lord? Why, I do believe you told me once I should not force my attentions on a gentleman—let alone kiss him!—for a man finds such boldness distasteful." It was her turn to arch a slender brow. "Your exact words, if I recall."

He smiled, his expression tender. "I think I will go quite mad if you do *not* kiss me. Besides, I am not just a gentleman. I am your husband." His smile faded. "And your husband would very much like to make love to his wife."

Tears sprang to her eyes, yet she was smiling, a smile he knew he would carry in his heart forever. Her arms tightened around him. The dewy softness of her mouth hovered just beneath his, a provocative invitation. "And your wife wishes you would wait no longer, my lord."

And indeed, Victoria knew beyond any doubt that this was all she wanted—*he* was all she wanted. With infinite gentleness, he kissed her, then lifted her in his arms and laid her on the bed. When he stretched out beside her, she pressed herself against his length, eager for all he would teach her.

Her shift was soon but a flimsy pile on the carpet. With her palms she skimmed the sleek outline of his shoulders. She could feel the knotted tension in his muscles, yet he did not hurry her. The touch of his hands on her breasts was a divine torment. With his thumbs he teased the sensitive peaks until they throbbed and stood up hard and erect. His head lowered. His tongue touched her nipple, leaving it shiny and wet and aching. She gasped as he took one deep coral circle into his mouth, sucking and circling, sweeping across that turgid peak with the wild lash of his tongue.

His hand drifted lower, down across the hollow of her belly, sliding through dark gold curls. Victoria's heart began to hammer, for there was a strange questing there in the secret cleft between her thighs. Surely he would not touch her there, she thought in half-panic, half-excitement. Surely she did not *want* him to, for such a thing was scandalous . . .

It was heaven. A jolt of sheer pleasure shot through her. The gliding stroke of his fingertips was boldly undaunting, skimming damp folds, dipping and swirling against the pearly button of sensation centered within.

Her eyes widened. Her nails dug into his shoulders. "Oh, dear," she whispered faintly. "Miles, I do not think—"

"It's all right, sweet." He stared down at her, his features were strained, his voice thick. "All I want is to please you." Sweat beaded his upper lip. His blood pounded almost violently. As she gave a muted little whimper, his shaft swelled still further, straining his breeches until he felt he would surely burst the bonds of his skin.

Her lashes fluttered closed. One long, strong finger slipped clear inside her, a blatantly erotic caress. Blistering flames leaped deep in her belly, for his thumb now worshiped that sensitive kernel of flesh. Her hips began to move. Seeking. Searching for something maddeningly elusive. And then it happened. Her body seemed to tighten, then explode in a blinding flash of ecstasy.

Her eyes opened, smoky and dazed. Miles had pulled away, but it was only to strip away his breeches. Lamplight flickered over his body, turning his skin to burnished gold. He looked like a god, she thought wonderingly, strong and proud and irresistibly masculine.

Tentatively, she touched the hair-matted plane of his chest. He sucked in a harsh breath. Emboldened, she dared to explore still further, brushing the grid of his abdomen with the backs of her knuckles. His eyes half-closed.

"Touch me, Victoria." His voice was taut. With his own hand, he dragged hers where he wanted it most.

Her cool fingers curled about his shaft. He was enormous, hot and thick. A fingertip traced the velvet-tipped crown. Even as she marveled that something so steely hard could be so soft, she swallowed, for she could not imagine how she could accommodate something so immense . . .

His breath rushed out. "God, Victoria. Oh, God..."

Then he was there between her thighs, kneeling between them. He levered himself over her, his features heated and searing. His belly was hard as stone against her—as was his manhood. One swift, stretching stroke of fire and virginity was no more; his shaft pierced hard and deep inside her, to the very gates of her womb.

A ragged sound broke from her lips. Above her, Miles went utterly still. Victoria blinked, for he lay buried to the hilt within her. Her velvet heat clamped tight around his swollen member, the pressure of his shaft stunningly thorough.

"Oh, my," she said shakily.

He braced himself above her. His lips grazed hers. His voice was but a breath of air. "Do I hurt you, love?"

She was stunned to find her body had yielded. Already the stinging pain was but a memory. She shook her head, wordlessly offering her lips... her body...

Her very soul.

He kissed her then, a lingering, binding caress. His shaft withdrew, only to return with a deft, sure plunge that stole her very breath. Pleasure, dark and heady, swirled all around her. The flame was back in her belly, burning higher and higher as their hips met again and again. His hands slid beneath her buttocks. Guiding even as she blindly sought... Lifting as she arched to meet each downward plunge...

The rhythm of their love dance was hot and driving, frenzied and urgent. She felt herself swept high and away, deep into a white-hot vortex of sheer rapture. She was only half-aware of crying out. Above her, Miles gave one final, piercing lunge. She could only cling to him while his climax erupted inside her, a fiery rush of molten heat.

The tension eased gradually from his body. His lips nuzzled the baby-soft skin behind her ear. "Sweet," he whispered. "So sweet."

Without warning she began to cry.

Warm fingers brushed the dampness from her cheeks, a touch of infinite tenderness. "Victoria. Victoria, love, what is this?" He froze, propping himself on an elbow and staring down at her. "Never say I hurt you!"

"It isn't that." She buried her face against his chest. "It's just that—I thought you did not want me," she sobbed. "I thought you didn't want me— I thought you would never want me!"

In some strange way, she knew he understood. A possessive arm locked around her, drawing her close and tight against him. A hand beneath her chin, he brought her gaze to his. "Never doubt that I *do* want you, sweet. Never doubt *me*."

And in that moment, she didn't.

Chapter 8

A soft rapping on the door woke the pair the next morning. Miles rose and reached for his breeches, then walked barefoot to the door. From the depths of the bed, Victoria stirred, vaguely aware of a low-voiced exchange.

The door shut. As he retraced his steps, she peered at him sleepily. "Miles? Who was it?" Her voice was still blurred from sleep. "Is something wrong?"

His features grave, he sat on the edge of the mattress. With his fingers he smoothed the tumbled hair from her shoulders, leaning forward to kiss her before he spoke. "I'm afraid so, sweet. I've an estate and holdings in Cornwall, and it seems a vicious storm has just swept through the area. It destroyed a number of tenants' homes and also damaged the manor house."

Victoria sat up, tucking the counterpane over her bare breasts. Despite the night just past, she was still a bit shy about Miles seeing her naked. Gently she touched his forearm. "Oh, no. I do hope no one was hurt."

"Luckily, there were no serious injuries." His gaze snared hers. "But I'm afraid I must be off as soon as I can to assess the damage."

She spoke quickly. "Would you like me to go with you?"

He considered but a moment. "I think not. It's a long, arduous journey in the best of times, and frankly, I'm not sure what I'll encounter when I arrive. If the manor house is damaged extensively, it might well be a hardship for you." He paused. "Will you wait for me here?"

"Of course," she said promptly.

His lips quirked. He patted a rumpled portion of the coverlet. "I mean here, love"—his gaze warmed—"in this very spot." The pitch of his voice grew seductive. "Preferably, dressed as you are, though perhaps I should say *un*dressed as you are."

Victoria blushed furiously. Miles chuckled, then rose to hurriedly bathe and pack. She remained where she was, content to watch him lazily.

At last he was ready. He looked dashing and handsome, and as he returned to the bedside, a tiny little thrill went through her. She slipped her arms around his neck. "Hurry back," she whispered.

He rested his forehead against hers. "Oh, I will, sweet," he murmured huskily. "Of that you may rest assured."

The kiss they shared was long and passionate.

Victoria spent the next few days quietly. Though she longed for Miles's return, her heart was filled with burgeoning hope. Their marriage was not the disaster she had feared. Miles had made her feel cherished and special in a way she'd never dreamed possible. Indeed, she was suddenly quite certain marriage could be all her heart had ever wanted . . .

Late one afternoon she returned from tea with Sophie. Nelson greeted her at the front door. "My lady, while you were out, a messenger arrived from Lyndermere Park."

Victoria frowned. Lyndermere was Miles's estate in Lancashire. "A messenger?"

"I didn't have the opportunity to speak with him

myself, my lady. But he brought with him this note for his lordship." Nelson picked up a small missive from a silver tray, extending it toward her. Victoria hesitated before picking it up.

"The maid who took it said the messenger was directed to deliver it in all due haste, my lady. Unfortunately, she neglected to tell him his lordship was in Cornwall at the moment." Nelson cleared his throat. "That's why I thought it best to direct it to your attention, my lady. If it should be a matter of importance . . ."

"Yes. Yes, of course. And thank you, Nelson." Victoria dismissed him with a smile.

Upstairs in her room, she laid the letter on the bureau, then stripped off her gloves and untied her bonnet. Laying the bonnet aside, she bit her lip.

Her gaze was drawn to the letter.

Should she open it? Despite Nelson's concern, she was reluctant to do so. She couldn't help but feel she would be trespassing where she should not. Yet that was silly, wasn't it? After all, she was Miles's countess. And if the contents should indeed be urgent . . .

With a sigh she went to retrieve it. Uncomfortable as she was, she decided it was best to open it after all. Before she could change her mind, she broke the seal.

The letter was short. It contained but a few sentences. Quickly she scanned it.

You've been gone a very long time. I miss you dreadfully. Please, please come home . . .

Love,
Heather

A faint, choked sound escaped her throat.

It was written in a precise, flowing . . . and unmistakably feminine hand.

Love, Heather.

There was a crushing pain in her chest.

Love, Heather.

How could he do this? she screamed silently. The memory of their night together rose swift and high in her mind. He had been so sweet. So tender. God! she thought brokenly. She had been almost certain that he cared—and cared deeply—for her. That perhaps he'd even begun to love her . . .

What was it he'd said? *Never doubt that I do want you, sweet. Never doubt me*.

It was all a lie. A *lie*.

Only one thing could have made it worse—oh, how great her humiliation would have been if she'd told him she loved him.

Because she did.

She just hadn't known how much . . . until now.

But his betrayal was too much for her wounded heart to bear. So Victoria did the only thing she could think to do. She ordered her bags packed and went home to Papa.

The marquess of Norcastle was quite astonished when his daughter appeared in the entrance hall, bags and baggage in tow.

"Victoria! Good heavens, girl, what is this?"

Victoria took one look at Papa and burst into tears.

Enfolded snugly in his ample arms, Victoria cried her heart out against his shoulder. Little by little, the story came out. How, against all odds—against all reason!—she had fallen in love with her husband. How she had only just discovered there was another woman in his life . . .

Her lips were tremulous. " 'Twould have been silly for me to expect to be the first, nor did I expect it. But he gave me every reason to believe that"— her voice caught—"that he truly cared. Papa, I believed him! And now I feel so—so foolish!"

The marquess sighed and touched her hair. "Victoria," he said slowly, "I have always taught you to judge fairly and without bias, have I not?"

Victoria nodded, her face still ravaged by tears.

"Then I ask you now to be fair, child. Give him the chance to explain."

Slowly she drew back. "Papa, no! You—you would defend him? Against your own daughter?"

He gestured vaguely. "No, of course not. But remember the night you were wed? I told you that he was not so cold as you believed. I was right, wasn't I?"

He detected a faint layer of bitterness in her tone. "Only yesterday I would have agreed wholeheartedly, Papa. Now I am not so sure. Indeed, I think he is cruel beyond words! He held me in his arms, knowing all the while that this woman named Heather awaited him in Lancashire! Perhaps she is his mistress. Or perhaps she is the one he meant to marry, for it was his intention that in time our marriage should be dissolved. He was only biding his time and awaiting the right moment." Her eyes blazed as she announced, "Either way I-I do not care. I shall consider myself well rid of him!"

The marquess cocked a shaggy brow. "You deceive no one, daughter, least of all yourself. You love him. You love him or none of this would matter." He studied her for a moment. "And it may not be as it seems, Victoria. Have you even considered this?"

"What need is there to—" she began, then stopped abruptly. Her eyes narrowed. "You confuse me, Papa. Why, I could almost believe that you know something you refuse to tell me—"

"No." He quelled her swiftly. "I know very little,

except that I would never entrust my daughter to a man I thought to be a scoundrel."

"And you believe Miles is *not* a scoundrel?"

"I do."

"Papa, you are a traitor!"

The marquess winced. "No, daughter, I am not, and I can say no more, for it is not my place." He sighed. "These doubts must be laid to rest, Victoria, and only Miles can do that. Go home. Go home and await your husband's return."

"I don't want to go to Miles," she cried. "I don't want to see him ever again. I-I am home and I want to stay here!"

The glaze of tears in her eyes was almost his undoing. The marquess spoke softly, yet there was no doubting his conviction. "No, Victoria. This is no longer your home. You are the countess of Stonehurst and for now, your home is with your earl. Look to him for answers. But know this, child. If all is as you believe, I will do everything in my power to see this marriage ended, for I could not bear to see you unhappy. But first you must find out the truth—and that must come from your husband."

Her shoulders drooped. Her anger fled as suddenly as it had erupted. Papa was right. Deep inside, Victoria knew it. But that didn't make it any easier to bear. Battling a feeling of helplessness, she kissed him good-bye and returned to Grosvenor Square. For the second time that day, a parade of servants traipsed through the house carrying an array of trunks and baggage.

Sleep eluded her that night. But by the next morning a righteous resolve had fired her blood—as well as an unfaltering purpose.

Papa had advised her to wait for Miles. Well, that was all well and good. But Victoria remained convinced that she fully understood why Miles had been so reluctant to speak of Lyndermere. Perhaps it was folly. Perhaps it was sheer foolishness . . .

But she would see for herself this woman named Heather—the woman she'd come to consider her rival.

She set out for Lyndermere the next day. By the following morning, she was rolling along the hills of Lancashire. It was a part of England she'd never before visited. Had her mood been more lively, she'd have exclaimed with delight over the brilliant green valleys and flower-strewn fields. Before long, the coach turned down a long lane bowered with dozens of gracefully arched trees. Soon the coach rolled to a halt before an E-shaped stone building.

Her stomach knotted and tight, Victoria peered through the carriage window.

Naturally the coach was emblazoned with the Stonehurst crest. Apparently it had already been spotted, for a dozen or more servants had filed out the front doors and down the wide stone steps. They stood in a scraggly line, beaming nonetheless.

Those smiles froze when Victoria descended from the carriage. Daniel, the driver, quickly introduced her.

"His Lordship's wife, the new countess of Stonehurst. She and the earl were married last month."

This was news, indeed, judging from the openmouthed expressions. But the servants quickly surrounded her, bowing and bobbing curtsies, their manner all warm friendliness. To Victoria, there was just a blur of faces and names.

"I'm delighted to meet all of you," she said crisply. She seized on the one name she could recall, that of the housekeeper. "Mrs. Addison, I would very much like to meet someone I believe is in residence here, someone named Heather. Could you please direct me to her?"

"Of course, ma'am. If you'll just follow me." Victoria was right behind her as the housekeeper trekked up a grand staircase and turned to the right.

She stopped at the first door and tapped lightly upon it. "Miss Heather? Someone to see you," she called. She stepped back toward Victoria, lowering her voice to a whisper. "You'll have to forgive her, my lady. I'm afraid she's very disappointed that it wasn't His Lordship in the coach."

Victoria's spine had gone stiff. *I should imagine*, she thought blackly. When the housekeeper withdrew, she reached for the door. Pushing it open, she braced herself. No doubt Heather was a beauty, for she couldn't imagine Miles with anything less.

Boldly she stepped within the room.

The room's sole occupant was perched on a window seat across the room. Indeed, she *was* a beauty, with hair like the darkest night tumbling down her back. And those huge, thick-lashed eyes . . . somewhere between blue and purple, like the flower for which she was named.

But in that mind-splitting instant, Victoria also received the shock of her life . . .

Heather was just a child.

Chapter 9

Shame coursed through her, for she had harbored such venomous thoughts! Fast on the heels of that was a relief which left her weak in the knees, yet a dozen questions flooded her mind. Who was this child? And why had Miles never mentioned her?

Gathering herself in hand, Victoria ventured a smile. "Hello, Heather," she said softly. "May I come in?"

The child hesitated, then nodded. As Victoria moved forward, something caught in her chest, for only now did she glimpse the unshed tears in the little girl's eyes.

She stopped several feet away, not wanting to upset the child any more than she was already. "Heather"—she tipped her head to the side—"is it all right if I call you Heather?"

Again that silent nod.

Carefully she felt her way. "Well, Heather, I understand you were expecting the earl. It was you who sent the note to London, wasn't it?"

The girl seemed to hesitate, then nodded. "Actually, I-I asked Mrs. Addison to write it for me. Her writing is so much better than mine."

"And I arrived instead of the earl," she said with a nod. "Well, Heather, I'm very sorry I disappointed you."

The girl dashed a hand across her cheek. "It's all right. It's just that I—I thought you were Papa."

Papa.

Victoria's mind reeled. So Heather was Miles's daughter? This was news, indeed. He'd never been married, or had he? Or was the child illegitimate? Yet none of that seemed to really matter in that moment, for Heather sounded so woeful that Victoria knew a sudden urge to gather her close against her breast and turn those tears to laughter.

"Well, Heather, your papa would be here if he could. But I'm afraid he's gone to Cornwall, where a storm damaged one of his estates there. But I am certain that as soon as he is able, he'll return here to Lyndermere."

"Soon, do you think?"

She sounded so hopeful that Victoria very nearly laughed. Yet she knew that to do so might well be a mistake. "Very soon, I daresay. And I daresay you don't have the foggiest notion who I am."

For the first time the merest glimmer of a smile tugged at the girl's rosebud mouth. "To be perfectly honest, my lady, I don't."

"That's what I thought." Victoria held her breath and moved closer. She eased down to her knees so that her eyes were on the same level as the little girl's. "Heather, your papa and I were married in London last month. I am Victoria, his wife." She spoke very gently, hoping she wasn't making a terrible mess of this. "I have the feeling I'm going to like Lyndermere very much, Heather. And I should like to stay on here because I'd very much like for you and I to get to know each other."

Heather gazed at her unsmilingly. "Are you quite certain you wish to?"

Victoria found the question quite baffling. "Of course I am."

"But why? Why would you wish to?"

"Because I suspect we're going to be spending a great deal of time together."

"Lady Sutherland didn't want to be with me. She wanted to send me away."

Victoria's smile froze. "Lady Sutherland?"

"Yes. Papa was going to marry her—oh, a long time ago!"

Lady Sutherland . . . So this was the woman he'd told her of, the woman he'd intended to marry.

"Oh, but surely you must be mistaken, Heather." Victoria strived for a light tone. "Lady Sutherland couldn't possibly have wanted to send you away."

"She did, my lady. She did. She hated me." Heather's tone was notably fierce.

Such strong words . . . from one so young. Gazing across into that somber little face, Victoria was struck by the fleeting sensation that Heather was old beyond her years. But before she could say a word, Heather's gaze slid away. Her voice very small, she added, "I heard Lady Sutherland with Papa one day. She called me a cripple."

"A cripple. Good heavens, why on earth—"

And in that moment Victoria discovered precisely why. Heather slid from the window seat and started across the room.

This bright and beautiful, charming little girl . . . walked with a limp.

Halfway to the door, she stopped and turned. She stood silently—waiting, Victoria knew, for her reaction. The child's expression was half-defeated, half-defiant.

Something caught in Victoria's chest, something that hurt as surely as Heather had hurt in that moment. But she didn't allow herself to pity Heather; she suspected Heather would never accept pity. And so she didn't flinch from those wide-set violet eyes.

Instead she swallowed her anger at Lady Sutherland
. . . and swallowed her heartache.

She held out her hand. "Heather, please come
here."

The little girl returned to stand before her.

"Heather, I want you to understand something.
Normally I do not presume to judge someone I do
not know—and I confess I do not know Lady Sutherland. But 'tis my opinion that Lady Sutherland
was quite addle-brained—and should have been
taken out and whipped for daring to say such a
thing!"

It was Heather's turn to blink. "That's what Papa
told me," she said slowly.

"Good for him. Heather, Lady Sutherland had no
right to judge you so harshly, especially without
knowing you." Victoria's regard was steady, her
tone firm. "Heather, I will not make that mistake,
for I am nothing like Lady Sutherland. It doesn't
bother me in the least that you have a limp. I
shouldn't care if the entire world should limp! And
now, I would ask something of you, Heather."

"Yes, my lady?"

Was it her imagination—or was Heather standing
a bit taller? Yes, she most definitely was!

"Please, do me the honor of not lumping me in
with the likes of Lady Sutherland!" A faint twinkle
in her eye, Victoria smoothed the muslin shoulder
of Heather's gown. "Do you think you can do that
for me, love?"

Heather's head bobbed up and down.

Victoria wanted very much to reach out and hug
the little girl close, but she sensed it was too soon.

"Now," she said crisply, "on to the business of
getting to know one another. I suddenly find I'm
quite thirsty. Why don't we go downstairs and have

a spot of tea and biscuits in the salon, just you and I?"

For an instant Heather seemed uncertain. Then she leaned forward. "Can we ask Mrs. Addison to use the best silver?" she asked in a whisper.

"An excellent idea, Heather. I'm glad you thought of it!"

Heather's face had begun to glow. "Papa says Cook makes the best plum cake in all of England, and I know she baked some just this morning. Do you think we could have plum cake, too?"

Victoria rose to her feet. "Do you know, I'm really quite famished! Plum cake sounds quite the thing. Why, we'll have a tea party!"

Heather's eyes had grown huge. "A tea party?" she breathed. "Like a grand lady in London?"

"Like the two grand ladies of Lyndermere Park," Victoria chuckled. Holding her breath, she held out her hand.

When Heather took it with no hesitation whatsoever, Victoria felt her heart turn over.

"It was quite odd, my lord. A messenger arrived from Lyndermere Park with a letter for you. He said it was quite important, so I gave it to my lady. Then my lady packed her bags and left for her father's, only to return that very evening! Then not two days later she set out for Lyndermere. It was really quite odd," Nelson repeated.

Miles had set a breakneck pace back to London in the pouring rain. He was exhausted, drenched, and ached from head to toe. All that had sustained him was the certainty of a warm, loving welcome from Victoria.

But now an awful tightness gripped his heart. "Where is this letter?" he demanded.

Nelson coughed. "I believe my lady took it with her."

"Damn!" Miles tore up the stairs, but Nelson was right. There was no letter in either his bedroom or Victoria's.

He stood in the middle of the floor, his mind racing. He could only guess at the contents of the letter, but he had the terrible feeling Victoria had found out about Heather. God, but he should have told her the truth long ago!

For now the truth might very well mean his downfall.

He set out for Lyndermere within the hour.

For the most part, Victoria spent the next few days quietly, coming to know Heather . . . but it was also a time of deep reflection.

She came to realize that she was no longer the desperate young woman who sought to avoid marriage at all cost; for in truth, marriage had changed her. Or perhaps more precisely, *love* had changed her.

It was odd, how she had come to want all she had dismissed with such disdain, all that she'd been so convinced was not important . . .

And it was here at Lyndermere Park that Victoria made a great discovery indeed.

She didn't want to spend her life alone, as she had proclaimed to Papa—and Sophie. She wanted a home—a home such as this!—that echoed with the sounds of laughter and love and life. She wanted children to cherish and nurture and protect . . .

And she wanted it with Miles.

She had thought he cared. She'd even thought he loved her just a little . . . She was furious with him. She felt betrayed—and so very confused as well! But it pained her unbearably knowing that Miles had chosen not to tell her of Heather's existence. It was as if he had some—some secret part of him that he would keep forever hidden from her.

Why? *Why* hadn't he told her? It was a question that caused her no end of torment. Miles loved Heather deeply; the way Heather spoke of him— and his behavior toward the child—left Victoria in no doubt that it was so. At first she'd thought Heather was his by-blow. But she'd learned from Mrs. Addison that Heather was Miles's ward; how and why it came to be, Victoria had yet to learn. Yet few men would have taken in another's child, and in Victoria's estimation, it was an act of tremendous generosity. So it was that she couldn't imagine that Miles was ashamed of Heather because of her limp; it was not in his character to be so petty.

Victoria was left with just one conclusion. He hadn't wanted her to know about Heather.

Did he trust her so little? Did he think she wouldn't care about this sweet, young child who waited so anxiously for her papa to come home?

It hurt to realize he thought so little of her—that he chose to share so little with her. But Victoria stifled her hurt and hid her troubled state of mind whenever Heather was near.

On this particular day, Victoria sat with Heather in the drawing room, one arm around the child's narrow shoulders. Heather's dark head was nestled against her shoulder, her expression quiet and tranquil, her eyes ever alert. The pose was reflective of all the pair had shared these past days. For both it was a time of discovery. At eight years of age, Heather was an extremely thoughtful, intelligent child. She also had quite a talent for watercolors. But she also possessed a maturity—and sensitivity—far beyond her tender years.

For Heather, it was a time of learning as well—

learning to trust someone other than her papa—the *way* she trusted her dear Papa.

Though she was quite capable of doing so herself, she loved it when Victoria read to her. And she listened raptly when Victoria told her stories.

"Tell me the story about the scandalous bride," Heather pleaded on this particular evening.

Victoria smothered a grin. The story about the scandalous bride was one which Heather never tired of hearing—one which Victoria was altogether familiar with . . . and for good reason.

"There once was a young woman whose father was a marquess. Like all fathers, the marquess was anxious for his daughter to make a suitable marriage. The young lady, however, had a mind of her own, you see, and had no wish to marry the boorish and foppish young men who offered for her. If she were to marry, she wanted to marry a man she could love, and who loved her in return. But after several Seasons in London, she'd begun to give up hope that such a man existed.

"But by now the marquess had grown ever so impatient with his daughter. The young lady knew this, but she'd decided it was better to live her life alone than to marry a man she didn't love. And so she concocted an outrageous scheme, a scheme she thought would put her beyond the pale."

Heather snuggled against her. "What did the young lady do?"

"She followed a man into a garden and kissed him—can you imagine, she dared to kiss him! But you see, Heather, the young lady was not quite so clever as she'd thought, for her father demanded she marry the fellow, a man who happened to be of good family—an earl, in fact. So it was that she ended up a bride, though as you can imagine, a rather scandalous bride."

Heather peered up at her. "Was her husband handsome?"

"Oh, yes, this lord was so handsome he made her heart flutter madly and she tingled clear to her very toes just looking at him! But you see, they both were a stubborn pair, and rather resentful of each other for being forced to wed."

"They didn't like each other, did they?"

"No, love, not at first." The corners of Victoria's lips lifted. Though she didn't realize it, her voice had gone all soft and dreamy. "But do you know, strange as it may seem, the young lady ended up falling hopelessly in love with her handsome young lord."

"And what about him? Did he love her?"

Victoria's heart twisted. *If only I knew*, a voice inside cried. *If only I knew* . . .

"Yes, pet, he loved her quite madly." Though she still smiled, her eyes were full of wistfulness. "He loved her, and they were happier than either dreamed possible."

Usually Heather was content to move on to the next story. But today, she was silent for a moment. Her dark head dipped low. It spun through Victoria's mind that she seemed troubled. Then all at once she spoke.

"I will never marry," she said.

Quiet as the child's voice was, there was a ring of finality that stunned Victoria. She frowned. "Heather, sweet, why on earth would you—"

"Lady Sutherland said I would forever be an encumbrance around Papa's neck. She said no man would want me for a wife. I-I heard her."

Victoria gritted her teeth. Lady Sutherland again. Anger simmered within her. She could cheerfully strangle the woman!

"Heather," she stated firmly. "I thought we'd established that Lady Sutherland hasn't a brain in her head."

Heather still had yet to look at her. "I think she is right. I think I will never marry. The boys in the village. They stare at me. They stare because I'm different than other girls."

Victoria's throat grew thick with tears. She wrapped her arms around Heather and pulled her close. "Oh, darling, I know it may seem impossible now, but nothing could be further from the truth! You're a beautiful little girl and you'll grow into a beautiful young woman. It may take some time, but someday there will be a man who loves you very much and you will be happy, I promise you."

Slowly Heather raised her head. Victoria nearly cried out when she saw that the little girl's eyes shimmered with tears. "As happy as the lord and lady in the story?" she asked in a tiny voice.

Something broke inside Victoria then. She ducked her head and rested her cheek against Heather's dark, shining cloud of hair. "Yes," she choked out, only barely able to speak. The ache in her breast was nearly unbearable.

Not wanting to distress Heather further, she gathered herself in hand and gave Heather a quick hug. Raising her head, she offered the little girl a shaky smile.

Heather regarded her curiously, tipping her head to the side. "Do you know," she said after a moment, "I'm still not certain what to call you. 'My lady' is so formal."

"I agree," Victoria said promptly. "What would you like to call me?"

Heather pondered a moment. "Well," she murmured, "Papa isn't really my papa. I'm his ward, you know."

Victoria nodded. "Yes, I know, dear. Mrs. Addison told me."

"Still," Heather went on thoughtfully, "I call him Papa." A tiny frown furrowed her brow. "My mother died when I was very young. Mrs. Addison and my nanny are very nice, but . . ." Her voice trailed off. She bit her lip, opened her mouth as if to speak, then abruptly closed it.

Victoria encouraged her gently. "Yes, love, what is it?"

A small hand stole into hers. "May I call you Mama?" she whispered.

"Heather. Oh, Heather, of course you may." Touched beyond words, Victoria pulled the little girl onto her lap and hugged her fiercely. She was laughing; she was crying, tears she couldn't withhold and didn't try to.

It was the faint click of a door that alerted her . . . They weren't alone. Someone else was in the room . . .

And that someone was her husband.

Chapter 10

❧

Conscious thought was but a blur. Despite every-thing, all she could do was stare, as if he were a veritable feast for the eyes.

Heather had spied him as well. "Papa!" she exclaimed. She slipped off Victoria's lap. But before she could take more than a few steps, Miles was there. He caught her high in his arms.

"My black-haired little poppet. I missed you, love."

Heather giggled. "Did you bring me a present?"

Miles's mouth quirked dryly. "I brought you a whole trunkload of presents, poppet."

"Can I see?" She fidgeted eagerly.

Miles kissed her cheek, his eyes tender. "In just a bit, love." He paused. "I see you've met my wife."

Heather glanced shyly back at Victoria. She curled her fingers around Miles's collar and bent her fore-head to his. "She said I could call her Mama."

Miles's gaze rested on his wife. "So I heard," he said softly.

Victoria's eyes flitted away. She linked trembling hands together in her lap. Her heart lurched. What else had he heard?

When she finally found the courage to glance back at him, she was disconcerted to find herself the ob-ject of his attention.

"I'd like to spend a few minutes with Heather and get her settled for the night." His eyes cleaved the distance between them. "Will you wait for me here?"

Victoria's nod was jerky; she could manage no more. To Heather, she called a wobbly goodnight.

The time passed all too quickly. Victoria sat and then paced. She paced and then sat. Then suddenly Miles was there before her, and it was just as she'd said in her story—he was so handsome her heart fluttered madly. The very sight of him made her tingle all the way to her toes.

He moved to stand directly before her. One corner of his mouth curled up in a half-smile. "I must say, Victoria, this is the last place I expected to find you."

Her head came up. "No doubt," she snapped. She was up and on her feet, her eyes blazing. She'd suddenly remembered how angry she was with him— and she was, so furious she was shaking with it.

"You're aware a letter came for you from Lyndermere?"

"Yes. Though I've yet to discover the contents."

"I opened it only because Nelson thought it might be urgent." She defended herself fiercely. "It was very brief, my lord. Something on the order of . . . 'I miss you terribly. Love, Heather,' " she quoted.

"And you thought Heather was a woman, didn't you? A woman I kept here in the country? A mistress perhaps?" When she glared at him, his lips quirked. "And that was what sent you packing to your father's?"

"Oh, I can see you find it vastly amusing," she flared hotly. "And I had every intention of never seeing you again, Miles Grayson! But Papa had the audacity to tell me you might not be such a scoundrel after all. He knew about Heather, didn't he?"

Miles's grin had faded. "Yes—and no. He was

aware of her existence—that she was my ward—but I had no way of knowing if he knew the truth . . ." He sighed wearily, running his fingers through his hair. "Victoria, it's a long story. And I know you're angry that I didn't tell you about Heather—"

Tears burned her throat. "Yes, I'm angry. Angry because in all the weeks we've been married, not once did you see fit to tell me about your ward! Why, when I came here, I had no idea Heather even existed—I've never felt so foolish! And I'm angry because all the time you were in London, this poor, neglected child was here alone—"

"Neglected? Come now, Victoria, you exaggerate. I have never neglected Heather, nor will I. And she was hardly alone, for there is a house full of servants who love her and care for her every need—"

"But it was *you* she needed, Miles. She wanted her papa, and you should have been here with her! For that matter, she—she needs a mother, too, though apparently it's never occurred to you that your *wife* could be the mother she needs."

Guilt flickered across his face. "Did you think it was easy for me? I stayed because of you, Victoria." His tone was intense. "Because I wanted to be with *you*. That's the truth."

"The truth!" The breath she drew was deep and shuddering. "How am I to believe you when you hid the truth from me—you didn't tell me about Heather! How am I to trust you when you refused to trust me? Because you didn't, did you, Miles? You didn't trust me with the truth about Heather, did you?"

Miles's face had gone pale. "No," he said very quietly.

Victoria began to cry openly. "Why?" she cried. "Why didn't you trust me? Did you think I'd fly into a rage? Did you think I wouldn't understand? Did you think I'd want to send her away like—like that witch Lady Sutherland?"

She saw him flinch, as if he'd been struck. And she knew then . . .

"That's it, isn't it?" Pain slashed through her, like a rapier through the heart. Her words were a trembling, broken whisper. "You—you thought I was like her . . ."

Miles's body had gone stiff.

"You're right," he said, his tone wooden. "I *did* think you were like Margaret. You see, I'd heard of you, even before that night at the Rutherfords, the beautiful—and much sought-after—daughter of the marquess of Norcastle who refused to choose a husband. Victoria, how can I explain . . . ? The next thing I knew we were wed. I knew you didn't want to be a wife . . . why would you want to be a mother, and to a little girl who wasn't even your own . . .

"I never loved Margaret, not really. I want you to know that, Victoria. I admit, I was swept away by her beauty and charm. I proposed to her because I thought Heather needed a mother—because I thought she could make us happy. I-I thought I was doing the right thing. Margaret came from an impeccable family. She loved the glitter of London, the parties, the gossip.

"But as the wedding date drew near, I'd begun to have doubts—to think her shallow and vain—but I kept them to myself. I brought Margaret to Lyndermere to meet Heather. Victoria, she was . . . horrified when she saw Heather. She looked at Heather as if she were a—a monster."

Tears coursed down her cheeks. Everything he said was like a knife turning inside her. "I know that, Miles. But you must have known later that I wasn't like her. I-I could never be so cruel! Yet still you didn't tell me. You refused to believe in me.

God, and I''—a jagged cry tore from her lips—''I
thought you cared for me.''

He seized her hands. She tried to snatch them
back but he wouldn't let her.

''I do. Victoria, I *do*.'' His tone was low and fervent. ''But I was still afraid, sweet, and you must
admit, you were scarcely at home those first weeks
of our marriage. It seemed you thrived on the parties, the crowds, the adoration from those silly
young bucks in London. I-I didn't think you could
be happy with a simple life in the country. I didn't
think you could be happy with *me*!''

His voice grew raw. ''But above all, I had to protect Heather. I've remained here at Lyndermere in
order to spare Heather the pain of gossip and whispers among the London highbrows. I couldn't let her
be scorned or disdained by anyone. I couldn't let her
be hurt again the way Margaret hurt her! Victoria,
the night we made love . . . I knew you were different or I wouldn't have let it happen. My God, I
wouldn't have *wanted* it to happen. But I did, Victoria. I wanted you so much it hurt inside. And then
the next morning I intended to tell you about
Heather, but the news from Cornwall came and I
had to leave . . .''

He pulled her shaking body into his embrace.
''I'm sorry, sweet,'' he said achingly. ''I'm so sorry.
I knew how wrong I'd been when I saw you with
Heather. I was so relieved and yet so ashamed!''

Victoria searched his face. The depth of emotion
reflected in his eyes nearly took her breath away. It
was going to be all right after all . . . With a tiny little
cry she wrapped her arms around his waist and
clung.

''I want you to know everything, sweet, how
Heather came to live here . . . everything. There was
a carriage accident nearby some years ago. The

coach carried three passengers—a man, a woman, and a child of about three."

Victoria's tears had begun to slow. She turned her tear-stained face up to his. "Heather?" she whispered.

Miles nodded. "The driver and the man were killed immediately. The woman lingered for several days."

"Heather's parents?"

"I believe so. I know for certain the woman was her mother. I brought her here to Lyndermere." An odd note entered his voice. "Victoria, never in my life have I heard such vileness! Her mother knew she was dying. She heaped curses on her daughter and spewed the crudest of obscenities—because Heather would live and not her!"

Victoria went cold inside. "The accident. Is that how she came to be lame?"

"No. Her injuries were serious, but her knee was already scarred and malformed. The physician said it was likely some other accident. She was too ill to be moved—and she was so small—that I kept her here with me to recuperate. By the time she was well—oh, I know it sounds strange—but I loved her too much to let her go."

Victoria rubbed her cheek against the soft wool of his jacket. "It's not strange at all," she whispered. "I feel the same already."

His arms tightened. "There's more, Victoria. Heather was an orphan. I do not condemn them, but her parents' clothing was ragged and unkempt. Had I let her go, she would have been called a gutter-snipe. I couldn't let that happen. Nor could I let her go to an orphan house—my God, the conditions in those places are deplorable!"

Victoria felt him swallow.

"I lied, Victoria. I asked the courts to declare her

my ward. I told the magistrate her parents were very dear friends of mine; that her father was an impoverished lord from France—Heather's mother told me her name was Duval—who'd married an English lady. I said they were on their way to see me, to resettle here in England, when the accident occurred."

His palm was warm upon her nape. With his thumb he urged her face to his. "Heather believes herself to be the daughter of a French aristocrat and an English lady. Until this moment, no one knew the truth but me." His eyes darkened. "It's a secret I will guard with my life."

For an instant Victoria couldn't speak. Her throat was too tight. "Why? Why do you tell me this? Why now?"

"Because I trust you with my heart, sweet. I love you, Victoria. *I love you.*"

To her utter shame, she began to cry all over again. Miles swept her close, so close their hearts beat together as one. "Shhh," he soothed. "I didn't mean to make you cry again, sweet. I'll make it up to you, I swear."

Her smile was tremulous. "It's all right. It's just that I—I never thought to hear you say that."

His gaze had fallen to her lips. "No? What about the story you told Heather?" he teased. "The lord loved his lady quite madly, did he not?"

"That was just a-a fanciful dream," she confessed.

His expression was incredibly tender. "It's no dream, sweet. I *do* love you. But I fear I must know—did the lady truly fall hopelessly in love with her lord?"

Victoria pressed her hand into his cheek, her smile misty. "Oh, yes," she whispered. "Quite hopelessly indeed . . ."

Epilogue

❧

Nearly a year had come full circle, and fragrant spring breezes rippled across the broad fields of Lancashire. It was late May, and on this warm spring eve, twilight cast a purple haze across the western sky.

Victoria and Miles had remained at Lyndermere Park for much of the year. She had come to love Lyndermere as much as her husband. Trips to London were few—a necessary nuisance, Miles called them. But while Victoria occasionally found herself missing a night at the opera or an evening of waltzing at Almack's, it was here at Lyndermere—with Miles—that her heart and hopes and dreams resided . . .

She could imagine no other life . . . nor a life more perfect.

But there had been an addition to the family. They were no longer three, but four . . .

Beatrice Louise Grayson had made her entrance into the world on a wild, stormy night in late February, much to her father's delight . . . and her mother's relief.

Beatrice had now reached the ripe old age of three months. Her belly had grown round and firm, her cheeks pink and plump. A cap of pale gold curls covered her head, and her eyes were as blue as sapphires; her grandpapa proudly proclaimed Beatrice the very image of her mother.

Now, having finished nursing the babe, Victoria smoothed a tender hand over the fine gold fuzz covering her daughter's scalp, then handed the babe into the waiting arms of her husband so that she could adjust her gown.

Miles pressed a warm kiss on that tiny brow. He chuckled when Beatrice flashed a sunny little grin, for such was her nature. He laid her in the cradle, his hold on her immeasurably gentle.

Heather looked up eagerly from where she sat reading in the window seat. "May I rock her, Mama?" she pleaded. "And tell her a story, too?"

Victoria's eyes softened. "Of course you may, love." Smiling, Victoria pulled a small chair next to the cradle so Heather could sit.

When Heather flashed her a beaming smile as she took her place, Victoria felt her heart squeeze. It was her most fervent wish that Beatrice would someday come to be like Heather, for there was no sweeter child on the face of this earth; and indeed, for Victoria there was no greater privilege than hearing this beautiful, dark-haired child call her "Mama" . . .

Heather extended a finger toward the babe. Beatrice curled a tiny pink fist around it and held on fast. "Now then, Beatrice. Here is the story I will tell you. There once was a young lady who was all the rage in London. But this young lady . . . I think we shall call her Lavinia, yes, Lavinia!"

Beatrice stared at Heather raptly, as if she understood every word.

Victoria's lips quirked, for Miles was shaking his head, an indulgent smile on his lips. When he held out his hand, she accepted it wordlessly.

Heather continued. "Well, Beatrice, Lavinia was very opposed to marriage, but she came up with a most unusual idea in order to lay to rest her papa's insistence that she marry. Can you imagine, Beatrice, Lavinia followed a man—an earl—into a garden and kissed him! But her plan failed, you see, for her papa demanded she marry this man!"

Hand in hand, Miles and Victoria quietly retreated. At the threshold, they paused to listen once more.

"Oh, but this scandalous bride was at wit's end, being forced to marry this earl, for though he was quite handsome, he was a wicked one indeed!"

Miles was taken aback. "Handsome, yes," he concurred in a whisper. "But wicked?" He shook his head in mild affront. "I think not!"

Victoria's eyes were dancing. "A woman's perspective," she informed him gravely. She pressed a finger to her lips, for Beatrice was yawning, and her eyes had begun to droop.

Heather hastened to finish. "And so, Beatrice, the scandalous bride Lavinia set about taming her wicked earl and making him fall quite madly in love with her . . ."

Miles pulled his wife into his arms. "She did indeed," he murmured against the smooth skin of her temple. He drew her into the hallway where he claimed her lips in a long, ardent kiss that sent their senses soaring.

When at last he released her, a teasing smile curled her lips. "Ah," she said playfully, "but the scandalous bride does have one regret."

One dark brow arched roguishly. "And what might that be, countess?"

Victoria twined her arms about his neck. "Had she known what fate awaited her that long-ago night, she'd have kissed her wicked earl much, much sooner . . ."

Samantha James

Born in the Chicago area, SAMANTHA JAMES now makes her home in the Pacific Northwest with her husband, three daughters, and two Shetland sheep-dogs. It isn't always easy juggling three careers—wife, mother, and romance novelist—but she can't imagine a life without writing. Known for her emotionally charged stories, Samantha is the bestselling, award-winning author of six previous novels: *Just One Kiss*, *My Lord Conqueror*, *Gabriel's Bride*, *Outlaw Heart*, *My Rebellious Heart*, and *My Cherished Enemy*. If you enjoyed this story, you can visit Heather, Miles, and Victoria again soon in *Every Wish Fulfilled*, a January 1997 release from Avon Books.

Beyond the Kiss

❧

Kathleen E. Woodiwiss

Chapter 1

Near Charleston, South Carolina
July 17, 1803

Gentle, rose-scented breezes wafted in through the open windows and French doors of Oakley Plantation house, filling the spacious rooms with the cooling air of a midsummer's evening. In a second-story bedroom, the refreshing zephyrs slipped inward with a silky sibilance of lace panels billowing beyond elegantly adorned velvet draperies. The swishing of the cloth was no more than a whisper in the hushed stillness, as soft as the tremulous sigh of the young bride as her new husband raised his lips from hers. Beneath his warmly admiring regard, her dark lashes slowly lifted, and Jeff Birmingham found himself immersed in radiant pools of aqua blue.

"When you look at me like that, my dear Raelynn," he breathed, mesmerized by her glowing beauty, "I can almost believe we've been in love since the dawn of time."

Raelynn's gaze leisurely followed the path of a slender finger as she traced it down his sun-bronzed cheek, past a tiny half-moon scar at the side of his mouth, and then along the boldly chiseled line of his jaw. He was so handsome, it was easy to imagine an impressionable young maid being instantly smitten.

How could she have guessed that she'd be just as susceptible? Yet, in the brief span of a single afternoon, she had both met and married this man.

Smiling into the green eyes that sparkled with a shining luster close above her own, Raelynn brushed the tips of her fingers caressingly across his lips. "Perhaps we *have* been in love all our lives, Jeff, and were only waiting to find each other."

"Then I'm a man immeasurably blessed," he stated huskily. "You were the vision I glimpsed in my dreams, and though the face and form of my enchantress were but vague shadows in my mind, I was driven by the hope that if I searched long and hard enough, one day she would become reality. When I saw you this afternoon, it was as if you had walked out of my dreams into my life. You're the one I've been yearning for, the sweet nectar I've been craving. Henceforth, I'm eternally bound to you."

Looping her arms around his neck, Raelynn sighed dreamily. "Little did I foresee when I slipped from my uncle's grasp that I'd be dashing into the arms of my future husband only a few blocks away." Her silvery laughter spiraled upward, melding with the soft tinkling of crystal prisms that the breezes bestirred in the chandelier above their heads. "And to think I nearly split your crown in front of Mrs. Brewster's hat shop."

Jeff's lips twitched with amusement as he recalled the discussion he had been having with the portly, middle-aged milliner just before he had stepped back in the path of this winsome beauty. Mrs. Brewster had been fretting about the possibility of him being able to find a wife who could equal the exquisite loveliness of his sister-in-law, yet scarcely ten minutes later he had discovered such a one struggling for balance beneath his very nose. "You have a distinct way of commanding a man's attention, my dear."

Raelynn giggled at his waggish humor. "I suppose I should apologize for my unseemly haste, sir, but how was I to know that a grand gentleman like yourself would be leaving a ladies' hat shop just when I'd be running past it?" Tilting her head at a coquettish angle, she contemplated him with playful skepticism. "You don't look the sort to be wearing bonnets, Mr. Birmingham. Or did you perchance go there to visit with Mrs. Brewster? Isn't she rather old for you?"

"About as old for me as you are young, my dear," Jeff replied with a deep, throaty chuckle. "If you must know what I was doing in her shop, my winsome little tease, I went there to buy my sister-in-law a bonnet for her birthday. Had I foreseen my own wedding ere the evening was done, I'd have found a bonnet of comparable beauty for you as well."

Raelynn pouted prettily as she smoothed his neatly tied stock. "To be sure, sir, ten and nine is for some the age when spinsterhood begins. So you must agree that I'm not so young."

Jeff's laughter challenged her claim. " 'Tis young when you've just married a man who's put the better part of thirty and three behind him this year. I'm sure the gossips will be speculating on which orphanage I found my child bride in."

She could not understand how a man of his splendid good looks had managed to reach so mature an age without acquiring a wife for himself, and siring a goodly number of offspring to boot. A veritable avalanche of wistful entreaties must have come from all the awestruck maids in the area. And if he had never yielded to the pleas of those doe-eyed maidens who yearned to marry him, then surely there had to have been a mistress or two who doted on him. Perhaps, even now, there was some sweet young thing he was wont to woo when his manly moods demanded.

"Tell me truly, sir," she begged with a coyly inquisitive smile. "Have you had many loves in your life? Do you tease me by saying that I'm the only one you've searched for all these many years?"

Jeff's eyebrows flicked briefly upward as he acknowledged, "In my lengthy quest for the woman of my dreams, I cannot deny that I've tested my heart with others, but they never assuaged that unsettled feeling gnawing at my vitals. I tell you no lie, madam, when I say that of those maidens I've courted, I favored none with a plea to be my wife. Whatever enticements inspired me to seek their company were ephemeral, as fleeting as the morning dew. Indeed, the longer I searched for my vision, the more resolved I became to remain a bachelor 'til I found her." His mouth curved slowly in a lopsided grin. "I never once supposed she'd have to cross the ocean to get to the place where we'd meet."

Raelynn was grateful that the grim residue which had darkened her thoughts after a disastrous voyage and the death of her mother had been whisked from the forefront of her mind by the joy and pleasure she was presently experiencing. Her hopes for a brighter future helped to ease the trauma of losing her last remaining parent. Still, her life in the past year had been marked much too often by tragedy for her to feel completely free of it now.

London had certainly seemed a cruel, despicable place to live after accusations of treason were hurled against her father by some of his less notable peers. Perhaps the ambitions of those particular viscounts and barons had been at the crux of their malicious attempts to defame the name of Lord Randall Barrett. Whatever their motives, they had succeeded in having him arrested, and though he had vehemently denied their allegations, her father had died in his cell without even being allowed a trial. Following his demise, the crown had stripped away his wealth and properties, leaving Raelynn and her mother with no recourse but to seek shelter in a tumble-down cottage on the outskirts of the city. With the small cache of coins her father had secreted away against a possible reversal of fortune, they had at least seen their basic needs provided for, but it had been a drab and joyless existence. They had found little compassion in the hateful slurs and glowers that the common folk in the area had liberally bestowed upon them.

It was no kindly act of providence that had brought Raelynn's uncle to their door barely a month after Randall Barrett's passing. Twenty years earlier, as a young cabin boy, Cooper Frye had been reported lost at sea. Raelynn's mother, Evalina, had listened solemnly to the stranger's claims that he had been swept overboard during a storm and marooned on an island for several months before being rescued by Baltic traders who, after taking him on board as cabin boy, had sailed off to foreign shores. But Evalina had glimpsed nothing in his features to remind her of that tall, lanky boy who had gone to sea with such lofty expectations. Still, he had known enough about the Frye family to finally convince her that he was, indeed, her brother.

His talk of the new land had led both mother and daughter to hope that things might be better for them across the ocean. Prudently conservative of their limited funds, Evalina had gone with Cooper Frye to arrange for passage aboard a ship, but she had later been forced to entrust their purse to him rather than see it stolen by some of the other passengers on the voyage. They soon had cause to regret their reliance on the man. While Cooper Frye had selfishly seen to his own needs, Raelynn and her mother had suffered diverse hardships, having barely enough to eat and finding little rest and privacy in the unbearable filth of a dank, crowded hole.

Three days after their ship had docked in Charleston, and precisely two weeks after he had knelt solemnly beside the crate that had first served her mother as a bed and later as a coffin, Cooper Frye had blandly dismissed his sacred pledge to see to the welfare of his niece. Having given Raelynn a feeble excuse to allay her suspicions, he had taken her to visit Gustav Fridrich, that bald-headed, ice-eyed German who was making himself harshly felt in his sector of the city and becoming well known among the rowdies working the docks. Earlier in the day they had witnessed an aging shopkeeper being beaten by Gustav's bullies because the man had been unable to make a payment on a loan. No doubt it was the catalyst that had caused her uncle to concoct his devious plan. As unscrupulous as the German apparently was, he would not likely fault another for trying to profit from the sale of a relative. Still, Gustav had haggled like one who had always sought a bargain, and Cooper Frye had given him a few hours to think about his proposition. If he wanted her, her uncle had boldly informed the man, he'd have to lay out two hundred fifty in hard Yankee coins before the matter could be settled.

Raelynn vividly recalled how trapped she had felt after leaving the German's warehouse. Enraged at the deceit of her uncle, she had jerked free of his bruising grasp and raced away, having no idea where she was heading, yet totally resolved toward putting as much distance between herself and Cooper Frye as her strength would allow. She had been so intent on thwarting his money-hungry plans for her that she had given no heed to the dangers of running helter-skelter through the streets of Charleston. She had rounded a corner and nearly knocked onto his backside the handsomest man she had ever seen. That was the moment when Jeffrey Birmingham had come into her life.

There hadn't been time for apologies. Spurred recklessly on by a shout from her uncle, she had bolted into a busy thoroughfare, completely oblivious to an approaching four-in-hand. Jeff had raced after her, whisking her up in his arms and to the far side of the street, well out of harm's way before she was even aware that she was in any danger. She could not have known, of course, that after he became her champion, she would most willingly accept him as her bridegroom . . . and, very soon now, her lover.

Considering how quickly she had been attracted to him, Raelynn was rather surprised that she had deigned to ask for time to get to know him better before they consummated their vows. Truly, in spite of the rush and furor of the day, she was convinced that she had gained for herself a husband the likes of which many of her gender would search a lifetime for.

Any woman would have been captivated by his handsome features and charming wit, but there had been something more between them, some strange magnetism that had bound them together in a brief span of hours. After such a whirlwind courtship, she could only wonder what the future would hold for them. Would she have cause to regret their hasty union? Or would she be completely content all the years of their lives?

"Here we are, Jeff, newly wedded and on our way to sharing a bed together, and yet we're little more than strangers," Raelynn mused aloud. "Are you truly as wonderful as you seem? Or have you bewitched me with some magical potion?"

" 'Twould seem we have both sipped the same heady brew, for I am no less entranced," he avowed huskily.

Tucking her arm in his, Jeff smiled down at her and escorted her through the French doors and out onto the veranda where arm in arm they strolled along, admiring the beauty of a black velvet sky that was bedecked with a myriad of twinkling stars and a silvery sliver of a moon reclining in indolent repose above the treetops. Beyond well-manicured grounds stretching out behind the main house, a line of majestic oaks formed a partial barrier in front of the servants' quarters. Lantern-lit windows marked several of the cabins through the swaying branches, and from one of them drifted the soft, haunting tune being played on a pan-pipe. Their senses were wonderfully stimulated by the sights and sounds around them and by the fragrance of flowers that made the air a heady delight. It was truly a night made for lovers.

Jeff slipped his arms about his wife's slender waist and braced his hips against the porch balustrade as he pulled her close between his legs. Turning his head, he gazed toward the neatly turned fields stretching endlessly toward the east. "Part of this land you see here was given as an English grant to my father, along with several thousand acres that make up the family plantation at Harthaven. After my parents died, Harthaven was handed down to my brother, Brandon, being the first born, and a warehouse and other properties of equal value were left to me. Until a few years ago, I lived with my brother and managed our properties while he sailed to foreign climes. He met Heather in England and brought her back to Harthaven as his wife. The gossips took great delight in the fact that Brandon had married Heather while still engaged to Louisa Wells, the woman who once owned this place. And I suppose to some degree I led the snoops on when I doted upon Heather. But by then, she was already well along with child, just as she is now, and it was hard for me to imagine anyone mistaking my brotherly regard for her as some deep, hidden passion. Later, when Louisa was found slain in this house, a few talebearers tried to say that Brandon had killed her in a fit of rage, but of course that wasn't true. By then, he was totally dedicated to Heather."

"You mean Louisa was slain here in this very house?" Raelynn queried in surprise.

Jeff's brows rose above a curious grin. "Not afraid of ghosts, are you?"

"No, of course not," his young wife hastened to assure him, but a blush suffused her cheeks when she realized just how much his revelation had startled her. "This place is so wonderful, it's hard to imagine that someone was actually murdered here. Did they ever catch the one who was responsible?"

" 'Twas an ugly little man who admired beautiful women. He later tried to do away with Heather, too."

"You mean . . . in this house?"

His green eyes gleamed as Jeff watched his young wife closely. She seemed so incredulous it was not difficult to guess what she was thinking. He could foresee himself spending many a delightful night assuring her that whether the house was cursed or not, she would always be safe in his arms. "He tried, my love, but Brandon came to her rescue. Later, a limb broke in a storm and fell on top of the man, crushing him beneath it."

Raelynn's shoulders shook with an expressive

shudder. "I think you're trying to frighten me, Jeffrey Birmingham."

Her husband laughed. "Now why would I want to do that, madam?"

"I don't know, but if you have a penchant for churlish tales and more of them to tell," she warned, peering up at him with a daring twinkle in her eye, "I may be better off with Gustav Fridrich after all."

"He'd never treasure you as much as I do," Jeff whispered as his mouth lowered toward hers. "You'll always be my dearest wife, the sweetest love of my life."

He kissed her with a leisurely thoroughness that made Raelynn's pulse throb with a new, chaotic rhythm. She clung to him, having no desire to break away, and when he finally lifted his head, she pressed close against him.

"You make me forget what we were even talking about," she murmured breathlessly.

"My family," he reminded her with a chuckle.

"Tell me more," she coaxed.

"I thought you didn't want to hear any more of my stories," he teased.

"Not if they're gruesome."

"Then you'll no doubt be happy to hear there are no more stories of murder and intrigue to be told about my family. At least, none that I'm aware of."

"I'm relieved to hear that," she replied with a smile. "Now tell me how you came here to Oakley."

"After Louisa was killed, I paid the debts against the property and added several thousand acres to the original tract of land. It's taken a lot of work and capital to make Oakley what it is today, but I've grown to love it here. This is where I'd like our children to be born and to grow up. A dozen or two would suffice."

Raelynn leaned back in his arms and laughed.

" 'Tis my guess that you intend to keep us both busy for many years to come."

"I've waited a long time to find you, my dear, and it's only right that we enjoy our lives to the utmost. I'd love to have a dozen or so daughters who look exactly like you."

"And I'd be thrilled with a dozen or so sons who are as handsome as their father," she rejoined gaily.

His grin grew broader. "We'll have to add a few more bedrooms to accommodate them all."

Raelynn lifted her shoulders in a pert shrug as she reasoned, "If this house has seen its share of tragedy in the past, it's only fitting that it be filled with joy and laughter in the future. 'Twould be a heavenly place to nurture our children and to grow old together."

"I can hardly wait to begin."

Dragging her eyes from his handsome face, she looked toward the fields to the east. "What sort of crops do you grow here on the plantation?"

Following her gaze, Jeff spoke with a measure of pride in his voice. "That's cotton growing there, and where the fields of cotton end, we've got rice thriving in the lowlands. There's a good market for both products across the Atlantic, as well as in some Caribbean ports. Brandon and I own equal shares in a sawmill, and what lumber we don't sell locally, we usually ship, but that's not too often. This area is growing fast enough to keep our men sawing logs for at least another ten years."

"If you own a warehouse, Jeff, then surely you must have come in contact with Gustav Fridrich, or at least know of him."

Jeff's answer came with a liberal measure of disdain. "I've heard enough talk about that scoundrel to make me cautious about getting involved with him. I know he's hired a lot of toughs to help his investments thrive, by force if need be. I've made it a habit to keep my distance. To put it mildly, madam, I'd sooner trust a wild boar than Gustav Fridrich."

"I'm glad you bought me, Jeff, but I've been reluctant to tell you something about your agreement with my uncle." Her eyes glimmered in the moonlight as she searched his face. "When Cooper Frye offered to sell me to Fridrich, he was only asking two hundred fifty Yankee dollars for me. You could have bought me for considerably less than the seven hundred fifty you paid for me."

Jeff chuckled, undismayed. "What Cooper Frye doesn't know, my dear, is that I'd have gladly paid a hundred times more than that. I would have deemed it worth every moment of this happiness I'm now sharing with you. You're the woman I've searched for all my life. How can I regret the cost, whatever the amount?"

Raelynn sighed. "In the short time I've known Cooper Frye, I've come to realize that he's not to be trusted. He's a thief, plain and simple. As long as he knows you have money, I'm sure he'll try to wheedle what he can from you."

"Your uncle had better keep his distance or I'll make him wish he had," Jeff replied. "He agreed to leave us alone. If he doesn't, he'll have to return the money I gave him. He'll not find me an easy taskmaster if he has to work the debt off."

"Since he first came to us in England shortly after my father died in prison, I've often wondered if he is really my uncle or just someone who knew the cabin boy, Cooper Frye, before he perished at sea. I feel uneasy about the way he showed up all of a sudden without a single letter ever reaching his family to say that he was alive. To be sure, if he wasn't whom he claimed to be, there wasn't much to be

gained from associating himself with us, certainly
nothing of monetary value, so I rather doubt he
sought us out for that reason. All we had was what
my father had managed to hide for us before he was
arrested, and it was too meager a sum to interest an
ambitious thief. Still, Cooper Frye took what was left
of our funds and provided for his own comforts during the ocean voyage. By the time we arrived, there
was nothing left. Selling me to Gustav Fridrich was
the easiest way my uncle had of getting his hands
on more."

Jeff gently kissed her brow, smoothing away the
troubled frown that briefly marred its perfection.
"Don't fret yourself about that wretch any more, my
love," he cajoled. " 'Tis highly unlikely that you'll
be seeing him again."

"I hope what you say is true, Jeff," Raelynn answered quietly, "but I fear 'tis not his way. If I know
Cooper Frye at all, I predict that he'll not be leaving
us alone."

Jeff wrapped his arms around her, pulling her
close. "Don't dread what the future holds for us, my
love. This night is ours alone, the beginning of our
marriage. Let us enjoy all the intimate pleasures to
be shared between a husband and his wife without
dwelling on that scoundrel any longer."

Raelynn could feel his long, muscular body
through the soft satin of her gown, and her blood
stirred with desire as his parted lips played provoc-
atively upon hers. At first, his kiss was gently in-
quiring, yet it soon became a flaming brand that
torched a quickening fire within her, setting her
senses ablaze with a passion that warmed her as
thoroughly as any bubbling cauldron. No longer
was she Raelynn Barrett, the proud, aloof maiden,
but a bride well roused and eager.

His face slowly retreated, leaving Raelynn adrift

in a deliciously giddy trance. "To be sure, sir," she sighed with a slight quaver in her voice, more than a little dazzled by his affect on her, "another kiss of the sort will see me so addled I'll be hard-pressed to dress myself for bed."

A shaft of light streaming from the bedchamber illumined his face, and she could see the emerald eyes shining above an hypnotic, white-toothed grin. "The word is undress, madam, and you needn't fret yourself about such minor inconveniences. Not when I'm eager to be of service."

Lifting a hand, Raelynn toyed with a wayward black lock that had fallen onto his brow. "I've been told that a bride should beg a few moments of privacy to adorn herself for her groom on their wedding night. You even bought me a gown to wear, remember?"

Jeff smiled into her dancing, moonlit eyes. "Lay out the gown for a later hour if you must, madam, but for now, you'll have little need of it."

Raelynn vividly recalled her mother telling her what to expect on her wedding night and encouraging her to offer herself as a rare, precious gift to her groom, for though she was virginal, it lay well within her power to make it a night she and her new husband would long remember. Such sage advice could not be lightly ignored.

"Is there no servant to pluck me free of the one I now wear and help me ready myself for my bridegroom?" she persisted. "Your housekeeper was very adept at helping me dress for the wedding. Could she not assist me now?"

"Your pardon for my lack of foresight, madam," her husband begged. "By now, Cora and her family are probably safe abed in their own quarters beyond that line of oaks you see behind me, too far to be summoned with a mere tinkling of a bell. I fear I've been a bachelor much too long. I lent little consideration to your needs when I gave the servants leave to retire after dinner. My butler would be the only one left in the house, and although Kingston is adept at what he does, he's not very handy as a lady's maid." A smile curved his lips as his eyes engaged hers with a mischievous glint. "Alas, my love, I fear there be none other to assist you in your boudoir, save myself."

Raelynn braced an elbow on his shoulder and seemed to seriously ponder his reply as she laid a slender knuckle against her cheekbone. "I do recall asking for some time to get to know you better before we shared a bed," she admitted, a smile twinkling at the corners of her mouth. "I just didn't know your kisses would make me change my mind so soon."

His gaze engulfed hers. "And what is your desire now, madam?" Jeff breathed, lowering his lips toward hers. "Would you rather stay here and enjoy this bejeweled night together for a while longer? Or shall we return to the bedchamber and ready ourselves for bed?"

His lightly caressing kiss was just as persuasive as all the others he had bestowed upon her lips, and it was a long moment before she could answer. "The night is truly delightful, sir," she said with a sigh, "and the company no less than intoxicating. Still, I'm curious to know what awaits me as a bride."

He smiled with pleasure. "I was hoping you'd say that."

Pushing away from him with a soft laugh, Raelynn swept across the porch with a whisper of silk and entered the bedchamber. Jeff followed, pausing briefly to close the French doors behind him, and was no more than a step behind her when she halted beneath the chandelier. Slipping an arm about her narrow waist, he pulled her back against him.

"Now I have you at last," he whispered, brushing his lips across her shoulder. His kisses wandered upward along her silken throat to her ear as his hands stroked down the sides of her hips. "You've haunted me too long as the enchantress of my dreams. I must soon be nurtured by your sweet delights or die of this ever-gnawing hunger."

Raelynn trembled against him and, at the urging of his hands, turned willingly to face him. For a moment their mouths played in sweet union, then Jeff stepped back. His smoldering eyes were like a warm tongue gliding leisurely over her flesh, consuming her with their intensity as he doffed his black silk frockcoat and tossed it over the back of a nearby chair. Affecting a courtly air, he swept an arm before him and showed a leg in a lissome bow.

"Madam, you have before you a most ardent and obedient servant. Your very wish is my command."

Melodic laughter evidenced her delight over his gallant courtship. Spreading her skirts of silver blue satin, Raelynn sank into a deep curtsy, unconsciously awarding him with a tantalizing view of her breasts. "Truly, sir, I've never seen a more eager knight. May I ascribe your haste to the exuberance of your passion?"

"Indeed you may, my love." Flames of green fire were kindled in his eyes as they swept the full, ripe curves of her bosom. When she straightened, his gaze delved into hers as his thin fingers untied his stock and unbuttoned his waistcoat with purposeful intent. "I'm a man at risk, madam, sorely tempted by your beauty."

Bewitched by his mesmerizing stare, Raelynn raised her arms and began to uncoil the ropes of pearls that entwined her hair. Soon the auburn tresses tumbled in carefree abandon around her pale

shoulders and down her back. Lifting the strands of
pearls before her face as if they were a silken veil,
Raelynn began a slowly swaying dance toward him,
enticing him with a sultry gaze. Her soft laughter
threaded through his mind like a siren's song, and
he had no will to resist. The pearls slid to the floor
unnoticed as his long, thin fingers encircled her
wrists and drew them behind his neck. Slipping his
arms about her waist, he moved with her in a slowly
circling waltz toward the tall four-poster where a
dozen candles burned atop the ornate branches of a
pair of silver candelabras that resided on tables on
either side. In the softly glowing candlelight his
leanly chiseled face seemed suffused with a sun-
bronzed radiance, and in that moment Raelynn was
certain that her husband was as splendid looking as
any mythical god of ancient lore.

Her breath came in quickening snatches as her
husband seemed to strum the very fibers of her being, awakening her to the sensual pleasure of his
caresses as his hands moved over her hips and buttocks and settled her closer against the manly heat
of him, igniting her imagination no small degree. It
was a new and rousing experience to be courted in
such a provocative manner, and Raelynn found herself being swept up in a whirlwind of excitement.

While his hands roamed with increasing boldness,
her own trembled with eagerness as she unfastened
the tiny studs of his shirt to the waistband of his
narrow-fitting breeches. There she paused in inde-
cision, wondering if he would think her brazen if
she continued.

Savoring the fragrance of her hair, Jeff pressed his
lips into the silken strands as he murmured encouragement. "Sweet love, I give you leave to do with
me as you desire. I am yours as you are mine." Still,
he plucked open the top of his trousers to ease her

doubts. "It would pleasure me to be disrobed by my bride."

His teeth nibbled at her ear, sending waves of tingling warmth racing through her. Aroused by the strange sensations he awoke within her, she hardly noticed her hand brushing against his tautly muscled abdomen as she reached into his trousers to pull the tail of his shirt free.

The unexpected contact snatched Jeff's breath, and for a reckless moment he stood rigid, his head erect, his eyes half-closed as his cravings pulsed like molten lava through his body. Goaded now by a raging hunger, he pondered the folly of snatching her up and having his way with her without further delay. Then reason returned, and he let his breath out haltingly as he drew hard rein on his racing passions. Almost calmly he shrugged out of his shirt and laid it aside.

Oblivious to the exquisite torture which her touch aroused in her husband, Raelynn sighed with admiration as she stroked her hands along his ribs. The lightest brush of her fingertips fueled the fires of desire, and Jeff was like a man on a slowly turning rack of intense pleasure, being stretched to the very limits of his control.

Raelynn was impressed by the steely hardness of his rugged muscles and the broad expanse of his shoulders. In his sleek and well-tailored garb he had seemed more slender than athletic, and she had assumed he would be thin beneath the subtle padding of his fine fitting clothes, but as she could now see, such was not the case. Handsomely refined and trim, Jeff Birmingham had a physique that rivaled Adonis.

"You're beautiful," she breathed in awe, threading her fingers through the crisp dark hair covering his chest. "More beautiful than I could have imagined."

Amused by her choice of words, Jeff raised a skeptical brow to a lofty angle and gave her a hint of a lopsided smile, the best his badly frayed restraints could manage at the moment. "Beautiful? Ah, madam, I fear you shade the truth with extravagance. Beautiful is a word I would use in an attempt to describe you."

Raelynn pressed her fingers to his lips and shushed him with a negative shake of her head. "You're beautiful to me, Jeffrey."

Slipping her arms about his neck, she raised on her toes and tested her rapidly expanding knowledge, snaring his lips in a seductive kiss. Jeff strove hard to convince himself that he had the discipline of a saint. If not for the tidal waves coursing tumultuously through his veins and crashing in ever-strengthening swells of excitement against the crumbling wall of his restraint, he might have succeeded. But then, he was only a man, and a newly espoused one at that.

His fingers played at the back of her gown as his mouth feasted on the sweetness of her response, searching, devouring, awakening sensual pleasures previously unknown to her. Raelynn found herself growing warm and pliant with the wine of desire. She hardly noticed when her bodice began to loosen over her breasts, only when his lips left hers. Her lashes trembled downward as his mouth trekked a searing trail along her pale throat, then his dark head dipped lower still to the fullness of her bosom, and she caught her breath at the ecstasy he aroused. The flames of passion licked upward, suffusing her woman's body with a fiery heat until she felt driven by a burning desire to make herself one with this man.

The gown slid with barely a whisper of defeat to the floor, and for a long moment Jeff liberally drank from the brimming chalice of her beauty. Clad only in a clinging chemise of satin and lace, his bride was a vision of perfection, a temptress whose creamy breasts rose and fell with her rapid breathing.

Jeff's own breath grew rushed as he struggled to curb the mounting demands of his body. His young wife fulfilled every facet of his desires, and he was hard-pressed to maintain a patient and courtly manner, and not startle her with the fierceness of his ardor.

Beneath the gentle urging of his hands, the satin straps slipped from her shoulders, and the shallow bodice slithered languidly down over the swelling fullness. On the very brink of full exposure, her breasts seemed to deliberately delay the descent of the garment as if to coyly tease him. Raelynn watched him with bated breath, yearning for his touch, impatient for that moment when he would gather her to him. Her senses quaked in anticipation, and she leaned toward him invitingly, sending the chemise to the floor with a small shrug of her shoulders. Then her heart quickened beneath the slow, tantalizing stroke of his hands. Her head fell back as she basked in the rousing pleasure of his caresses and the scalding heat of his mouth on her breasts.

Inhibitions were more quickly shed than the last of their clothing, and ere the latter settled breathlessly on the floor, no trace of hesitation could be found. As if borne on a cloud, they drifted downward to the snowy white sheets of their marriage bed. It was a seductive, hypnotic ritual of lovers, the pulsating thrill of search and discovery, a sweet and intimate prelude to the delights yet to come. It was the hunger of ravenous kisses, of passions unleashed, of silken limbs twining eagerly around a muscular body, and of hard flesh meeting soft. . . .

They were two beings bound in a sensual embrace as old as time itself, intent upon each other and their newly found ecstasy, poised on the very brink of ultimate possession. A long moment passed before either of them noticed a distant rumbling in the stillness of the night. A frown flickered across Jeff's brow as he realized the sound was not born of the wind blowing through the trees. Indeed, no bridegroom could have been more determined to ignore the intrusion, but try as he might he could not banish the noise to the farthermost reaches of the universe. It grew increasingly louder until it became the rattle of many hooves thundering up the lane in front of the house.

Having failed to relegate the clamor to some distant clime, Jeff raised himself on an elbow and glared toward the bedroom door through which the offending clatter drifted, totally incensed that some of his blundering acquaintances might have chosen this precise moment to pay him a visit.

"I'll kill them!" he growled low. "So help me, if this is some kind of prank my friends have concocted, I'll kill the whole bloody lot of them!"

Sharing his disappointment, Raelynn trembled in frustration beneath him. Even now she could feel the fires cooling in his loins, while the ones in her own body still raged, yearning to be sated. "Who would visit at such an hour?"

Jeff heaved a frustrated sigh. "I'm afraid, my love, we're about to find out."

In the next instant, the front door slammed open, reverberating throughout the house, and a loud shout, heavily tinged with an accent, filled the halls.

"Vhere is zhe master of zhis house? Vhere is zhat rat who stole my voman?"

Raelynn gasped, vividly recalling her revulsion

and rage when her uncle had tried to sell her to the German. "That voice! Oh, Jeff! I'd know it anywhere!" She clasped his arm in distress. "It's Gustav Fridrich!"

Jeff muttered a curse as he rolled from her and came to his feet. Scooping up her chemise, he tossed it to her. "Quickly, my love! Dress yourself!"

As he reached for his breeches and pulled them on, Raelynn slid to her feet and hurriedly settled her undergarment into place. "What will you do, Jeff?"

"Gustav may reign like a ruthless barbarian over feeble old men, but here at Oakley, he'll soon learn he faces a different kind of adversary," he answered. "No man forces his way into my house without answering for it."

His words made his young bride quake with fear. " 'Tis foolishness to think that you can confront Gustav and his men alone, Jeff. You'll not remain unscathed. You've got to flee to safety before it's too late!"

" 'Pon my word, madam. What kind of man do you think me?" Jeff stared at her in astonishment. "I cannot flee and leave so many of mine at the mercy of that brute. I'd be a coward in my own eyes, as well as in yours."

Even before uttering her plea, Raelynn had known he would deny her request, but she had felt strongly compelled to beg him just the same. His reply was no different than her father's had been when Evalina had begged him to make haste and flee from England on a ship. Having had truth on his side, Lord Barrett had thought he'd be victorious over his enemies, but of course that had not been the way of it. Intuition had warned Raelynn that Jeff was a man who took honor and responsibility seriously, even at the expense of his own life, but lofty principles offered little solace to a bereaved widow.

"It didn't take long for Gustav to find out about us," she said, knowing only too well where the information had come from.

"I was wrong to think Cooper Frye would leave us alone," Jeff conceded. " 'Tis sure that he has had some hand in this matter and has deliberately sent the German to vie with me."

"You will be careful, won't you, Jeff!" Raelynn pleaded in deep consternation. "No one can predict what Gustav will do if he's crossed. He could even kill you if he gets the chance."

" 'Tis not my intent to yield him the opportunity, madam," Jeff replied, tossing her a grin as he strode across the room. "Now that I've found you, I have much to live for."

Opening the doors of a large armoire, he took a wooden box from the middle shelf and removed a pair of matching flintlocks. After checking the priming on both, he slid one into the top of his breeches and clasped the other firmly in hand as he went to the bedroom door. Laying a hand on the knob, he turned to face her. "Lock the door behind me, Raelynn," he urged. "I'd not take it kindly if some wayward rogue slipped past me and bundled you off to Gustav's lair."

The door swung closed, and Raelynn stared in frozen dismay at the portal. She waited, expecting to hear some slight sound as Jeff moved down the hall, but there was only the commotion created by the invasion of the brigands. The loudness of their entry stripped away any hope that Jeff would be successful in holding so many men at bay. To be sure, if Kingston no longer was in the house, then her husband would be completely alone when he faced the ruthless rogue and his lawless band.

Her conscience reared up accusingly. This was her fault! Gustav Fridrich would never have come to

Oakley if she hadn't defied her uncle and run away! Burdened by a growing dread of what terrible disaster might befall her husband, Raelynn cringed inwardly as a deep gloom settled its murky shroud over her spirit, coming nigh to smothering her. If the dreaded reaper wreaked the same degree of havoc upon the one she now loved as he had those she had cherished in the past, then surely calamity would have its day. She'd be powerless to stop it!

Chapter 2

Kingston's outraged protests rang out above the din as he confronted the miscreants. "What y'all mean marchin' in here without so much as a purty please or a how yo' do? Y'all acts like yo' done bought this place, lock, stock, an' barrel! But ah knows dat ain't true 'cause Mistah Jeffrey'd die befo' sellin' Oakley ta no-account white trash! Y'all better hightail it on outa here befo' he hears this racket an' comes down ta have a look-see at what's afoot. Or purty soon y'all gonna wish yo'd never laid eyes on this place."

Gustav leaned back his bald head and guffawed loudly toward the ceiling, setting the crystal chandelier a-tinkling with his mirth. "Ja! And you maybe get your throat cut too, black man."

Jeff moved with silent, barefoot tread to the landing above the stairs and stealthily descended until he could see all that transpired in the entrance hall below. He half-perched, half-leaned against the balustrade as he counted better than a score of scruffy, pistol-toting brigands milling about. But instead of watching the doors or stairs for occupants of the house who might come to see what was amiss, they seemed far more intrigued with the bric-a-brac that was temptingly near at hand.

Casually directing the bore of the flintlock toward the huge, bald-headed German, Jeff calmly inquired,

"You are looking for me, Herr Fridrich?"

The shiny pate snapped up with a surprised start, and for a moment Gustav stared in wide-eyed alarm at the threat directed toward him. Then he seemed to rein in his fear. His pale, ice-blue eyes narrowed above a sneer as he threw up a hand in a gesture of defiance. "Are you brave enough to kill Gustav when zhere are at least a score of my men in zhis hall who vill avenge me?"

Jeff lifted his bronze shoulders in an indolent shrug. "I'm sure your men will lose much of their incentive when they realize there's no one left to pay them. In any case you'll be dead, Gustav, and I'm willing to take my chances with your men. As I see it, they'll be like a body without a head, mindless, so to speak."

"*You stole my voman!*" Gustav shouted, shaking a meaty, hammerlike fist at Jeff. "*I pay two hundred fifty Yankee dollars for Cooper Frye to bring zhe vench to me, and you stole her!*"

Jeff thoughtfully contemplated his own forearm as he rubbed the barrel of the flintlock across it. "'Twould seem ol' Cooper Frye has been paid twice for his niece," he pondered aloud, then his eyes rose, and the cold steel of his stare was as threatening as the pistol. "But you'll have to retrieve your money from him or consider it a loss. You see, I gave him more than enough to pay you, seven hundred fifty Yankee dollars to be exact, and since I've already claimed Raelynn Barrett in marriage, I strongly suggest that you and your men leave my house before someone is killed, because I'm not sharing my wife with you or any other man." As if to make his point, Jeff pulled the hammer back on the flintlock. "And I promise you, Herr Fridrich, if you persist in this foolishness, you'll be the first to die."

"*You wouldn't . . .*"

The ear-splitting roar of a pistol being discharged startled the German and made him leap for cover. His bulk slowed his movements, and when a second pistol barked on the heels of the first, he was catapulted backwards by the force of a lead ball plowing into his shoulder. A roaring scream was torn from his throat as he clutched a hand over his wound and writhed in agony on the floor, but his movements cost him dearly as his arm swung limply from a shattered socket. Grinding his teeth against the anguishing pain, he struggled to his knees and lifted a raging snarl toward the man who had challenged him a brief moment ago. His wrath ebbed to an expression of stunned disbelief, for the master of the house had toppled forward from his perch and now was sprawled face-down upon the stairs. A thin wisp of smoke drifted from the bore of his pistol, which was still loosely clutched in his hand, and from the tousled head that dangled over the edge of a step, blood streamed onto the polished surface of the next level, forming a rapidly growing pool of glistening red.

A harsh scream of rage shredded the sudden silence, bringing Gustav around with a start.

"Yo' shot the mastah!" Kingston wailed and vented a tormented sob as he ran toward the stairs.

Gustav snatched his own pistol from his holster and swung it around, leveling it at the servant. He vividly recalled seeing another flintlock in the top of his host's breeches and could only imagine what might befall them if the butler got his hands on it. Snarling a warning through gnashing teeth, he brought the black man to a sudden halt. "Stay where you are or I vill kill you myself!"

"But the mastah!" Kingston sobbed. "He's wounded! Maybe dead!"

"It's too late for him now!" Gustav roared. "If he

is still alive, he vill not be for long, not vith zhat head wound! Now stay vhere you are!"

Kingston moved his eyes carefully askance as he detected the rasping sound of pistols being cocked close behind him. Several ruffians had stepped forward with drawn weapons and were now intimidating him at very close range. Standing very still, he raised his hands in helpless submission.

Gustav turned from the servant and swept a dark scowl over the faces of his men. "Vhich one of you shot Herr Birmingham?"

A curly-haired young scamp named Olney Hyde swaggered forward with a cocky grin and boldly perused the fallen master of the house as he tucked a smoking pistol into his holster. "We couldn't rightly let this here gent kill ye, Gustav, not after ye promised each of us a purse for helping ye, so I aimed for his head and shot him dead." Unaware of Gustav's rapidly approaching advance, he snapped his fingers as he boasted, "The gent fell like a brick! Never knew what hit him."

"*Dummkopf!* You nearly got me killed!" Gustav bellowed, drawing back his good arm and flinging it across the ruffian's face.

Olney was sent flying from the force of the blow, and after sliding across the polished planks of the flooring, he came to rest near the bottom of the stairs where he lay for a moment in a dazed stupor. Shaking his head to clear his befuddled senses, he pushed himself up and stared bleary-eyed at the German.

"Vhen you shot Herr Birmingham," Gustav explained at the top of his lungs, "his pistol vent off and hit me! Now see vhat you've done!" His lips curled with derision as he gestured to the arm that hung slack, then he shook a fist threateningly at the younger man and laid upon him every foul curse that came to mind. His tirade dwindled at last, but not before he vented a final warning. "If I lose zhis arm, Olney Hyde, I swear I vill chop off *yours!*"

His shout reached to the four corners of the house, but Raelynn was already on the run, having heard the shots. Shortly after Jeff had left her, she had rolled her long hair into an untidy knot at her nape and dragged on the drab gown and worn shoes that she had been wearing when she met him. Even shabbily garbed, she was truly a fetching sight. She drew every eye in the hall, and the hired henchmen who stared suddenly understood why Gustav had refused to yield possession of this young woman to another and why he'd been willing to pay a fortune to get her back.

A sudden chill swept Raelynn, turning her blood cold as she approached the landing. For a moment she glared back at the rapscallions, then her gaze descended to the long manly form sprawled motionless on the stairs. A rending cry of despair escaped her as she half-slid, half-stumbled in a hasty descent. A rivulet of blood flowed over the steps from the ever-widening puddle beneath Jeff's head, but she was heedless of the gore soaking into her homespun dress as she gathered her husband's head onto her lap.

"What have I done? What have I done?" She rocked in misery, bewailing her widowhood which had come much too swiftly upon her. Then her gaze fell upon Gustav, and an overwhelming fury was unleashed within her. Shaking uncontrollably, she glared at him through brimming tears. *"Murderer!"*

Gustav pointed to her with a bloody hand as he ordered his men, "Get her!" Pain permeated his voice despite his tone of command. "Ve must go before others come!"

Raelynn pushed Jeff's head from her lap and scrambled up the steps in a desperate attempt to escape, but Olney Hyde was eager to regain his good standing and clambered up the stairs behind her.

"Run, Miz Raelynn!" Kingston shouted and started to follow, but a pistol was quickly directed toward his head.

"If you value your life, black man, you vill think twice before you interfere," Gustav warned gravely.

Olney sprinted quickly up the stairs behind Raelynn, but as she reached the landing, she whirled with an unladylike snarl and kicked at him, nearly catching him in the face. He easily ducked and brought an arm around, sweeping her other leg out from under her. She tumbled forward on top of him, and together they made a rather rapid and bruising descent of the wide stairs, with Olney bearing the brunt of their combined weight. At the bottom of the stairs, Raelynn found her arms seized by two men who hauled her struggling before their leader.

Clasping his shoulder, Gustav stepped forward and jeered in pain-twisted mockery as his pale eyes swept her faded, blood-smeared garb. "For a rich man, your late husband vas not overly generous with you, *mein Liebchen*. Perhaps you'll admire Gustav vhen he buys you pretty clothes, eh?"

"The world will cease to exist ere that day comes, Gustav." Her voice transmitted the sneer visible on her lips. Then her tone grew hushed, and the softness of her velvet-edged threat set the German's heavy nape crawling. "For what you've done, I swear I will take vengeance or die trying."

Gustav forced a grin. "I like a *frau* with spirit. Zhere is more pleasure in conquering her."

Raelynn blanched at his taunt and did not bother to quell a shudder of revulsion as she gazed into his grimacing face. He seemed to revel in the fact that only a weak female opposed him. She saw a cruel savagery in the harsh lines of his countenance that clearly bespoke the true nature of the man. If she had hoped to find some hidden niche of warmth or compassion in this rogue, she realized that here was one who appeased his self-serving interests without regard for those he hurt or maligned along the way. He had no conscience where others were concerned. They were merely beasts to be made to serve his burgeoning will or else be destroyed.

Like shards of blue ice, his eyes pierced to the depths of her searching gaze, bringing a chill to her heart as he lifted a brow in amusement at her stunned incredulity. Others had found cause to fear him, and at that very moment Raelynn knew only too well that she was no exception. Earlier in the evening she had dared to believe that her future would be filled with blissful contentment. Now she foresaw only a living hell.

Gustav clutched his arm tightly against his side, sparing himself the excruciating agony of splintered bones piercing torn flesh. He tore a velvet cord free from a nearby drape and, beckoning one of his cohorts near, bade him to bind the arm close against his side. Though the pain he suffered almost caused his knees to buckle, he stood still while the man complied. White-lipped and stiff-faced, he finally turned to his men. "Two of you ride on ahead to Charleston and fetch *Doktor* Clarence to zhe varehouse. Drag him zhere if you must, but have him vaiting vhen I arrive!"

A pair of men rushed from the hall, and the thundering hoofbeats of their racing steeds gave evidence of their haste. Gustav followed with the rest of the men at a slower pace and was carefully hoisted by four stout-armed cohorts into the back of a buckboard that had been confiscated, along with a harness and team, from the Birmingham stables. Raelynn was lifted to the back of a horse, but any attempt to make good her escape was useless, for the reins were firmly clasped by the man who led her steed behind his own.

The sound of their departure dwindled beneath the loud, wailing moan of the butler as he rushed to the stairs. Kneeling beside his fallen master, Kingston carefully searched the thick crop of short hair and found a long bloody crease in the scalp. As he pulled the gooey strands away from a deep gash of oozing red, he thought he felt a faint stirring of breath on his arm. When he reached down and clasped the lean wrist anxiously between his fingers, he could detect no pulse. But then, his own hands were shaking so hard he could not have discerned the thudding of a steel hammer.

Gathering Jeff's long body in his arms, Kingston staggered unsteadily beneath the burden as he struggled to get to his feet. As he climbed the stairs, tears made wet paths down his dark face as he muttered to himself, "Ah'm gonna kill that bald-headed man, jes' as soon as ah'm able."

As if in answer to his threat, a sudden moan from the man in his arms sent a jolt of prickling surprise through Kingston, threatening to send him sprawling backward down the stairs. He gaped down in wonder as a wincing grimace flickered across the face of his master, and with a sudden thud, Kingston dropped to his knees.

His eyes flicked upward as if he fully expected to see some heavenly being looming above him, but he saw nothing more astonishing than the gleaming crystal chandelier with its brightly glowing tapers, which he had been in the process of snuffing when Gustav and his bullies had bolted through the door. Suddenly he grinned and blinked back new tears, this time of joy.

"The mastah's *alive*! He's alive!"

Drifting upward from a hazy darkness, Jeff clasped a hand to his throbbing head and groaned a question. "What happened?"

"Ah doan know!" Kingston shrugged. "Maybe it was an angel whad touched ya' or some'in.'"

"An angel?" Jeff's confusion deepened as he squinted up at the servant, but his head hurt too much for him to make any sense of the butler's statement. He struggled to sit up and managed to brace himself on the next higher step. Moving his eyes slowly and carefully about in spite of the anguish it caused him, he peered around the hall. He was almost sure that a second ago it had been filled with a bunch of wild and unruly ruffians. Or had he dreamed it all? "Where are Gustav and his men?"

"They left, Mistah Jeffrey, an' they took Miz Raelynn wid 'em."

With a curse Jeff came to his feet, then promptly regretted his rash movement as a harrowing pain filled his head. The world dipped precariously around him. He swayed dizzily on his feet and clasped both hands over his face as he waited for the torment to ease and his equilibrium to return.

Seeing his master's unstable balance, Kingston quickly braced a shoulder beneath the younger man's and carefully turned him toward the upper landing. "Ah'd best get yo' in bed, Mistah Jeffrey, where yo' can rest whilst yo' recollect 'bout whad happened. Ah 'spect yo'll be wantin' ta gather up a body o' men an' ride out aftah Miz Raelynn an' that ol' devil Mistah Fridrich. Ah'll send a rider over ta fetch Mistah Brandon. Won't do for yo' ta go ridin' off widout him, not the way yo' is feelin'."

"I don't even know where they've taken her," Jeff lamented as the servant lent him support down the hall.

"Don't go worryin' 'bout that none, Mistah Jeffrey. Mistah Fridrich told his men ta fetch Doc Clarence so's that ol' man could mend his wounds. Wid Doc Clarence a-thinkin' the Birmin'ham family is mighty special, he'll be tellin' yo' what yo' needs ta know or my name ain't Kingston Tucker."

Jeff's brows creased together, conveying his confusion. "How did Fridrich get hurt?"

Kingston grinned as he pushed open the door to the master bedroom. "Yo' did it, Mistah Jeffrey. When that other young scamp shot yo', your pistol went off, an' the ball went straight inta Mistah Fridrich's shoulder an' made his arm hang like it was broke. Yo' maybe didn' know it at the time, but your aim was nigh as true as ever."

Kingston carefully lowered his wounded master to the edge of the bed, and for a long moment Jeff sat rubbing his temples, trying to massage away the piercing discomfort. When he drew his hands away, he stared at his fingers that were now liberally covered with blood. " 'Twould seem I've got a new part in my hair, Kingston."

The butler chuckled at his master's undaunted humor. "They left here a-thinkin' yo' was dead, Mistah Jeffrey, or at least near 'bouts. Miz Raelynn was a-thinkin' so, too. She swore she'd make Mistah Fridrich pay or die tryin'."

"They'll be a bit more careless if they think I'm dead," Jeff remarked as Kingston spread several linen towels across the pillow to protect it from the bloodstains. "But I must find them before Gustav turns his attention upon Raelynn."

"Ah s'pect that man'll be hurtin' too much ta be thinkin' o' doin' anythin' like that, Mistah Jeffrey, so's yo' can just rest yo'self a spell whilst yo' wait for Mistah Brandon ta get here." Kingston eased Jeff back upon the bed and swung his legs onto the mattress. "Ah ain't no doctor, but the way it looked ta me, that ol' pirate might never use that arm again."

Kingston poured water from a pitcher into a wash basin and, dampening a cloth, began to gently dab at the wound.

"Don't bother about me now, Kingston," Jeff urged, taking the rag from him. "I need you to go now and send a rider over to fetch my brother. Send another to Charleston to tell Sheriff Rhys Townsend what has happened. Make sure he understands how many of Gustav's toughs we'll be facing. We'll have need of every man who's willing to help us."

"Yassuh, Mistah Jeffrey!" With that, Kingston hurried from the room, leaving Jeff to close his eyes against the throbbing torment in his head.

Raelynn stood in a shadowed corner of the cluttered warehouse apartment and watched in darkly brooding silence as Gustav tipped a jug of whiskey to his mouth and gulped down a long draught. The doctor, an elderly gentleman with white hair and a small neat mustache and beard, was in a highly agitated state of irritation when they arrived and was not above verbally venting some of that frustration upon his patient.

"I told you before, Gustav! Now it's evident that I'll have to tell you again! I'm tired of patching you up!" he ranted. "No sooner do I get you sewn up and on your feet again, than you're off battling some other rascal. You'd better start considering the dangers of associating with riffraff or learn to rein in your temper while you're among them. Or one of these days your men will be bringing you back in a pine box."

"Leave off zhe preaching," Gustav muttered irascibly. "I hurt too much to take it kindly."

The physician snorted in contempt. "Well, I don't mean it kindly at all! I told you the last time I patched you up that I was fed up with being summoned here! If you foolishly ignore my advice, then I don't want anything more to do with you!"

"Yu fix my arm zhis time. Next time maybe I vill listen."

"Not likely!" Dr. Clarence scoffed. Still, he cut away the bloody shirt with gentle concern and carefully examined the wound. Then he voiced his prognosis with a heavy sigh of exasperation. "The ball will have to come out, of course. Otherwise, 'twill poison your blood. If that happens, you'll likely lose your arm . . . or your life. I'll have to remove it without delay, plus whatever loose splinters of bone I can find."

"You tell me nothing I do not know already!" Gustav growled. "Get on vith it!"

"You'd have fared better if the shot had gone clear through your shoulder," Dr. Clarence prodded.

"Just do vhat you must. I'll not abide zhe loss of *mein* arm."

"Better the loss of your arm than your life."

Raelynn mentally jeered at the wise counsel. *If not for this brutish oaf*, she wanted to scream at the doctor, *my husband would still be alive and I'd be safe in his arms!* In silent hostility she scanned Gustav's massive, barrel chest as she remembered her husband's tautly muscled torso that only a few short eons ago she had been admiring.

Tears filled her eyes as a vision of Jeff lying on the stairs with his life's blood flowing from him came back to haunt her. The truth chafed accusingly as it turned inward. Jeff would still be alive if not for her. In agreeing to marry him, she had brought the sentence of death upon him. She could not even hope for a child to remember him by. Although definitely more mature in her knowledge of men since she awoke that morning, she was still a virgin, a fact

which could only be attributed to Jeff's gentle care
of her.

And now, this was to be her punishment. She
would be the plaything of this foul, despicable brute
who knew no kinder emotion than lust and greed.
He would ravish her, having no care how he bruised
and violated her. Her only quest in life now would
be to see him die, not swiftly but a slow torturous
death, for surely that was how she would suffer for
leading this monster to Jeff.

Gustav's harsh scream wrenched Raelynn from
her musings, seeming to fulfill her wishful bent. At
present, three of Gustav's men were holding him
down on the mattress as the doctor probed the
wound with metal instruments. Quietly she moved
forward to stand at the end of the bed, and when
her eyes met Gustav's, he ground his teeth to sub-
due another outcry and shuddered in silence against
the anguishing torment.

"How brave you are, Gustav," Raelynn chided
tauntingly. "Indeed, you squall as loudly as a babe
who's lost his sugar-sop."

Dr. Clarence glanced at her in surprise, convinced
that Gustav had chosen a cold-hearted bit of baggage to wile away his nights with. Then he followed
her penetrating glare back to his patient. Her hatred
was almost tangible, which he could not as yet understand. For all he knew, she had come willingly
to the warehouse apartment. But then, if one cared
to take note, the young man, Olney Hyde, seemed
to hover threateningly near her.

"Make yourself useful, girl," Dr. Clarence ordered, piercing her with a scowl before he jerked his
head toward the jug of whiskey. "Wash away some
of this blood with that brew."

Raelynn raked Gustav's paunchy form with a contemptuous perusal, then she raised a bland stare to the doctor. "Why should I?"

In the next moment Olney grabbed her arm in a painful vise and pressed the bore of a pistol against her temple. " 'Cause if'n ye don't, ye red-headed tart, ye're gonna be layin' six feet under."

At the metallic scrape of the weapon's hammer being drawn back, Raelynn's blood chilled in her veins. Death was only a heartbeat away, yet the memory of her slain husband made her consider the benefits of her own demise. At least her conscience would no longer accuse her.

Lifting her slender shoulders in a challenging mood of indifference, Raelynn sneered in the face of his threat. "Better that than bedding down with the filthy boar."

For a split second, Olney stared down at her in slack-jawed amazement, never having seen a man, much less a woman, who could scoff so easily with a cocked pistol pressed to the head.

Dr. Clarence straightened indignantly. "Put that damn cannon down before it blows a hole through that girl's head!" he rumbled in outrage. "Or so help me, I'll let this man die beneath my scalpel!"

"Olney! Do vhat he says!" Gustav barked. Snatching up the jug again, he swilled down several more gulps in an effort to dull his senses, shaking all the while against the agony that raked him.

With an indolent shrug of his shoulders, Olney relented and lifted the bore of the pistol away from Raelynn's head. Mimicking a courtly bow, he stepped back several paces, giving her breathing room.

"If you're not too squeamish, girl," Dr. Clarence persisted impatiently, "I could use your help."

Raelynn swept a hand about the room, indicating the half-dozen scamps who stood around guzzling from their own jugs. "I'm sure these men are far more willing to see Herr Fridrich survive than I am. I was married tonight and that German oaf killed my husband before bringing me here to this den of murdering thieves. 'Tis only a matter of time before I take my revenge, and if I help you, I'll do everything I can to see that Gustav doesn't last through the night."

Gustav snorted through his pain. "Maybe I let my men have you first, eh Frau Birmingham."

"Birmingham?" Dr. Clarence repeated incredulously. Glancing at the German and then at Raelynn, he gruffly demanded, "Do you mean to say, girl, that you married Jeffrey Birmingham this evening and that he is now dead?"

Sudden tears brightened Raelynn's eyes as she nodded. "Gustav and his men broke into Oakley Plantation house and shot him while I was upstairs."

With a muttered curse, Dr. Clarence threw down the scalpel and began to pace about the room in deepening perturbation. "Thirty-odd years ago, I brought Jeff Birmingham into this world. I was sent for when they discovered he was breech. His mother valiantly endured the pain to give life to her babe. Since then, I've seen few men who could equal the worth of the Birminghams. Now you tell me Jeff has been killed and I must tend the wounds of his murderer! Devil take you all, you filthy rodents! I will not!"

Gustav's eyes shot bolts of fire at the doctor. The pain in his shoulder was of far more consequence to him than the slaying of Jeff or any discomfort the girl might have felt over the loss of her new husband. With an angry snarl and a snap of his fingers, Gustav sent Olney back to Raelynn's side with the flintlock. Once again, the weapon was pressed to her temple and the hammer pulled back. "The girl vill die, *Doktor*, if you do not mend my shoulder. And I promise you this, if Olney kills her, I vill kill you."

Dr. Clarence glowered back at him for a moment. Then, having no other choice, he nodded once in mute acquiescence. Taking up the instruments again, he waited until the pistol was raised from Raelynn's head and then bent to his labors again.

Gustav lost consciousness as the ball was removed. Several pieces of splintered bone were taken out as well. It was then that Raelynn consented to give aid, but only to wipe the elderly doctor's brow. Even so, Olney stood close behind her, ready to take her life if the scalpel slipped.

At last, the wound was closed and dressed in a heavy bandage that bound the arm tightly against the German's side. Gustav roused briefly while this was being done, but he was in so much pain he was eager to swallow the draught of laudanum which the old man spooned into his mouth. When the German slipped into the nether depths of slumber, Dr. Clarence began to gather his tools.

"I'm going home to clean up," he informed Gustav's men, "but I'll be back in two hours to check on him. If the bleeding starts again, send a rider over to fetch me, but let me warn you men. If I should find the girl harmed in any way upon my return, Gustav will rot in his own gore, that much I promise you."

Dr. Clarence made his departure, reluctantly leaving Raelynn behind to watch over her captor. Though his home was no more than five blocks away, it seemed a thousand miles had been traversed before he finally pulled his horse-drawn buggy to a halt near the stable and climbed down.

"Dr. Clarence?"

The old man squinted as he peered into the shadows from whence the voice had come. He had cause to be apprehensive, for it was the second time in a few hours that a voice had called to him from the darkness. He could only consider the consequences to Raelynn if someone else had dictated that he be taken elsewhere. "Who is it? What do you want?"

"We need your help, Dr. Clarence."

The voice came again from the deep gloom, and the doctor watched warily as a pair of tall, darkly garbed men approached. They passed through a mottled patch of moonlight shining through the branches of a towering oak, prompting Dr. Clarence to gawk in disbelief as he recognized the leaner one of the two. "Jeffrey Birmingham! What great miracle is this? I was told you were dead."

"He very nearly was," Brandon Birmingham answered ruefully, laying a hand on his brother's shoulder. "He's got a deep gash in his head from a lead ball to prove it."

"We need your help, Dr. Clarence," Jeff repeated as he halted beside the elder. "You've got to tell us where they've taken my wife, Raelynn."

"I'll gladly tell you, Jeff," Dr. Clarence readily replied, "but the two of you can't go after those thugs alone. You'll both be killed!"

"We have seven mounted riders hidden in the trees behind your house, and hopefully another dozen or so will be coming with the sheriff. We sent word on ahead, so Rhys will know how many of Gustav's men we'll be facing. It all depends on how many deputies he's been able to summon at this time of the morning."

"They'll kill Raelynn if you're not careful," the old doctor cautioned. "They forced me to mend Gustav's shoulder by holding a pistol to her head. That young whelp, Olney, might do it just for the sheer pleasure of killing someone. I heard some scuttlebutt about him being the one who shot you, Jeff. Believe me, he's as dangerous as a coiled rattler."

"If Olney kills her, then he'll have to answer to Gustav," Jeff reasoned, "and I don't think he wants to do that. It might mean his life. When do they expect you to return?"

"In two hours or less."

"Tell us where they're hiding," Brandon urged. "We'll need to know as much about the place as you can offer, then we'll be able to lay out a plan."

"You two should know the place. They're at old Milburn's warehouse, just a few blocks from here."

"I thought they'd be hiding out somewhere else," Jeff remarked.

"When Gustav has an army of men always around to protect him, why should he be afraid that someone will disturb him in his den?" Dr. Clarence reasoned. "Besides, the man has as many lives as a cat."

"We're familiar with the warehouse," Brandon informed the surgeon. "In fact, Jeff almost purchased it at one time, but he decided it was too far away from the docks to be of much benefit for the shipping trade."

"Gustav has taken residence in an apartment that he's created for himself on the ground level of the warehouse," Dr. Clarence advised them. "Most of his men will probably be in there with him, but you can expect there will be several guards watching for trouble on the outside."

Jeff faced Dr. Clarence as a strategy began to take shape in his mind. "After you return and finish with Gustav, try to stand near the door with Raelynn. When you hear a soft bird chirp from outside, suggest that she'll feel better after a breath of air. Insist upon it. If Gustav is awake, ask him if she can go for a walk outside. As long as he thinks his men are guarding the place and can watch over her, he should give his consent. By that time, I hope I'll have replaced his sentries with some of our own men."

Dr. Clarence rubbed his bearded chin reflectively. "Your plan might work if all goes well. At least it will allow me to get Raelynn out before any gunshots are fired."

A flash of white teeth gleamed in the moonlit gloom as Jeff grinned. "And I'll be there at the door to whisk her to safety."

Dr. Clarence laid a hand on his arm. "Just remember, lad. Raelynn thinks you're dead. It will be quite a shock for her when she sees you."

"I'll try not to frighten her unduly," Jeff assured him. Facing the doctor's house, he contemplated the large striped cat that sat preening himself on the front porch and quickly added the finishing touches to his plan. "Do you mind if we borrow that old tomcat of yours?"

"Felix?" Dr. Clarence was confused by the request but readily complied. "You're welcome to him, Jeff. But why?"

"Felix just might create the kind of diversion we'll need to get the guards' attention, especially if the cat is being chased by the sheriff's hound. We'll also need that muzzle you once fashioned to fit over Felix's head when he was meowing after every female cat in town."

Dr. Clarence glanced at Brandon, who was just as baffled, but after a moment the physician suddenly found reason to chortle. "I pity Townsend's hound if he catches Felix. That old cat has been known to tear up quite a few mongrels in his time."

His comment drew chuckles from the other two, but Jeff went on to reassure him. "Townsend has a special whistle that brings the dog back to him at a run. If all goes well, neither of the animals will get hurt."

"I'm not worried, Jeff. I know you'll take care of

Felix. He's always enjoyed the tidbits you've brought him on your visits." The elder grew serious. "But I do fear for you and your friends. I've made several trips to the warehouse to tend Gustav and his men, and at various times I noticed long crates stacked way back in the warehouse almost to the ceiling, the sort that muzzle-loaders and such are shipped in. It wouldn't surprise me at all to learn that Gustav has set up a large armory for himself inside the warehouse. He certainly has enough men to use whatever weapons he may have amassed. You could start a war, you know."

"Once Raelynn is safe, the sheriff can deal with Gustav and his men as he sees fit," Jeff replied. "There's been some talk lately about smugglers in the area. Townsend may decide to look through the warehouse, just to see what he can find."

The old man thumped Jeff's chest gently with an aging forefinger as he chuckled. "Advise your friend to have a close look at my patient while he's there. Gustav could stand a long rest in jail to recuperate from his wounds. Considering the frequency of his injuries, he might live longer if he's locked away."

"I'm sure Townsend will do what he can to accommodate your request. He's as curious about Gustav as we are."

Dr. Clarence grew solemn again. "Gustav isn't what you'd call a forgiving sort, Jeff. If you manage to get Raelynn back, he'll likely come after her again . . . if he isn't put away."

"I intend to see that he is," Jeff assured the physician. "If Gustav's not a smuggler, then at the very least he's a kidnapper."

" 'Twill only be a matter of time before he's out again, then what?"

"I just might have to kill the man myself."

Chapter 3

Two tall men in dark apparel flitted along the alley-way until they reached a corner of the structure that stood across the street from the old Milburn build-ing. There, from the protective darkness, the pair observed the sentries who were guarding the warehouse. Several lanterns had been hung to light the area in front of the edifice, and as the two guards strode back and forth across the full length of it, they were wont to pause in passing and exchange a bit of conversation before moving on to the opposite ends. There they turned and strolled back.

A broad-shouldered hulk of a man joined the pair who watched from hiding and, with a low disgruntled grunt, shoved the muzzled cat into the arms of the one who stood nearest him.

"Here!" Sheriff Rhys Townsend leaned near Jeff to hiss. "This was your damn fool idea, so I'll let you have the divine privilege of holding this infernal beast. With all these claw marks on my arms, my wife is bound to wonder what she-cat I've been bedding down with, and we haven't even been married long enough to have had our first fight yet. Besides, it looks like the two of you will be needing this wild-cat more than Farrell and I will."

With a grin, Jeff gathered the struggling cat against him and almost immediately Felix quieted, recognizing a familiar friend. When Jeff scratched him behind the ear and stroked his back, the animal began to purr in delight.

The sudden change in Felix's disposition drew another disgusted snort from the sheriff. "I tried doing that, just like you told me," Rhys Townsend grumbled in a raspy whisper, "but that ornery critter refused to mind his manners."

Brandon wiped a hand across his mouth to curb his own mirth. It was a known fact that this huge hunk of a sheriff didn't like cats any better than he did poisonous snakes. "Never mind the excuses, Rhys," he murmured through a grin. "We understand that you're skittish around cats and don't hold it against you. The problem, as I see it, is that Felix knows it, too."

Townsend cut his eyes sharply, fixing his friend with an exasperated glower. "I haven't seen you nuzzling up to the thing!"

Brandon spread his hands to protest his innocence. "Can I help it if I like dogs better?"

"Humph! No one can make me believe that Jeff Birmingham prefers cats over dogs," the sheriff commented. "Not with all those hounds I've seen around Oakley."

Brandon grinned at the very idea. "Jeff would have had a menagerie in the house if Ma had let him."

Jeff approached the more pressing matter at hand as he asked the lawman, "What did you find in the back?"

"Two guards, just like here in the front, but the area's not as well lighted, so we'll have the advantage. Farrell said he could wait around the far corner without being seen and grab the guard closest to him when he makes his turn. I'll take the other one about the same time. What about the two of you?"

"Once Felix has claimed the guards' attention, Brandon and I can take care of these two." Jeff laid a hand on his friend's arm and urged, "When you grab the two in back, make sure they don't have a chance to set up a hew and cry beyond what the cat and dog will make. We'll have to get Raelynn and Dr. Clarence out alive, and we can't charge into the warehouse until we do."

Rhys Townsend chuckled softly as he unhooked a heavy cudgel from his belt and slowly slapped it in the palm of his hand. "Once we smack 'em alongside their heads with a pair o' these, those guards'll collapse like flies who've given up living."

"Just leave 'em breathing, will ya?" Brandon quipped with wry humor. "I've sparred in fun with Farrell Ives enough to know he packs a powerful wallop."

Townsend's broad shoulders shook briefly with silent amusement before he leaned forward to whisper, "You can bet that fancy man didn't learn to fight like a warrior in that elegant clothier shop he owns."

Brandon grinned. "You'd better not let Farrell hear you calling him a fancy man or you'll get the chance to count your teeth when you pick 'em up off the floor."

Rhys shrugged. "Oh, he's heard me all right, but he knows I'm just jealous of his good looks and all those fine clothes he wears. I wouldn't intentionally insult him in his hearing. My mama didn't raise a nitwit."

With a casual salute, the sheriff grinned and crept away. Soon his large bulk was shrouded by darkness. A moment passed before the two guards came together again in front of the warehouse. Jeff lifted a hand and silently motioned to his brother, sending Brandon flitting quickly along the side of the building where they stood. Rounding the back corner at a run, he disappeared behind it.

Jeff waited, giving Brandon time to get into position at the far end of the structure, then he removed the muzzle from the cat and tossed him gently in the direction of the warehouse. Felix lit on all fours without emitting a sound, then paused to casually survey his surroundings. He began to stroll leisurely along the street toward the guards, but when the silence was abruptly rent by a loud barking, the tomcat crouched in sudden alarm and looked back along the dark street in the direction from which the disturbance was coming. When a huge dog bounded into view, Felix took off with a shriek, setting the two guards to guffawing as the animal tore down the street toward them. The hound gave chase, and only Jeff saw Brandon dart across the street behind the laughing guards and disappear into the inky blackness at the far end of the warehouse. When the two sentinels turned to watch the animals, Jeff dashed to the opposite end and pressed back into a wedge of ebony shadows.

The front door of the warehouse opened, and Olney leaned out to demand, "What the devil's going on out there?"

One of the guards waved away his concern. "Nothing to worry about. Just a dog chasing a cat. How's Gustav?"

"Much better. The doc is with him now, givin' him more o' that sleepin' potion. Ye boys keep it quiet out there so's he can rest."

The door closed, and the guards resumed their pacing, passing each other as they strolled to the far corners of the warehouse. As they made their turn, a sudden sharp blow on the head sent each of them into a state of unconsciousness. Soon they were tied up, gagged, and dragged around the corner of the building, where they were dumped.

Inside the warehouse apartment, Dr. Clarence closed his satchel and, taking it in hand, approached Raelynn. She sat slumped in a chair near the door, looking completely exhausted and thoroughly dejected. It seemed unusually good timing that he heard a soft chirp just outside the portal as he laid a comforting hand upon her shoulder.

"A walk outside will do you good, child," he advised. "You've breathed enough of this foul, dank air to make you sick. Come outside and see me off, then you can spread a blanket near Gustav's bed and try to get some sleep. None of his men will dare bother you."

Raelynn came slowly to her feet and glanced questioningly at Olney. "May I go outside for a while with the doctor?"

"Ye may," he answered with a smirk, basking in the authority he had been given over the two, "but remember . . . If ye try to escape, I'll shoot the doctor and chain ye to Gustav's bed. Ye'll be the first face he sees when he wakes."

Raelynn trembled, too fatigued to ignore his threats. She nodded meekly, and the doctor opened the door for her. Crossing her arms beneath her bosom, she heaved a disconcerted sigh and stepped out into the lantern-lit darkness. Beyond the buildings to the east she could detect a subtle lightening of the night sky that heralded the coming of dawn.

Olney came to stand in the portal behind her and called to the tall, darkly garbed man striding to the far corner. "Ye watch them real good now. The girl's not to leave, do ye hear?"

"I hear," came a mumbled reply.

The door closed, and suddenly the guards whirled and came running toward them. The doctor grabbed

Raelynn's hand and, bending low, pushed his face near hers, claiming her complete attention.

"Take hold of yourself, girl. You're in for a shock."

Raelynn moaned in distress and tried to withdraw. "Please, I'm too tired to cope with anything else."

One of the guards stepped beside the doctor, no doubt to prevent any trickery they might have been discussing, but she turned aside, refusing to acknowledge his very presence. She had had her fill of Gustav's toughs.

"Raelynn?"

Her breath caught in her throat. The rogue's voice was soft and cajoling, sounding very much like . . . like Jeff's!

But surely her beleaguered brain was playing tricks on her. . . .

"Dear Raelynn, will you not look at me?" the man softly queried.

She whirled, glaring through sudden tears. No filthy charlatan had a right to mimic the genteel manners of her husband . . . or his voice!

Then her eyes lit on the all-too-familiar face, and the shock came with as much force as a blow. Her knees buckled beneath her, and if not for Jeff springing forward and catching her, she would have slumped to the ground.

"You're alive! You're alive!" she raved excitedly as he drew her up against him. She clutched at him, hardly able to believe this moment was real, that he was really alive! Her hand shook as she touched his cheek. "But I saw you lying deathly still upon the stairs! And there was so much blood! I thought you *were* dead! Did my eyes deceive me? How can you be standing here now as if nothing had happened?"

"I was only wounded, my love," he averred with

a smile. "The shot creased my scalp and knocked me unconscious. That was all."

Brandon had halted nearby and glanced toward the far end of the warehouse as the sheriff came running around the corner. Laying a hand on his brother's arm, he urgently implored, "Jeff, we've got to get Raelynn out of here now. Townsend and the men are ready to storm the warehouse, and if she's still here when Gustav's bullies put up a show of resistance, she may get hurt in the crossfire."

"Let me take her to Oakley," Dr. Clarence urged. "My buggy is nearby."

"Heather will be there to take care of her," Brandon informed them. "She was going to have one of the servants drive her over after I left. She'll be relieved to have Raelynn back safe and sound."

Despite the offers of help, the young bride clung desperately to her husband, too afraid to chance letting him go. "But can't you take me home yourself, Jeff?"

Dr. Clarence kindly offered an explanation. "Your husband will be needed here, my dear, to set aside any lie Gustav may try to pass off on the sheriff." The old man laid a gentle hand on her arm and cajoled, "Come, child. You can find the rest you need at Oakley. Brandon's wife will be there to watch over you and give you comfort, and Jeff will come as soon as he's able. Doctor's orders, you know."

Raelynn was deaf to the old man's logic and resisted his efforts to draw her away. "But what if something should happen to you, Jeff?" she argued, her voice choked by tears. "I thought I had lost you before. I would simply die if I lost you now."

Gathering her close, Jeff laid his cheek against her sweetly scented hair as he turned her statement around. "And what would I do, my love, if you were wounded or killed in the fray?" he asked tenderly. "What if some of Gustav's men escaped and found you? I'd never forgive myself if they stole you away again. The safest place for you to be right now is on your way back to Oakley. I'll send a couple of men back with you to make sure you and the doctor arrive safely."

Raelynn groaned, understanding his reasoning, yet unwilling to be parted from him. Still, she could not easily ignore the men who were waiting to rush the warehouse. It seemed she had no choice but to relent. "I'll go to Oakley," she mumbled gloomily. "But I won't rest until I know you're safe."

Jeff leaned down to press his lips near her ear. "Wait for me in my bed, my love. Ere the sun rises and sets again, we'll share it together as man and wife."

Sheriff Rhys Townsend laid a hand on the sturdy iron grip of the door and, without so much as a knock or a salutation, threw the heavy portal open and rushed inward with a pair of pistols drawn. Several miscreants scrambled for cover, firing their weapons as they went. The deafening din wrenched Gustav awake with a startled jerk. He lay in paralyzed fear upon his bed as lead balls zinged in a crisscrossed pattern overhead. Even in his dazed stupor, he realized the folly of trying to rise.

Jeff bolted through the door, discharging his dueling pistols toward the crates from whence other shots were being fired. Brandon followed hard on his heels, and bedlam erupted as a dozen men charged in behind him, brandishing arms of one kind or another. The deputies quickly dispersed inside the warehouse apartment, and a mad scramble ensued as the rogues tried to find a way of escape. But the windows were barred and the doors could not be safely reached. Firing haphazardly to cover their retreat, the brigands turned and fled into the main warehouse where they hid behind stacked crates or hunkered down in whatever nook or cranny afforded them protection. The air fairly cracked with a barrage of gunfire, and all the while Gustav lay in frantic confusion upon his bed. Dazed by the heavy draught of laudanum, he could only wait for someone to come to his rescue.

Raising a hand, Jeff caught Townsend's attention and gestured to the bed. The leader of the ruffians was obviously at their mercy, and what better way to end the conflict than to point that fact out to his men. The sheriff grinned, catching Jeff's meaning, and sprinted quickly across the apartment to force his presence upon their unwilling host.

Gustav gulped as he stared in wide-eyed alarm into the bore of the pistol that was suddenly thrust into his face.

"Now, you hold still, ya' hear," Townsend advised with an exaggerated drawl and a disturbingly complacent grin. "Else I'm gonna have to hurt you a *lot*."

Gustav tightened his slackened jowls and glared at Townsend over the barrel of the gun. "Vhat is zhe meaning of zhis?" he demanded. "Vhat right do you have to barge in here and threaten me and my men?"

"Why, I can't believe ya don't know me, Mistah Frederick. 'Round these here parts I'm known as the sheriff." Townsend was enjoying himself immensely and gestured casually with his weapon as he talked. After several moments elapsed, he noticed the German's rapt attention with the bore of the pistol as it bobbed up and down before his eyes. Raising the sights charitably to the ceiling above their heads, Townsend grinned down at the man. "But let me introduce myself, Mistah Frederick. I'm Sheriff Rhys Townsend."

"I know who you are, you imbecile!" Gustav snarled in rampant disgust. "And my name is *Fridrich*! Gustav Fridrich!"

"Well, *Fridrich*, let me tell ya another thing. If'n your men don't put down their weapons, y'all gonna be in a mighty heap o' trouble. So what's it gonna be? The surrender of your men . . . or your immediate arrest?"

"Do I have a choice in zhe matter?" the German queried derisively.

"Nope," Townsend replied with cocksure certainty.

Gustav fixed him with a stony glare as he mulled over his options, but even with his thoughts muddled, he grasped the full import of the situation. The sheriff had offered him no alternative; he had to comply or be arrested. And no telling what would happen if he left the warehouse to the lawman's discretion.

"Zhis is Gustav speaking! I say to my men, lay down your veapons," he called out, straining to be heard. "If you can hear me, tell zhose who cannot! The sheriff vill take me in if you continue to resist." The gunfire began to slacken as other voices passed his message on. "Believe me! A mistake has been made. Do not fear vhat zhe sheriff vill do to you. He cannot arrest you without a reason."

Townsend considered the German with blatant skepticism. "Seeing as how you and your rowdies barged into Mistah Jeffrey's house, shot him and made off with his bride, not to mention a few horses and gear, I'd say I've got some dastardly good reasons to arrest the lot of you."

"Zhat thief stole my voman!" Gustav railed. "I have zhe bill of sale to prove zhe girl is mine, bought and paid for in Charleston zhis very afternoon!"

"You mean yesterday afternoon, don't ya?" Townsend needled. "Maybe you don't know it, but the sun is coming up on a new day."

"Vhatever! It makes no difference!"

"Well, I'd like to be straight about the time," the sheriff prodded. " 'Cause it might clarify your motives and mean the difference between your arrest for kidnapping and horse thieving or your release on the grounds that you were attempting to retrieve some property you actually laid out money for."

"No matter vhat time I bought her, she is still mine! And I can prove vhat I say!" Gustav looked around until he spied Olney. He gestured imperiously toward a desk as he bade the younger man, "Fetch zhat paper Cooper Frye signed."

A tall, good-looking gentleman, who sported a flawlessly clipped Vandyke beard, approached the foot of the bed. Briefly his eyes passed over a rumpled and rather gaudy frockcoat and a feathered hat hanging on a nearby clothes tree, but the pained frown that flickered across his brow was short-lived. His own clothes were dark and suitable for the mission he had been called upon. Even so, the garments were stylish and fit his muscular, square-shouldered frame superbly. Returning his gaze to the occupant of the bed, he bestowed a dazzling white-toothed grin upon the injured man as he presented himself.

"I'm Farrell Ives, and although we've never met, I've heard of you. I own a clothier shop here in Charleston, which you obviously know nothing about, but I can assure you it was right there on the boardwalk in front of my establishment that Jeffrey Birmingham bought Miss Raelynn Barrett from her uncle, as I and . . ."—he inclined his head toward his companions—"a goodly number of these gentlemen here can attest to. I understand that my friend married her, too, so I rather think that makes her his."

"*Zhe vench is mine!*" Gustav bellowed. Receiving a folded piece of parchment from Olney, he issued a snort of derision as he sailed it toward the sheriff. "Zhere is my proof! Let Herr Birmingham provide evidence zhat the girl is his, *if* he can! Let him stake his claim to her, *if* he is here!"

A shuffling of feet marked the opening of a passage as the men who had crowded into the apartment stepped back, allowing the Birmingham brothers to approach the bed. Gustav and Olney gaped in shock, for they could not mistake Jeff Birmingham. The one who followed had to be closely related, for the resemblance he bore to the other was astounding.

Halting beside the bed, Jeff gave the German a bland smile as he handed Townsend a lading bill upon which he had written out his contract with Cooper Frye. He now used it as a receipt to verify his purchase of Raelynn. "I'm not a ghost," he assured Gustav. "Your lackey was just a poor shot, that's all."

Olney bristled at the insult, but he rushed to his own defense. " 'Twas an accident!" he cried. "I didn't mean to shoot ye!"

Brandon's brief, sardonic laugh assailed his assertion. "That's not what I've heard."

Jeff settled a dubious stare upon the young hellion. "Nor I. You remember my butler, don't you? Well, Kingston swears he heard you boasting about aiming your pistol at my head and shooting me. That doesn't sound like an accident to me."

Olney sneered. "Who'd take a black man's word over mine?"

Townsend paused in his scrutiny of the receipts and settled a baleful squint on the man until Olney, feeling the penetrating heat of his stare, turned a questioning gaze to him.

"You're looking at the man," Townsend informed him bluntly.

"Looking at the m-man?" Olney stammered. "What do you mean?"

"What cha do, boy? Forget what ya said?" Townsend goaded, drawing hearty laughter from his deputies. "You're not very smart, are ya? Maybe I need to spell it out for you so there won't be any question about it. I'll take Kingston's word over yours anytime, any day."

Olney had a strong sense of self-preservation. Flying into a temper, he jabbed a finger accusingly at Jeff. "This fella was threatenin' Mr. Fridrich with a loaded pistol! And ye can see that he shot him, too!"

"How easily you forget, boy!" Townsend admonished. "Mr. Fridrich was an intruder in the Birmingham house! He went there to steal this man's *wife!*"

Gustav broke into the verbal fray with a shout of denial. *"Nein!* She is mine! Bought and paid for!"

With a wry grimace, Townsend scrubbed a hand over his bewhiskered chin as he glanced down at Jeff's voucher. Then he cleared his throat. "Well now! 'Tis clear that Cooper Frye signed his name to both documents, but if it's a matter of who paid more for the girl, Mr. Birmingham's got you beat, Mr. Fridrich, by three times as much."

"It does not matter who paid more! Vhat is important is who bought her first!" Gustav ground his teeth against the pain evoked by his movements as he braced himself up on an elbow. "Cooper Frye came to me about four in zhe afternoon and said zhis man had made an offer to buy his niece. Right zhen, I gave him two hundred fifty Yankee dollars for her and made him sign a receipt. Vhen I sent my man to fetch her to my varehouse, Cooper Frye told him zhat Herr Birmingham had stolen his niece and taken her home vith him. He said *noth*ing about Herr Birmingham paying for her! If he has a receipt, zhen he must have bought her after zhat!"

" 'Twould seem that Cooper Frye has cheated you, Herr Fridrich," Jeff informed him bluntly. "By the time four o'clock rolled past, ol' Coop was already richer by seven hundred fifty Yankee dollars. 'Twas at least an hour earlier when he acquired that sum from me as payment for his niece."

"*Nein!*" Angrily Gustav shook his head. "Cooper Frye vould not dare cheat me!"

Jeff smiled derisively. "I surmise, Herr Fridrich, that your confidence in the integrity of the man may be based on some mistaken idea that he's frightened of you." He indulged the German by explaining with terse impatience. "After taking money from me, Cooper Frye met with you and sold his niece for a second time in so many hours. Face it, Gustav. You've been duped, by an Englishman right off the boat from London."

Farrell Ives stepped forward again, capturing the sheriff's attention. "I was there, Rhys. I saw it all happen. At a quarter till two yesterday afternoon, I heard Cooper Frye say that he had promised his niece to Gustav Fridrich. By two-thirty, Jeff had already given Cooper Frye his money and the man had gone on his way. Nearly half the town was there to witness the event."

At least half a dozen men nodded in affirmation, prompting Townsend to return Jeff's receipt to him. Tilting his head aslant, the sheriff considered Gustav at some length. " 'Twould appear you've been rooked by a crafty old crow, Mr. Fridrich. But since you've provided proof that you actually bought the girl, I guess I can't arrest you for kidnapping. Horse-thieving maybe, but I expect you were in a bit of an anxious rush to get fixed up by Dr. Clarence. Still, I'd advise you to stay away from the Birminghams from now on. Otherwise, I'll have to consider you a menace to the peace of this area." He handed over the German's receipt as he continued. "On another unrelated matter, I'd like your permission to look through your warehouse. I've heard some allegations that you and your men have been smuggling, and if I can, I'd like to put down such rumors as pure speculation."

Gustav's pale eyes grew chilled as he stared back at the lawman. "And if I deny your request?"

Townsend grinned pleasantly. "Well, seeing as how you were responsible for getting Mr. Birmingham shot, I might have to arrest you anyway, along with that young whelp you hired." He glanced up to fix that one with a pointed stare, only to realize that Olney had slipped out of sight. Townsend quickly pushed through the gathering of men to look for him, but it soon became apparent that Olney was nowhere to be found. Perplexed, Townsend looked toward his deputies. "Where'd that young scamp get to, anyway? Didn't I tell you to watch all the doors and windows so no one would escape?"

"We did, Sheriff!" one of his men insisted. "He must be in the main warehouse somewhere. 'Tis sure no one could've escaped through the doors."

Several deputies walked through the warehouse, while a trio of others went outside to look around the area. After a futile search, they all returned. "He's gone, Sheriff!" one man announced breathlessly. "He must have slipped out while y'all were arguing over the ownership of Mrs. Birmingham."

"Well, damme," Townsend swore, flushing red with chagrin. "That boy might be slow-witted, but he sure knows how to make himself scarce in a hurry." Lifting a hand, he gestured to a deputy.

"Take some men and ride around town to see if you can find that rascal. I'll be along as soon as Fridrich here lets me have a look-see through this here place."

Gustav sneered in contempt. "And if I do not, you vill arrest me, eh? It vould seem I have no choice but to let you. Still, I should varn you, Sheriff, that I vill hold you personally responsible if anyzhing goes missing. Do you understand?"

"I'll let you search me and my men before we leave," Townsend assured him with a laconic grin.

"Do you even know vhat you are looking for?" Gustav inquired with disdain.

The sheriff lifted his broad shoulders in a casual shrug. "Anything at all that you can't verify ownership of with lading bills or papers of charter."

"You vill see zhat my papers are in order, Sheriff."

"Good! Then maybe I won't have to arrest you."

Chapter 4

Sweltering heat had settled over the countryside with unusual tenacity, and without a whisper of air stirring, a murky haze hung over the land, holding the heat close above the ground. Jeff and Brandon reached Oakley nigh the noon hour and were nearly spent from the long, hot ride and the night they had passed without sleep. They dismounted in the lane near the front steps of the mansion and wearily yielded the reins to a groom, who led their horses away. Heather had been watching from the house and came out on the porch to greet them. Wiping her hands on an apron she had tied above her swollen belly, she glanced from one to the other apprehensively.

"You two don't look very happy," she ventured worriedly. "Is it the heat? Or are you distressed about something else?"

Brandon mounted the steps and brushed a reassuring kiss upon her brow. "We won't have to bury anyone, sweet, if that's what you mean."

Heather released a sigh of relief. "No need to tell you both how we've all been fretting. I thought Cora and Kingston would wear out the floorboards going to the windows to watch for Jeff's return. Still, 'tis apparent the two of you are put out about something, and since I'm not a mind-reader, I guess you'll have to tell me what it is."

Jeff slapped his hat against his booted leg as he climbed to the porch. "It didn't go as well as we had hoped, Tory. That's all."

The pet name, which Jeff had pinned on her years before, lacked the usual teasing lilt, giving her further cause to chafe with uneasiness. "What happened?"

Jeff exhaled a long, wearied breath and shrugged. "'Tis simple enough, really. Sheriff Townsend couldn't find an iron-clad reason to arrest Gustav. The man had a signed receipt from Cooper Frye affirming the fact that he had paid two hundred fifty dollars for Raelynn. When he sent for her, ol' Coop told the man that I had stolen her away. Gustav rode out here, intending to get her back, and Townsend agreed that it would have been his right if I hadn't bought her first. As for trying to prove Gustav is a smuggler, all of his papers appeared to be in order. Townsend questions their validity, but his hands are tied."

"But you were shot in your own home!" Heather protested. "Couldn't Sheriff Townsend arrest Gustav for trying to kill you?"

Jeff shook his head. "He wasn't the one who shot me, and Gustav's men claimed before they ever came out here that they were given orders not to shoot anyone. It seems Gustav had meant to intimidate me by the sheer number of men he brought with him and thought I would give him Raelynn without a fight."

"He didn't know you very well, did he?" Brandon observed with a rueful chuckle.

"But what about the young man who actually shot you?" Heather queried. "Why couldn't the sheriff arrest him?"

Her husband laughed again, with even less humor. "You won't believe this, my sweet, but Olney disappeared right from under our very noses."

"What do you mean, disappeared?" Heather's lovely brows gathered in confusion. "Did he escape?"

Jeff's smile was a trifle grim, and he shook his head, as perplexed as she was. "Olney was gone before any of us realized it. All the windows were barred, and our men stood guard at the doors. No one could have left the warehouse without being seen. There were so many men inside, it was hard to keep track of everyone. Townsend was talking to Gustav at the time, and the next thing any of us knew, Olney had gone missing. There were crates stacked in the main warehouse, too many for Townsend to thoroughly examine when he conducted his search for smuggled items, but whatever open crates he found, he had them checked."

Heather's brows came together in a troubled frown. "The fact that Gustav is still free will not sit well with Raelynn. I had some difficulty convincing her that you would be all right, Jeff, and that she should get some rest before your return, but when she hears this news, she may never sleep again, and I wouldn't blame her in the least."

"Don't borrow trouble, my love," Brandon cajoled, turning his wife to face him. He touched her lips with a soft kiss and stroked a hand over her rounded belly as he admired the fetching aura of her childbearing state. "You wouldn't want to upset our unborn daughter with your worrying, now would you?"

Heather smiled and yielded readily to his gentle fondling until she glanced past him and noticed her brother-in-law watching them with a merry twinkle brightening his eyes. Blushing, she hurriedly pushed away from her husband and busied herself straightening her apron. A chuckle from Jeff drew Brandon's attention and lent some insight to her sudden reserve.

"Don't mind me, Tory," Jeff urged. "I didn't see a thing." He crossed to the front door and paused there to grin back at the couple. "At least, nothing I haven't seen my brother doing before."

Chuckling at his remark, Brandon laid an arm again about Heather's shoulders and whisked her along with him as he walked into the house. When they entered the hall, they found Jeff already leaping up the stairs, and they smiled at each other, understanding his eagerness.

"Madam, I believe it's time for us to go home," Brandon said thoughtfully. "By now, Beau must be wondering where his parents are. And I think Jeff has designs on going to bed . . . if Raelynn is agreeable, that is. For that matter, I wouldn't mind going to bed either, once we're at home."

Heather sympathized with her husband, knowing he hadn't slept at all during the night just past. She brushed a damp curl from his brow and noticed that his face was rather flushed. "You must be exhausted, but you'll have to sleep in one of the lower bedrooms to find any relief from this heat."

"Who said anything about sleep?" he queried with a meaningful gleam in his eyes.

Heather's lips curved upward as her deep sapphire eyes glowed with love. "Forgive me, my dearest. I thought you were tired and not feeling very well. You do look rather feverish."

"Feverish for you, madam," Brandon breathed, placing another kiss on her lips. "And you ought to know by now that I'm never too tired for what we do best together."

When he reached the upper landing, Jeff strode

down the hallway to his right until he reached his bedroom door. There he paused to listen, but no sound of movement came from within. Quietly turning the knob, he pushed the door slowly inward, not at all certain that Raelynn would be there. What he found delighted him. His young wife was slumbering peacefully on the far side of his bed with her long auburn hair reaching out behind her in shimmering waves across his pillows. His heart quickened with an overwhelming joy and a variety of other inexplicable emotions.

Strange how different his feelings were now that he had a wife to come home to, he mused, reflecting back on the nights when he had gone to bed with a book to read, hoping to banish that damnable, pathetic sense of solitude that had plagued him. Indeed, this heady felicity was a far more pleasing concoction than he could have ever imagined it would be. Mrs. Brewster was right, he decided emphatically, recalling the previous day when the milliner had urged him to make haste to marry. Nothing was quite as tiresome as coming home to an empty house and an even lonelier bed. But that was all behind him now. He had a beautiful wife awaiting him.

Leaning forward, Jeff reached out to awaken his young bride, but the sight of his own gunpowder-blackened hands made him draw back in repugnance. This would never do! He was filthy, hot, and sweaty! She was fresh, clean, and as sweet-smelling as jasmine in bloom. He could not think of intruding into her sleep while the acrid stench of black powder was still pungent in his nostrils. Their first moment of blissful union had to be perfect in every sense of the word.

Leaving his shirt and trousers hanging over the door of his armoire, he moved quietly across the room to his dressing chamber. The servants brought water for a bath, and after their departure, he sank into the brimming tub with a deep sigh of appreciation. For a moment he leaned his head back against the raised rim and closed his eyes, feeling the warm liquid relax his tense muscles, then he realized the folly of getting too comfortable. He was too exhausted to stay awake.

Ending his bath, he toweled himself dry and quietly returned to his bed where he stretched out beside his sleeping wife. His lack of sleep weighed him down both mentally and physically, and he knew that to make the moment of their intimacy the best it could be, he would have to rest for at least a few moments to revive both his mind and his energy.

Gustav came awake with a start as quietly approaching footsteps intruded into his sleep. His eyes flew wide, and like a man half-crazed with fear, he searched into the gloom of his warehouse apartment, unable to shake the lingering effects of the laudanum he had taken. With an effort he focused his gaze on the shadowy figure of a man standing a discreet distance from his bed, and the cold prickling panic finally dissipated, leaving in its stead a weak feeling of relief as he realized the man was not the sheriff, but Olney Hyde.

"Vhere have you been?" Gustav growled gruffly.

Olney flashed him a confident grin. "I thought you might enjoy a visit from an old friend."

"Ha!" Gustav threw up his good hand in disgust. "If not for you, I vould be in one piece now. And I vouldn't have zhat sheriff breathing down my neck, vatching every move my men make! I should never have shown you zhat secret passage. Otherwise, I vould now have the pleasure of knowing zhe sheriff had locked you away."

Olney pressed a hand to his breast, making much of the other's disparagement. "And here I've been tearing the whole of Charleston apart trying to find a suitable bauble to bring back to ye." With a wily grin he tugged sharply on the rope he held, rudely yanking the large bulk of Cooper Frye forward into the light. A filthy rag had been stuffed into the Englishman's mouth, and another one, tied around the lower part of his face, secured it in place.

"I found him hidin' out in a henhouse on the waterfront," Olney explained. "He was plannin' on sailing to New York before the week is out. He even paid one of the strumpets to make all the arrangements for him so he wouldn't be seen by any of our men."

Gustav relaxed back into his pillows and smiled gloatingly at the Englishman. "You vere very foolish, my friend, for cheating me. No man makes a fool of Gustav Fridrich and lives to tell of it. It is not so much the money, you understand. It is zhe loss of your niece I resent. I vould have made her *mein frau*, but now, she belongs to Herr Birmingham, and he vill not give her up unless I kill him. But if I do, zhe vench vould never forgive me."

Cooper Frye shook his head frantically and gestured to the gag in his mouth. Then pleadingly he pressed his fettered hands together.

"Vhat's this?" Gustav queried mockingly, amused by the man's pantomime. "Vould you like to speak before I let Olney take you out and dump your foul carcass in the ocean?"

Eagerly Cooper nodded, and with affected boredom Gustav flicked his hand casually toward him, giving Olney permission to remove his gag.

"Now, vhat do you have to say zhat's so important, eh?" the German inquired arrogantly. "I varn you, vhatever it is, it better be vorth my time."

Cooper Frye was more than willing to cooperate. "I knows of a way ta make me niece hate the Yankee an' send her runnin' back ta ye. An' I wouldn't charge ye a bloomin' farthin' for makin' it all 'appen."

Gustav raised a brow sharply as he regarded the Englishman with narrowed eyes. "I vouldn't like you to do anyzhing zhat vould bring the sheriff back here again. My affairs are of a most delicate nature, and I vould not have zhem disrupted again by zhat rude barbarian."

Cooper Frye chortled and shook his head. "This 'ere idea o' mine wouldn't involve the sheriff none at all. Ye see, I met this 'ere girl ... ten an' five years at the most she be, small an' pretty wit' bright gold hair...."

"Get on vith it!" Gustav interrupted impatiently.

"Well, this 'ere Nell cooks an' sews for the ladies at the brothel, an' we did some talkin' whilst the strumpets were entertainin' the gents. Nigh on ta nine months ago she was workin' at Oakley, sewin' sheets an' linens wit' all 'em fine, fancy initials like her poor dead mother taught her ta do. Whilst she was there, this Nell got real caught on that Birmingham gent, even slipped inta his bed one night whilst he was sleepin' and got him all hot and ready for her, but when the bugger woke up, he started rantin' an' ravin' 'bout how she weren't 'ardly old enuff ta know 'bout such things. He told her ta pack up her belongin's 'cause he couldn't trust her ta leave him be if'n he let her stay. Right then and there in the dead o' night, he woke his driver an' sent her off ta Charleston in his carriage. He told his man ta make sure she had a room at the inn for a brace o' nights and gave her the money she'd earned from sewin'. Beyond that, he says to her, he wants never ta see her at Oakley 'gain long as he lives."

Gustav jeered as he ridiculed Cooper's reasoning. "So! You say zhis vill make your niece hate Herr Birmingham? Your pardon, Englishman, but I do not zhink much of your logic. Raelynn vill only admire her husband zhe more."

Grinning with unmeasurable confidence, Cooper Frye lifted his tethered hands and scratched his bristly cheek with a grubby finger. "Not if'n she's led to believe the little twit is carryin' his babe."

Gustav's interest was considerably heighten by the idea. "Vhat vould cause Raelynn to zhink such a zhing?"

Cooper extended his rope-bound wrists to his captor with a hopeful grin. "Cut me free, and I'll be tellin' ye gents."

Olney glanced at the German to receive a consenting nod, then drew his knife and sliced through the bonds that bound the Englishman's wrists.

"Give an ear ta what I've got ta tell ye, me friend," Cooper urged Gustav, " 'bout a tall, dark-haired, green-eyed Irishman what took the little wench inta his bed at the inn an' got her wid babe afore he set sail the next morn'n. It just happened to be the very same night Mr. Birmingham kicked her outa his, it were, close to nine months ago."

Gustav arched a brow as he considered the merits of the idea. "Vhat vould it take to get zhis Nell to say zhat Herr Birmingham is zhe father of her babe?"

Cooper Frye lifted his massive shoulders in a careless shrug. "Maybe a few pretty gowns ta wear and five hundred Yankee dollars, just a little somethin' ta make it better for her an' the babe when it comes."

Gustav fixed the other man with an icy stare. "And vhat vould yu have me do for you, Cooper Frye, other than allowing you to live?"

The Englishman knew when to be cautious. "I wish only ta serve ye, yer lordship."

Gustav smiled with meager toleration. "Zhat's good, Cooper Frye, because you vill do just zhat . . . and you vill prove your loyalty to me . . . or die."

A deafening clap of thunder seemed to shake the large plantation house right down to its foundation, rattling windows, frightening servants, and sending dogs scurrying off the porch to find another place of shelter. Upstairs in the master bedchamber, the new mistress of Oakley came awake with a startled gasp, having been rudely snatched from the depths of sleep. Unable to recognize her surroundings, she glanced about her in confusion. The bed wherein she lay was unfamiliar, yet the place beside her had been slept in, evidenced by the rumpled bedclothes and the top sheet that had been thrown aside. A pair of dark trousers and a shirt were hanging over the door of an armoire, but she saw no sign of the one who had worn them.

Lightning flashed, briefly chasing the storm-borne gloom from the room. A loud rumbling intruded into the flickering display, severing the silence with a crescendo of riveting peals that made her flinch at every horrendous crack of thunder. When the deafening din faded, delicately tinkling chimes began to play. Charmed by the music, Raelynn sat up and swept her gaze over the unfamiliar furnishings until her eyes lit on the porcelain clock residing on the marble mantel at the far end of the room.

The fourth hour!

Raelynn gasped in dismay, realizing she had slept nearly the whole day away without putting to rest the matter that had plagued her most, the welfare of her husband. Though she had to assume he was the one who had been sleeping beside her, at least for a short time, she could not rest until she saw him for herself.

A strong gust of wind swept inward through the open windows, fluttering silken panels and bringing with it a cooler breath of air. A delicate floral essence, mingled with the scent of rain, filled the chamber, drawing Raelynn from the bed. She went to stand near the window and gazed out upon a wind-swept terrain. Off in the distance she could see the rain marching across the fields toward them. With the force of the strengthening gale, it would only be a matter of moments before the storm reached Oakley Plantation.

As predicted, the downpour came, but just as quickly it passed, leaving the air sweet and pleasantly cool in its wake. Raelynn felt greatly refreshed by her lengthy respite, and after a careful toilette, she went downstairs to see if she could find Jeff.

The butler was hurrying across the front foyer when she reached the upper landing. He seemed in an anxious dither to escape toward the back, but he failed in his quest when she halted him with a question.

"Kingston, could you tell me where Mr. Birmingham is?"

Shame-facedly the servant turned and lifted a hand lamely toward the front of the house. "Mistah Jeff's out on the porch, Miz Raelynn. He's got a visitor, but I s'pect he'll be comin' in shortly if'n yo' wants ta wait in the parlor for him." Kingston smiled more hopefully. "I'll bring yo' some refreshments ta tide yo' o'er 'til din . . ."

An enraged scream came from the porch, squelching his offer and serving quick death to the peace of the hall.

"You had no right to marry another after you did this to me!" a woman shrieked in shrill tones. "Here

I am, about to give birth to your child, and you tell me you want nothing more to do with me! I wonder what your highfalutin' friends will say when I let it be known that I'm carrying your bastard."

The suddenly flustered Kingston tried to redirect Raelynn's attention to something less disturbing than the accusations being hurled on the porch. "That was a mighty fierce storm we had for a spell, wasn't it, Miz Raelynn?"

His words might just as well have never been spoken, for they fell on ears that were completely attentive to the jeering threats that came from the porch.

"Maybe I should talk to your new wife, too, and tell her what she can expect when her back is turned!"

"You're talking nonsense, Nell, and you know it!" Jeff barked.

"Nonsense, is it?" Her tone was snide. "You didn't think it was nonsense when you took me into your bed and made love to me!"

"You little liar! You slipped into my bed like a sneak-thief in the night when I was asleep," he accused. "I may have been a bit dazed, but this much I know! I woke up before anything of this nature happened between us!"

"I'll soon be carrying proof in my arms for all the world to see that you had your way with me!" Nell muttered suddenly. "And if the babe looks like his father, then everyone will know who fathered the poor li'l thing!"

Jeff didn't know why the girl had waited so long to make such claims except that with the birth of her child imminently near she had perhaps begun to worry about how they would get along. "If it's money you're after, Nell, you'll not be blackmailing me to get it," he gritted. "I won't be coerced by the threat of you spreading lies against me. If you're so destitute, go talk with the father of the babe. Perhaps he'll take pity on you and do what is right."

"I'm talking to him right now!" Nell insisted. "And you're turning a deaf ear to my pleas!"

The front door was pulled slowly open, and Jeff swung around in surprise as his wife stepped out onto the porch. For the life of him, he couldn't wipe away his distressed frown and present for her a more noble, reassuring countenance. He was certain he looked as guilty as Nell made him out to be.

Raelynn met his gaze warily and blushed in confusion. "I couldn't help but hear with all the shouting going on."

"So!" With a cold, disdaining glare Nell marked Raelynn's progress across the porch. "This is your new woman, eh?"

Resenting her inference, Jeff stressed a correction. "This is *my wife*."

"My! My! My! You are touchy nowadays, Jeffrey. But not so long ago you were calling *me* your woman."

"You're a child! Maybe fourteen! Fifteen, at the most!" he ground out. " 'Twould be a cold day in hell before I'd think of molesting a chit barely weaned!"

"Well, your missus ain't so old either!" Nell snapped with jealous rancor. Her eyes blazed as they swept the beautiful pale green gown that Raelynn had donned. She could not deny that Cooper Frye's niece was beautiful, but if she had rich garments and a houseful of servants to wait on her, she was sure she'd be just as appealing to the only man that mattered to her. How could he stand there looking so handsome in his casual attire and not understand how desperately she wanted him for her own? Prodded by envy, she voiced her conjecture in hurt tones. "I'd look just as fetching if you'd buy me a pretty dress or two like you promised that night you planted your seed in me belly. Oh, Jeffrey, don't you see how I care for you despite the way you've used me?''

Jeff's scowl turned as black as the storm clouds that had recently passed over the land. Turning from Nell in disgust, he faced Raelynn and found her watching him with a troubled frown. It was obvious that she was upset by their exchange, yet the words that could adequately assuage her suspicions and convince her of his innocence were beyond his ken.

He knew he had a stubborn streak as wide as the sky was high and that he'd never yield to whatever it was that Nell was trying to get from him. If she wanted a job, he could probably get Farrell to hire her on as a seamstress, for she was very talented with a needle and thread, but she apparently wanted more than he was willing or able to give her.

He gathered his wife's trembling hands in his to gently kiss the back of each. "I beg you to believe me, my love," he murmured for her ears alone. "I'm innocent of what this girl accuses me of."

"You can turn your back on me if'n you want, Mr. Jeffrey Birmingham." Nell's voice hardened as she observed the tender attention he bestowed on his wife. "But you'll not be so high and mighty when I get through with you!"

Jeff whirled to face the pregnant woman. "Just what in the devil are you after, Nell? What do you expect from me? Do you honestly think I'll roll over like a well-trained dog and submit to the mischief you've brewed in your mind? Did I wrong you so badly when I refused your overtures and sent you away, that you must now wreak vengeance with fabrications? You and I both know what happened that night, and it was nothing that I'm ashamed of. If you were as smart as I once thought you were, you'd see how futile and feeble your lies are. There's absolutely nothing to be gained from this confrontation."

"All I'm wanting is a father for my babe," Nell insisted, "and a husband. You owe me that much."

"That's beyond my capability . . . or my desire," he replied bluntly. "I'm married now. . . ."

"You can get the vows annulled. . . ."

"*Noooo!*" he roared.

Nell stumbled back in sudden trepidation at the force of his denial. She hadn't imagined that the chivalrous Mr. Birmingham could react so strongly toward one of her gender. His vehemence gave her pause, to be sure. Cooper Frye had promised her fifty dollars for causing the breakup of the newly wedded couple, and with her baby coming any day now, she needed whatever money she could get her hands on. Besides, it wasn't so much the monetary rewards that had compelled her to do this thing as much as it was a dream she had once savored, and that was to become the bride of Jeffrey Birmingham. The Irishman had looked so much like him that she had allowed herself to dream that it was Jeff making love to her. But Jeff was the one who had coldly rejected her and hauled her from his bed like a naughty child, and now she had grave doubts that he would ever change his mind about her. Indeed, she'd be lucky to leave of her own accord.

"I see you're set against doing what's right," she badgered, gathering her courage. "So I'll be leaving you to reap your just due." With a sweep of her hand she indicated the hired livery she had arrived in. "I was hoping you'd take pity on me for what you'd done and at least pay my driver for the fare out here." She dropped her gaze to her rounded belly and heaved a disconcerted sigh. "Here I am, burdened nigh to bearing, but I can see you're not in a generous mood, and certainly not when your wife is standing there listening to every word we say. I don't know what hold she has on you, but I can see that you've made up your mind, and I'll be saying no more. Goodnight to you, Jeffrey."

Pressing a hand to her distended stomach, she carefully descended the steps and approached the carriage. The driver handed her in, closed the door behind her, and then, tipping his hat politely to the couple on the porch, climbed to his seat and slapped the reins, setting his single horse into motion.

Jeff turned slowly to face his wife as the conveyance rumbled down the lane, but she moved stiffly across the porch to stand near its edge. Leaning a shoulder against a Doric column, she gazed solemnly into the distance, oblivious to the beauty of the rain-speckled scenery and the tall, majestic oaks with their gracefully sweeping limbs. She was so confused that she felt numb inside. Only one thing she grasped with startling clarity. She could not give herself to this man until she had settled the matter of his innocence in her heart.

"I'll need some time to consider what effect these accusations may have on us, Jeff," she said soberly. "I hope you'll understand my reservations. In view of what I've just heard, I have much to sort out. I cannot join you blithely in your bed while questions about Nell . . . and her baby torment me."

"I was hoping to enjoy the evening with you as man and wife," Jeff murmured, coming to stand behind her. The fragrance of her hair wafted through his senses. How he longed to kiss her, hold her, make love to her. . . .

"If you don't mind, I'd rather eat alone tonight," she managed without her voice breaking.

His heart grew heavy. "If you insist, Raelynn. I'll have a tray sent up. . . ."

Her throat was tight, and she was so close to bursting into tears, it was a long moment before she could answer. "Send it to the bedchamber I would have had if I had not yielded to your kisses. I need some privacy to think this matter through."

"What can I say to convince you of my innocence?" Jeff asked in an anguished tone. "Am I to be judged by the words of Nell, who obviously thinks she can milk me for a fortune with the lies she's willing to tell against me? If your faith in me is so fickle, madam, then I can assure you, we'll be constantly at odds in our marriage. You'll have to learn to trust me, for if you're always attentive to the tales of others who, for their own malicious purposes and aspirations, will try to tear us apart, you'll be forever wondering about me. I'm sure there will be others who will make the attempt, perhaps because of some infatuation for you, or a desire to extract a bit of wealth from me, yet I must believe in your integrity as you must believe in mine." He released a sigh and spread his arms in futility. "But as we are only strangers barely met, I must allow that you need time to get to know me. I'm willing to grant you that favor. The only thing I ask in return is that I be allowed to court you as your betrothed. Tonight you may dine alone, but in the future I must insist upon your presence at my table and, when we are in public, your hand within my arm, for I could not bear the agony of others knowing we are estranged."

" 'Tis but a small favor you ask," Raelynn murmured in reply. "And I find no difficulty in complying with your wishes. 'Tis what we agreed upon at the beginning, if you'll remember."

"How could I forget?" Jeff mumbled softly. Thinking it best to leave her to her thoughts, he brushed past her and descended the front steps. Never looking back, he turned and strode toward the stables at the back of the mansion, feeling in desperate need of some activity that would turn his frustration into complete exhaustion. It would be the only way he could face retiring to a lonely bed again.

Racing one of his steeds was usually a sport Jeff both reveled and excelled in, but this afternoon he took no pleasure in urging his swiftest stallion to a reckless pace and taking every challenging jump he could. He now understood what Brandon had gone through when once upon a time his brother had been kept from Heather's bed. There was just so much a man could tolerate in good humor, and after having tasted the sweetness of Raelynn's response, it was ludicrous for him to imagine that he'd be able to push that memory from his mind once he fell into bed. Instead of finding the rest he sorely needed, it would become a place of torment wherein visions of his young wife in various stages of dishabille would tantalize him unmercifully. Knowing she would be only a few doors away, he'd be like a man cast into the depths of hell.

The tray of food that had been sent up to Rae-lynn's bedchamber remained untouched as she stood on the porch, staring toward the live oaks that stretched in a row across the back lawn. She was vexed with worry and fear, having seen Jeff race away from the stable on the back of a glistening black stallion, and though she had urged the servants to tell her about the animal, none had dared elaborate on his temperament. Still, their concerned frowns had told her more than she had really wanted to know. It was no gentle beast that Jeff was riding, and she could only blame herself if anything happened to him.

Lanterns had been lit in several of the servants'

quarters behind the oaks, but a handful of children, reluctant to stop their play, still chased each other in the deepening twilight. Their laughter rang with the excitement of their game, but as night stole the last light from the sky, they reluctantly parted and returned to their homes. Raelynn knew that Cora was still in the main house, as well as Kingston and a few of the other servants, for they were awaiting the master's return. Only Kingston had dared to make a muttered comment about Nell's visit within Raelynn's range of hearing, and that was to say that the girl had left just as quickly this time as she had nine months ago, when the master had sent her packing in the middle of the night.

With a dismal sigh Raelynn leaned her head against one of the posts that lent support to the porch balustrade and the overhanging roof. She knew only too well that she had not allowed Jeff to explain in detail what had happened that night with Nell. She had been far too intent upon getting away from him and allowing herself time to think over what she had heard. In doing so, she had been less than fair to him. Even a condemned man had a right to answer his accuser, but she had not wanted to listen to his arguments for fear she would find some flaw in his character that would totally shatter her illusions and make a mockery of the kind of man she had thought him to be. Her first impressions of Jeff were of a gallant, heroic gentleman, but if he was guilty of all that Nell had claimed, in her mind he would be no better than Gustav, appeasing his own prurient desires, regardless of the hurt he caused others.

Rapid hoofbeats intruded into her thoughts, and Raelynn felt a great flood of relief as she espied Jeff astride the black. Horse and rider passed through a shaft of light streaming from the house, and she watched as they neared the stable. Jeff swung down from the steed as the groom came out to greet him, and handed the reins over to his servant. Their voices drifted back to her.

"Take your time cooling him down, Sparky," Jeff called back as he left the stable. "He's had a hard ride."

"Don't yo' worry, Mistah Jeffrey. Ah'll be careful with this here beast. And may I say, suh, it's a relief ta have yo' back safe and all in one piece."

Jeff chuckled and waved his crop, acknowledging the young man's comment. "For once, Brutus didn't try to buck me off. He's flying higher over all the jumps, too."

"Ah still wouldn't trust him if'n I were yo', Mistah Jeffrey. He's just waitin' ta catch yo' unawares so's he can break yo' neck."

"I'll be careful, Sparky."

Raelynn retreated into the deeper shadows as Jeff leapt up the stairs at the far end of the porch. Crossing the veranda, he pushed open the French doors to his bedchamber and stepped within, unaware of the blue-green eyes that followed his progress. She heard him step to the inside hall and call down for a bath to be brought up. As his voice rang through the house, the servants' moods revived almost immediately. Once again there was laughter and the teasing chatter of long-established friends drifting through the halls.

Raelynn smiled, feeling her own spirits take wing. She couldn't help but wonder at this man who was able to bring life back into a house with his mere presence. She could only assume from the anxious concern recently demonstrated by the blacks that her husband was well liked, perhaps even loved by those who served him. If he were truly a man void of compassion, as Nell had tried to portray him, then surely the servants wouldn't have cared whether he came back or not.

A sudden scream rent the silence, and with a start of surprise, Raelynn looked around to see the black woman, Cora, running across the back lawn toward the servants' quarters. A mottled brightness pierced the lush greenery of one of the live oaks that stood between the main house and the cabins. To her horror, Raelynn saw flames leaping from the roof of one of the larger shacks.

"My baby! My baby's in there!" Cora screamed hysterically as she ran beneath the low branches. "Somebody save her!"

"Fire! Fire in one o' the cabins!" a deep male voice shouted from the mansion.

Someone clanged a warning on the iron triangle hanging outside the kitchen, and a short moment later Raelynn saw Kingston sprinting across the lawn. Jeff snatched open the French doors of his bedchamber and ran out onto the veranda, still wearing the shirt, trousers, and boots he had ridden in. Raelynn stared in amazement as he crossed the width of the porch in two leaping strides. Catching hold of the balustrade, he hurled himself over it and, like a cat in the wilds, landed in a crouched position on the lawn below. He sprang easily to his full height and was off and running toward the burning cabin before Raelynn realized she was still holding her breath. She did not pause another moment. Lifting her gown and wrapper to her knees, she ran along the porch toward the stairs and was soon racing after him.

Flames were leaping up the outer wall of the cabin near the front door, which had been flung ajar in an aborted attempt to rescue the youngster. Cora tried repeatedly to approach the entrance, but the heat drove her back again and again. From within, a young child shrieked in terror, unable to find a way of escape. Her screams set spurs to Cora, who sobbed in panic as she dashed across the porch, dipped a bucket into a rain barrel that stood near the edge, and ran back to fling the contents over the fire. The short-lived spray did little to deter the bright, greedy flames that were already licking through the boards of the porch.

"Oh, sweet Lord o' mercy, save my little girl!" Cora wailed through her weeping. "Please! Somebody save my Clara!"

Upon reaching the cabin, Jeff leapt onto the porch and, with Kingston's help, overturned the rain barrel, sending the water skimming across the planks in a forceful wave. It drove back the flames licking at the floor and splashed through the front door. Seizing an ax from a wood pile that was stacked nearby, Jeff brought its blade down with a mighty stroke, cleaving the rain barrel completely in half on one side. With another blow he knocked away the bottom, then divided the far side in much the same manner, sending several staves flying from the metal binders. The top band he bent beneath a booted heel, turning it into a handle of sorts. Then he hefted the larger portion of the barrel in front of him, using it as a shield against the intense heat that flared outward from the flames.

Raelynn clasped a trembling hand over her mouth, squelching audible sounds of fright as Jeff charged through the front door of the cabin. Standing in throat-constricting fear, she watched through the portal as he searched about for the little girl, then he turned and stepped into an interior room. Raelynn held her breath as the other side of the cabin became a raging inferno. Part of the roof began to collapse, sending sparks flying upward and eliciting frightened gasps from those who waited for Jeff to reappear. He did so at a run, clutching the tiny girl against him with one arm, while he clasped the halved barrel in his other hand.

He burst from the front portal and set wings to his booted heels as he sprinted across the porch to the safety of the lawn. Raelynn breathed a deep sigh of relief and, for a few moments, was content to watch him being thanked and clapped on the back by the blacks. The child's lusty cries confirmed that she was frightened but miraculously unharmed.

Jeff deposited the toddler into the arms of her mother, who sobbed in gratitude. "Thank yo', Mistah Jeffrey! Thank yo', an' God bless yo'! God bless yo' real good!"

Jeff glanced around in search of Cora's husband. "Where did Jeremy go? I thought he was watching Clara until you finished at the main house."

"My brother went bullfroggin', Mistah Jeffrey," a young girl of fourteen announced as she stepped near. "He asked me ta look aftah Clara 'til he got back. Ah was fryin' some fish fo' supper over a fire in the hearth, but the kettle slipped off the hook an' overturned. The grease spilt clear across the room an' caught fire. It was like a wall between Clara an' me. The fire spread so fast, ah couldn't reach her in the other room. Ah had ta climb out a window ta save myself. When ah ran around ta the front, the heat was so bad, ah couldn't go back in. Ah'm mighty sorry ah burned down Cora's cabin, Mistah Jeffrey."

"It was an accident, Ali. No need to fret," Jeff replied, dropping a reassuring hand on the girl's shoulder. "I'm just thankful no one was hurt."

Cora hugged her daughter tightly, drawing a squeal of protest from the toddler. "Ah doan want another scare like that as long as ah live!"

Jeff looked toward the cabin that was now engulfed in flames. "You'll be needing a new place to live now."

"Ah 'spect so." The woman sighed. "But right now, ah ain't gonna worry 'bout what ah lost when ah'm holdin' my little Clara *alive* in my arms!"

Raelynn moved forward to stand near the servants, and when Jeff looked around, she offered him a smile that was both tender and pleading. He stepped close and gazed down at her with a questioning expression.

"Will you forgive me, Jeff, for not allowing you a chance to explain before I drove a wedge between us?" she asked timidly.

He could understand her reservations. "Considering what you heard from Nell, I cannot blame you for trying to keep me at arms' length. We *are* strangers, and although we are now wed, we have much to learn about each other."

"As you have said, we need to learn to trust each other," she replied softly.

"Aye, that we must do, madam, but it will come in time, as we become better acquainted."

"I think I will enjoy getting to know you, Jeffrey," she murmured with a smile. Her eyes glowed more brightly than could be credited to the blazing fire. "Any man who'd risk his life to save a servant's child is truly an exceptional individual. The compassion you demonstrated toward Cora gives me cause to seriously doubt Nell's assertions, yet if you wouldn't mind, before I fall even more deeply in love with you, I'd like us to spend some time together becoming friends."

Jeff might have felt some disappointment, except for the fact that she had said she loved him. His heart soared to jubilant heights, and his widening grin expressed his elation as he offered her an arm. "Madam, may I escort you back to the house? And if you have not eaten, I'd consider it an honor if you'd share a late supper with me . . . wherever you'd deem appropriate."

Raelynn slipped an arm through his and ignored the sooty smudges on the back of his hand as she laid her palm upon it. "If you will not press me overmuch, I'll dine with you in your bedchamber if you'd like."

"For you, I'll be a blessed saint," he assured her, then grinned. "But only if you'll allow me to kiss you, as I so desperately long to do."

Raelynn lifted a challenging brow and chuckled at the merriment twinkling in his eyes. "I do perceive a wily ruse in your plea, sir. I shall be more wary of your kisses during the affirmation of our friendship and take them in limited doses, lest I find myself yielding once again to your amorous bent even before the night is spent."

"Have you a set time in mind for this exploration of friendship?" Jeff queried somewhat apprehensively.

Raelynn leaned her head upon his shoulder and smiled in secret pleasure as she felt his arm slip around her waist. "I don't think it need take too long, do you, Jeff?"

"No time at all, madam," he replied, his heart soaring. "No time at all."

Kathleen E. Woodiwiss

KATHLEEN E. WOODIWISS is America's preeminent author of historical fiction. She has written eight novels, all of which have become multimillion-copy bestsellers. Her novels have been translated into fifteen languages. Ms. Woodiwiss lives in Louisiana, where she is currently at work on a new novel.